After thirty-five years as a nurse, **Patricia Davids** hung up her stethoscope to become a full-time writer. She enjoys spending her free time visiting her grandchildren, doing some long-overdue yard work and traveling to research her story locations. She resides in Wichita, Kansas. Pat always enjoys hearing from her readers. You can visit her online at patriciadavids.com.

Anna Schmidt is an award-winning author of more than twenty-five works of historical and contemporary fiction. She is a three-time finalist for the coveted RITA® Award from Romance Writers of America, as well as a four-time finalist for an RT Reviewers' Choice Award. Critics have called Anna "a natural writer, spinning tales reminiscent of old favorites like *Miracle on 34th Street*." One reviewer raved, "I love Anna Schmidt's style of writing!"

USA TODAY Bestselling Author

PATRICIA DAVIDS

Plain Admirer

&

ANNA SCHMIDT

Second Chance Proposal

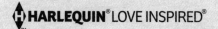

HARLEQUIN® LOVE INSPIRED®

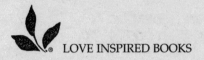

LOVE INSPIRED BOOKS

Recycling programs
for this product may
not exist in your area.

ISBN-13: 978-0-373-83896-7

Plain Admirer and Second Chance Proposal

Copyright © 2016 by Harlequin Books S.A.

The publisher acknowledges the copyright holders
of the individual works as follows:

Plain Admirer
Copyright © 2013 by Patricia MacDonald

Second Chance Proposal
Copyright © 2013 by Jo Horne Schmidt

CONTENTS

PLAIN ADMIRER

Patricia Davids

This book is lovingly dedicated to my father, Clarence—a man who can look at any stretch of water and tell just where the fish are. Thanks for teaching me, my daughter and my grandchildren to bait our own hooks. Love you. Let's go fishing soon.

And God blessed them, and God said unto them,
Be fruitful, and multiply, and replenish the earth,
and subdue it: and have dominion over the fish
of the sea, and over the fowl of the air, and over
every living thing that moveth upon the earth.
—*Genesis* 1:28

Chapter 1

"This isn't easy to say, but I have to let you go, Joann. I'm sure you understand."

"You're firing me?" Joann Yoder faced her boss across the cluttered desk in his office. For once, she wasn't tempted to straighten up for him. And she didn't understand.

"*Ja.* I'm sorry."

Otis Miller didn't look the least bit sorry. Certainly not as sorry as she was to be losing a job she really needed. A job she loved. Why was this happening? Why now, when she was so close to realizing her dream?

She'd only been at Miller Press for five months, but working as an assistant editor and office manager at the Amish-owned publishing house was everything she'd ever wanted. How could it end so quickly? If she knew what she had done wrong, she could fix it. "At least tell me why."

He sighed heavily, as if disappointed she hadn't accepted her dismissal without question. "You knew when you came over from the bookstore that this might not be a permanent position."

Joann had moved from a part-time job at the bookstore next door to help at the printing shop after Otis's elder brother suffered a heart attack. When he passed away a few weeks later, Joann had assumed she would be able to keep his job. She loved gathering articles for their monthly magazine and weekly newspaper, as well as making sure the office ran smoothly and customers received the best possible attention. She dropped her gaze to her hands clenched tightly in her lap and struggled to hang on to her dignity. Tears pricked the back of her eyelids, but she refused to cry. "You told me I was doing a good job."

"You have been. Better than I expected, but I'm giving Roman Weaver your position. I don't need to tell you why."

"*Nee,* you don't." Like everyone in the Amish community of Hope Springs, Ohio, she was aware of the trouble that had visited the Weaver family. She hated that her compassion struggled so mightily with her desire to support herself. This job was proof that her intelligence mattered. She might be the "bookworm" her brothers had often called her, but here she had a chance to put her learning to good use. Now it was all being taken away.

She couldn't let it go without a fight. She looked up and blurted, "Does he really need the job more than I do?"

Otis didn't like conflict. He leaned back in his chair and folded his arms across his broad chest. "Roman has large medical bills to pay."

"But the church held an auction to help raise money for him."

"He and his family are grateful for all the help they received, but they are still struggling."

She'd lost, and she knew it. Only a hint of the bitterness she felt slipped through in her words. "Plus, he's your nephew."

"That, too," Otis admitted without any sign of embarrassment. Family came only after God in their Amish way of life.

Roman Weaver had had it rough, there was no denying that. It was a blessing that he hadn't lost his arm after a pickup truck smashed into his buggy. Unfortunately, his damaged left arm was now paralyzed and useless. She'd seen him at the church meetings wearing a heavy sling and heard her brothers say the physical therapy he needed was expensive and draining his family's resources.

Her heart went out to him and his family, but why should she be the one to lose her job? There were others who worked for Miller Press.

She didn't bother to voice that thought. She already knew why she had been chosen. Because she was a woman.

Joann had no illusions about the male-dominated society she lived in. Unmarried Amish women could hold a job, but they gave it up when they married to make a home for their husband and children. A married woman could work outside the home, but only if her husband agreed to it.

Amish marriage was a partnership where each man and woman knew and respected their roles within the *Ordnung,* the laws of their Amish church. Men were the head of the household. Joann didn't disagree with any of it. At least, not very much.

It was just that she had no desire to spend the rest of her life living with her brothers, moving from one house to another and being an unwanted burden to their families. She'd never had a come-calling boyfriend, although she'd accepted a ride home from the singings with a few fellas in her youth. She'd never received an offer of marriage. And at the advanced age of twenty-six, it wasn't likely she would.

Besides, there wasn't anyone in Hope Springs she would consider spending the rest of her life with. As the years had gone by, she'd begun to accept that she would always be a maiden aunt. Maybe she'd get a cat one day.

Otis folded his hands together on his desk. "I am sorry, Joann. Roman needs the job. He can't work in the sawmill with only one good arm. It's too dangerous."

"I must work, too. My brothers have many children. I don't wish to burden them by having them take care of me, as well."

"Come now, you're being unreasonable. Your brothers do not begrudge you room and board."

"They would never say it, but I think they do." She knew her three brothers had taken her in out of a strong sense of duty after their parents died and not because of brotherly love. Hadn't they decided her living arrangements among themselves without consulting her? She stayed with each brother for four months. At the end of that time, she moved to the next brother's home. By the end of the year, she was back where she had started. She always had a roof over her head, but she didn't have a home.

She wanted a home of her own, but that wasn't going to happen without a good-paying job.

"Joann, think of Roman. Where is your Christian compassion?"

"I left it at home in a jar."

Otis scowled at her flippancy. She blushed at her own audacity. Modesty and humility were the aspirations of every Amish woman, but sometimes things slipped out of her mouth before she had time to think.

Why couldn't someone else give Roman a job he could manage? She dreamed of having a home of her own, a small house at the edge of the woods where she could keep her books and compile her nature notes and observations unhindered by her nieces and nephews. Best of all, she'd be able to go fishing whenever she wanted without her family's sarcastic comments about wasting her time. The only way she could accomplish that was by earning her own money.

She was so close to realizing her dream. The very house she wanted was coming up for sale. The owners, her friends Sarah and Levi Beachy, were willing to sell to her and finance her if she could come up with the down payment by the end of September. If she couldn't raise the agreed-upon amount, they would have to sell to another Amish family. They needed the money to make improvements to their business before winter.

What only a week ago had seemed like a sure thing, a gift from God, was now slipping out of her grasp. Joann didn't want to beg, but she would. "Can't you do anything for me, Otis? You know I'm a hard worker."

"All I can offer you is a part-time position—"

"I'll take it."

"One day a week on the cleaning staff."

"Oh." Her last bit of hope vanished. Her book learning wouldn't be needed while she swept the floors and emptied wastepaper baskets.

Otis leaned back in his chair. "Of course, your part-time position at the bookstore is yours if you want it."

A part-time salary would be far less than she needed. Still, it was better than nothing. She wasn't proud. She'd do a good job for him. In time, she might even get a chance at an editorial position again. Only God knew what the future held.

She nodded once. "I would be grateful for such work."

Otis rose to his feet. "*Goot.* You'll work afternoons Monday through Wednesday at the bookstore, and here on Saturdays. But there is something I need you to do for me before you switch jobs."

"What is that?"

"I need you to show Roman how we do things here. He's only worked in the sawmill and on the farm. The publishing business is foreign to him. I'm sure it won't take you more than two weeks to show him the ropes. He's a bright fellow. He'll catch on quickly. You can do that, can't you?"

He gets my job, but I have to show him how to do it? Where is the justice in that? She kept her face carefully blank.

Otis scowled again. "Well?"

"I'll be glad to show Roman all I've learned." It wasn't a complete lie, but it was close. She would do it, but she wouldn't be happy about it.

Otis nodded and came around the desk. "Fine. I hope

my nephew can start on Monday morning. After you get him up to speed, you can return to the bookstore. That's all, you can go home now."

"Danki." She rose from her seat and headed for the door. Pulling it open, she saw the man who was taking her job sitting quietly in a chair across the room. Did he know or care that she was being cast aside for him? They had attended the same school, but he had been a year behind her.

After their school years, she saw him and his family at Sunday services, but their paths rarely crossed. He'd run with the fast crowd during their *rumspringa,* their running-around teenage years. She had chosen baptism at the age of nineteen while he hadn't joined the faith until two years ago. His circle of friends didn't include her or her family. She studied him covertly as she would one of her woodland creatures.

Roman Weaver was a good-looking fellow with a head of curly blond hair that bore the imprint of the hat he normally wore. His cheeks were lean, his chin chiseled and firm. He was clean-shaven, denoting his single status. His years of hard physical work showed in the muscular width of his shoulders crisscrossed by his suspenders. He wore a black sling on his left arm. It stood out in stark contrast to his short-sleeved white shirt. His straw hat rested on the chair arm beside him.

Compassion touched her heart when she noticed the fine lines that bracketed his mouth. Was he in pain?

He looked up as she came out of the office. His piercing blue eyes, rimmed with thick lashes, brightened. He smiled. An unfamiliar thrill fluttered in the pit of her stomach. No one had ever smiled at her with such warmth.

His dazzling gaze slid past her to settle on Otis, and Joann realized she'd been a fool to think Roman Weaver was smiling at her. She doubted he even saw her.

"Hello, *Onkel,*" Roman said, rising from his chair.

"It's *goot* to see you, nephew." Otis stepped back to give him room to enter his office. Roman walked past her without a glance.

She kept her eyes downcast as an odd stab of disappointment hit her. Why should it matter that his smile hadn't been for her? She was used to being invisible. She'd long ago given up the hope that she'd become attractive and witty. She wasn't ugly, but she had no illusions about her plain looks. She was as God had made her.

She consoled herself with the knowledge that what the Lord had held back in looks He'd more than made up for in intelligence. She was smarter than her brothers and her few friends. It wasn't anything special that she had done. She was smart the way some people were tall, because that was the way God fashioned them.

For a long time, she thought of her intellect as a burden. Then, an elderly teacher told her she was smarter than anyone he'd ever met and that God must surely have something special in mind for her. That single statement had enabled Joann to see herself in a completely new light.

Being smart wasn't a bad thing, even if some others thought it was. When she landed this job, she knew being smart was indeed a blessing.

As Roman Weaver closed the door behind him, old feelings of being left out, of being overlooked and unvalued wormed their way into her heart. They left a painful bruise she couldn't dismiss.

Crossing to her desk, she lifted her green-and-white quilted bag from the back of her chair and settled the strap on her shoulder. Roman Weaver might look past her today, but come Monday morning, he was going to find he needed her. He wouldn't look through her then.

Roman forced a bright smile to his lips in order to hide his nervousness. The summons from his uncle had come out of the blue. He had no idea what his mother's brother wanted with him, but the look on her face when she relayed the message had Roman worried. What was going on? What was wrong?

The better question might have been: What was right? He had the answer to that one: not much in his life at the moment. The gnawing pain he endured from his injury was constant proof of that.

Otis indicated a chair. "Have a seat."

Roman did so, holding his injured arm against his chest, more from habit than a need to protect it. "I've often wondered what it is that you do here."

He glanced around the room filled with filing cabinets, books and stacks of papers. The smell of solvents and ink gave the air a harsh, sharp quality that stung his nostrils. Roman preferred the clean scent of fresh-cut wood.

His uncle was the owner of a small publishing business whose target audience was Old Order Plain People, Amish, Mennonites and Hutterites. A small bookstore next door housed a number of books he published as well as a small library. Although Roman occasionally read the magazine his uncle put out each month, he'd only visited the office and bookstore a few times. He wasn't a reader.

"How's the arm?" Otis asked.

"It's getting better." Much too slowly for Roman's liking.

"Are you in pain?"

"Some." He didn't elaborate. It was his burden to bear.

"I'm sure you're wondering why I've asked you here. Your parents came to see me last Sunday," Otis said, looking vaguely uncomfortable.

"Did they?" This was the first Roman had heard of it.

"Your father asked me for a business loan. Of course, I was happy to help. I know things have been difficult for all of you."

Roman's medical bills had already cost his family nearly all their savings. His inability to do his job in the sawmill was cutting their productivity, making his father and his brother work even harder. If his father had come to Otis for a loan, things must be dire.

"You have my gratitude and my thanks. We will repay you as soon as we can."

"I know. I'm not worried about that. Before they left, your mother spoke privately with me. My sister is very dear to me, but I will admit to being surprised when she asked if I would offer you a job here at my office."

The muscles in Roman's jaw clenched. "I work at my father's side in the sawmill. I don't need a job. I have one," he said.

Sympathy flashed in his uncle's eyes. "You have one that you can't continue."

"My arm is better. I'm making progress." He concentrated on his fingers protruding from the sling. He was able to move his index and middle finger ever so slightly.

He could tell from the look on his uncle's face that he wasn't impressed. If only he knew how much effort it took to move any part of his hand.

"I give thanks to God for His mercy and pray for your recovery daily," Otis said. "As do your parents, but your father needs a man with two strong arms to work in the mill if he is to earn a profit and meet his obligations."

"He hasn't said this to me."

"I don't imagine he would. I'm asking you to consider what is best for your family. I have work, worthy work, for you to do that requires a good mind but not two strong arms. Besides, your mother will rest easier knowing you aren't trying to do too much."

A sick sensation settled in Roman's stomach. "She told you about the incident last week?"

"Ja."

"It was a freak accident. My sling got snagged on a log going into the saw. The strap broke and freed me." He tried to make it sound less dire than it had been. He would relive the memory of those horrible, helpless moments in his nightmares for a long time. His confidence in his ability to do the job he'd always considered his birthright had suffered a harsh blow.

"I understand you were jerked off your feet and dragged toward the saw," Otis said.

"I was never in danger of being pulled into the blade." He was sure he could have freed himself.

Maybe.

"That's not how your mother saw it."

No, it wasn't. Roman's humiliation had been made all the worse by his mother's fright. She had come into the mill to deliver his lunch and witnessed the entire thing. Her screams had alerted his father and younger brother, but no one had been close enough to help. God had answered her frantic plea and freed him in time.

"I'm sorry *Mamm* was frightened, but sawmill work is all I know. I don't see how I can be of use to you in this business," Roman said.

"I fully expect you to give me a fair day's work for your wage. Joann Yoder will teach you all you need to know about being a manager and an editor."

Roman barely heard his uncle's words. He stared at his useless arm resting in the sling. It was dead weight around his neck. He didn't want to be dead weight around his family's neck. Could he accept the humiliation of being unable to do a man's job? He wasn't sure. All his life he'd been certain of his future. Now, he had no idea what God wanted from him.

"Say you will at least think about it, nephew. Who knows, you may find the work suits you. It would please me to think my sister's son might carry on the business my brother and I built after I'm gone."

Roman glanced at his uncle's hopeful face. He and his wife were childless, and his recently deceased older brother had never married, but Roman had no intention of giving up his eventual ownership of the sawmill. If he did accept his uncle's offer, it would only be a temporary job. "Who did you say would train me?"

"The woman you saw leaving just as you came in."

"I'm sorry, I wasn't paying attention. Is she someone I know?"

"Joann Yoder. The sister of Hebron, Ezekiel and William Yoder. I'm sure you know her."

Roman's eyebrows shot up. "The bookworm?"

Otis laughed. "I had no idea that was her nickname, but it fits."

"It was something we used to call her when we were kids in school." She was a plain, shy woman who always stayed in the background.

"Joann can teach you what you need to know about this work."

Roman clamped his lips shut and stared down at his paralyzed arm. He had trouble dressing himself. He couldn't tie his own shoes without help. He couldn't do a man's job, a job that he'd done since he was ten years old. Now, he was going to have a woman telling him how to do this job, if he took it. How much more humiliation would God ask him to bear?

He looked at his uncle. "Why can't you show me how the business is run?"

"I'll be around to answer your questions, but Joann knows the day-to-day running of the business almost as well as I do."

So, he would be stuck with Joann Yoder as a mentor if he accepted. Was she still the quiet, studious loner who chose books over games and sports?

Otis hooked his thumbs under his suspenders and rocked back on his heels. "What do you say, Roman? Will you come work for me?"

Chapter 2

Joann trudged along the quiet, tree-lined streets of Hope Springs with her head down and her carefully laid plans in shambles. Early May sunshine streamed through the branches overhead, making lace patterns on the sidewalk that danced as the wind stirred the leaves. The smell of freshly mowed grass and lilacs scented the late afternoon air.

At any other time, she would have delighted in the glorious weather, the cool breeze and the fragrant flowers blooming in profusion beside the neatly tended houses of the village. At the moment, all she could see was more years of shuffling from one house to another stretching in front of her.

If only I hadn't dared dream that I could change my life.

A small brown-and-white dog raced past her, yipping furiously. His quarry, a yellow tabby, had crossed the street just ahead of him. The cat shot up the nearest tree. From the safety of a thick branch, it growled at the dog barking and leaping below. The mutt circled the tree several times and then sat down to keep an eye on his intended victim.

As Joann came up beside the terrier mix, he looked her way. She stopped to pat his head. "I know just how you feel. So close and yet so far. Take my word for it, you wouldn't have liked the outcome if you had caught him." The cat was almost as big as the dog.

Joann walked on, wondering if there was a similar reason why she couldn't obtain the prize she had been working so hard to secure. Would the outcome have been worse than what she had now? Only the Lord knew. She had to trust in His will, but it was hard to see the good through her disappointment.

After a few more minutes, she reached the buggy shop of Levi Beachy at the edge of town. She passed it every day on her way to and from work. Across the street from the shop stood the house that had almost been hers.

Sarah Wyse, a young Amish widow, had lived there until shortly after Christmas when she married Levi. For a time they had rented the house to a young Amish couple, but they had moved away a month ago and the small, two-story house was vacant again.

Vacant and waiting for someone to move in who would love and cherish it.

Joann stopped with her hands on the gate. The picket fence needed a coat of paint. She itched to take a paintbrush to it. The lawn was well-kept, but if the home belonged to her, she would plant a row of pansies below the front porch railing and add a birdhouse in the corner of the yard. She loved to watch birds. They always seemed so happy.

She would be happy, too, if all it took to build a snug home for herself was bits of straw and twigs. However, it took more. Much more.

She gazed at the windows of the upper story. She'd been a guest in Sarah's home several times. She knew the upstairs held two bedrooms. One for her and one for visitors. Downstairs there was a cozy sitting room with a wide brick fireplace. Off the kitchen was a room just the right size to set up a quilt frame. Joann longed for a quilt frame of her own, but she didn't have a place to keep one.

"Joann, how nice to see you," Sarah Beachy said as she came out of the shop with her arms full of upholstery material. She did all the sewing for the business, covering the buggy seats and door panels her husband made in whatever fabric the customer ordered.

"Hello, Sarah," Joann returned the greeting but couldn't manage a cheerful face for her friend.

"Joann, what's wrong?" Sarah laid her bundle on a bench outside the door and quickly crossed the narrow roadway.

Unexpected tears blurred Joann's vision. She didn't cry. She never cried. She rubbed the moisture away with her hands and folded her arms across her chest. "Nothing," she said, gazing at the ground.

"Something is definitely wrong. You're scaring me." Sarah cupped Joann's chin, lifting gently until Joann had no choice but to meet her gaze.

She swallowed and said, "I've come to tell you that

you don't have to wait until September to put your house on the market. You can do it right away."

"You mean you've decided that you don't want it?"

"I'm afraid I can't afford it now."

"I don't understand. Just two weeks ago you told us you were sure you could earn the amount we agreed upon by that time."

"I was fired today."

"Fired? Why on earth would Otis Miller do that?"

"To give the job to someone who needs it more. He's keeping me on as a part-time cleaning woman, and I can have my old job at the bookstore back, but I won't earn nearly enough to pay you what you need by the end of the summer. It was really nice of you and Levi to offer to let me make payments over time, but I know how much you want to make improvements to the business before winter."

"Levi would like to get the holes in the roof fixed and a new generator for the lathe, but I would rather see you happy. If you want, I can talk to him about giving you more time. Perhaps, instead of selling it we could rent it to you. We would both be delighted to have you as our neighbor."

"*Danki,* but that isn't fair to you. Selling your house outright makes much more sense. Besides, with only a part-time job, I wouldn't be able to afford the rent, either. There will be another house for me when the time is right."

She said as much, but she wasn't sure she believed it. Her brothers didn't feel she should live alone and they weren't willing to cover the cost of another house. The local bank had already turned her down for a home loan. She didn't have enough money saved to make a substantial down payment and her employment record wasn't long enough. Only Levi and Sarah had been willing to take a chance on her.

Another home might come along in the distant future, but would it have such a sunny kitchen? Or such an ample back porch with a well-tended garden that backed up to the woods, and a fine sturdy barn for a horse and buggy? This house was perfect. It wasn't too large or too small, and it was close to work.

To the job she didn't have anymore. Her shoulders slumped.

"Come in and have a cup of tea," Sarah said. "There must be something we can do. Perhaps you can find a different job."

The wind kicked up and blew the ribbons of Joann's white prayer *kapp* across her face. She glanced toward the west. "*Danki,* but I should get going. It looks like rain is coming this way."

"I'll have one of the boys hitch up the cart and drive you."

Joann managed to smile at that. "I'm not about to get in a cart with Atlee or Moses. People still talk about how they rigged the seats to tip over backward in Daniel Hershberger's buggy and sent him and his new wife down the street, bottoms up."

Sarah tried not to laugh but lost the struggle. She giggled and pressed her hand to her lips. "It was funny, but my poor Levi was so upset. You will be safe with either one of the twins. Levi's mischief-making brothers have been a changed pair since our wedding."

"How did you manage that?"

Sarah leaned close. "I only feed them when they behave. They do like my cooking."

Joann laughed and felt better. "Ah, Sarah, your friendship is good for my soul."

"I cherish your friendship, as well. Who did Otis give your job to?"

"Roman Weaver. I'm to teach him everything I know about the business."

"I see." A thoughtful expression came over Sarah's face. "So you will be working with Roman. Interesting."

"Only until he has learned enough to do my job. What's so interesting about it?"

A gleam entered Sarah's eyes. "Roman is single. You are single."

Joann held up her hand and shook her head. "Oh, no! Don't start matchmaking for me. Roman doesn't know I exist, and it wouldn't matter if he did. I'm not the marrying kind."

"You will be when God sends the right man your way. I'm the perfect example of that. I didn't think I would marry again after my first husband died, but Levi changed my mind. Roman's a nice fellow. Don't let the disappointment of losing your job color your opinion of him."

"I'll try. Just promise me you won't try any of your matchmaking tricks on me."

"No tricks, I promise."

After refusing a ride once more, Joann bid Sarah farewell and glanced again at the lovely little house on the edge of town before heading toward her brother's farm two miles away. Her steps were quicker, but her heart was still heavy.

* * *

Roman left his uncle's publishing house and stopped on the narrow sidewalk outside. The realization that he couldn't do the job he loved left him hollow and angry.

He'd never once wanted to work anywhere except in the sawmill alongside his father. The business had been handed down in his family for generations. His mother used to say that he and his father had sawdust in their veins instead of blood. It was close to the truth. Now he was being asked to give it up. The thought was unbearable. He'd already lost so much. He tried not to be bitter, but it was hard.

He wouldn't accept his uncle's offer until he'd had a chance to talk things over with his father. Roman had to know if his father wished this. It hurt to think that he might. The gray clouds gathering overhead matched Roman's mood. Thunder rumbled in the distance.

"What did *Onkel* Otis want?" The question came from Roman's fifteen-year-old brother, Andrew, as he approached from up the street. His arms were full of packages.

"He wanted to see how I'm getting along. Did you find all that *Daed* needed at the hardware store?" He held open the door so his brother could put the parcels on the backseat. The job offer was something he wanted to discuss with his father before he shared the information with Andrew.

"I checked on our order for the new bearings, but they haven't come in yet. I have everything else on father's list."

When Andrew climbed in the front, Roman moved to untie his mother's placid mare from the hitching post. Meg was slow but steady and unlike his spirited gelding, she wouldn't bolt if he lost control of the reins. Managing his high-stepping buggy horse with one arm was just one more thing that he couldn't do anymore.

Maybe his uncle was right. Maybe he should move aside so his father could hire a more able man. It wouldn't be forever.

His parents and Bishop Zook had counseled him to pray for acceptance, but he couldn't find it in his heart to do so. He was angry that God had brought him low in this manner. And for what reason? What had he done to deserve this? Nothing. He climbed awkwardly into the buggy.

"Do you want me to drive?" Andrew asked.

"*Nee,* I can manage." Earlier, Roman had tied the lines together so he could slip them over his neck and shoulder as he often did when he worked behind a team in the fields. That way he couldn't accidently drop the reins. By pulling on first one and then the other, he was able to guide Meg along the street without hitting any of the cars lining the block. Driving still made him nervous. He cringed each time an *Englisch* car sped by, but he was determined to return to a normal life.

Just beyond the edge of town, they passed a woman walking along the road. She carried a green-and-white quilted bag slung over her shoulder. He recognized it as the one that had been hanging from a chair in his uncle's office. This had to be Joann Yoder. He glanced at her face as he passed her and was surprised by the look of dislike that flashed in her green eyes before she dropped her gaze.

What reason did she have to dislike him? The notion disturbed his concentration. He tried to ignore it, but he couldn't.

Dark gray clouds moved across the sky, threatening rain at any moment. Lightning flashed in the distance. The thunder grew louder. He pulled Meg to a stop.

Andrew gave him a quizzical look. "What are you doing?"

"A good deed." He waited.

When the woman came alongside, he touched the brim of his hat. "Would you like a lift?"

"Nee, danki," she replied coldly as she walked past without looking at him.

He studied her straight back and determined walk. If she were this unfriendly, it wouldn't be a joy working with her. Why was she upset with him? He'd rarely even spoken to her.

Roman looked at his brother. "What do you know about Joann Yoder?"

"What is there to know? She's an old *maedel.* She does whatever old maids do. Can we get home? I have chores to do yet this evening, and I'd rather not do them in the dark."

The road ahead was empty. The next farm was over a mile away. A few drops of rain splattered against the buggy top. Roman clicked his tongue to get Meg moving. She plodded down the road until she came even with Joann and then slowed to match the woman's steps. They traveled that way for a few dozen yards. Finally, Joann stopped. The mare did, too.

She smiled as she patted the animal's neck. When she turned toward Roman, her smile vanished. She kept her eyes lowered. He was surprised by a sharp desire to make her look at him again. He wanted to see if her eyes were as green as he thought.

"Did you need something?" she asked.

"*Nee.* We are just on our way home."

"At a snail's pace," Andrew added under his breath.

Roman ignored him. "Allow us to give you a ride. We are obviously going in the same direction. It looks like rain."

"I won't melt."

"But you will be uncomfortable."

"I'll be fine."

"Won't your books get wet?"

She looked down at her bag and back at him. A wary expression flashed across her face. It had been a guess on his part but it appeared he was right about the contents of her bag.

As she stared at him, he saw her eyes *were* an unusual shade of gray-green. They seemed to shift colors according to the light or perhaps her mood. Why hadn't he noticed that about her before now? Maybe because she was always looking down or away. A raindrop struck her cheek and slipped downward like a tear.

For a moment, she didn't say anything, then she nodded and wiped her face. "A lift would be most welcome."

"*Goot.* Where can we take you?" He was ashamed to admit he didn't know where she lived.

"I'm staying with my brother, Hebron Yoder. His farm is just beyond the second hill up ahead."

"We don't go that far," Andrew said under his breath.

"It won't hurt us to go a little out of our way." Roman ignored Andrew's put-upon sigh and waited as Joann rounded the buggy and opened the door on the passenger's side. Maybe he could find out why she disliked him.

* * *

Joann wasn't sure what to make of Roman's unusually kind gesture. He'd passed her dozens of times when she was walking along this road without offering her a lift. What was different about today? Did he know she was being fired in order to give him a job? She didn't believe Otis would share that information, but perhaps he had.

Was Roman feeling guilty? If so, then it was up to her to grant forgiveness and get their working relationship off to a good start.

She leaned forward to look around his brother, determined to overcome the shyness that had gotten ahold of her tongue. "Congratulations on your new position."

"What new position?" Andrew demanded.

She caught the annoyed glance Roman flashed at her. She sat back and looked straight ahead. So much for a good start.

"*Onkel* Otis offered me a job at his publishing office," Roman admitted reluctantly.

"Why?" Andrew looked incredulous.

Roman didn't reply. Joann immediately felt sorry for him. The answer was so obvious.

The reason finally dawned on Andrew. "Oh, because of your arm. You didn't take it, did you?"

Joann hadn't considered that possibility. Hope sprang to life in her heart. Was her job safe after all? She waited anxiously for his reply.

"I'm considering it," he said.

Considering meant he hadn't said yes. Was there some way she could convince him to turn down the offer? She had to try. "I'm sure the job wouldn't be to your liking."

"Why do you say that?" he asked.

She racked her mind for a reason. "The work is mostly indoors."

"Not working in the hot sun this summer sounds nice."

She chewed the corner of her lip as she tried to think of another reason he wouldn't want the best job in the world. "It's very noisy when the presses are running."

"I seriously doubt it's noisier than a sawmill." His amusement brought a flush of heat to her face. How silly of her.

All that was left was the truth. She took a deep breath. "It requires hours of reading, excellent comprehension and a firm grasp of writing mechanics as well as an inquisitive mind," she said.

He pulled the mare to a halt and turned to face her. Andrew looked from his brother to Joann and then leaned back out of their way. Roman's brow held a thunderous expression that rivaled the approaching storm. "You don't think I possess those skills?"

She swallowed hard. The truth was the truth. Just because he was upset was no reason to change tactics now. Her chin came up. "I doubt that you do."

"Is that so?"

Joann was tempted to tell him his uncle only offered the job out of pity, but she wisely held her tongue. Nothing good could come from speaking out of spite. She tried to match his stare, but her courage failed. She dropped her gaze to her clenched hands. Why had she started this conversation? It was up to God to decide which one of them was best suited for the job.

In the growing silence, she chanced a glance at Roman's face. His dark expression lightened. Suddenly, he burst out laughing.

"What's so funny?" Andrew asked.

"She's right. I'm not a fellow who enjoys reading or writing."

Joann's hopes rose. "So you don't intend to take the job?"

Roman slapped the reins to get the horse moving. "We'll see. I can learn a new thing if I set my mind to it. Do you always speak so frankly, Joann Yoder?"

Embarrassed, she muttered, "I try not to."

"And why is that?" he asked.

Did he care, or was he trying to make her feel worse? She repeated the phrase her brothers often quoted. "Silence is more attractive than chatter in a woman."

"Says who?" he asked.

"A lot of people."

He wasn't satisfied with her vague answer. "Who, specifically?"

"My brothers," she admitted.

Andrew nodded sagely. "I have to agree."

"I think it depends on the woman," Roman replied.

She glanced at him and thought she caught a glimpse of humor shimmering in his eyes, but she couldn't be sure. Was he laughing at her? Most likely he was. He held her gaze for a long moment before staring ahead again.

Raindrops began splattering against the windshield and roof of the buggy. Joann was every bit as uncomfortable inside as she would've been out in the rain but for a very different reason. Being near Roman made her feel fidgety and on edge, as if something important were about to happen. Thunder cracked overhead and she jumped.

"How long have you worked for our uncle?" Roman asked, looking up at the sky.

"About five months."

"He said that you'll be my teacher if I take the job."

"That's what he told me, too."

"What kind of things would you teach me?"

Andrew interrupted. "I don't know why you're considering it. *Daed* and I need your help in the sawmill. We can't do it all alone."

"I didn't say I was taking it, but I need to know enough to make an informed decision. What things would I have to learn?"

"Many things, like how to set type and run the presses and how to use the binding machines. Eventually, you will have to write articles for the magazine. Many people send us stories to be printed. You'll have to learn how to check any facts that they contain. We don't want to hand out the wrong advice."

"Give me an example."

She thought a moment, and then said, "People send in home remedies for us to publish in our magazine all the time. Sometimes they are helpful, but sometimes they can be harmful to the wrong person, such as a child. When in doubt, we check with Dr. White or Dr. Zook at the Hope Springs Clinic."

He glanced her way. "Have you written any articles?"

"A few."

"What were they about?"

"I wrote a piece about our history in Hope Springs. I've submitted several tips for the Homemaker Hints section that were published. I've even done a number of poems."

"Interesting. What else would my job entail?"

Andrew rolled his eyes. "I can just see you writing homemaker tips and poetry, *bruder*."

Roman paused a moment, then said, "Roses are red, violets are blue, pine is the cheapest wood, oak is straight and true."

Roman chuckled and smiled at his brother. Andrew grinned and said, "That's not bad. Maybe uncle will use it."

The affection between the two brothers was evident. Joann wished for a moment that she could joke and laugh with her brothers that way. They were all much older than she was. She had come along as a surprise late in her parents' lives. Hebron, the youngest of her brothers, had been fifteen when she was born. They were all married and starting their own families by the time she went to school. Her brothers pretty much ignored her while she was growing up. It was only after their parents died that they decided they knew what was best for her.

Roman clicked his tongue to get Meg to pick up the pace. "Tell me what else I would have to learn."

"You would have to proofread the articles that Otis writes or that others send in to be published. You'll have to attend special meetings in the community in order to report on them, such as the town council meetings and school board meetings. We report the news weekly as well as publish a monthly magazine."

"Sounds like a piece of cake."

"Do you think so?" If he didn't value what they did, how could he do the job well?

When he didn't say more, she leaned forward to glance at him. His face held a pensive look. Was he thinking about taking the job or rejecting it? If only she could tell.

Finally, her brother's lane came into view. By the time they reached the turnoff, the rain had slowed to a few sprinkles. "I'll get out here," she said. "Thanks for the lift."

Roman stopped the buggy. Joann bolted out the door into the gentle rain and hurried toward the house. Once she gained the cover of the front porch, she watched as he turned the buggy around and drove away. At least she could draw a full breath now that she wasn't shut in with him.

What was it about being near him that set her nerves on edge? And how would she be able to work with him day in and day out if he did take the job?

"Please, Lord, let him say no."

Chapter 3

Roman sat at the kitchen table that evening with his parents after supper was done. His conversation with green-eyed Joann earlier that day hadn't helped him come to a decision. He wasn't sure what to do. What would be best for him? What would be best for his family?

Although he lived in the *dawdy-haus,* a small home built next to his parent's home for his grandparents before their passing, he normally took his meals with his family. He waited until his younger brother left the kitchen and his mother was busy at the sink before he cleared his throat and said, "*Daed,* I need to speak to you."

"So speak," his father replied and took another sip of the black coffee in his cup. Menlo Weaver was a man of few words. Roman's mother, Marie Rose, turned away from the sink, dried her hands on a dish towel and joined them at the table. Roman realized as he gazed at her worried face that she had aged in the past months, and he knew he was the reason why.

He took a sip of his own strong, dark coffee. "I spoke with *Onkel* Otis today," he said.

"And?" his mother prompted.

"He offered me a job."

There was no mistaking his father's surprise. Menlo glanced at his wife. She kept her gaze down. Roman knew then that it hadn't been his father's idea. That eased some of his pain. At least his father wasn't pushing to be rid of him.

As always, Menlo spoke slowly, weighing his words carefully. "What was your answer, *sohn?*"

Roman knew his father well. He read the inner struggle going on behind his father's eyes. Menlo didn't want his son to accept the job, but he also wanted what was best for Roman. "I told him I'd think it over."

His mother folded her dish towel on her lap, smoothing each edge repeatedly. "And have you?"

"Of course he's not going to take it," Menlo said.

Roman knew then that he had little choice. His father would keep him on, but the cost to the business would slowly sink it. If Roman had an outside job and brought in additional money for the family, they could afford to hire a strong fellow with two good arms to take his place and make the sawmill profitable again.

He looked his father square in the eye. "I've decided to accept his offer. I hope you understand."

Menlo frowned. "Are you sure this is what you want?"

Roman didn't answer. He couldn't.

"You'll come back to work with me when your arm is better, *ja?*"

Roman smiled to reassure him. "*Ja,* Papa, when my arm gets better."

Menlo nodded. "Then I pray it is a good decision and that you will be healed and working beside me soon."

Roman broached the subject weighing heavily on his mind. "You will have to hire someone to take my place. Andrew and you can't do it all alone."

"We can manage," his father argued.

"You'll manage better with more help. Ben Lapp is looking for work. He's a fine, strong young man from a good family," his mother countered.

Menlo glanced between his son and his wife. He nodded slowly. "I will speak to him. I thought you were going to tell us you had decided to wed Esta Barkman."

Roman had been dating Esta before the accident. He'd started thinking she might be the one. Since the accident, he'd only taken her home from church a few times. It felt awkward, and he wasn't sure how to act. He didn't feel like a whole man. He avoided looking at his father. "I'm not ready to settle down."

"You're not getting any younger," his mother said. "I'd like grandchildren while I'm still young enough to enjoy them."

"Leave the boy alone. He'll marry soon enough. The supper was *goot.*"

"*Danki.*" She smiled at her husband, a warm smile that let Roman know they were still in love. Would Esta smile at him that way after thirty years together? He liked her smile. Her eyes were pale blue, not changeable green, but it didn't matter what color a woman's eyes were. What mattered was how much she cared for him.

He wanted to wait until his arm was healed before asking her to go steady, but his mother was right. He wasn't getting any younger. Now, more than ever, he felt the need to form a normal life.

Menlo finished his coffee and left the room. Roman stayed at the table. His mother rose and came to stand behind him. She wrapped her arms around him and whispered, "I know this is hard for you, but it will all turn out for the best. You'll see."

If only he could believe that. Ever since he was old enough to follow his father into the mill, Roman had known what life held for him. At the moment, it felt as if his life had become a runaway horse and he'd lost the reins. He had no idea where it was taking him. He hated the feeling.

"Are you worried about working for my brother? Otis is a fair man."

"It's not *Onkel* Otis I'm worried about working with. It's his employee, Joann Yoder. She's taken a dislike to me for some reason." It was easier to talk about her than about his self-doubts.

"Nonsense. I can't imagine Joann disliking anyone. She's a nice woman. It's sad that no man has offered for her. She has a fine hand at quilting and a sweet disposition."

"Not so sweet that I've seen."

"She is a little different. According to her sister-in-law, she spends all her time with her nose in a book or out roaming the woods, but it can't be easy for her. Be kind to her, my son."

"What do you mean it can't be easy for her?"

"Joann gets shuffled from one house to another by

her brothers. I just meant it can't be easy never having a place to call home."

"I don't understand."

"She's much younger than her brothers. When her parents died, her brothers decided she would spend four months with each of them so as not to burden one family over the other. I honestly believe they think they are being fair and kind. I'm sure they thought she would marry when she was of age, but she hasn't. She's very plain compared to most of our young women."

"She's not that plain." She had remarkable eyes and a pert nose that matched her tart comments earlier that day. Why hadn't he noticed her before? Perhaps because she seldom looked up.

His mother patted his arm. "She's not as pretty as Esta."

"*Nee,* she's not." He rose from the table determined to put Joann Yoder out of his mind. He had much more important things to think about.

"Joann, we're going fishing. Come with us."

Looking up from her book, Joann saw her nieces come sailing through the doorway of the bedroom they shared. Ten-year-old Salome was followed closely by six-year-old Louise.

Joann didn't feel like going out. Truth be told, all she wanted was to sit in her room and pout. Tomorrow they would all travel to Sunday services at the home of Eli Imhoff, and she was sure to see Roman Weaver there. She had no intention of speaking to him.

On Monday, she would learn if she still had her job or if she had lost her chance to buy a home of her own. Last night she prayed to follow God's will, but she really hoped the Lord didn't want Roman to take the job any more than she did. She had tried to find pity in her heart, but the more she thought about him, the less pity entered into the picture. He seemed so strong, so sure of himself. She'd made a fool of herself trying to talk him out of working for Otis.

Why couldn't she stop thinking about him?

Because he was infuriating, that was why. And when he turned his fierce scowl on her, she wanted to sink through the floor.

"Come on, Papa is waiting for us." Louise pulled at Joann's hand.

She shook her head and said, "I don't think I'll come fishing today, girls."

"You love fishing, *Aenti* Joann. Please come with us," Salome begged.

Louise leaned on the arm of the chair. "What are you reading?"

Joann turned her attention back to her book. She'd read the same page three times now. "It's a wonderful story about an Amish girl who falls in love with the Amish boy next door."

"Does she marry him?" Louise asked.

Joann patted the child's head. "I don't know. I haven't finished the book. I hope she does."

Louise looked up with solemn eyes. "Because you don't want her to be an old *maedel* like you are?"

Joann winced. Out of the mouths of babes.

"That's not nice, Louise," Salome scolded. "You shouldn't call *Aenti* Joann an old maid."

Louise stuck out her bottom lip. "But Papa says she was born to be a *maedel*."

Joann was well aware of her brother's views on the

subject of her single status. Perhaps it was time to admit that he was right. A few months ago, she had cherished a secret hope that Levi Beachy would one day notice her. However, Levi only had eyes for Sarah Wyse. The two had wed last Christmas. Joann was happy for them. Clearly, God had chosen them for each other.

Only, it left her without even the faintest prospect for romance. There was no one in Hope Springs that made her heart beat faster.

She closed her book and laid it aside. "Salome, do not scold your sister for speaking the truth."

Joann wanted to know love, to marry and to have children, but if it wasn't to be, she would try hard to accept her lot in life. When did a woman know it was time to give up that dream?

Salome scowled at Louise. Louise stuck her tongue out at her sister and then ran from the room.

Salome turned back to Joann. "It was still a rude thing to say. Never mind that baby. Come fishing with us."

Joann shook her head. "I don't think so."

"But your new fishing pole came. Don't you want to try it out?"

Joann sat up. "It came? When?"

"The mailman brought it yesterday."

"Where is it?"

Salome pointed to the cot in the corner of the up-stairs bedroom. "I put it on your bed."

"It's not there now. It wasn't there when I went to bed last night."

"Maybe Louise was playing with it. I told her not to," Salome said, shaking her head.

Joann cringed at the thought. If the younger girl had

damaged it, she wouldn't be able to get her money back. She'd foolishly spent an entire week's wages on the graphite rod and open-faced spinning reel combo. In hindsight, it was much too expensive.

Oh, but when she'd tried it out in the store, it cast like a dream. Maybe she should keep it.

No, she gave herself a firm mental shake. She couldn't afford it now. If her hours were cut, she would have to make sacrifices in order to keep putting money in her savings account. Otherwise, she faced a lifetime of moving her cot from one household to another.

Salome dropped to the floor to check under the other beds in the room. Finally, she found it. "Here it is."

Joann breathed a sigh of relief when Salome emerged with the long package intact. Taking the box from her niece, Joann checked it over. It bore several big dents.

"Did she break it?"

"I don't think so." Joann carefully opened one end and slid out the slender black pole. The cork handle felt as light and balanced in her hand now as it had in the sporting goods store. She unpacked the reel. It was in perfect shape.

From the bottom of the stairs, Joann heard her brother call out, "Salome, are you coming?"

"Yes, Papa. Joann is coming, too." She ran out the door and down the stairs.

Joann stared at the pole in her hands. Why not try it out once before sending it back? What could it hurt? It might be ages before she had a chance to use such a fine piece of fishing equipment again. She bundled it into the box, grabbed her small tackle box from beneath her cot, exchanged her white prayer *kapp* for a large black kerchief to cover her head and hurried after her niece.

On her way out of the house, Joann paused long enough to grab an apple from the bowl on the kitchen table. Outside, she joined the others in the back of the farm wagon for the jolting ride along the rough track to a local lake. It wasn't far. Joann walked there frequently, but she enjoyed sitting in the back of the wagon with the giggling and excited girls at her side.

The land surrounding the small lake belonged to an Amish neighbor who didn't care if people fished there as long as they left his sheep alone and closed the gates behind them. Joann had been coming to the lake since she was a child. Joseph Shetler, the landowner, had been friends with her grandfather. The two men often took a lonely little girl fishing with them. Occasionally, Joann still caught sight of Joseph, but he avoided people these days. She never knew why he had become a recluse. He still came to church services, but he didn't stay to visit or to eat.

The wagon bounced and rumbled along the faint wheel tracks that led to the south end of the lake. It had once been a stone quarry that had filled with water nearly a century ago. When they reached the shore, everyone piled out of the back of the wagon and spread out along the water's edge. The remote area was Joann's favorite fishing place. She knew exactly where the largemouth bass, bluegill and walleye hung out.

She'd spent many happy hours fishing here peacefully by herself, but each time served to remind her of the wonderful days she'd spent there with her grandfather. He had been the one person who always had time for her.

If she closed her eyes, she could still hear his craggy voice. "See that old log sticking out of the bank, child?

There's a big bass right at the bottom end of it. Mr. Bass likes to hole up in the roots and dart out to catch unwary minnows swimming by. Make your cast right in front of that log. You'll get him."

Joann smiled at the memory. It had taken many tries and more than a few lost lures before she gained the skill needed to put her hook right where she wanted it. Her *daadi* had been right. She caught a dandy at that spot.

She was always happy when she came to the lake. She kept a small journal in the bottom of her tackle box and made notes about of all her trips. She used the information on weather conditions, insect activity and water temperature to compile information that made her a better angler.

Normally, she released the fish if she was alone. Today, she would keep what she caught and the family would enjoy a fish fry for supper.

When everyone was spreading out along the lakeshore, she said, "I haven't had much success fishing on this end of the lake. The east shore is a better place."

"Looks *goot* to me." Hebron threw in his line.

Joann shrugged and headed away from the lake on a narrow path that wound through the trees for a few hundred yards before it came out at the shore again near a small waterfall. This was where the fishing was the best.

Carefully, she unpacked her pole and assembled it. From her small tackle box, she selected a lure that she knew the walleye would find irresistible and began to cast her line. Within half an hour, she had five nice fish on her stringer.

She pulled the apple from her pocket and bit into

the firm, sweet flesh. The sounds of her crunch and of the waterfall covered approaching footsteps. She didn't know she wasn't alone until her brother said, "Joann, I've been calling for you."

Startled, she turned to face him. "I'm sorry, Hebron, I didn't hear you. What do you need?"

"We're getting ready to go. The fish aren't biting today."

"I've been catching lots of walleye. Have you tried a bottom-bouncing lure?" She set her apple beside her on a fallen tree trunk and opened her tackle box to find him a lure like the one she was using.

He waved aside her offering. "I've tried everything. What's that you're fishing with?"

"An orange hopper."

"I meant the rod. Where did you get that?"

She extended her pole for him to see. "I ordered it from the sporting goods store in Millersburg."

"Mighty fancy pole, sister."

"It works wonderfully well. Try casting it, you'll see. You'll be wanting one next."

"My old rod and reel are good enough."

She turned back to the water. "Okay, but I'm the one catching fish."

"Be careful of pride, sister. The *Englisch* world has many things to tempt us away from the true path."

"I hardly think a new fishing pole will make my faith weaker."

"May I see it?" he asked.

"Of course. You can cast twice as far with it as your old one. Give it a try." She handed it over, delighted to show him how well-made it was and how nicely it worked. She picked up her apple and took a second bite.

Hebron turned her rod first one way and then another. "A flashy thing such as this has no place in your life, sister."

"It does if I catch fish for you and your children to eat."

"Are you saying I can't provide for my family?"

"Of course not." She dropped her gaze. Hebron was upset. She could tell by the steely tone creeping into his voice.

He balanced the rod in his hand, nodded and drew back his arm to cast.

Eagerly, she sought his opinion. "Isn't it light? It really is better than any pole I've owned."

He scowled at her, and then threw the rod with all his might. Her beautiful pole spun through the air and splashed into the lake.

"No!" she cried in dismay and took a step toward the water. The apple dropped from her hand.

"False pride goes before a fall, sister," Hebron said. "I would be remiss in my duty if I allowed you to keep such a fancy *Englisch* toy. Already, I see how it has turned your mind from the humble ways an Amish woman should follow. Now, come. We are going home. I will carry your fish. It looks as if God has given us enough to feed everyone after all." With her stringer of fish in his hand, he headed toward the wagon.

She stood for a moment watching the widening ripples where her rod had vanished. Now she had nothing to return and nothing to show for her hard-earned money. Like the chance to own a home, her beautiful rod was gone.

Tears pricked against the back of her eyes, but she refused to let them fall.

* * *

Late in the afternoon on Saturday, Roman took off his sling and began the stretching exercises he did every day, four times a day. His arm remained a dead lump, but he could feel an itching sensation near the ball of his shoulder that the doctors assured him was a good sign. As he rubbed the area, the uncomfortable sensation of needles and pins proved that the nerves were beginning to recover. He had been struck by a pickup truck while standing at the side of his buggy on a dark road just before Christmas. The impact sent him flying through the air and tore the nerves in his left shoulder, leaving him with almost complete paralysis in that arm.

Dr. White and Dr. Zook, the local physicians he saw, were hopeful that he would regain more use of his arm, but they cautioned him that the process would be slow. Unlike a broken bone that would mend in six or eight weeks, the torn nerves in his arm would take months to repair themselves. Even then, there was no guarantee that he would regain the full use of his extremity.

Roman tried to be optimistic. He would work for his uncle until his arm was better. When it was, he would return to working with his father in the sawmill as he had always planned. He held tight to that hope. He had to.

The outside door opened and his brother Andrew came in. He held a pair of fishing poles in one hand. "I'm meeting some of the fellows down at the river for some fishing and a campout. Do you want to come along?"

Roman put his sling back on. He didn't like people seeing the way his arm hung useless at his side. "I don't think so."

"Come on. It will do you good. You used to like fishing."

"I like hunting, I like baseball, I like splitting wood with an ax, but I can't do any of those things. In case you haven't noticed, I've only got one good arm." The bitterness he tried so hard to disguise leaked out in his voice.

"You don't need to bite my head off." Andrew turned away and started to leave.

"Wait. I'm sorry. I didn't mean to snap at you."

Andrew's eyes brightened. "Then you'll come? There's no reason you can't fish with one arm."

"I'm not sure I can even cast a line. Besides, how would I reel in a fish? That takes two hands."

"I've been thinking about that and I have an idea. It only takes one hand to crank a reel. What you need is a way to hold the rod while you crank. I think this might work."

Andrew opened his coat to reveal a length of plastic pipe hooked to a wide belt and tied down with a strap around his leg.

Roman frowned. "What's that?"

"A rod holder. You cast your line and then put the handle of your pole in this. The inside of the pipe is lined with foam to help hold the rod steady. This way it won't twist while you're cranking. See? I fixed it at an angle to keep the tip of the rod up. All you have to do is step forward or backward to keep tension on the line."

Roman looked at the rig in amazement. "You thought of this yourself?"

It was a clever idea. It might look funny, but the length of pipe held the rod at the perfect angle. "It just might work, little brother," Roman said.

"I know it will. With a little practice, you'll be as good as ever. Come with us." Andrew unbuckled his invention and held it out.

Roman took it, but then laid it on the counter. "Maybe next time."

He didn't want his first efforts to be in front of Andrew and his friends. A child could cast a fishing pole but Roman wasn't sure he could.

Andrew nodded, clearly disappointed. "Yeah, next time," he said.

He left Roman's pole leaning in the corner and walked out. After his brother was gone, Roman stood staring at the rod holder. He picked up his brother's invention. Surely, he could master a simple thing like fishing, even with one arm.

There was only one way to find out. After checking to make sure no one was about, he gathered his rod and left the house. Since he knew Andrew and his friends were going to the river, Roman set off across the cornfield. Beyond the edge of his father's property lay a pasture belonging to Joseph Shetler. Wooly Joe, as he was called, was an elderly and reclusive Amish man who raised sheep.

It took Roman half an hour to reach his destination. As he approached the lake, he saw Carl King, Woolly Joe's hired man, driving the sheep toward the barns. Roman knew Carl wasn't a member of the Amish faith. Like his boss, he kept to himself. The two occasionally came to the mill for wood for fencing or shed repairs, but Roman didn't know them well. When Carl was out of sight, Roman had the lake to himself.

He glanced around once more to make sure he was unobserved. In the fading twilight, he faced the glass-like water that reflected the gold and pink sunset. Lifting his rod, he depressed the button on the reel and cast it out. He hadn't bothered adding bait. He wasn't ready to land a fish and get it off the hook with one hand. Not yet.

He slipped the handle of his rod into the holder his brother had made. It was then he discovered that actually reeling it in wasn't as difficult as he had feared. When he had all the line cranked in, he pulled the rod from the holder and flipped another cast.

This wasn't so bad. Maybe he should have brought some bait. He'd only reeled in a few feet when he felt his hook snag and hang up. He yanked, and it moved a few feet but it wouldn't come free. What was he snagged on?

Chapter 4

Roman discovered just how hard it was to crank his rod with something on the other end. It wasn't a fish, just deadweight. Suddenly, it gave a little more. He half hoped the line would break, but it held. Whatever snagged his hook was being pulled across the bottom of the lake. When he finally managed to wrestle it in, he stared at his prize in amazement. It was someone's fishing pole.

When he stepped down to the water's edge, he noticed a half-eaten apple bobbing at the shoreline. There were fresh footprints in the mud at the edge of the water, too. He'd stumbled upon someone's fishing spot, and they hadn't been gone more than an hour or two.

It was easy to tell that the pole hadn't been in the water long, either. There wasn't a speck of rust on the beautiful spinning reel. The rod and handle were smooth and free of slime.

Whoever had lost the nice tackle had done so recently. Had Carl been fishing before Roman showed up? Was this his pole? It wasn't a run-of-the-mill fishing pole. This was an expensive piece of equipment. Far better than the one Roman owned.

He'd found it. Should he keep it?

He carried his prize to a fallen tree and sat down. It didn't seem right to keep such a high-priced rod and reel. How had it come to be in the lake? Maybe the unfortunate angler had hooked a fish big enough to pull his unattended gear into the water. Whatever happened, Roman was sure the unknown fisherman regretted the loss. He certainly would.

He debated what to do. If he left it here, would the owner return to fish at this spot, or would another angler chance upon it?

He decided on a course of action. From his pocket, he pulled the pencil and small notebook he normally carried to jot down wood measurements. Keeping it handy was a habit.

He wrote: *Fished this nice pole from the lake. Take it if it's yours or you know who owns it.*

That should suffice. He left the pole leaning against the log and weighted his note down with a stone. If the owner returned, it would be here for him. He'd done the right thing. He would check back later in the week. If the rod was still here, then the good Lord wanted him to have it.

Gathering up his old pole, Roman tucked it under his arm and headed for home, content that he'd be able to enjoy an evening of fishing with his brother in the fu-

ture without embarrassment. At least one thing in his
life was looking up. Hopefully, his new job would be
just as easy to master.

Joann followed her sister-in-law and her nieces into
the home of Eli Imhoff on Sunday morning. She took
her place among the unmarried women on the long
wooden benches arranged in two rows down the length
of the living room. Her cousin, Sally Yoder, sat down
beside her.

Sally was a pretty girl with bright red hair, fair skin
and a dusting of freckles across her nose. While many
thought she was too forward and outspoken, Joann considered her a dear friend. She often wished she could be
more like her outgoing cousin. Just behind Sally came
Sarah and Levi with Levi's younger sister, Grace. Sarah
sat up front with the married women. Grace took a seat
on the other side of Joann. Levi crossed the aisle to sit
with the men.

Joann's eyes were drawn to the benches near the
back on the men's side where the single men and boys
sat. She didn't see Roman.

"Are you looking for someone?" Grace asked.

Joann quickly faced the front of the room. "No one
special."

"Is Ben Lapp back there?" Sally asked with studied
indifference. She picked up a songbook and opened it.

Joann wasn't fooled. Sally was head over heels for
the handsome young farmer. Ben was the only one who
didn't seem to know it.

Joann glanced back and saw where Ben was sitting
just as Roman came in and took a seat. Their eyes met,

and she quickly looked forward again. She whispered to Sally, "Ben is here."

"Is he looking at me?"

"How should I know?"

"Check and see if he's looking this way."

Joann glanced back. Ben wasn't looking their way, but Roman was. Joann quickly faced forward and opened her songbook.

Sally nudged her with her elbow. "Well? Is he?"

"No."

"Oh." Disappointed, Sally snapped her book closed. After a moment, she leaned close to Joann. "Is he looking now?"

"I'm not going to keep twisting my head around like a curious turkey. If he's looking, he's looking. If he isn't, he isn't."

"Fine. What's wrong with you today?"

"I'm sorry. I'm just upset because I may lose my job."

"Why? What happened?" Grace asked.

"Otis wants his nephew to take over my position."

Sally gave up trying to see what Ben was doing. "Which nephew?"

"Roman Weaver."

Grace shot her a puzzled look. "What does Roman know about the printing business?"

"Whatever I can teach him in two weeks. After that, I go back to my old job at the bookstore. Oh, I'm the cleaning lady now, too."

"That's not fair," Sally declared. "You do a wonderful job for the paper. My mother says the *Family Hour* magazine has been much more interesting since you started working for Otis."

Joann sighed. "I love the job, but what can I do?"

"Quit," Sally stated as if that solved everything. "Tell Otis he can train his own help and clean his own floors."

"You know I can't do that. I need whatever work I can get."

Esta Bowman came in with her family. Grace nodded slightly to acknowledge her. Esta moved forward to sit on a bench several rows in front of Sally. The two women had been cool toward each other for months.

According to gossip, Esta had tried to come between Grace and her come-calling friend, Henry Zook. Happily, she had failed. Grace confided to Sally that she and Henry would marry in the fall. Although Amish betrothals were normally kept secret, Sally shared the news with Sarah and Joann. Joann hadn't told anyone else.

Grace whispered to her. "Esta has been at it again. Everyone knows she's walking out with Roman Weaver, but according to her sister, she's just doing it to make Faron Martin jealous. Two weeks ago, Henry saw her kissing Ben Lapp."

"Ben wouldn't do that," Sally snapped.

Grace waved aside Sally's objection. "I think she was only trying to make Faron notice her. Anyway, it worked. She left the barn party last Saturday with Faron, and I saw them kissing. I noticed he drove his courting buggy today. Mark my words, she'll ride home with him this evening and not with Roman."

Joann discovered she wanted to hear more about Roman's romantic attachment, but she knew church wasn't the place to engage in gossip. She softly reminded Grace of that fact. Grace rolled her eyes but fell silent.

Joann resisted the urge to look back and see if Roman's gaze rested tenderly on Esta. It was none of her business if he was about to be dumped by a fickle woman.

Joann turned her heart and mind toward listening to God's word.

After the church service, the families gathered for the noon meal and clustered together in groups to catch up on the latest news. There were two new babies to admire and newlyweds to tease. Then Moses and Atlee Beachy got up a game of volleyball for the young people that kept everyone entertained. It was pleasant to visit with the friends she didn't see often. Joann was sorry when it came time to leave. She found herself searching for Roman in the groups of men still clustered near the barn but didn't see him. Nor did she see Esta among the women.

Hebron walked up to her, a scowl on his face. "Have you seen the girls?"

She looked around for her nieces. "I think they were playing hide-and-seek in the barn with some of the other children."

"See if you can find them. I'm ready to go."

Joann walked into the barn in search of her nieces. It wouldn't be the first time the girls had stayed hidden to keep from having to go home when they were having fun. They often played this game. After calling them several times, Joann accepted that she would have to join the game and find them herself. She climbed the ladder to the hayloft. A quick check around convinced her they weren't hiding there. So where were they?

Joann returned to the ground level and began checking in each of the stalls. She didn't believe the girls would be hiding with any of the horses, but she didn't know where else to look. One stall was empty. A rustling sound from within caught Joann's attention. She stepped inside but her search only turned up a cat with a litter of kittens curled up in a pile of straw in the far corner. She took a moment to reassure the new mother. Stepping closer, she stooped to pet the cat and admire the five small balls of black-and-white fur curled together at her side. It was then she heard Roman's voice.

"Esta, I wish to speak to you alone."

"You sound so serious, Roman. What's the matter?"

"May I speak frankly?" Something in his voice held Joann rooted to the spot.

"Of course. We're friends, aren't we?"

"I hope that we have become more than friends. That's what I wish to talk about."

"Why, Roman, I'm not sure I know what you mean." Esta's coy reply sent Joann's heart to her feet. She needed to let them know she was present, but she dreaded facing Roman. Maybe if she stayed quiet, they would leave and she wouldn't be discovered. She held her breath and prayed. To her dismay, they stopped right outside the stall where she crouched beside the kittens.

"Can I take you home tonight?" Roman asked.

"Did you bring your courting buggy? I thought you came with your family."

"I did come with my family, but it would make me very happy if you would walk out with me this evening."

"I've already told Faron Martin that he could take me home. He brought his courting buggy."

"Tell him you've changed your mind."

"But I haven't."

"Esta, don't do this to me."

"Don't do what? I want to ride in Faron's buggy. He's got a radio in it, and his horse is a mighty flashy stepper. Almost as pretty as your horse, but of course, you can't drive him anymore, can you?"

Joann heard the teasing in Esta's voice. She was toying with Roman. Did she care who took her home as long as they had a tricked-out buggy? Joann wanted to shake her. How could a woman be so fickle?

"Esta, I'm ready to settle down. Aren't you?"

"Are you serious?"

"Very serious."

Joann wished she was anywhere else but eavesdropping on a private conversation. She shouldn't be listening. She covered her ears with her hands and took a step back. She didn't know the mother cat had moved behind her until she stepped on her paw.

The cat yowled and sank her teeth into Joann's leg. She shrieked and shook the cat loose as she stumbled backward. She lost her balance and hit the stall door. The unlatched gate flew open and Joann found herself sprawled on her backside at Roman's feet.

Esta began laughing, but there was no mirth on Roman's face.

"What do you think you're doing?" he demanded.

"I'm sorry," she sputtered, struggling to her feet.

Esta crossed her arms. "She's making a fool of herself, as usual."

"I was looking for my nieces, if you must know." Joann said as she dusted off her skirt and straightened her *kapp.*

A smug smile curved Esta's lips. "She's just eavesdropping on us because she can't get a boyfriend of her own."

Joann's chin came up. "At least I don't go around kissing everyone who walks out with me."

Shock replaced Esta's grin. "How dare you."

Growing bolder, Joann took a step closer. "Which one is a better kisser? Ben Lapp or Faron Martin?"

"Oh!" Esta's face grew beet red. She covered her cheeks with her hands and fled.

It was Joann's turn to sport a smug grin. It died the second she caught sight of Roman's face. The thunderous expression she dreaded was back.

"What have I ever done to you?" he asked in a voice that was dead calm.

She looked down, unable to meet his gaze. "Nothing."

"Then why your spiteful behavior?"

"You call the truth spiteful?" She glanced up, trying to judge his reaction.

"What truth is that?"

"Esta Barkman is a flirt, and she's using you."

"I won't listen to you speak ill of her."

"Suit yourself." She swept past him, wishing that she had kept her mouth closed. What did she care if Esta was leading him on? It was none of her business what woman he cared for. Joann only hoped she had opened his eyes to Esta's less-than-sterling behavior even if it cost his good opinion of her.

On Monday morning, a faint hope still flickered in Joann's heart as she walked up to the front door of the publishing office. She didn't see Roman's buggy on the street. Perhaps he wouldn't come, and she could continue with her job as if nothing had happened. Oh, how she prayed that was God's will.

She paused with her hand on the doorknob. "Please,

Lord, don't make me work with that man," she whispered.

She pushed open the door and came face-to-face with the object of her prayers. Roman Weaver stood behind the front counter. He scowled at her and glanced over his shoulder at the clock on the wall. It showed five minutes past nine. Looking back at her, he said, "You're late."

Great. Just great. He was here in spite of her prayers. This was going to be a long day.

Joann hung her bag on the row of pegs beside the door as she struggled to hide her disappointment. "I'm not late. That clock is ten minutes fast. I've been meaning to reset it. Welcome to Miller Press. We publish a monthly correspondent magazine with reports from scribes in a number of Amish settlements, plus other news and stories. We also publish a weekly paper that has sections on weddings, births, deaths, accidents and other special columns. Besides those two, we also do custom print jobs."

Two straw hats hung on the pegs. That meant only Otis and Roman had come in. Gerald Troyer and Leonard Jenks would be in anytime now. Hopefully they would come quickly. She was running out of things to say.

The thought no sooner crossed her mind than the outside door opened and Gerald walked in. A tall and lanky young man, his short, fuzzy red-brown beard proclaimed him a newlywed. "Morning, Joann. Did you have a nice weekend?"

"Well enough. And you?" She refused to look at Roman. She would need to apologize at some point for her behavior yesterday.

Although he was Amish, Gerald belonged to a congregation from a neighboring town. He sighed heavily. "My wife's family came for a surprise visit."

"And how did that go?" Joann asked.

"Her mother is nice enough, but I don't think her father likes me. He didn't say more than four words to me the entire weekend."

She saw him glance pointedly at Roman. She couldn't delay the moment any longer. She gestured toward Roman. "Gerald, this is Roman Weaver. Roman is going to be working with us."

"Excellent. Are you a pressman, reporter or typesetter?" Gerald asked as he held out his hand.

Roman shook it. "None of those, I'm afraid, but I'm willing to learn."

Joann said, "Otis wants Roman to learn all aspects of the business. Gerald is our typesetter and helps with local news reporting."

"Minding my p's and q's, that's me," Gerald said with a wide grin.

Joann noticed the puzzled look Roman gave him. He really didn't know anything about the business. She explained. "All type is set in reverse so that when it's printed it's in the correct position. The p and the q look so much alike that it is easy to mix them up. Typesetters have to mind their p's and q's. It's a very old joke."

Roman didn't look amused. "I see. Minding my p's and q's is my first lesson. What's next, teacher?"

He stressed the last word. To Joann's ears it almost sounded like an insult. Any hope of a good working relationship between them was fading fast.

"I guess we'll start with the layout of the building." She indicated the high front counter with a tall chair behind it. "The business consists of six separate spaces. Here in the front office, we take orders for printing jobs, accept information and announcements for the paper and take payments for completed orders."

Otis had his office door closed so she knew not to disturb him. "To the left is your uncle's office. Otis oversees all aspects of the business. Any questions I can't answer, he'll be able to."

The front door opened again and a small, elderly gray-haired man entered. He wore faded blue jeans and a red plaid shirt with the sleeves rolled up. His fingernails were stained with ink. He nodded to Joann.

"Leonard Jenks, I'd like you to meet Roman Weaver," she said.

"You're Otis's nephew, aren't you? He told me he offered you a job. Don't expect special treatment."

"I don't," Roman replied, meeting the man's gaze with a steady one of his own.

Leonard nodded, and then said, "Once I get the generator started, we can run those auction handbills. You have them ready, right Joann?"

"I need to put one through the proof press before we get started. I wanted to wait and show Roman how that's done."

"Then you'd best get to it. Make sure he knows I won't waste my time and my eyesight trying to read his chicken scratching. Block print every order," Leonard said, then crossed to a door at the back of the room and went out.

"Friendly fellow," Roman said.

"You have to give him a chance to get to know you. As he mentioned, no one uses cursive writing here. Everything must be printed legibly. Anything you've written that you want to go into print must be typed up. Can you type?"

He arched one eyebrow. "No."

Joann could have kicked herself. Of course he couldn't type with just one hand. She rushed on to cover her mistake. "Leonard's wife will type up your work. Just let Otis know when you need her."

"I'll learn how to do it. I'm surprised to see an *Englisch* fellow working here. I thought they all went in for computer printing these days."

"Leonard worked for fifty years at a printing company in Cleveland. When they upgraded to more modern presses, he found himself out of a job. Your uncle purchased their old equipment. When Leonard learned where the equipment was going, he asked Otis for a job and moved to Hope Springs. He's invaluable. He knows the equipment inside and out and he can fix anything that goes wrong."

"Is that why his unsociable behavior is tolerated?"

"In part. As I was saying, these are the front offices. Through this door is the makeup room and the table where the type is kept along with our proof press."

She opened the door and went in. Gerald was putting on a large leather apron. "I'll show you how type setup works when Joann is finished with you," he said to Roman.

The sooner she was finished with him the better. Having Roman following her was like having a surly dog at her back. She expected him to snap at her at any second. Her nerves were stretched to the breaking point.

Should she apologize for her comments yesterday or should she go on as if nothing had happened? She certainly wasn't about to mention their meeting in front of Gerald.

"Next door to this building is a bookshop where our books are available to the public," she said. "The store is run by Mabel Jenks, Leonard's wife."

"My uncle hired the wife, too? That's surprising."

"She isn't an employee. He sold half the bookstore to her. Your uncle's business needed to expand beyond the borders of this town. He had books and pamphlets for sale in the store as well as a library of important Amish works. Many are quite rare. Selling part of the bookstore to Mabel, an *Englisch* partner, allowed Otis to expand to the internet so that people from all over the world could find information about the Amish and search for our books. Mabel runs our website, too."

"I had no idea this was such a big operation."

At least he finally seemed impressed with something she was showing him. "Beyond this setup room are the presses. We have four. You'll learn to run each one."

"Leonard will show me that?"

"Ja."

"I can hardly wait."

She ignored his sarcasm. "In keeping with the *Ordnung* of our Amish congregation, we don't use electricity. The lamps are gas. A diesel generator that sits behind the building runs the equipment that isn't hand-operated. It's Leonard's baby, but he'll show you what to do in case you have to run it in a pinch."

"I took a look at them earlier. They're the same type we use at our sawmill."

"I'm glad you're familiar with them." At least he was qualified to do something at his uncle's business.

She wasn't sure why he had accepted the position.

She'd never met anyone less suited to become an editor and office manager, a job that fit her like a glove. Somehow, she was going to have to get him up to speed and quickly. If she couldn't, would Otis let her stay? She doubted it. He was getting on in years. Was he thinking about who would take over after he was gone? If he wanted it to be his nephew, well, she understood, but she didn't have to like it.

She kept walking with Roman close on her heels as they passed between the presses. Hopefully, Otis would want Roman to spend the rest of the day with him or with Leonard. She was going to be a nervous wreck if he was breathing down her neck all day.

"Back here is our storage room." She opened the door and stepped inside. Roman followed.

She'd never noticed how small the room was until he took up all the available space and air. "We keep paper, solvents for cleaning ink off the type and such in here along with rolls of wire for our binder," she said breathlessly. "I'll give you a list of what we stock and how to find it."

"All right."

She turned to face him and gathered her courage. "That's the grand tour. Any questions?"

"Not really." He leaned casually against the doorjamb blocking her only exit.

Now what should she do?

Chapter 5

Her voice held a funny quality that Roman couldn't quite identify. Was it resentment, fear or something else? Before he could decide, she clasped her hands together and said, "About yesterday."

He wondered if she would bring it up. She had spoiled more than his opportunity to take Esta home. He had doubts now that hadn't existed before. What if she was telling the truth? Did he want to know?

"What about yesterday?"

"I want to apologize."

"For what?"

She stared at the floor. "You know."

"I'm not sure I do. Why don't you explain." He couldn't help the amusement that crept into his voice. It wouldn't hurt her to squirm a little before he forgave her. She had been rude to Esta. Although, he had to admit Esta shared part of the blame for the exchange.

He almost missed the baleful glare Joann flashed at him before she looked down at her hands. No wonder she didn't look up often. She gave herself away when she did. Those green eyes of hers reflected her emotions the way still waters reflected the sky and clouds overhead.

"I'm sorry I didn't announce myself when I realized you were having a private conversation," she said. "I should have."

"And?" he prompted.

"And I shouldn't have said those things to Esta," she added in a rush. She tried to move past him, but he continued blocking the doorway.

"And?"

The color rose in her cheeks, making them glow bright pink. He wanted to see how far he could push before that outspoken streak she tried so hard to curtail came out. He didn't have to wait long.

Her gaze snapped up and locked with his. Sparks glittered in the depths of her eyes. "And I'm sorry it was all true!"

He struggled not to smile, having gotten the reaction he wanted. "That's hardly an apology."

Her eyes narrowed as she glared at him. "It's all you're going to get. Your uncle hired you to work here. Don't you think you should get started?"

Roman stepped out of the door and swept his arm aside to indicate she should go first. She hesitated, then squeezed past him. He caught a whiff of a pleasing floral scent. Roses maybe. It had to be from her shampoo or soap. Amish women didn't wear perfumes. Whatever it was, he liked it.

She marched ahead of him to the front of the office. His uncle was behind the front counter waiting on a customer. He called Roman over and showed him the price list they used for ads and single-page flyers and posters. It was easy enough to understand. When the customer left, Otis asked, "How is your first day going?"

Roman lowered his voice. "Joann doesn't seem happy to have me here."

Otis frowned as he looked around Roman to where Joann was gathering a stack of papers from her desk. "Has she said something to that effect? I'll speak to her if she has been rude."

"No, it's probably just me."

"All right, but let me know if she or anyone makes you feel unwelcome. This is my shop, and I say who works here."

Joann crossed the room to join them with several letters clutched to her chest. Her smile was stiff. "Are you ready to learn how to use the proof press?"

"Absolutely, teacher. Lead on."

Her smile stayed in place, but he knew she was annoyed by his pet name for her. All she said was, "Please follow me."

Her instructions were precise and to the point. She quickly showed him how to operate the small press that made a single copy of the handbill they were doing. She handed the first printed page to him. "Read it over and look for mistakes. If you have set the type, get someone else to read it. Errors can slip by because you read it knowing what it should say instead of what is actually on paper."

He scanned the paper carefully and immediately spotted a misspelling. "This should be 'working baler' not 'woking baler,' unless someone does bale woks, whatever that would be."

She frowned at him and leaned close to examine the paper in his hand. Again, he caught the fresh scent of flowers. She glanced up at him and quickly moved a step away. "You're right. I'll let Gerald know. Once he has corrected the letters in the composition stick, we'll turn the project over to Leonard. He'll print the size and number of handbills that were ordered."

"Okay, teacher, what's next?"

He caught a glimpse of the sparks that flashed in her green eyes again before she looked away. With deliberate calm, she said, "The mail. We'll go through it and sort it into letters for the newspaper, ones that might go in the magazine and those that need Otis's attention."

She strode toward the front of the building, and he followed, amused by the square set of her shoulders and intrigued by the gentle sway of her hips.

That thought brought him up short. She had done nothing but cause trouble for him. The last thing he expected was to find her attractive in any way. He quickly dismissed his reaction and focused on what she was saying.

She indicated a stack of mail and offered him a letter opener. She read the first letter. "Alma Stroltzfus is going to be one hundred years old on the twenty-fifth of this month. Her family is hosting a get-together in honor of the day. Family from all across the state will be there. This should go in the weekly paper. Our magazine doesn't come out until after the date, but we could mention it there, too."

He opened his first letter. "This is from a farmer on Bent Tree Road. He is offering forgiveness to the youth who set fire to his haystacks. Magazine or newspaper?"

"Newspaper, I think." She opened the next letter. "This is a poem about losing a child and dealing with that grief. Definitely a piece for the magazine."

They both reached for the stack of mail at the same time. Their hands touched. She jerked away as if he were a hot stove, her eyes wide with shock. "We can finish this later. Let's have Gerald show you how to set type."

As she hurried away, he noticed again the soft curve of her hips beneath her faded dress. There was definitely more to Joann Yoder than met the eye.

By noon, Roman's head was spinning with all the information Joann poured onto him like syrup over a stack of hotcakes. Some of it was soaking in, but a great deal of it slid off his brain and pooled around his feet. He had no idea there was so much to his uncle's business. He hated to admit it, but he was impressed by Joann's scope of knowledge.

There had been a steady stream of customers into the shop all morning. Some placed orders, but many stopped in simply to leave notices and announcements to run in the paper. Joann took care of the customers, accepted payments, filed the notes and continued to serve him a steady diet of information about what his work would entail.

This wasn't going to be an easy job to master. It wasn't one job. There were dozens of new skills he'd have to learn. He clung tight to the thought that if a woman could manage the place so easily after only five months, then so could he.

Otis came out of his office and said, "Time for lunch."

Joann went to the front door and turned the open sign to closed. Below it, she hung a second sign that said they would return at one o'clock.

"Roman, you are welcome to come home with me. My wife would be delighted to feed you," Otis said.

"I'm sorry, I can't join you today. I have an appointment with Doctor Zook. Please tell *Aenti* Velda I'll be happy to eat with you tomorrow."

"I'll do that. I go right by the clinic on my way home. I'll walk with you." He settled his hat on his head and held open the door. Roman grabbed his own straw hat from the peg and stepped out ahead of him.

As they walked side by side on the narrow sidewalk, they passed a few buggies and cars parked alike in front of the various businesses. It was Monday, and quiet in the small village that nestled amid the farms and pastures of rural Ohio. The main activity seemed to be near the end of the street. Roman noticed his mother's cart parked outside a shop.

Otis asked, "Well, what do you think?"

"I think there is a lot to know."

Otis chuckled. "I do more than shuffle papers all day."

"I'm learning that. It's sure not what I expected."

They stepped aside to let a group of women pass in front of them. They were headed into the fabric shop. Roman caught sight of his mother through the window. Otis saw her, too, and waved. She smiled brightly and waved back.

Otis said, "I see the ad and flyers I printed for the

big sale today at Needles and Pins are bringing in customers. That's good. That will mean repeat business."

Roman looked at his uncle. "What made you start a printing shop? Your father ran a dairy farm, didn't he?"

"*Ja.* I worked on the farm with my brothers, but I saw a need among our people for decent things to read. There was a series of articles in one of the local newspapers by an unhappy ex-Amish fellow who believed his new ways were better, and he urged others to follow them."

"We face that all the time. Our life is not for everyone."

"True, but a man must be careful what he reads. Without meaning to, he can allow unholy thoughts to take root in his mind. I started thinking about getting a small press because of those writings and because a friend told me about an old Amish book he wanted to see reprinted. My brother and I printed the book in our barn. It was no thing of beauty, but people bought copies. Not long after that, a woman I knew wrote a manuscript and she asked our Bishop how she might get it published. The Bishop sent her to me. I soon realized the Lord was nudging me to start a business where good Amish folks could find appropriate reading material."

"You print more than books now."

Otis smiled and nodded. "That we do. The magazine grew out of letters people wrote to us after reading some of our books. Once the magazine became popular, people wanted to read the news about their Amish neighbors every week instead of once a month. I bought a bigger press and hired people to help me. Running the press only one day each week wasn't cost-efficient so we started printing flyers, pamphlets and advertisements."

"Not everyone who came in today was Amish."

"We do work for *Englisch* customers as long as the content is acceptable according to our ways. We now print schoolbooks and cookbooks, too. Tourists love our Amish cookbooks. I truly believe the good Lord has caused my business to prosper because I stayed true to His teachings."

"You have created a fine thing, uncle."

"No more than your father has done. Men need good solid wood to build strong houses and barns. I believe we also need good solid books to build strong minds."

They had come to the corner in front of the Hope Springs Medical Clinic. Otis walked on toward his home and a hot lunch while Roman entered the waiting room of the clinic. His uncle's words about good books stayed in his mind. Roman had always considered reading to be something he needed to get by in business and for church. He'd never thought of it as a way to improve his mind.

His father led the family in prayers and Bible reading each morning and evening. Roman read the Bible sometimes at night, but not as often as he should. He wondered what books his uncle would suggest he read. He would make a point to ask him. The thought of books brought Joann to mind. What did she like to read?

He shook his head. Why was he thinking about her, again? She was like a cocklebur stuck to his sock. Not exactly painful, but irritating and difficult to get rid of.

Fortunately, his name was called, and Roman followed the nurse back to a small exam room. Dr. Zook came in a few moments later. Roman waited quietly as he read his chart.

He looked up at last. "I received a letter from the neurosurgeon that did your surgery," Dr. Zook said. "He's optimistic about your recovery."

"I'm glad one of us is."

Dr. Zook closed the chart. "He believes with therapy you should recover some of your hand functions."

"Some, but not all?"

"Are you doing your exercises regularly?"

"*Ja,* but I still can't move my arm."

"I'm not surprised. Brachial plexus injuries such as the one you sustained take a long time to heal. Nerves grow very slowly. Only a fraction of an inch in a month. It may be a few months to a few years before your recovery is complete."

"No one will tell me if I'll be able to use my arm again. Will I?"

"We simply don't know. The brachial plexus, the network of nerves that carry signals from your spine to your shoulder, arm and hand, was badly damaged. Two of your nerves were torn apart. While the surgeon was able to repair them, we're not sure they will function as they once did. Other nerves were stretched drastically when that pickup hit you. It was a blessing you weren't killed."

"Somehow, this doesn't feel like a blessing."

Dr. Zook rose and helped Roman remove his sling. He examined the arm, moving it gently. "Have you noticed any changes at all?"

"I've had some twitches in my forearm."

"That's good. As the nerves start to regrow, you'll feel twitching in the muscles they supply. We can start specific exercises to improve those muscles when it happens. Keep up with your stretches. It's important to keep your joints limber. Once they freeze, there isn't much that can be done for them. How is the pain?"

"Always there."

"Have the pills I've given you helped at all?"

"Some. Keeping my mind occupied helps, too."

"I wish there was more I could do to help, but it is going to take time and it's going to be painful."

"So I've been told."

"I want you to be very careful at work. You could injure your arm badly and never feel it. A sawmill can be a dangerous place at the best of times."

Roman slipped his arm back in the sling. "I'm not working at the mill right now."

"Oh?"

"I'm working at my uncle's print shop."

"That's good. While it may be less physically demanding there, it has its own set of dangers. I've bandaged a few crushed fingers and put some stitches in your uncle, too. Just remember to pay attention."

"I will."

"This injury was life-changing for you, Roman. It can't be easy making the adjustments you've had to make. How are the flashbacks?"

"Less frequent."

"Are you sleeping okay?"

"Sometimes."

"Nightmares?"

"Sometimes."

"Roman, depression is natural after an injury like yours. Anger and sadness are symptoms that can be treated if they persist. Don't be afraid to tell me if you have that kind of trouble."

"It was God's will. I must accept that."

"I believe everything happens for a reason, and that God has a plan for everyone, but He invented doctors to help people along the way. So let me do my job, okay? I'll see you in two weeks or sooner if you need me." The young doctor smiled and left the room.

Roman saw no reason to smile. He was crippled, and no one could tell him when, or if, he would recover.

Joann jumped when the front door banged open, but it wasn't Roman returning. It was only her cousin, Sally.

"Hi, Joann. I brought the sketches that Otis wanted. Is he here?" Sally's cheerful face never failed to brighten Joann's day. Her talent as an artist was well known in the community, and she often supplied the black-and-white line drawings that were the only graphics used in the *Family Hour* magazine. Otis would give her a list of things he wanted for the next month's layout and what size they should be. Her beautifully drawn images of ordinary Amish life never failed to amaze Joann.

"Otis isn't back from lunch yet. Can you wait for him?"

"Sure. I've already done my shopping. I got the prettiest lilac material at Needles and Pins for half off. You should get over there and get some. It's going fast."

"I don't have need of a new dress. Mine are fine."

"They may be fine as you see it, but they are getting a little threadbare and stained. Besides, that gray isn't your best color."

Joann looked down at her dress and matching apron.

It was an old dress, but it was comfortable. "I like it be-cause it doesn't show the ink stains so readily."

"I'm just saying it wouldn't hurt to take a little more care with your appearance. You might have the chance to impress a fine fellow who comes in to place an ad," Sally said.

What did Roman think of her attire? Why should he think of her at all? Deciding it was time to change the subject, Joann reached for the folder her cousin held. "May I see your sketches?"

Sally beamed. "I was hoping you'd ask."

After laying the sketches side by side on the coun-tertop, Sally shifted her gaze to Joann. "Do you think these are what Otis had in mind?"

The outside door opened, and Roman entered the shop with a deep frown creasing his forehead. Had the doctor given him bad news? "I hope he feels bad about taking your job," Sally whispered to Joann as she gave him a cool stare.

Joann gripped Sally's arm and said under her breath, "Please don't say anything."

Fortunately, Gerald came out of the typesetting room at that moment. "Sally, have you brought us some more of your artwork?"

"I brought in four pieces to see if this is what Otis wanted."

"He should be back any minute. Let's see what you have. Roman, Sally is our artist. She can draw almost anything."

Sally blushed. "I have a small talent."

Gerald moved to stand beside the women. Roman hesitated, as if unsure what to do. Joann said, "Come look at these, Roman, and tell us what you think."

He came forward and studied the array. "They're nice. I like this one best."

"I do, too." Joann held up the sketch of a small girl handing her mother jars from a basket.

"It reminds me of my mother's storeroom in the cellar," he said. "She has hundreds of jars on her shelves."

Sally nodded. "I sketched it while my mother was helping my sister put up green beans last summer. The little girl was inspired by my niece."

"It's darling, Sally," Joann said. "I hope Otis will use it on the cover of the next issue. He's writing a series of articles about stewardship. What a great way to show people how being good stewards is really a part of everyday life."

"I didn't know if he would object to the partial view of the child's face. I know some of your customers belong to more conservative churches."

Joann studied the picture closely. Sally had been careful to draw the woman's figure from the back so that her face wasn't seen, but the child had been sketched in profile.

"I think it's fine. What do you men think?"

"Looks good to me," Gerald said.

"If it's controversial, I say don't use it," Roman added his two cents.

Joann saw the joy go out of Sally's eyes. Roman didn't realize how much Sally's artwork meant to her. She never signed her work or took credit for doing it, but she wanted to use the talent God had given her to glorify Him. This was her way of doing that.

"Otis has the final say," Joann said. "It's up to him."

Otis returned a few minutes later. He looked over Sally's sketches and agreed with Joann's assessment.

Thankfully, he kept Roman with him the rest of the afternoon, and Joann had a chance to relax. Roman left a few minutes before five. Joann stayed behind to tidy up the shop.

When she left the building, she was surprised to see Roman come out of the bookstore next door. He had two novels tucked inside his sling. He paused when he caught sight of her. After a moment of hesitation, he said, "My buggy is just around the corner. Would you care to share a ride?"

There wasn't a cloud in the sky. He had no reason to offer her a lift today. "It doesn't look like rain."

"I thought since we were going the same way…" His voice trailed off. He cocked an eyebrow and waited.

It was a long walk after a long day, but she'd rather crawl home on her hands and knees than spend another minute in his company. Thankfully, she managed not to blurt out her opinion. "I have errands to run. I'll see you tomorrow."

Tomorrow would arrive all too quickly.

"Suit yourself." Without another word, he walked away and turned the corner.

Had he actually sounded disappointed? She couldn't imagine why unless he'd come up with a new way to torment her and wanted to test it out.

She started walking, determined not to look back. She was being unkind, but the thought of spending the next two weeks showing him how to do her job was almost more than she could bear. She wasn't herself when he was near. She had to be careful not to trip on her words or run into a desk. He made her feel awkward and jumpy and she had no idea why.

The sad part was that her two weeks with him

wouldn't be the end of it. She'd still be coming in to clean. Would he ask why she'd changed jobs? Or why she was cleaning when she knew so much about printing? What would she say?

The answer to those questions would have to wait. There was no sense worrying about it before it happened.

She did have an errand to run. It hadn't been just an excuse. She stopped at the public library to inquire if the latest copy of *Ohio Angler* had come in. It hadn't.

The *Angler* was the one *Englisch* magazine that she read cover to cover. She suspected that her brothers wouldn't approve, so she never checked it out. She simply read it at the library. It was from those glossy pages that she had gleaned much of her knowledge about fishing. That and spending hours and hours with a pole in her hand.

Disappointed, she left the library and walked through town toward her brother's home. She passed Sarah's house without stopping. That dream was over. She would just have to learn to accept it. When she reached the lane to her brother's farm, she stopped. She didn't feel like going home yet. She needed to be alone and think. She needed the solace of the lake.

Chapter 6

Roman's spirits lifted when he walked into his mother's kitchen. The wonderful aromas of baking ham, scalloped potatoes and hot dinner rolls promised a delicious meal would soon be ready. His mother, with beads of sweat on her upper lip, was stirring applesauce in a large pan on the stove.

She looked over at him and smiled. "You're just in time. Your papa has gone to wash up. How was it? Was Otis kind to you?"

"It was fine. I'll go wash up, too. Where is Andrew?" His bottomless pit of a brother was always in the kitchen trying to sneak a bite of this or that before his mother got it on the table.

A worried frown creased her brow. "He said he wasn't hungry."

Roman stared at her in shock. "Andrew said that? He must be sick."

Roman's father came into the room. "He's not sick. He just doesn't like change. Can't say that I do, either."

"We change when we must," Marie Rose stated quickly. "It's ready. Have a seat." She opened the door of the oven and pulled out the ham.

Roman could tell his father wanted to say more, but he simply took his place at the head of the table.

Marie Rose scowled at Roman. "Go wash up. Don't make your father wait on you."

Joann rounded the bend in the narrow path that led to her favorite spot at the lake and stopped dead in her tracks. A fishing pole, exactly like her new one her brother had thrown into the water, was leaning against a log where she liked to sit. She glanced around expecting to see another angler, but there was no one in sight. She called out, but no one answered.

The breeze off the water caused a bit of paper on the log to flutter. She moved closer and saw the paper had been weighted down with the stone. Picking it up, she read the note and her heart gave a happy leap. It wasn't a pole like hers. It was hers.

By the grace of God, someone had snagged her pole and pulled it from the depths of the lake. She hugged the note to her chest as she spun around with joy.

"Oh, thank you, thank you, thank you," she shouted. If only the unknown angler were present, she would thank him or her in person.

As quickly as her elation bubbled up, it ebbed away. She had her pole back, but she could hardly return it to the store after letting it soak in the lake. Nor could she take it to her brother's home. Hebron would never allow her to keep it after he had made such an issue of her owning it. So what now?

Hebron rarely came to the lake. If she kept the pole here, he would never know. The fallen log she normally sat on was hollow on one end. She knelt down to check and see if it would work as a storage locker. The rotted-out area was almost big enough to hold the rod. Looking around, she found a long pointed branch and worked at making the cavity bigger. After five minutes, she had an adequate space. If she stuffed a little grass into the hollow, she would have a perfect hiding spot.

Dusting off her hands, she sat back on her heels. Somehow, she had to thank the person who'd rescued her rod. Surely, he would return to check on his find. She quickly opened her tackle box and took out her journal. She tore off a sheet of paper. After searching through her lures, she found the blue and green rattle-trap she was looking for. It was a homemade lure, but she'd caught plenty of bass with it. She pondered what to say for a few minutes, then wrote a brief letter. She folded the paper over with the lure inside it and laid the note on the log. She put the same stone on top of it, took a step back and smiled.

At least one thing had improved in her life. She had her pole back. She jotted a few quick notes in her journal about the wind direction and the temperature, then she tied a spinner on her new rod and cast it out into the water. The lure landed exactly where she had aimed. A second later, she had a hard strike and she spent the next half hour happily catching and releasing fish. Her one regret was that the friendly fisherman wasn't here to enjoy the evening, too.

When she judged it to be about suppertime, she put her rod back inside the hollow tree and headed for home. During the long walk, thoughts about the kind fisherman who had given her back her pole kept going around and around in her mind.

Was it someone she knew? Joseph Shetler, perhaps, or his hired man? She thought his name was Carl King, but he wasn't Amish. There was speculation that he had been once but had left the faith.

Who else could her friend be? She couldn't tell from the brief note if he was *Englisch* or one of the Plain people. Maybe it was a woman. That didn't seem likely. The handwriting had been bold, strong and to the point.

Whoever it was, she hoped one day she would have the chance to thank him or her face to face.

Roman stepped off his parents' front porch into the cool evening air. The days were getting longer. It wouldn't be dark for another hour. Supper had been an awkward meal. His father didn't ask about his day. Roman wouldn't have known what to say if he did ask. Andrew had remained absent from the table. Roman didn't want his new working arrangement to put a strain on his relationship with his brother.

He went in search of Andrew and found him sweeping the sawmill floor. The boy was attacking the accumulated sawdust with a vengeance. "I should go get *Mamm*," Roman said. "She would be impressed. She's never seen you intent on getting this place so clean. It would do her heart good."

Andrew stopped sweeping but didn't look at Roman. "I'm not doing it to impress anyone."

"I know. I'm just trying to make conversation, but

I'm not doing such a good job. This is awkward for me, too. I realize you're upset with me for taking the job in town."

He looked at the stacks of new two-by-fours sitting against the wall. They'd had a productive day without him. He'd made the right decision.

Andrew started sweeping again. "So how is your new job?"

"Complicated. *Daed* said he hired Faron Martin to work here. Do you think he'll work out?"

"It's too soon to tell. I guess he is all right, but it's not like working with you."

"Yeah, he has two good arms."

"But he doesn't know up from down about our business."

Roman chuckled. "I'm pretty sure the people at our uncle's office feel the same way about me."

"I don't believe that. You're twice as smart as they are."

Roman pulled a whisk broom from its hook on the wall and began cleaning wood chips off the counter near the doorway. "Thanks for the vote of confidence, but I'm like a babe in the woods. Everything is new. It's not like this place where I know every nook and cranny and every piece of equipment as well as I know the back of my hand."

"So come back." Andrew didn't look up, but Roman didn't need to see the tenuous hope in his eyes, he heard it in his voice.

"If only it were that simple, Andy."

"I miss having you around."

Roman stepped close to his brother and ruffled his hair. "I miss you, too."

"It's not the same. I've worked beside you since I was old enough to hold a handsaw."

"Andy. I've been meaning to thank you for your gift."

Andy stopped sweeping and looked up with a puzzled expression. "What gift?"

"Your fishing rod holder. It works pretty well."

"It does? You tried it out? When? Did you catch anything?"

"I tried it the other evening when you went fishing with your friends, and I did catch something."

"Wait a minute. You went fishing by yourself? Why didn't you come with me?"

"I wasn't eager to embarrass myself in front of others."

"I didn't think about that. I'm sorry."

"The fault lies with me, little brother, not with you. Anyway, I wanted to thank you."

Andrew brightened. "Hey, do you want to go fishing this evening? We caught some nice catfish below the bridge at the river."

"Sure, but let's go over to Woolly Joe's lake. I caught a new rod and reel there."

"What?"

"Honest. I pulled a brand new rod with an open-faced reel out of the water. It was a beauty."

"What did you do with it?"

"I left it there with a note in case the owner came back. I'm curious to see if someone claimed it, so I'm going over there now. Want to come with me?"

Andrew tossed his broom in the corner. "Sure. Can I get my rod? We've got time to get in a little fishing, don't we?"

Roman smiled at his excitement. "Get your rod and

go get a sandwich from mother. I know you missed supper."

"Good idea. I'm starving." He took off toward the house at a run. He reappeared with a sandwich in one hand and a second one in a plastic bag sticking out of his pocket.

It was nearly dusk by the time Roman and Andrew reached the north end of the lakeshore. "Is this the place you left the pole?" Andrew asked.

"*Nee,* it's farther along on the east side."

Roman nearly missed the path, but he managed to locate the fallen log after a brief search.

Andrew turned around once in the small clearing. "I don't see it. Looks like somebody took it home."

"But they left my note." He picked up the piece of paper weighted down with a rock. Once he had it in his hand, he realized it was a larger sheet of paper than the one he'd left the other day. It had been folded in half. When he opened it, something fell out. It was a fishing lure in the shape of a small fish, a plug, obviously hand-carved and painted with iridescent blue and green colors.

He held the page to catch the fading light from the setting sun.

Dear Friendly Fisherman,
You have no idea how happy I was to see my new rod and reel resting against this log today. I knew when I read your note that a true sportsman had recovered my possession. At a time when everything seems to be going wrong in my life, you have created a bright spot with your kindness. As a small token of my thanks, I'm leaving this jig. It

isn't much, but if you cast it along the rocky out-cropping to the west, you should land a nice bass or two with it. Thank you again.

A Happy Angler

Roman grinned. He'd managed to make someone happy. He was glad that he'd left the fishing pole behind. The good Lord had used him to comfort a stranger.

"What's that?" Andrew asked.

"A note of thanks and a fishing lure for my trouble." The pole had done more than make a stranger happy. It had given Roman a reason to come to the lake with his brother. How strange to think a lost rod and reel was God's tool to mend the rift between them.

"That's cool. Why don't you give it a try?"

Roman hesitated. He didn't want to look like a fool in front of Andrew. He couldn't tie on the lure. Besides, what if he hooked a fish and couldn't reel it in? He almost said no, but something in his brother's eyes stopped him.

Instead, he said, "I believe I will if you rig it for me. I'm not very good at knots with one hand yet." It was the first time he had asked Andrew for any kind of help.

"Not a problem." Andrew grinned from ear to ear. He soon had the iridescent fish secured to the end of Roman's line. When he stepped back, Roman approached the shore and located the spot the thank-you note had mentioned. On his fourth cast, he felt a strike. "I've got one."

"Do you need me to help?" Andrew put his own pole down and moved to Roman's side.

"I think I can manage." It was hard to crank the reel

one-handed with a fighting fish on the other end, but Roman realized he was enjoying the challenge.

"Lean back and keep your rod tip up. Giving him a little more line." Andrew continued to call out instructions until Roman landed the fish. At that point, he raced to the water to grab their prize.

Roman realized he was grinning from ear to ear now, too. If he could do this, he could do other things. He sat down on the log and laughed aloud. "Did you see that? I did it."

Even in the fading twilight, he could see Andrew's happy smile as he held the fish aloft. "You did it, all right. It's a beauty of a bigmouth bass. Must be four pounds if it's an ounce. If we catch a few more, *Mamm* can fry them up for supper tomorrow."

"I'm game if you are, but you know you're going to have to clean them all. I don't think I can manage that with one hand just yet."

Andrew's grin faded and then quickly returned. "That's a deal."

Later, when Andrew had walked a little farther along the shore, Roman took a moment to admire the colors of the sunset reflected perfectly on the still surface of the water. The sun rose and the sun set, no matter what troubled him. The world unfolded as God willed. Roman pulled the note from his pocket and read it again.

At a time when everything seems to be going wrong in my life, you have created a bright spot with your kindness.

He knew exactly how it felt to have everything going wrong. Yes, he had recovered the pole and left it here. It had been a simple thing to do, not really a kindness on his part, but he was glad that he had brightened someone's day in much the same way as the letter and the lure had brightened his.

The Happy Angler had more than repaid Roman's offhand kindness with a true gift. The lure was homemade. The maker had surely spent hours carving and painting the piece. Its value was much more than wood and paint. Using it had shown Roman he could ask for help without feeling helpless. He could do the things he used to do. He just had to learn to do them in a different way.

He turned the piece of paper over and wrote a note of his own on the back. Hopefully, the happy angler would return to the spot and learn that the small gift was greatly appreciated and it was so much more than a fishing lure. When he finished the note, he hesitated to sign it.

It was possible the happy angler was someone he knew. Like Roman, the anonymous writer wasn't looking for praise for what he'd done and had chosen not to sign his own name. Perhaps he had a reason for wanting to remain unknown. Roman decided to close the letter with the name the happy angler had given him.

"Andrew, did you save your sandwich bag?"

"*Ja,* mother likes to reuse them, you know."

"Do you think she'll mind if I keep it?"

"I doubt she'll notice. Why?"

"I'm going to write a note thanking this fellow for the plug. I thought I should put it in a plastic bag in case it rains."

"Good thinking. And tell him how well it worked."

Joann was on her way to town the next morning when Roman passed her in his buggy. He stopped the horse a few yards ahead of her and waited. When she came alongside, he said, "Good morning. I'm going your way."

It wasn't exactly a warm invitation. She thought she would have another two miles to mentally prepare herself to spend the day with him. That hadn't happened. She tried to find an excuse, but none came to her. Oh, well, she could hardly refuse a lift this morning without appearing rude.

"Danki." She climbed into the passenger's side, and he set the horse in motion. She wished she had taken more time with her appearance that morning. She had picked her oldest work dress, determined not to think about what Roman Weaver thought of her. Now, she was sorry she hadn't chosen a newer dress. She felt dowdy and small next to him.

The silence stretched uncomfortably as the horse clipped along at a good pace. The steady hoofbeats and jingling harness supplied the only sounds. Joann racked her mind for something to say. She wasn't much good at small talk, especially with men. Finally, she said, "It's a nice morning."

"Ja."

She waited, but he didn't say anything else. Apparently, he wasn't one for small talk, either. As he concentrated on his driving, Joann had a chance to study him.

He seemed more at ease today, although he glanced frequently in the rearview mirror that was mounted on his side of the buggy. He held the reins in one hand. He hadn't looped them over his neck as he had the first time she'd ridden with him. He was dressed as usual in dark pants with black suspenders over a short-sleeved pale blue shirt. It looked new. She couldn't help noticing that he had missed two buttons in the middle of his chest.

She didn't realize she had been staring until he said, "What?"

She jumped and looked straight ahead. "Nothing."

He glanced down and gave a low growl of annoyance. "I was trying to hurry."

He attempted to do up the buttons and hold the reins, but the horse veered to the left into the oncoming lane. He quickly guided the mare back to the proper side of the road.

Joann held out her hand. "I'll drive for you."

He hesitated, then finally handed over the lines. From the corner of her eye, she watched as he struggled with the buttons for several long seconds without success. Another low growl rumbled in his throat. "I'm as helpless as a toddling *kind*."

Roman didn't remind her of a child. Just the opposite. To her, he seemed powerful and sure of himself in spite of his injury. She'd never been more aware of being a woman. He gave up fumbling with his shirt with a sigh of exasperation.

She said, "Let me get them for you."

He took the reins from her and raised his chin as he half-turned toward her. Joann felt the heat in her face and knew she was blushing bright red. This was the kind of thing a wife did for a husband, not a casual acquaintance. Her fingers fumbled with the buttons much longer than she would've liked. When she had them closed at last, she jerked her hands away from his broad chest. "Got it," she said breathlessly.

"Danki." His gruff reply held little gratitude.

"You're welcome. Have your mother cut open the

buttonholes a little more. It will make it easier to get the buttons through them."

"I don't need my mother to do it for me."

It was impossible for her to say the right thing to him. They rode the rest of the way in silence. Joann thought the ride would never end.

The awkwardness between them persisted through-out the morning. Joann tried to show him how to use the saddle binder but quickly realized it took two hands to position the pages and then remove them even though the actual staples were driven in by pressing a lever with her foot.

She pulled the pamphlet off the machine. "I'm sure Gerald can do any of the binding work that's needed."

Roman said, "I'll find a way to make it work."

"Of course." Determined to get past the awkward moment, she said, "Over here we have the Addresso-graph and our address files. One set of cards is for the newspaper, the other is for our magazine."

"This looks like something a one-handed fellow can manage," he drawled.

Thankfully, she heard the jingle of the bell over the front door and went out to greet their customer. A mid-dle-aged man in a fancy *Englisch* suit stood waiting at the counter with a briefcase in his hand. His black hair was swept back from his forehead. He wore a heavy gold ring on one hand.

"Good morning. How can we be of service?" she asked. He wasn't someone she recognized.

"I was told that Roman Weaver works here. I'd like a few words with him."

The man's serious tone sent a prickle of fear down her spine. "He's in the back. I'll get him."

She turned around, but Roman had followed her and was standing a few feet away. "I am Roman Weaver," he said.

"Good morning, sir. Your father told me that I might find you here. I'm Robert Nelson. I'm an attorney. I represent Brendan Smith. Is there somewhere we can talk privately?"

Otis had taken a carton of books to the bookstore next door. "We may use my uncle's office if this won't take long," Roman said.

"Not long at all," the *Englischer* assured him.

Joann had trouble stifling her curiosity as the two men went into the empty office.

Chapter 7

Roman closed the door and turned to face the attorney representing the man responsible for the accident that had altered his life forever. He didn't invite him to sit down.

Mr. Nelson opened his briefcase on top of the desk. "As I'm sure you are aware, the trial for my client is under way. The jury has heard closing arguments, and we expect a verdict tomorrow or the next day."

"Your *Englisch* law is of no consequence to me. I follow God's laws."

"Yes, that's very admirable. I've heard the Amish offer forgiveness to those who have wronged them. Is that true?"

"I have forgiven Brendan Smith. I have already told your partner this."

The junior attorney had come to Roman's hospital room with a letter from Mr. Smith's insurance company.

They offered money to pay Roman's hospital bill and repair his carriage. Roman rejected their offer.

"Yes, I was informed of the conversation. As you were told then, if you change your mind, the insurance company is still willing to make a settlement."

"That is not our way. It would not be right to profit from this misfortune. It was God's will."

Mr. Nelson smiled. "If everyone felt the same way, attorneys such as myself would soon be out of business."

"I am not responsible for how other people feel. Have you come to discuss something else? If not, I must get back to work."

"Actually, I have come for a different reason. It is possible the jury will find my client guilty of vehicular assault. If they do, it will mean jail time for Brendan. As you know, he has had several run-ins with the law, minor things."

"He deliberately destroyed Amish property. He and several of his friends beat an Amish man for no reason."

"Bad judgment, bad company and too much alcohol. He has paid for those crimes according to the law. Hitting your buggy was nothing but an accident. Pure and simple."

Roman wasn't so sure. He remained silent.

"My client also has a family. He has a wife and a small child. He has parents and a younger brother who depend on him. If the judge gives him the maximum allowable sentence, it will be a hardship for more than Brendan."

"I am sorry for his family. I will pray for them."

"I was hoping that you could do more than that. We, Brendan and I, would like to ask you to come to the sentencing hearing if he is found guilty. We're hoping for an acquittal, of course."

"I have no wish to become involved with your *Englisch* court."

"I can understand that, but if you come and speak on Brendan's behalf, ask for leniency for him, the judge might be persuaded to hand down a lighter sentence."

Roman remained silent as anger boiled inside him. He saw no reason to beg for mercy when Brendan had shown no remorse.

The attorney rushed on. "The Amish are well-known for their generous and forgiving nature. I'm asking you, I'm begging you, to speak on this young man's behalf. Enough grief has already been caused by what was a terrible accident. We'll be happy to reimburse you for any expenses involved. We realize you would have to hire a driver to take you to Millersburg, take time off from work, that sort of thing."

This man had no idea of the damage that had been done to Roman's life, yet he stood there offering to pay for his help. To buy forgiveness. In the *Englisch* world, money solved everything, but it couldn't give Roman back a useful arm.

"Is he sorry for the pain he caused? I have not heard him say so."

"I'm sure he is sorry, but we entered a plea of not guilty. You must shoulder some of the blame for the accident. You were parked in a poorly-lit location. You didn't have hazard lights out."

Bitterness swelled up inside Roman. He barely managed to keep his voice level. "I have said I have no wish to become involved with your *Englisch* court."

He turned around, jerked open the door and left the room.

* * *

Joann watched as Roman stormed out the front door. A few moments later, Mr. Nelson came out of the office. He stopped at the counter, opened his briefcase and held out a card. "Tell Mr. Weaver if he changes his mind he can contact me at the phone number on the back of this. It's my cell phone. He can reach me day or night."

Joann took the card. "I'll give him the message."

"I thought you Amish were a forgiving people. That's the way you're portrayed on television."

She didn't care for his snide tone. "We are commanded to forgive others as we have been forgiven."

"You might want to remind Mr. Weaver of that." Mr. Nelson snapped his briefcase closed and left.

Roman returned fifteen minutes later. He didn't say anything when she handed him the card. He simply tore it in two and threw it into the trash.

For Joann, the rest of the week passed with agonizing slowness. She constantly managed to irritate Roman while he seemed to delight in irritating her. It got to the point that even Gerald and Leonard noticed the friction.

Gerald approached her when Roman had gone out with his uncle to purchase supplies they were running low on. He stood in front of her as she sat at the front counter. "Joann, what's going on?"

"What do you mean?" She continued working.

"I've never known you to be so on edge. What's going on between you and Roman?"

"For some reason we rub each other the wrong way. I'll make more of an effort to be nice."

Leonard came in wiping his stained hands on an equally stained rag. He scowled at her. "Joann, my wife told me this morning that you're going back to the bookstore."

"I am."

"Why?" the two men asked at the same time.

Sighing, she propped her hands on the countertop. "Because that's the way Otis wants it."

Gerald crossed his arms over his chest. "We thought Roman was here as added help, not to replace you."

Leonard grunted his annoyance. "He doesn't know enough to replace her. Although, he does know the generator inside and out."

She said, "He will learn what he needs to know. We just have to give him time. Please don't tell him that he's taken my job or hold it against him. I was here on a temporary basis, and now I'm going back to my old job."

"It ain't right," Leonard grumbled as he turned away.

Gerald gave her a sympathetic half-smile. "Well, that explains a lot. I know you like what you've been doing here. It's got to be hard giving it up."

"It is, but all good things must come to an end, right?"

"So they say." Gerald went back to his typesetting table.

Joann waited for Roman to return, determined to be kinder and more helpful. If only he didn't insist on calling her teacher in that snide way.

No matter what had been said between them, each evening when she went out the door, Roman was waiting in his buggy to drive her home. Each morning, he was waiting at the end of her lane to give her a lift into town. When Friday evening rolled around, he was there as usual. She was delighted to have a real excuse not to ride with him.

"I'm staying in town this evening. I'm having supper with Sarah and Levi Beachy."

Was that a look of disappointment in his eyes? It was gone before she could be sure. He said, "I reckon I will see you on Monday, then."

"Actually, I'm driving my cart in on Monday so you won't have to pick me up."

"I see."

He nodded toward her and then drove away, leaving Joann feeling oddly bereft. She watched until his buggy rounded a bend in the road and vanished from sight.

At Sarah's home, Joann found her friend tending her garden. Long rows of green sprouts promised a bountiful harvest in the fall. Sarah was busy making sure the occasional weed that dared to sprout didn't stand a chance of growing to maturity.

"Why don't you put the boys to work doing that?" Joann called from the fence.

Sarah looked up from her work and leaned on her hoe. "Because I want my garden to flourish and not be chopped to pieces."

"Are you saying the twins can't tell a tomato plant from a dandelion?"

"I'm sure they can but it's safer if I do this myself. I'm so glad you could come for supper. Sally and Leah are coming, too."

"Wonderful." The women had all become close friends after Sarah's aborted attempt at playing matchmaker for Levi. The whole thing had been the brainchild of Grace, his sister. In spite of all the women Sarah had put in his path, he only had eyes for her.

Sarah chopped one last weed and then walked toward Joann. "How are you and Roman getting along?"

Joann sighed and shook her head. "Like oil and water. Like cats and dogs. Like salt and ice."

Sarah grinned. "In other words, just fine."

"Please, can we talk about something else?"

Sarah's grin faded. "Is it really that bad?"

"Every time I open my mouth, I manage to say something stupid."

"I always thought you would make a nice couple." Sarah carried her tools to a small shed at the side of the barn and hung them up.

Joann was sure she hadn't heard correctly. "You thought Roman and I would make a good couple? We barely knew each other. Why would you think that?"

From behind them a man's voice said, "It's just a feeling she gets. She can't explain it. It comes over her like a mist. She sees two people groping their way toward each other."

Sarah turned around and fisted her hands on her hips. "Do not make fun of my matchmaking skills, Levi Beachy. I found a wife for you, didn't I?"

He moved to stand close beside her. "If I remember right, I'm the one who found a husband for you," he said softly.

Joann chuckled. "If you two are gonna start kissing, I'm going to leave. However, I would like to point out that I knew before you did, Sarah, that Levi was in love with you. And I told you that, didn't I?"

Levi slipped his arms around his wife. "I remember all the effort she put into convincing me that she loved fishing. It was a ploy to get you and me together on a fishing trip, Joann. She hates fishing."

Sarah cupped his cheek with one hand. "I don't mind fishing. As long as I don't have to touch them, clean them or take them off the hook. If you wanted a fishing buddy instead of a wife you should've asked Joann to marry you."

Levi looked at Joann. "If I had only known, I would've given you much more serious consideration."

Joann giggled. "I'm afraid Sarah is the only one brave enough to take on you and the twins. I wouldn't have the heart for it."

"Speaking of the twins," Levi said as he looked around, "where are they?"

"They went to a singing party at David and Martha Nissley's place." She whispered to Joann, "The Miller twins are going to be there."

Levi scowled. "Those girls are too young to be going out."

Sarah patted his arm. "They're old enough to catch our boys' attention. Get used to it, Levi. Once Grace is married, the boys will soon follow suit."

"Hey, that will leave us all alone, my love. Nice."

"Until the babies start arriving," Joann added with a chuckle.

Sarah took Levi's hand and began walking toward the house. "We should go in. I'm sure Grace has supper about ready."

He stopped in his tracks. "Grace is cooking supper?"

Sarah blew a strand of blond hair off her face. *"Ja."*

He turned to Joann. "If we hurry, we can beat the crowd to the Shoofly Pie Café."

Sarah yanked him toward the house. "Stop it. Grace's cooking has gotten much better."

He gave her a quick peck on the cheek. "She'll never make a peach pie better than yours, *liebchen*. Remember that, Joann. The way to a man's heart is through his stomach. Good looks fade, good cooking never does."

Joann followed her friends to the house. Finding a way to a man's heart wasn't an issue for her. Her looks were nothing special, so it wouldn't matter if they faded. Her last thought before she stepped into the house was to wonder what type of pie Roman liked best.

It wasn't until early Saturday morning that Joann had a chance to get away and go fishing again. She packed a couple of pieces of cold fried chicken left over from lunch, a few carrots and an apple along with a pint jar filled with lemonade into her quilted bag. She left a note for her brother and his family telling them she wouldn't be home for the noon meal. When she arrived at the hollow log, she wasn't surprised, but she was disappointed when there was no message waiting for her.

She left her pole in its hiding place. She didn't really feel like fishing. She just needed to be by herself. The day had been warm, so she slipped off her shoes, gathered up her skirt and waded knee-deep into the cold water.

The muck and moss squished between her toes. When she stood still, she could see tiny minnows swimming around her feet, eager to investigate the new intruder in their watery domain. She looked over the calm surface of the lake and blew out a deep breath. It was such a good place. She always felt happy when she was here.

A splash off to the left made her look that way. She didn't see the fish, but something white caught her attention. She waded toward a stand of cattails. Nestled among the reeds at the edge of the water was a plastic bag. She picked it up and recognized her letter tucked inside. With growing excitement, she opened the bag and pulled out her note. On the back, she saw her unknown friend had written another letter. Quickly, she waded back to shore and sat down to read it.

Dear Happy Angler,
I'm glad the pole has been returned to its rightful owner. Strange how things work out sometimes. You don't owe me any thanks, but I appreciate the lure. I caught two nice four-pounders with it in the spot you suggested. Your gift brought me much more than a pair of fish. It brought me closer to someone I care about. Thank you for that. Like you, little seems to be going right in my life. I won't bore you with the details. I will say that something about this peaceful spot makes my troubles seem smaller. Perhaps it's only that I've gained some perspective while enjoying the quiet stillness of this lake. It's a good place to sit and refresh my soul. I hope it has refreshed yours. The sunset tonight leaves me in awe of the beauty God creates for us. It is a reminder for me that He is in charge and I am not. Sometimes, it is hard to accept that.
    Have you caught anything good lately?
A Friendly Fisherman

Joann hugged the letter to her chest. How strange and yet how wonderful that this person had found the lake was a place to soothe away the problems of life. What problems did her unknown friend face? She wished she knew. She wished she could help.

Joann smoothed the letter on her lap as she considered what to do next. Her first impulse was to write a note to the Friendly Fisherman, but was that wise? Was she really going to start a correspondence with someone she knew nothing about? Her innate good sense said it would be foolish.

Yet something in the letter she held called to her. Someone else faced troubles and was still able to appreciate the beauty of the natural world.

She read the letter again. There was nothing to tell her if the author was Amish or *Englisch,* single or married. She strongly suspected it was a man. He'd signed it the Friendly Fisherman, not Fisherwoman. Joann had encountered few of her gender who enjoyed fishing as much as she did. And there was the rub.

The unknown writer probably assumed she was a man, too.

What would he think if he learned she was an Amish maiden? Would he laugh at the thought that she spent her free time making fishing lures and studying the lakes and ponds around Hope Springs? Would he even reply to her note if he knew the truth?

She wrestled with her conscience. It was wonderful to find someone who saw this place the way she saw it: as a God-given gift that refreshed her soul.

On the other hand, exchanging letters with a stranger would be frowned upon by her family. If he were *Englisch,* her brothers might forbid it outright. Joann realized she had started down a slippery slope. First, by hiding the pole her brother had tossed in the lake. Now, she was considering a secret correspondence, as well. The thought of doing something forbidden was romantic and exciting. When would something exciting come into her life again? Quite likely, never.

She read the letter for a third time. This fisherman, whoever he was, wasn't eager to be known. Otherwise, he would've signed his true name. He might be someone she knew who was troubled. Didn't she have an obligation to help in her own small way?

The smart thing to do would be to toss the note away and not write another one.

Joann, who had long accepted that she was a smart woman, chose the unwise course. She pulled out her journal and wrote another letter.

When she was finished, she read it over. Nothing hinted that she was a female. She'd taken pains to make her writing dark and bold. Nothing hinted that she was Amish, either, only that she had faith in the healing power of God's love. She hoped it would find its way into the Friendly Fisherman's possession and cheer him.

With that in mind, she drank the rest of her lemonade, then rinsed and dried the jar with a corner of her apron. She tore the page out of her journal, put the letter inside the jar and screwed on the lid. The log had a knothole in its side where a branch had broken off the tree long ago. The jar fit perfectly inside the cavity.

Would the Friendly Fisherman find it? It wasn't apparent to the casual observer and that was the way she wanted it. She gathered a handful of small pebbles from the shore and laid them on the ground in the shape of an arrow pointing to the knothole. It was a subtle clue, but if the other fisherman was looking for a reply, he would see it.

Joann ate the remains of her lunch and enjoyed a pleasant few hours watching a family of ducks paddle and dunk for food in the lake. Glancing at her note's hiding place one last time, she realized she couldn't do it. She couldn't continue the correspondence unless she was completely truthful. She didn't have to add her name, but her unknown friend deserved to know he was writing to a single, Amish woman. If he was a married man, his wife might take a dim view of their perfectly innocent letters. She took out her note and added a postscript. Then, she started for home with a new and profound sense of excitement bubbling through her. She'd come as often as she could to check her make-shift mailbox.

Perhaps she might even meet her Friendly Fisher-man.

Chapter 8

"What's the lesson for today, teacher?"

Joann kept her temper in check by praying for patience. It was finally Wednesday morning. Only two more days of his constant company. She could hardly wait.

Roman leaned on the counter in front of her with that annoying grin on his face. He knew she hated it when he called her teacher in that mocking tone. Oh yes, he knew, and he made a point of calling her that every day since he'd started.

"What's the matter, teacher? Has the cat got your tongue?"

She was determined to be pleasant in spite of his taunts. "We're going to the Walnut Valley school board meeting."

Walnut Valley was one of several Amish schools that

dotted the county. Leah Belier was the teacher there. The school stood a few miles west of Hope Springs, on Pleasant View Road.

He grinned. "So my teacher is taking me to school."

"*Ja.* Be careful, or you'll learn something," she snapped as she walked out the door. He followed close behind her.

She had driven her pony and cart to work that day, so she wouldn't waste as much time getting to and from the school. She unhitched Barney and climbed into the cart. Roman climbed in beside her and reached for the reins. "I'll drive."

"I'm quite capable of driving my own cart to Walnut Valley without any assistance from you."

His hand closed over her wrist in a firm grip. "No point in taking two vehicles. I may only have the use of one arm, but I can handle a pony cart. I drive or we sit here all day."

"Okay." She quickly relinquished her hold and tried to rub away the tingling sensation his touch caused.

He frowned at her. "Did I hurt you?"

"*Nee,* I'm fine." She folded her arms tightly across her chest and scooted to the far edge of the seat. She'd never admit his touch did funny things to her insides. It wasn't that she liked him. It had to be something else.

Roman glanced at the woman seated beside him. She looked as jumpy as a cricket in a henhouse. Why was she so nervous? Surely, she wasn't afraid to be alone with him. Her tongue was sharp enough to fend off any man.

She noticed his gaze. "It would be nice if we weren't late," she said tartly.

No, she wasn't afraid. He backed the tawny-brown pony into the street and sent him trotting down the road. After traveling in silence for a mile, he asked, "What kind of things will you report from this meeting and others like it?"

She began to relax. "Not me. You'll be writing up this report. Did you get a notebook as I suggested? If not, I have one you can use."

"I brought a notebook and two pens, teacher. I'm prepared."

She bristled. "Basically, you should take note of things that are important to the community. People want to know if the school has enough funds for the coming year. They want to know who the new school board officials are and if there are any needs among the children."

"What kind of needs?"

"Well, last year one of the children starting in the first grade was in a wheelchair. The school needed to install ramps and make all areas of the school wheelchair accessible. Your uncle ran the story in his paper and a large number of people, including your father, showed up to help remodel the building."

"I remember the day. He took a load of wood with him to donate."

"Were you there?" she asked.

"I stayed to work in the sawmill, but my mother and brother went to help."

She fell silent for a while. He concentrated on driving. "I haven't asked what your father thinks of you working for Otis," she said.

"My father looks forward to the day I can return and work with him."

"So you see this job as a temporary one. I get it now."

"You get what?"

"Why you don't seem interested in learning the business."

"Maybe I don't seem interested because I don't have a good teacher."

That silenced her. She clamped her lips closed and looked off to her side of the road. He regretted the harsh remark almost instantly, but before he could apologize, a red sports car whizzed past as they were cresting a hill. It narrowly missed an oncoming car and had to swerve back quickly in front of them. Roman closed his eyes.

He heard the crack of splintering wood a split second before the truck hit him. He heard squealing tires as he flew through the air. He landed with a sickening impact and tumbled along the asphalt. There was blood in his mouth. He couldn't get up.

"Roman, watch out!"

He opened his eyes to see the pony had swerved dangerously close to the edge of the deep ditch. He managed to bring the animal back into the roadway without upsetting them. As soon as he could, he pulled to a stop.

He drew a ragged breath. "I'm sorry."

Joann didn't make the snide remark he expected. "Are you all right?" she asked quietly instead.

It was too late to disguise how shaken he was. He wiped the cold sweat from his face with his sleeve. "I think so."

She took a deep breath and sat back. "Take your time. We can go when you're ready."

"I thought you didn't want to be late."

She didn't reply. He couldn't bring himself to look

at her. He didn't want to see pity in her eyes. "I expect you'll insist on driving now."

"There's nothing wrong with your driving. Barney can get skittish when traffic is heavy."

The placid pony was standing with his head down and one hip cocked. He could have been asleep on his feet except his tail swished from side to side occasionally.

Roman had to smile. "I think you're maligning your horse's character to make me feel better."

"Do you feel better?" she asked softly.

"I'm getting there." His pounding pulse was settling to a normal rate.

"Then Barney is glad he could help. Does it happen often?"

Did he really want to talk about it? Something in her quiet acceptance of the situation made it possible. "*Nee,* and I'm thankful for that. The doctor calls them flashbacks. It feels as if I'm caught in the accident all over again."

"I never knew exactly what happened. Would it help to talk about it, or would that make it worse?"

"I don't know. I've never talked about it before."

"Maybe you should. It happened at night, didn't it?"

"It was dusk, but not full dark."

"Were you going someplace special?"

"I was coming home from seeing Esta." He clicked his tongue to get Barney moving.

"So you were alone when it happened."

"*Ja.*"

"I imagine you were thankful she wasn't with you."

"It wasn't a pretty sight, that's for sure." He stopped

talking as he thought back to that evening. Some of it was a blur. Some of it was painfully clear.

"My horse had started limping. I thought that maybe he'd picked up a stone in his shoe. I pulled over to the side of the road and got out. It was a cold and windy winter evening. I left the door open. I don't know why I did that."

"Maybe to block the wind off you while you checked the horse."

"Maybe. I don't remember. The man said he didn't see me. He went around thinking he had left enough room. Only, he hit the door and then me. It happened so fast. One second I'm standing by the side of the road and the next second I'm lying face down, and I can't get up."

"It must have been terrible."

"I could taste blood in my mouth but couldn't get any air into my lungs. I thought I was dying. We're supposed to think about God when we're dying. I didn't. I just wanted to get up and take a breath." He was ashamed of that. It was a betrayal of his faith. Why had he told her that?

She was quiet for a time, then she said, "You may not have been thinking about God, but He was thinking about you. We really are his children, you know. Children sometimes get frightened. That doesn't make them bad children. Our Father understands that."

She had managed to hit the nail on the head. He had been terrified of dying. The fear still lingered.

The sound of a siren startled them both. They turned to look behind them. The sheriff's cruiser, with red lights flashing, swept past them. He turned off the roadway a quarter of a mile ahead of them.

Joann stood to get a better look. "I think he's going to the school. I wonder what's wrong."

"Sit down and I'll get us there a little faster." He slapped the reins against the pony's rump. Barney responded with a burst of speed. Within a few minutes, they were turning into the schoolyard. A dozen buggies were already there. Men were clustered in a group at the side of the building. Some of the women and children were weeping openly. The smell of smoke lingered in the air from a charred hole in the side of the schoolhouse.

Joann looked frantically for Leah and was relieved to see her being comforted by Nettie Imhoff and Katie Sutter. Sheriff Nick Bradley stood talking to them, a notebook in his hand. Joann jumped down from the cart and raced toward them. "What has happened?"

Leah looked up. Her eyes were red and there were streaks of tears on her face. "Someone tried to burn down the school."

"Who would do such a thing?" Joann was shocked.

"We don't know, but we must pray for them, whoever they are," Nettie said. Everyone nodded in agreement.

"Tell me exactly what you saw when you arrived, Leah," the sheriff said.

She wiped her face on her sleeve, and then stretched her arm toward the building. "I came early to get ready for the school board meeting, and I found it like this. Someone had piled the school's books and papers against the building and set it on fire. All the children's artwork, all my grade books and papers, all gone." She broke down and started crying again.

Nettie enfolded her in a hug. "God was merciful.

The rain last night must have put out the fire before the whole building went up."

"Have you noticed anything suspicious in the last few days or weeks?" Sheriff Bradley asked.

Leah shook her head. "Why would they burn our children's books?"

"I don't have anything but speculation at this point. Maybe it was a group of kids horsing around and things got out of hand. Maybe it was something more sinister. Not everyone loves the Amish." Nick Bradley had family members who were Amish. He understood the prejudices they sometimes faced.

"You think this was a hate crime?" Joann asked in disbelief.

"It's my job to find out." He walked to where the men were gathered at the front of the building.

Leah gave a shaky laugh. "I've been complaining that we need new schoolbooks. I hope no one thinks this was my way of getting them."

Joann managed a smile. "No one would possibly think that."

"At least we'll have time to get the damage repaired before school starts again in the fall."

Roman, along with Nettie's husband Eli Imhoff, the new school board president for the coming year, joined the women. "This is not how I expected to start my term," Eli said. "Do not worry, Leah. We'll have our school back together in no time. Roman, please tell Otis I'll be in to see him about ordering new textbooks."

Roman glanced back to where Sheriff Bradley was speaking to the men. "I'm surprised to see the sheriff involved in this."

"None of us sent for him," Leah said.

Eli stroked the whiskers on his chin. "I wonder how he knew about it."

The Amish rarely involved outsiders in their troubles. What happened in the community normally stayed in the community. Their ancestors had learned through years of persecution to be distrustful of outsiders. It was a lesson that had not been forgotten. "I'll see what I can find out," Joann said.

The sheriff had left the men and moved to examine the charred side of the school. He squatted on his heels and used his pen to move aside the remains of partially burned book covers and bindings. He lifted an aluminum can out of the ashes. Joann stopped beside him and withdrew her pen and notebook from her pocket. She flipped it open. "Sheriff, have there been other attacks on Amish property?"

The moment she asked the question, she remembered the letter they had received from an Amish farmer whose hay crop had been burned.

The sheriff stood and pushed his trooper's hat back with one finger. "Nothing that I've heard about."

He glanced toward the group of men clustered at the far end of the school where Bishop Zook had just arrived. "You're more likely than I am to hear about something like this. The Amish don't usually call in the law. Makes my job harder sometimes, but I accept that your ways are your own."

"We appreciate that, Sheriff." Should she mention the letter? Like many of the notes they received, it hadn't included a name or return address.

"Could you run a reminder in the paper that people should report anything suspicious to the law? It's part of being a good neighbor to watch out for each other."

Perhaps the man would read the notice and contact the sheriff himself and she needn't say anything about it. "I'm sure Otis will agree to that. How did you know about today's incident?"

"I received an anonymous tip. It was a woman's voice. She said to hurry or someone was going to get hurt out here." He placed the can in a plastic bag.

"That sounds like a threat." She glanced around, reassured by the presence of only her Amish friends and their families.

"I thought so, too. I took it seriously."

Roman came to stand beside Joann. "Sheriff, the men want to know if they can start cleaning up."

"Tell them I need them to hold off until I have my crime scene people out to look this over. They should be finished by the end of the day. Have there been any problems in your local church group? Any disagreement between members?"

Joann spoke up quickly. "Our brethren would not do this no matter what kind of disagreements they were having."

Nick shrugged. "People are people. I won't rule out anyone. How are you doing, Roman?"

"Goot."

"Is the arm better?"

Roman looked at his sling. "Not much."

"I'm sorry to hear that. The jury found Brendan Smith guilty of vehicular assault yesterday. His attorney told me that he asked you to speak at the sentencing next month, but you declined."

A cold look came over Roman's face. His voice shook as he spoke. "I have forgiven him. It is your law that seeks to punish him. His fate is in God's hands."

Joann had never seen Roman so angry. "Who is Brendan Smith?"

"He's the young man who struck Roman with his pickup. His attorney was hoping that Roman would speak on Brendan's behalf, talk about Amish forgiveness and all that. He was hoping it might persuade the judge to go easy on Smith. He's facing jail time."

The sheriff rubbed a hand over his jaw as he looked at the scorched building. "Quite a coincidence that we have a fire at an Amish school the next night, isn't it?"

Joann glanced from Roman to the sheriff. "What are you saying?"

"That I'm not a big believer in coincidences." He touched the brim of his hat. "Take care, Roman, Miss Yoder. I'll be in touch."

As the sheriff walked away, Joann turned to Roman. "Why would you refuse such a request?"

"I don't want to talk about it." He stalked off, leaving her wondering just how much hurt and anger he still carried inside. Forgiveness was the only way to heal such sorrow.

Roman couldn't help wondering if this was somehow his fault. Was it retaliation by the friends of Brendan Smith? If he had agreed to speak on Brendan's behalf, would the school have been spared? He was deeply troubled by the idea.

As the sheriff marked off the school with yellow tape, Eli Imhoff stood on the back of his wagon to address the crowd. Bishop Zook stood at his side along with several men who were also members of the school board. Eli said, "We will hold our meeting here. It will not take long."

The people moved to gather around them. The Bishop spoke first. "Let us give thanks to our heavenly father that no one was injured, and let us pray for those who tried to carry out this grievous deed. May God show them mercy and the error of their ways. Amen."

The crowd, standing with their heads bowed, muttered, "Amen."

"The first order of business is to clean up the building and assess what needs to be torn down and what can be repaired," Eli said. "The sheriff will let us know how soon we can do that. Once we know what needs to be done to make the school safe, we will set a date to start rebuilding."

"We can put an announcement in the paper," Joann said. "We will need it by Thursday morning in order to make Friday's edition."

Bishop Zook nodded. "That can be done. I will send notices to our neighboring churches so that they may make a plea for donations at this coming Sunday's preaching. Please spread the word about our need. And do not worry, Leah, the school will be as good as new come the first day of class in the fall."

Eli looked at Roman. "Please tell your uncle that I will be in to see him as soon as we know what books must be replaced."

They went on to discuss other issues. Roman took careful notes. This was a story everyone needed to know about.

On the drive home, Joann sat quietly beside him. Roman wasn't up to making small talk or teasing her. She seemed to feel the same way. About a half-mile out of town, she finally spoke. "Did you tell the sheriff about the letter we received?"

The fact that there had been two fires on Amish property had struck him as odd, too. "*Nee,* did you?"

"I was afraid to, but now I wonder if I was wrong."

"What's done is done. The school will be repaired."

"I know, but what if this happens again and we could have prevented it?"

"Romans 12:19, Dearly beloved, avenge not yourselves, but rather give place unto wrath: for it is written, Vengeance is mine; I will repay, saith the Lord."

"You're right. We must leave it in God's hands." She didn't say anything else, but he could see she was troubled.

Back at the office, he told Otis what had happened. Otis shook his head sadly. "We shall do what we can for the school. I would like to see your notes when you're finished with them. I will want to add something about this to our magazine this month."

Roman struggled through the afternoon to type up his notes for Otis to review. Typing with one hand was a laborious process that he was sure he would never master. Across the room, Joann made quick work of her notes and handed them to Otis before Roman had finished a single page.

She came and stood in front of Roman's desk. She reached for his notebook. "I can help."

He slapped his hand down on it to prevent her taking it.

Annoyance flashed across her face. "I was only offering to type your notes for you."

"I can do my own work."

"I can do it faster."

Like he needed to be reminded of that. "I must learn to do it myself. You won't always be around to help."

"That's for certain," she said cryptically. She left and went back to work at her desk. When it was time to leave, Roman was glad she had her cart to drive. He wasn't up for company.

He learned when he arrived home that evening that news of the fire had preceded him. When he entered his father's house, he found his father and brother seated at the kitchen table. Faron Martin sat with them.

Roman's mother stood by the sink dabbing the corner of her eye with her apron. "Who would do this terrible thing?"

"Only God knows," his father said with a sad shake of his head.

Andrew looked at Roman. "Is it true the sheriff questioned you?"

"He spoke to everyone who was there."

"Nick Bradley is a good man. He will get to the bottom of this," Marie Rose declared.

Roman poured himself a cup of coffee and took a seat at the table. "*Daed,* do you know of a fellow on Bent Tree Road that had his haystacks burned recently?"

"I heard something about it from Rueben Beachy just yesterday. Why?"

"Did the fella know who started the fire?"

Menlo shook his head. "If he did, he didn't mention it."

"It seems like an odd coincidence, don't you think?"

"*Ja,* it does. Andrew, Faron, I reckon we can get a few more board cuts before supper." Menlo set his coffee cup in the sink, put on his hat and walked out the door. Andrew followed him.

Faron said, "Roman, could I speak to you outside?"

"Sure." Now what? Was this about Esta? Roman took

a last sip of his coffee and got to his feet even though this was a conversation he was sure he didn't want to have.

When the two men were out of earshot of the house, Faron said, "I reckon you should know that I've been stepping out with Esta."

So Joann had been telling the truth. "I heard something like that."

"I didn't mean to go behind your back while you were laid up. Esta said there's nothing serious between you. If that isn't the case, you should tell me now and I'll stop seeing her."

Roman was surprised by how little it hurt to know Esta didn't see him as a serious suitor. He'd been foolish to think she would find a one-armed man a good catch. "*Danki,* Faron, I reckon Esta is the one to decide that."

"All right then. Just wanted to set that straight. Didn't want any bad blood between us, what with my working for your dad and all." He held out his hand.

Roman shook it. "How's the job going?"

"It's the best work I could have asked for. Your father is a good teacher and a patient man, but I don't think your brother is very happy that he took me on."

"Andrew will get over it. Give him time."

"I hope that's true. What about you? How do you like working for your uncle?"

"It's not what I expected, but I'm starting to like it." To his amazement, he realized his words were the truth. He was starting to enjoy the job. Reporting and sharing information with the Amish community was important if they were to stay connected and strong in their commitment to care for each other.

As Faron went to finish his work, Roman began

walking down the lane thinking about Esta and Faron. Were they meant for each other? If so, who was the woman God had in mind for him? He couldn't think of anyone. Before long, his thoughts turned to Joann and her conflicting feelings about reporting another fire to the sheriff. He shared the same feelings. What was the right thing to do?

It was a fundamental part of his faith to live separate from the world. Yet, like Joann, he remained uncertain in his heart as to what he should do.

He didn't realize until he was at the fence to Woolly Joe's pasture that he had been headed toward the lake. Well, why not? It was a good place to ponder the rights and wrongs of life. Maybe the Happy Angler had written him another note.

Cheered by the thought, he made his way into the woods and down to the small clearing on the shore. To his disappointment, there wasn't a message on the log. He wondered if his last letter had been found. He wanted the Happy Angler to know his gift had been appreciated.

Roman sat down and stared out at the placid lake. High cliffs topped with lush trees made up the north shore. He caught sight of a lone doe walking along the rim briefly before vanishing into the trees. Barn swallows swooped across the surface of the water catching insects and taking drinks while zipping past the surface. Their agility was amazing.

"Little swallows you fly away but return each spring on the very same day."

With a start, he realized he'd just spoken the beginning of a poem. He took out his notebook and balanced it on the log. "Where do you go when you leave this home? What draws you afar, what makes you roam?"

While he was groping for his pen, his notebook fell off the log. The calm peacefulness that the evening brought his soul vanished. Frustration hit him like the kick of a mule. Would he ever learn to manage with just one arm?

Why him? Why had he been crippled? Because some foolish *Englischer* had one too many beers before getting behind the wheel of his truck? Where was the justice in that?

He looked to heaven and shouted, "Why me? What am I to learn from this?" The birds he'd been watching scattered.

He closed his eyes and listened, but only the croaking of frogs and the drone of insects answered him.

God wasn't speaking to him tonight. He'd just have to muddle on. He leaned down to pick up the notebook and noticed a row of pebbles on the ground. They had been laid in the shape of an arrow. It pointed toward the log. He stood and looked over the gray bark. There was a knothole in the side of the log he hadn't noticed before. Something shiny caught his eye.

He reached in and pulled out a glass canning jar. Inside, he saw a folded piece of notebook paper. He smiled, opened the jar and took out the note to read it.

Chapter 9

Dear Friendly Fisherman,
If you are reading this, you have found my make-shift mailbox. The last letter you left had blown into the water. If you hadn't been wise enough to put it in a plastic bag, it would have been gone forever. I didn't want to risk losing one of your notes again, so I came up with this idea.

I'm humbled and happy that my small gift has been of value. You won't bore me if you'd like to talk about your troubles. I've been told that troubles shared are troubles halved. Here in this beautiful spot, they do seem less important. I'll share my story with you and hope you feel free to return the favor.

I had plans to buy a house of my own soon. It's been a longtime dream of mine, but recently

I lost my job. I can't afford the house now. The new job I accepted doesn't pay as well. To top it off, I have to work with someone I don't much care for. He has made it plain that he doesn't care for me, either.

I'm determined to make the best of it, and I hope I can one day call him a friend. Until that time, I shall come here often to refresh my soul and regain some perspective. If I can't do that, I can sit here and imagine tossing him headfirst into the cold water. What a scare that would give the poor fish.

I shouldn't complain about my circumstances. My troubles are small compared to some. After all, how bad can it be if I have time for fishing? They only seem big because I can't see beyond them.

There, I've unburdened myself to you. I expect your troubles are worse than mine and you're laughing at me. Actually, I do feel better for having shared them with you.

The sky is overcast this morning, but I can imagine the colors of the sunset you saw. Were there clouds in the west? Were they fiery gold and rose pink? From this spot, all the colors must have been reflected in the lake. Two sunsets for the price of one. That's a good bargain in anyone's book.

I didn't fish today. The wind was in the north. Another reminder that we are not in charge, God is. I hope the fishing is good for you. You might want to try an orange, bottom-bouncing hopper to tempt a big old walleye that lives in the deep part of the lake. I had him once, but he broke my line.

I must close now, I've run out of paper.

P.S. I must add that I'm a single woman. (I almost didn't.) I'll understand if you choose not to write again. Please know that I have enjoyed your letters, and thank you again for returning my pole.

Your Happy Amish Angler

A woman!

Roman certainly hadn't expected that. A single Amish woman, to boot. Who was she? Did he know her? Was she a grandmother or someone's little sister?

No, the note said she had planned to buy a house. That was an uncommon thing for an Amish maid. Single women past marrying age sometimes lived alone, but most often, they lived with family members the way Joann did. If they desired to live by themselves, their father or other male members of the family would see to it that they were given a suitable dwelling such as a *dawdy-haus* as he lived in. He didn't know of any woman who had purchased her own house. His letter-writing friend was one very unusual woman.

Oddly, it did feel as if she were a friend, as if she were offering kind advice and gently steering him toward a better path. What would she think of him if she knew who he was?

"She would probably think I'm a poor, pitiful excuse for a man," he muttered as a wave of self-pity hit him.

He glanced at the letter again. No, she'd likely toss him headfirst into the lake and tell him to quit feeling sorry for himself.

Roman folded the letter in half and tucked it in the

pocket of his shirt. To own a house was a fine dream. It was a shame she had to give it up. It took a good person to make the best of a bad situation and work toward creating friendship where none existed. Roman knew a moment of shame for his treatment of Joann. He hadn't tried to make friends with her. He gained delight in teasing her, in making her snap back at him. It wasn't well done on his part.

Tomorrow, he would turn over a new leaf and be kinder to her. She was only trying to do her job. It wasn't her fault that he was ill-suited to the work and found it so difficult.

Roman considered what he should do. Finally, he brought out his notepad and started a letter of his own. Before he realized it, the note was two pages long, and he felt better for having unburdened himself. The Happy Angler was right. A burden shared was a burden halved.

He sealed the letter inside the jar and returned it to the knothole in the log as the evening light faded. He headed for home determined to do better at the job his uncle had given him and treat everyone there with fairness. Including Joann Yoder.

When he reached the house, he saw his mother weeding in her garden. He opened the gate and joined her. Stooping, he pulled a dandelion that had sprouted among the peas.

His mother paused and leaned on her hoe with a heavy sigh. "*Danki,* Roman. I appreciate the help. I declare, these weeds grow faster every year. I can hardly keep up with them."

"I'll take over the weeding from you this summer. My town job leaves me with extra time on my hands."

"Oh, that's sweet of you, but I enjoy being out here.

I like the smell of growing things. I feel closer to God in my garden. It would be a blessing if you could do it once in a while."

"Whenever you want, *Mamm*."

"Where have you been?" She started hoeing again.

"Over to Woolly Joe's lake."

"Ach, that's a pretty place."

"*Mamm,* do you know any Amish women who like to fish?"

She laughed. "Goodness, I know plenty of women who like to fish. Your grandmother loved to sit on the riverbank with a pole in the water. Sometimes, I think she didn't even put a worm on the hook, she just sat there and enjoyed the day. Why?"

"No reason. I heard a local Amish woman was trying to buy her own house but lost her job. Do you know who it was?"

His mother frowned as she concentrated. "*Nee,* I know of no one like that."

"Then I must have heard wrong." He took the hoe from his mother and set to work.

It seemed that the identity of his pen pal would remain a mystery. Maybe it was for the best this way. He hadn't revealed his name, either.

Joann stepped off her brother's front porch and scowled. She could see the end of the lane from the house. Roman wasn't waiting for her this morning. Now she was going to be late.

She'd grown accustomed to accepting a ride from him. She made a point of telling him when she would drive herself and she hadn't mentioned anything like that yesterday.

She didn't have enough time to walk all the way to town by nine o'clock. She started running. Oh, she could just see Roman standing behind the counter and glancing pointedly at the clock when she finally got there. He'd be happy to tell her she was late. She could hardly point out that it was his fault. Odious man.

She reached the road just as a horse and buggy came into view. She slowed to a walk. Roman pulled up beside her. "Sorry I'm late. I had trouble getting Meg hitched up. My brother normally does it for me, but he was sick in bed with a fever so I had to do it myself."

"That's okay. I hope he feels better soon." She was a little winded as she climbed in beside him.

"Why were you running?"

"I thought you'd decided not to come for me today. I didn't want to be late."

His brow darkened. "I'm sorry you thought I would deliberately make you late for work. That was never my intention."

Joann hugged her book bag to her chest and remained silent as he set off down the road. That was exactly what she had been thinking. Who was the odious one now?

She gathered her courage and said meekly, "I'm sorry for thinking poorly of you. Please forgive me."

"I reckon I've given you some cause."

"Still, I was in the wrong."

A smile twitched at the corner of his mouth. A touch of humor slipped into his voice. "I never expected to hear you say that."

She sat up straighter. "I can admit when I'm wrong. It just doesn't happen very often."

He chuckled, but then cleared his throat. "What's on our agenda for today?"

He hadn't called her "teacher" in that annoying tone. Perhaps her goal of eventual friendship was possible, after all.

"We'll be putting together the magazine. They need to be finished before five o'clock tomorrow night so we can get them to the post office."

"How many copies do we print?"

"Twelve hundred."

"Are you serious? We don't even have twelve hundred families in Hope Springs."

"The *Family Hour* goes all across the county to Amish and Plain folk and even some *Englisch* subscribers."

"There's still so much I don't know."

"You're doing okay. It takes time to learn it all. On Friday, we'll get out the newspaper as usual."

"That sounds like a lot of work for the week."

"I thought you found our work easy." Oh, why did she have to say that? Just when things were getting better. She could have cheerfully bitten her tongue.

He glanced at her and then laughed. "I have seen it is not as easy as I once thought. When I'm wrong, I say so."

She managed a slight smile. "I don't imagine that happens very often."

"More often than you might think, Joann Yoder. More often than you might think." He grinned at her, and she blushed with delight.

They rode the rest of the way into town in companionable silence. Joann's high hopes for a pleasant day vanished when they turned the corner and saw an ambulance in front of the office with its red lights flashing.

Leonard and his wife, Mabel, were standing outside. The front window had been broken.

Joann jumped out of the buggy before it rolled to a stop. "Leonard, what happened?"

"Someone threw a brick through our window. Otis was standing just inside. The brick hit him in the head. He was knocked unconscious."

Leonard's wife Mabel said, "We called an ambulance right away."

Roman rushed past them and into the building. Joann tried to follow him, but Mabel held her back. "There's broken glass and blood everywhere, dear. He's being taken care of. They said we should stay out of the way until the sheriff arrives."

A crowd was gathering around them. Leonard said, "Did anyone see who did this? Did the brick come from a car or from a buggy?"

Everyone shook his or her head. Mabel said, "It was early, businesses aren't open, there weren't many people on the street, but someone must have seen something."

Joann glanced over the crowd. No one stepped forward. The ambulance crew came out of the building with Otis on a stretcher. Roman came right behind them. As they put the stretcher in the back of the ambulance, Roman spoke to Leonard. "Will you drive me to my uncle's house to get his wife and take her to the hospital?" The nearest hospital was more than thirty miles away. Too far for a buggy.

"Of course."

Mabel said, "I'll go and get her. Leonard, you should stay and talk to the sheriff. You were inside when it happened. Roman, would you like to come with me?"

"*Ja,* I would. I should tell my mother what has happened."

Joann spoke up to reassure him. "I will take your buggy and let your mother know where Otis has been taken. Leonard, will you call Samuel Carter, the van driver, and see if he can take her to the hospital as well?"

Leonard pulled a cell phone from his pocket. His hand shook as he tried to dial the number. "I can't believe this. Otis is such a fine man. He wouldn't hurt a flea."

Mabel put her arms around him. "It's going to be all right."

Leonard wiped at his eyes. "He gave me a job when everyone else said I was through. I don't know what I'll do if anything happens to him."

Roman laid a hand on Leonard's shoulder. "We will keep the paper and the magazine running just as he would want."

Leonard looked at him, his eyes bright with unshed tears. "You're right. Just as he would want. I'm sorry now that I wasn't nicer to you."

"We will start anew, you and me."

Gerald came jogging down the street as the ambulance was pulling away. "What's going on?"

Roman said, "My uncle was hurt when someone threw a brick through the window. They're taking him to the hospital now. The sheriff will be here soon. When he is done, I want you to get some plywood to board up the window. Mabel, we should go before my aunt hears about this from someone else."

She kissed her husband on the cheek and hurried toward her car with Roman at her side. Joann and Gerald ventured as far as the doorway and looked in. There was broken glass everywhere. In the center of the mess was a pool of blood. A bloody towel had been discarded on the counter.

"What is happening to our town?" Gerald asked sadly.

Joann understood his sense of loss. First the school and now this. Was it a coincidence that it had happened during Brendan Smith's trial or was something more sinister at work?

Joann said, "I must go and tell Roman's family what has happened. I'll be back as soon as I can."

Gerald shook his head. "Don't hurry. I doubt we'll get any work done today."

"We'll get it all done. We have a magazine to get out and a business to run. That's the best thing we can do for Otis."

"It'll take twice as long without him."

"Then we must work twice as hard."

She made the trip out to Roman's home as quickly as she could. Poor Meg was covered with flecks of sweat and foam by the time they reached the mill.

Marie Rose and Menlo were grateful that she had brought the news and had thought to send for Samuel Carter. It wasn't long before his gray van pulled into the yard. The retired *Englischer* earned extra money as a taxi driver for his Amish friends.

Joann helped Marie Rose bundle together what they might need and saw them off. Andrew and Faron stood beside her as the dust from the vehicle settled. "I'll hitch up another horse for you, Joann. Meg is getting a little old to be making so many trips to town," Andrew said.

He led the mare away and returned a short time later

with a piebald pony hitched to a two-wheeled cart. "This is Cricket. He'll get you there and back."

"*Danki,* Andrew. I'll take good care of him. I must let my family and Bishop Zook know what has happened."

"I'll see that the bishop knows," Faron said.

"*Danki,* that will save me many miles of travel," Joann said.

She stopped by her brother's farm. Salome was pushing Louise on the swing in the front yard. They ran to her as she stopped the pony by the front gate.

"*Aenti* Joann, did you get a new horse?" Louise asked as she petted the animal's nose.

"*Nee,* Cricket belongs to Andrew Weaver. He only loaned him to me. Where is your father?"

"He and Mama are weeding the corn patch behind the barn."

"*Danki.*" She watched the two girls return to their play. What if it had been one of them injured by a thrown brick? Who might be next? She made up her mind. She would tell the sheriff what she knew. It was little enough, but someone had to try to put a stop to what was happening.

Joan hurried around the barn and met her brother and sister-in-law as they were heading in with their hoes over their shoulders. She quickly explained what had happened. They were both as shocked as she had been.

Hebron found his voice first. "You must stop working at that place."

She couldn't believe she'd heard him right. "Why?"

"It is too worldly for you. To have dealings with the *Englisch* law twice in one week tells me it is best you stay here and help on the farm."

"I'm sorry, Hebron. I gave my word to Otis Miller

that I would do a good job for him. I intend to honor my promise. I will be very late tonight. Don't wait supper on me."

She turned on her heels and left them staring after her, though she knew she hadn't heard the last of Hebron's opinions on the subject.

By the time Joann got back to town, the sheriff had gone and Gerald was nailing a large piece of wood over the broken window. He took a pair of nails from his mouth and said, "Leonard's wife just called and said that Otis is in the emergency room at the hospital in Millersburg. He's still unconscious, but they say his condition is good."

"Praise God for that news. What did the sheriff have to say?"

"He took the brick, but he has little hope of finding who did this unless someone comes forward to say that they saw the crime committed."

"Did he think this was related to the school fire?"

"If he does, he didn't say so." Gerald put the nails back in his mouth and finished hammering the one he had started into the woodwork.

Joann went inside. No one had started cleaning up, so she got a broom and a dustpan and began sweeping up shards of glass. She had most of it cleaned up, when someone came in the front door. Expecting Roman, she turned around quickly to ask about Otis, but it was a young *Englisch* woman. Joann said, "I'm sorry. We're closed for business today."

The woman shoved her hands in the front pockets of her jeans and hunched her shoulders. Her eyes swept around the room and focused on the blood Joann hadn't had a chance to wash off the floor.

"I heard that the old man who runs this place was hurt. Is that true?" the woman asked.

Joann dumped her dustpan full of glass into the trashcan. "*Ja,* they took him to the hospital in Millersburg."

The woman finally looked at her. "Is he going to be okay?"

"We don't know yet, but he is in God's hands, so we do not fear for him. Do you know Otis Miller? I can give his family a message if you want."

She started backing toward the door. "No, that's okay. I don't know him."

She turned around and ran into Roman who was just coming in. Her face turned ashen white. She bolted past Roman and out the door. Joann stepped to the unbroken window and watched her. She got into a red car parked halfway down the block and took off. Joann grabbed a piece of paper and wrote down the license plate number.

Roman came to stand beside her. "Who was that?"

"I don't know, but does that look like the car that almost ran us off the road on the way to school?"

"I didn't get a good look at the car."

She turned to face him. "She wanted to know if the old man who worked here had been hurt. She seemed upset when I told her what I knew. How is Otis?"

"Awake and worried sick that *Family Hour* and the paper won't go out on time. The doctor said they needed to run more tests. They're going to keep him for a few days."

"We can see that the magazine and paper get out on time. There's nothing wrong with the presses. I'm willing to stay late, and I'm sure everyone else is."

"*Danki,* that will mean a lot to my uncle. What did you write down?" He pointed to the notepad in her hand.

"I wrote down the license plate number of that woman's car."

"What do you intend to do with it?"

She gazed at his face trying to judge what his reaction would be if she admitted what she'd been thinking.

"You plan to give it to the sheriff, don't you?"

"I think the woman knew more about today's event than she let on," Joann said.

"Many in our church will tell you it's none of our business. We must forgive the transgressors. My uncle has said this from his hospital bed."

"I do forgive them. I just don't want anyone else to get hurt."

He held out his hand. "Give it to me."

Joann's shoulders slumped in defeat. She reluctantly handed it over without looking at him.

Roman stifled a twinge of pity and took the note from her. He didn't want her getting in to trouble with her family or with the church.

"What are you going to do with it?" Joann challenged Roman with a hard stare.

"That is my business. Forget the number, forget you ever wrote it down." He waited for the outburst he could see brewing behind her eyes.

Instead, she lowered her gaze. "I need to get the rest of this cleaned up."

"Is the sheriff on our mailing list for the *Family Hour* magazine?"

"*Nee,* but he gets our newspaper."

"Then I want the notice from the farmer whose hay

was burned put in the magazine and not in the news-paper."

"I'll have Gerald reset the type."

"Goot."

She started to turn away, but Roman caught her by the arm. "I want to thank you for letting my parents know about Otis. He was grateful to have his sister at his side."

"You don't owe me thanks. I would've done the same for anyone."

Her tone had a sting to it. Clearly, she was implying that he wouldn't. He didn't say anything else. It didn't matter what she thought of him. He would do what was best for all of them.

Once the office was cleaned, they set to work finishing the magazine layout and printing the twenty pages both front and back that would be bound into the final project. Joann was everywhere, running proofs, carrying paper, refilling the ink when Leonard hollered that it was low and pausing to speak to the steady stream of people who stopped in to inquire about Otis and offer help. By late afternoon, the hardware store owner was supervising the installation of a new window.

Roman tried his best to keep up with the flow. Otis normally ran the saddle binder, the machine that stapled the magazine pages together. Roman had already spent some time thinking about how he could operate it with one hand.

Joann had shown him how to use the machine on his first day of work. She laid the open pages across the bar with her right hand and pressed the stapler with her foot. The machine moved the papers into the proper position and inserted a pair of wire staples. She then removed the pages with her left hand and laid the finished product in a container, making the task seem almost effortless. It wasn't for him.

He found a leftover length of plywood to make a slide and positioned it against the end of the machine. He had seen that he didn't have to take the papers off the bar. He simply put the next set on the machine and when it moved the work into the proper position, it kicked the previous magazine off the bar, onto the slide and down into the box. He could bind the pages almost as fast as Otis and Joann had done. He was feeling quite pleased with his ingenuity.

Leonard, his arms loaded with boxes of paper, didn't see Roman's invention until he banged his shin on it. He muttered under his breath as he hobbled to a nearby chair.

He dropped the boxes and rubbed his leg with both hands. "Who put that dumb board in the way? Are you trying to cripple me?"

"*Nee,* one cripple at this company is enough," Roman said.

He added another set of pages to the binder and stomped on the foot pedal with extra force.

Joann came and picked up the boxes Leonard had dropped. "It's a clever idea, Roman, but you should have warned us you put it here. A few words would have spared our friend this pain," she said.

Leonard stood and took the boxes from Joann. Grudgingly, he said, "I'm sorry about the crippled remark."

"Forget it. We've got work to do," Roman said, then continued to bind sets as his embarrassment subsided. Joann's gaze clashed with his briefly before she walked away. She was right. He should have warned them, but he knew she was speaking about more than a bruised shin.

The license number was still in his pant pocket. Would turning it over to the law prevent another attack? He struggled with his conscience as he tried to decide the right thing to do.

Chapter 10

Was he ever going to speak to her again?

Joann endured the rest of the day without a word from Roman. Mostly, she kept her head down and stayed out of his way. He knew she'd been talking about the license number when she made that comment about warning folks. She'd seen the look of annoyance that flashed across his face.

It seemed that every time she made a little progress with understanding him, they clashed over something else. She should just give up and accept that they would never get along.

It was almost eight-thirty in the evening before they stopped working, but when they closed the front door, stacks of the *Family Hour* had been printed, stapled and addressed. All that was left was to take them to the post office first thing in the morning.

The sun was setting by the time they gathered in front of the building. Cricket was still waiting patiently at the hitching rail. However, the two-wheeled cart Andrew had loaned Joann wasn't equipped for nighttime driving.

"Roman, I have an extra set of battery-operated flashing lights you can use to get you home," Gerald said.

"Danki," Roman went with Gerald to get them and the two men made short work of affixing them to the tailgate of the cart.

Leonard and Mabel stood with Joann. Mabel said, "We're going to run over to the hospital and see if Otis needs anything. Can we give you a lift home?"

The couple already had a sixty-mile round trip ahead of them after a long and tiring day. They didn't need to go out of their way to drop her off. "No, you go on. I'll be fine. See you in the morning and please send word if Otis is worse. Tell him we are all praying for him," Joann said.

Mabel kissed Joann's cheek. "We will."

After she and Leonard drove away, Joann stood on the sidewalk and watched Roman climb into the cart. She said, "Good night. I'll see you tomorrow."

"Get in." His first words in four hours.

"Nee, really, the walk will do me good."

He sighed heavily with frustration. "Get in. I'm not letting you walk home in the dark."

It wasn't exactly an invitation, but she really didn't want to walk after such a long day. She climbed up onto the small benchlike seat. The cart was much narrower than the normal buggy. She and Roman were pressed together from hip to knee. The high arms of the seat left no room for her to move away from him. The result was a long, dark and exquisitely uncomfortable ride. He didn't say a word, and she couldn't think of anything to say that wouldn't sound foolish.

When they finally reached her brother's lane, she jumped down. "*Danki,* I appreciate the ride. I'll be driving myself after this, so you won't have to pick me up. Good night."

She raced up the lane like she had a pack of wild dogs coming after her. When she stepped into her brother's kitchen, she realized she'd been right about one thing. Hebron had more to say on the subject of her job. He was waiting for her.

She endured an hour-long lecture about being content with the simple life their ancestors had envisioned. She knew that Hebron believed what he was saying. She also knew he had her best interests at heart. She accepted his admonishment quietly. When he was finished, she explained she would only be working as a cleaning woman at the office starting on Monday, and he was content with that.

The following morning, she arrived at the office just as Leonard and Gerald were carrying boxes of magazines out to Leonard's small pickup. He would take them to the post office as soon as it opened. The usually dour Leonard was smiling. "Otis is being released from the hospital in the afternoon."

"That's wonderful news." She glanced inside the building. "Where is Roman?"

"He's gone to the hospital to help his aunt get Otis home and settled, so he won't be in today. It's just the three of us."

That would make it another busy day if they were to

get the paper out on time, but at least she wouldn't have to be on her tippy-toes around Roman all day. What a relief to have a day without him.

She thought that was what she wanted, but she found herself thinking about him constantly and wondering how he and Otis were getting along. As it turned out, he was on her mind as much when he was gone as he was when he was hovering beside her. No matter what, she couldn't escape him. In all the excitement she hadn't mentioned it was their last day together. Would he care?

On the drive home that evening, she passed the turn-off to the sawmill and was tempted to stop. Would he be there yet? What excuse would she give for showing up like this? She realized how foolish she was being and hurried on, determined to forget about Roman Weaver. Come Monday, she would be back at the bookshop in the afternoons, three days a week. She would clean on Saturday when the printing office was closed. Their paths weren't going to cross very often anymore, and that was a good thing.

That night, she dreamed about meeting the Friendly Fisherman, a kindly Amish man who looked like her grandfather with his long gray beard, who laughed with her and not at her, and who admired her keen mind. She awoke early with a bubbling mixture of hope and dread churning her stomach. The sun wasn't yet up when she slipped out of her brother's house and made her way to the lake.

Please, please, please let there be a letter from him.

As dawn broke, Joann entered her favorite spot and saw a raccoon washing his breakfast of clams on the rocky shore. She smiled. "Good morning, sir. Are you the Friendly Fisherman?"

The raccoon paused, his tiny hands grasping a cracked shell. He bared his teeth at her, then waddled away to eat in peace somewhere else. She called after him. "*Ja,* go away you old grump. I know a fellow just like you."

Annoyed with herself for letting thoughts of Roman spoil the glorious morning, she crossed the clearing to the log and pulled out her jar. There was a new letter inside. She sat down, unfolded the small pages and began to read the strong, bold writing with eager anticipation.

Dear Happy Angler,
Your idea for a mailbox is quite clever. I never would have thought of it. Now I know I can look forward to your notes come fair weather or foul. I'm truly sorry to hear about your troubles. To own a house is a fine dream, and it must be a hard thing to give up. I pray your circumstances will change.

Don't ever think your concerns are small or unworthy. I thank you for sharing them with me. I'll do you the courtesy of returning the favor. I also work with someone who would benefit from a dunking in the lake. Stubborn, willful, hard to please, quick to call attention to my failings. I sometimes wonder if it wouldn't be better to leave my job, but alas, others are depending on me so I must stay.

You're trying to make the best of a bad situation and develop a friendship with your coworker. You put me to shame. I must confess I've done nothing to better our relationship at work. With your wise words in mind, I plan to change that. I will be kinder. I will listen more and judge less. If I make the effort, perhaps the tension between the two of us will lessen over time. It's worth a try.

You are right about the sunset. Its beautiful colors were reflected perfectly in the water. It was a remarkable sight. Explain to me why a north wind kept you from fishing. It certainly hasn't been cold. I used to fish a lot, but not as much in recent years. I remember now why I liked it so much when I was a boy. It's the peacefulness. Well, landing a big fish is fun, too, although I have trouble holding a rod these days.

I'll be sure to try the orange hopper. Any tips, fishing or otherwise, will always be welcome from you.

As ever,
Your Friendly Fisherman

Joann laid the pages on her lap and stared out at the lake. A strong south wind was starting to blow, and it made the water gray and choppy. She should go over to the north shore and try fishing for bass along the rocky outcropping there. It was spawning season for them, but she didn't unpack her pole. Instead, she spent a long time thinking about the Friendly Fisherman's letter.

He found her advice sound and wise. That made her feel good. It took away some of the uneasiness she felt about continuing the correspondence.

How was it that a stranger understood her feelings and took her words to heart when so few others did?

She read the note again. So he didn't know the rhyme about the wind in the north. He surely had to be an *En-*

glisch fellow. Her Amish grandfather had taught her the saying years ago. She assumed everyone knew it.

Her conscience pricked her at the thought that he might be a married man. He hadn't said one way or the other. Although she knew her letters were harmless, not everyone would think so. If he were *Englisch,* she should give up writing to him.

She pushed the nagging doubts aside. She didn't know that for sure. He enjoyed her letters. He looked forward to hearing from her and she enjoyed hearing from him. There was nothing wrong with that. She wouldn't give it up. She had already given up so much.

She took out her pencil and notebook and started a new letter.

When she was finished, she tucked the jar back in the knothole and headed for home, where she had a full day of farm work waiting for her.

Later, her family took Otis and his wife a basket of food. They stayed briefly to visit and to do whatever chores the pair needed help with. Hebron might disagree with Joann working at the paper, but he would never neglect a neighbor in need. Joann had half-hoped to see Roman there, but his mother told her he'd already gone home. Try as she might, Joann couldn't stifle her disappointment. It didn't make sense, but she missed seeing him even if they did sometimes clash.

Roman spent the day helping his father and brother stack lumber at the sawmill. His mother had stayed the night with Otis and his wife. She wouldn't be back until late afternoon. Her men were left alone to fend for themselves when it came to cooking, but they managed. His father knew how to make scrambled eggs and cook bacon. They had the same meal for breakfast and lunch.

Roman was pleased to see that Andrew and Faron were becoming friends. The two joked around and worked well together. He was glad for his brother. He knew Andrew missed his company.

It felt good to get back to physical labor, but he realized by early afternoon that he'd put too much stress on his arm. It began to ache and throb wildly. He was going to be in for a long, uncomfortable night.

When evening came, his mother returned and soon had a hot supper ready for them. After that, the family retired early, leaving Roman alone in his small house. The days were growing longer and it wasn't yet dark.

He was restless. His arm hurt. There was no point in trying to get to sleep early. He wondered if Happy Angler had left him a new letter. He couldn't believe how much he looked forward to hearing from her. Maybe it was because she didn't know about his disability. They were equals, simply two people who enjoyed the same pastime. Roman didn't feel inferior or pitied. He pictured her as an elderly aunt, someone who loved the outdoors and freely gave good advice. What was she like? Should he try to find out? Would her next letter tell him more?

Finally, he gave in to his curiosity and walked to the lake. He didn't bother taking a fishing pole.

When he reached the clearing, he was happy to find he had a new letter. He lowered himself to the grass and used the log as a backrest while he read the latest note from his friend by flashlight.

Dear Friendly Fisherman,

When I arrived at the lake this morning, I saw a raccoon in our spot. I asked him if he knew you, but he grumbled and waddled away without answering me. Make sure you screw the lid of the jar on tightly if you leave me a letter. Raccoons are curious by nature and enjoy the challenge of opening things.

I'm surprised you don't know the rhyme about fishing and the wind. I thought everyone knew it. This is how it goes.

Wind from the West, fish bite the best.

Wind from the East, fish bite the least.

Wind from the North, don't venture forth.

Wind from the South will blow bait in their mouth.

My grandfather taught it to me when I was little. He would only fish when the wind was in the west or in the south, and he always had good luck. I, on the other hand, have not had much success improving my relationship at work. Don't think me wise. I'm not. I have a terrible tendency to say the worst possible thing at the worst possible moment.

Did you ever wish for the ability to call back the words you've said the second they leave your mouth? I wish that every day. Often, I think it would be better if I couldn't talk at all.

Perhaps that's why I enjoy writing these letters. I can always erase the words before you see them if I make a blunder. I hope you are faring better than I am with your troublesome work partner.

I will limit my advice here to fishing in the fu-

ture. I've had success with spinner baits and rub-
ber worms on this lake. Both are good choices no
matter what the weather and temperature. Another
bait you may want to try is a jig-and-pig. The bass
really seem to like them, even in the winter.
As always, your friend,
A Happy Angler

Roman chuckled at the idea of questioning a raccoon about his identity. His unknown friend had a good
imagination and a good sense of humor. As he read the
lines of the fishing rhyme, he vaguely recalled hearing
them in the past. His father didn't enjoy fishing but Roman's grandfather had. Maybe he was the one who had
recited the poem. He died when Roman was only six.
He had very few memories of the man. Roman's grandmother had lived with them until she passed away at
the age of ninety-two.

He pulled his small notebook and pencil from his
pocket and started a new letter. It took him a long time
to get the words just right.

When he finished his note, he tucked the jar securely
in the hollow space. He didn't mind the walk in the dark.
There was a full moon to light his way and he didn't
need to use his flashlight.

To his surprise, he did see a light on the far side of
the lake. Was it his unknown friend? Or was Woolly
Joe looking for a lost lamb? One day, Roman figured he
was bound to meet his friend face-to-face, but he wasn't
sure he wanted to. Discovering her identity would likely
end their unusual friendship. And he didn't want it to
end. He could put his feelings and fears into words on
paper better than he could speak them aloud.

On Sunday morning, Roman joined his family in the buggy for the eight-mile drive to the preaching service. It was being held for the first time at the home of Jonathan Dressler, a rare convert to their Amish faith. Jonathan was a horse trainer who took in unwanted and abandoned horses for an equine rescue organization. He had lived among the Amish for several years now and had married Karen Imhoff, the eldest daughter of Eli Imhoff, the previous fall.

The church service lasted the usual three hours. The bishop and two other ministers took turns preaching about forgiveness and about suffering persecution for the sake of their faith. In between, the congregation sang hymns from the *Ausbund,* their sacred songbook.

From his place on the benches near the back of the barn, Roman could see Joann Yoder sitting between her cousin, Sally Yoder, and her friend, Grace Beachy, on the benches to his left. Esta Bowman sat two rows behind them. Several times, he caught Esta smiling at him. Was she tired of Faron already?

Roman was glad he had realized Esta wasn't the woman for him. He was happy he'd discovered that before things had gotten more serious between them. He didn't find her sly smiles, overly sweet voice and flighty ways as attractive as he once did.

He glanced toward Joann. He hated to admit it, but he had her to thank for that. She might not have a sweet and attractive way about her, but she had a knack— a sometimes painful knack—of helping him see the truth. About himself and about others. He had come to respect that about her.

Perhaps it was time he told her that.

At the end of the service, Bishop Zook addressed the

crowd once more. "We are taking up two special collections today. One is to help purchase supplies to rebuild and replace what was lost at our school. We will have a workday at the school next Saturday and all are invited to come.

"The second collection is for our annual road use and repair. Our *Englisch* neighbors pay for road maintenance through gasoline taxes, revenue from driver's licenses, and money collected through tolls. However, we use the roads and bridges the same as they do, only we don't have to put gasoline in our horses or pay for a license to drive them. Our horse's shoes damage the roads in ways their car tires don't, so we must pay our fair share to keep them in good order."

Roman flinched at the thought of paying for road repairs. Why should he help the *Englisch* pay for road upkeep? So they could drive even faster and collide with more buggies?

The bishop continued, "Driving on well-maintained roads is a privilege. It is not a right. I urge you to give what you can. Last year our Amish churches in this area raised over a quarter of a million dollars for the fund. That money was divided between the state, the county and the township in which we reside."

Bishop Zook paused and then grinned. "For that amount, you would think I could get the potholes filled on the road that runs past my farm, but I reckon I'll have to give a little more to get that done." A ripple of laughter passed around the room. Roman didn't join in.

When the congregation was dismissed, Roman went out with the intention of speaking to Joann as soon as he had the chance. If he made an effort to mend fences

with her, he could tell his pen pal he was making progress in becoming a better man.

In spite of his best intentions, the chance never arrived. Everyone wanted to know about Otis and about
what had actually happened. He retold the story many
times. By the time he managed to get free, Joann was
sitting with her friends and eating, so he went in with
his brother and filled his plate. A half hour later, he went
in search of her again, but couldn't find her.

He learned later that her sister-in-law had become
sick and the family had gone home. He consoled himself with the fact that he would see her at work tomorrow morning.

That evening, he headed to the lake in hopes that
there would be another letter for him. He was disappointed to find his own note still in the jar. On the
walk home, he pondered why he cared so much about
exchanging letters with a stranger. He realized it was
because he could say whatever he pleased without the
fear of appearing foolish or weak. He had troubles, but
so did the Happy Angler. Together they had found a way
to share their burdens and make them lighter. Should
he suggest meeting in his next letter?

Perhaps not. If his unknown friend wanted to meet,
wouldn't she have suggested it by now? Besides, it
might be awkward if they found that they knew each
other. They would surely stop leaving notes for each
other if that were the case.

He found himself wondering why his pen pal hadn't
signed her letters in the first place. Roman hadn't signed
his first note because he didn't want to take credit for
a simple kind deed. So what reason did the Happy Angler have to keep her identity secret? Was it as simple

as Roman's reason? Or was there a darker motive behind the omission?

The thought troubled him until late in the night.

The following morning, he drove to work through the pouring rain and arrived mud-splattered and damp. His uncle was already there ahead of him along with Leonard and Gerald.

Roman said, "*Onkel,* should you be here? Didn't the doctor tell you to rest for a few days?"

"I'm sick of resting. I need to get back to work."

"Velda was driving you nuts, wasn't she?" Leonard said with a knowing wink.

Otis laughed then winced and put a hand to the bandage on his head. "*Ja,* she means well, but it was time to get out of the house. She can fuss over a body more than anyone I've ever met. Are the pillows too high? Would you like some tea? Shall I close the window? Do you need another pillow? Shall I open a window?"

"It's nice to have the love of a good woman," Gerald said.

Otis grinned. "I'm blessed and I know it, but even people who are in love irritate each other once in a while."

Roman glanced at the front door. "Speaking of irritating women, Joann isn't here yet. I wonder if something is wrong."

"She has gone back to her work at the bookshop. I'm not expecting her until noon today," Otis said.

"Are you serious?" Roman stared at Otis in stunned disbelief.

Otis nodded. "Perfectly serious. She has returned to her old position, but she'll do the cleaning here on Saturdays."

Leonard muttered under his breath, "We finally had someone who could do nearly everything in this office, and she goes back to shelving books and mopping floors. I don't think it's right but no one asked my opinion."

Roman wasn't sure what to think. Was this what she meant when she said she wouldn't always be around? Why hadn't she mentioned anything about it?

Otis scowled at Leonard. "Roman will soon master all of the tasks that Joann did."

Maybe he would and maybe he wouldn't. Her feet might be smaller than his, but she had left some mighty big shoes to fill. Was he the reason for her job change? Had she decided she couldn't work with him? It disturbed him to think that might be true. He hadn't been exactly friendly toward her.

"Now, let's get to work," Otis said. "We're going to be reprinting the schoolbooks this week, all of them, grades one through eight. I have the list here. Leonard, the plates are stored in the back of the bookshop."

Roman glanced at the clock. His uncle had said she'd be in after noon. Fine, he could wait a little longer. He had a lot to discuss with her when she came in.

Chapter 11

Would there be a letter waiting for her today? Oh, how she hoped there would be.

Joann left her brother's house an hour before she needed to leave for work. Instead of driving into town, she headed her pony and cart to the lake. It was raining steadily, but she didn't care. She had a sturdy umbrella.

She glanced out from under it at the leaden sky.

"Please, Lord, if I'm driving all this way in the rain, let there be a letter waiting for me today."

She needed something to cheer her, something to get her through the day.

Thoughts of Roman had occupied far too much of her time over the past several days. He needed to let go of the anger he carried, but she didn't know how to help him. She prayed for him and for herself. She wasn't angry about what had happened to the school and to

Otis, only saddened by the harmful actions of others. She offered up her forgiveness for the people who had committed the crimes. That should have been enough, but it wasn't. She wanted to prevent other incidents.

She hadn't forgotten the license plate number she had written down. If she gave it to the *Englisch* sheriff, would it be because she was following God's will or her own? Was she harboring a desire to prevent other such attacks, or was she seeking revenge? She wasn't sure of her own motives.

Vengeance was the Lord's. It had no place in her heart. However, she was human enough to admit she wanted the person who had injured Otis to face worldly justice.

She put her worries aside as she stopped in front of the gate leading to Joseph Shetler's pasture. Before she got down from the cart, a figure loomed out of the rain in front of her.

The shepherd's hired man stood with his shoulders hunched against the weather and water dripping from the brim of his dark hat. "How can I help you?"

Was this the author of her letters? Her heart beat faster. She'd never met him, she'd only heard stories about his reclusive ways. Carl King was much younger than she had expected. "I was on my way to the lake to do a little fishing."

"In this weather?" His voice was deep and gravelly, and held a hint of distrust.

She gave him a nervous smile. "I reckon the fish are already wet, so they shouldn't mind."

"You've been coming here a lot."

"Is that a problem?" What would she do if he turned her away?

"I guess not." He swung open the gate. "Just make sure that you don't let the sheep out when you leave. Keep an eye out for an ewe and lamb. They're missing from our flock."

Relieved that he wasn't going to stop her, she said, "I'll do that. Please tell Joseph that Joann Yoder says hello."

"I know who you are."

He certainly wasn't a friendly fellow. She would be surprised if it turned out that he was her pen pal. "You're Carl King, aren't you?"

"Yes."

Slapping the reins against her pony, she sent him through the open gate. As Carl swung it closed behind her, she looked over her shoulder. "Have you noticed anyone else coming here a lot?"

"No."

He looked impatient to end their meeting. She was keeping him standing in the rain. "Did you happen to pull a rod and reel out of the lake recently while you were fishing?" If he were the Friendly Fisherman, would he admit it?

"Nope."

"*Danki.* Have a pleasant day." In a way, she was thankful that he wasn't the one, but it was odd that he hadn't seen anyone coming and going frequently. He lived in the shepherd's hut near the pasture gate.

"Is there another way in to the lake?" she asked as she turned around. Carl was already gone. He had vanished into the mist as silently as he had appeared.

Happily, she found a letter waiting for her when she arrived at the log. She sat down and eagerly began to read, taking care to keep it out of the rain.

Dear Happy Angler,
I'm surprised Mr. Raccoon didn't stay and speak to you. I'll tell him that he was rude. I'm sure he will have more to say to you the next time you meet.

Joann grinned. It seemed her pen pal shared her sense of humor.

As for my work-related troubles, they have doubled. It is amazing how cruel and heartless some people can be. It saddens and sickens me. More than ever, I find I need the peace this place brings me. I'm bound up in a struggle between what I know is right and what others think is right.

That was exactly the dilemma she faced. To do what she thought was right, or to do what others told her was right. They were so much alike, this unknown writer and she. It was as if they faced the same challenges. It surely had to be someone she knew. But *Englisch* or Amish?

I never thought I lacked moral courage, but I fear that I do. Forgiveness is an easy word to say, but it's hard to mean it deep in your heart. I say it, but I don't mean it. I don't know if I ever will and that frightens me.

As for our troublesome coworkers, I suggest a trade. You can take my headache for a week and I'll take yours. I hope you don't think I'm making fun of your troubles. I'm not. I'm just grumpy and aching today. I think we're in for a weather change.

Don't be too hard on yourself. We all say things we don't mean. As for your coworker. Look for his strengths instead of his weaknesses. I know you'll find them.

It was good advice. Roman was irritating and reluctant to take her advice, but he had to have his own strengths. She would look for them more diligently.

And when she couldn't find any, she would think more about chucking him headfirst into the lake.

Shame swept over her at her unkind thoughts. Somehow, even when Roman wasn't around, he brought out the worst in her. She continued reading.

I plan to invest in a few jig-and-pigs. Thanks for the tip. Truthfully, I haven't been fishing lately, but I'll let you know what I catch in the future.

A Friendly Fisherman.

P.S. Please don't judge me harshly.

How could she judge him harshly? It was clear he struggled as she did with doing the right thing. She wrote out a heartfelt reply.

She folded the finished letter, tucked it into the jar and placed it inside the fallen log. She wished she could speak to her unknown friend in person. Wouldn't it be wonderful to meet here and enjoy a day of fishing together. She considered adding a request to meet, but shyness stopped her. He might enjoy exchanging letters, but who would enjoy spending time with a plain, lonely old maid? She didn't want his eagerness to read her notes turning to pity for her. It was better this way. For now. If he would reveal his identity, she might find the courage to reveal hers.

The rain stopped as she climbed back into her cart and headed toward town. Today, she would look for a hidden strength in Roman. If she discovered a positive quality about him, perhaps he would be on her mind less often.

When she arrived in town, she turned down the alley at the side of the building where Otis had a small shed for his employees' horses. She settled her pony on the fresh straw someone had laid down that morning. She made sure he had a pail of water and an armful of hay to munch on.

She entered the back door of the bookstore. Mabel was busy dusting the bookshelves in the small store. She held out a second dust rag for Joann. "I thought I would get started cleaning. I haven't had a customer all morning, and I'm bored to tears."

Joann slipped on a large apron and tied it behind her. She took the rag from Mabel. "I never complain if someone wants to clean."

"There is enough dust for both of us. I started by the front windows. If you want to start with the back shelves, we'll meet in the middle. How does that sound?"

"It sounds like a *goot* plan. Have you heard how Otis is doing?"

"I think he's doing okay. Leonard popped over earlier to tell me Otis had come in to work."

Joann frowned. "I thought he had strict orders from Dr. Zook to rest this week."

"You know men. They ignore their doctor's orders

and do what they want to do anyway. Then they complain like small children when they don't get better. I have half a mind to go over there and drag him home by the ear. He scared the life out of me when I saw him lying amid all that broken glass and blood."

Joann began dusting. She pulled out a handful of books, wiped down the shelf and replaced the volumes. "Have they found out who did it?"

Mabel stood on a step stool to wipe off the top of the bookcase. "Not that I've heard. I hope someone wasn't deliberately trying to hurt him. It does make me wonder since Roman is working here, too."

Joann paused in her work. "Why would that make a difference?"

"Because of the trial. Brendan Smith is known to dislike the Amish. He comes from a family that makes no bones about feeling the same way. It's sad, really. If they would just take the time to get to know their neighbors, I think they would feel differently."

"Is there a young woman in his family with white-blond hair, about my height, very pretty?"

"Not that I recall. Why?"

Joann dropped to her knees and began dusting the bottom shelves and books. "A young woman like that stopped in to ask about Otis that afternoon."

"A lot of people stopped in here to ask about Otis. I don't remember seeing anyone like that. The whole community was upset by what had happened. *Englisch* and Amish folks."

"It was probably just a coincidence, but I saw a car like the one she was in the morning of the school fire."

"Did you tell the sheriff?"

Joann shook her head. She had hoped to put her suspicions about the young woman to rest. All she had now was more questions.

"Joann, I don't mean to pry, but I was surprised when Otis told me that you wanted your job here at the bookstore back. I know you loved working in the printing office. Did it have anything to do with Roman Weaver coming to work there?"

It was the question she had been dreading. What should she say? The truth was always the best answer, but she didn't want to make it sound like Roman had forced her out. Otis had the right to hire anyone he wanted.

"It was time for a change." She finished dusting the bottom shelf and moved to the next bookcase.

"After only a few months?"

"I wasn't needed once Roman learned his way around. I'm happy doing this. It gives me more time to go fishing."

Mabel shook her head. "You and your fishing. I don't see how anyone can like touching slimy, smelly fish. Yuck."

Joann was saved from having to explain her fascination with the sport by the bell over the entrance. Mabel went to take care of her customer. Joann finished dusting, ran the vacuum sweeper over the carpet runners between the rows of shelves and mopped the uncarpeted areas of the floor. She was cleaning the two large windows facing the street when she saw Roman walk past. He caught sight of her at the same moment and stopped. To her dismay, he turned around to enter the shop.

Roman stood inside the entrance to the bookstore and watched Joann scrubbing the window so vigorously he was astounded that she hadn't worn a hole through it. She was deliberately ignoring him.

Mabel was helping another customer. "I'll be with you in a minute," she said.

He nodded and stepped over to the nearest bookshelves where he had a clear view of Joann. Was she still upset with him about the license plate number he'd taken from her? He'd been waiting all day to talk to her. Now that she was within sight, he suddenly didn't know why he'd been so keen on it. He rubbed a hand over his jaw and started browsing through the titles in front of him without really seeing them. He glanced her way several times, but she continued to work at cleaning the windows.

Finally, he spoke. "It must be on the outside."

She stopped scrubbing and glanced at him. "Were you talking to me?"

He replaced the book he held and picked up another. "You've been working on the same window pane for five minutes. If the spot hasn't come off by now, it must be on the outside."

She took a step back from the window. "You're right."

"What did you say?"

"I said you're right," she repeated in a louder voice.

He chuckled. "How hard was that to say?"

She rolled her eyes and picked up her supplies. "Laugh if you like, I have work to do."

He put the book away. "Otis told me you decided to come back to your old job. Why?"

"How is he today?"

She avoided his question by asking one of her own,

he noticed. "He has a bad headache. I tried to get him to leave, but he insists on staying."

"Stubborn must run in your family," she said.

"Tell me, why does someone who loves research, reading and writing as much as you do, give it up to scrub floors?"

She glared at him, her green eyes snapping. "There's nothing wrong with cleaning floors. Cleanliness is next to godliness."

He held up his hand. "I didn't say there was anything wrong with it. I only wondered why you chose it over working on the magazine and newspaper."

She looked down at the floor. "It was time for a change."

"Are you sure it's not because I work there now?"

She still didn't look at him. "I accepted this job before you accepted yours."

He wasn't sure he believed her, but he decided to give her the benefit of the doubt. He picked up another book and pretended to read the back cover. "Otis wants me to write an article for next month's magazine."

"On what?"

Mabel came over to him. "Are you interested in child-rearing?"

He looked at the book in his hand and hastily returned it to the shelf. "I'm just browsing."

"That's fine. Let me know if I can be of assistance." Mabel walked back to the counter and sat down. He turned to find Joann smothering a grin.

He liked her smile. He liked the way it made her eyes sparkle. Her grin slowly faded. She looked down. "What are you writing an article about?"

"The law and our responsibilities."

"Because of what's been happening?"

"I assume that's why Otis chose the topic. Perhaps because of my accident, as well."

"It is a relevant topic."

"What is your opinion? Should an Amish person call or notify the police when they are the victim of a crime? Does that go against our teachings of nonresistance and nonviolence? The Bible says in Matthew 5:39, 'But I say unto you, That ye resist not evil: but whosoever shall smite thee on thy right cheek, turn to him the other also.'"

She folded her arms and nibbled at her lower lip. "If you're asking me what I want done about the license plate number I wrote down, I would like to give it to the sheriff."

"There is a larger question besides what you or I would *like* to do. It's about what we *should* do."

"You believe we should do nothing."

"I'm not sure."

"By doing nothing, aren't we leading weaker souls into temptation?"

"How so?"

"Might someone decide it's easier to rob an Amish home because he thinks that crime won't be reported? What is our responsibility to him?"

"You think we should take temptation out of his way."

"Yes, but how? By keeping our money out of sight and in a safe place, or by letting it be known his crime will be reported to the *Englisch* law? Paul urged Christians to give civil authorities their dues with regard to taxes, respect and honor."

The fire was back in her green eyes. Why had he

ever thought she was homely? He said, "You've given me a lot to think about."

"I look forward to reading your article. Do you have your answer?"

"I think so. We should feel we can report a crime and answer police questions if we're asked, but we shouldn't seek revenge. We shouldn't file charges or seek damages from others. I think in this way we will remain true to the teachings of Christ."

"You have forgotten the most important thing."

"What's that?"

"We must forgive those who harm us."

Trust her to point out his failings. Why did he think she might understand his struggle? He took a step back. "I haven't forgotten. Enjoy your new job." He left the bookstore, slamming the door behind him.

He worked the rest of the afternoon on the article his uncle had assigned him. Three times he painstakingly typed out his thoughts and three times he tore the page out of the typewriter, wadded it up and tossed it toward the trash can. He left work that evening hoping something would occur to him out at the lake.

He was happy to discover a new letter waiting for him when he reached his now favorite spot. This time, he had taken his pole and hoped to get in a few hours of fishing before dark. He opened his note.

My Friend,
It seems we share the same sense of the absurd.
Mr. Raccoon has not put in another appearance.
Clearly, he is ashamed of his earlier behavior and
is trying to avoid me.
    I'm sorry your troubles at work are getting

worse instead of better. I, too, am saddened by the cruel and senseless behavior I've seen lately. Are we perhaps talking about the same events in our community? I'm referring to the Amish schoolhouse fire and the injury of Otis Miller when someone threw a brick through the window of his business. These nameless individuals may think they are hurting the Amish, but they are only hurting themselves. I feel sorry for them.

As for your personal struggle, I urge you to do what you know is right. That is usually the truest course. If you can, seek the wisdom of men you admire and take their words to heart. Very few people have lived a life free of pain. Some may even have faced the same issue that is troubling you. We do not travel though this world alone.

Forgiveness is not easy. Some hurts are so deep that we can see only despair and question why God has chosen this for us. Forgiveness is God's mighty gift to the giver. It heals the one who was harmed. It can also heal those who have caused harm if they acknowledge what they have done and seek redemption.

I hope you continue to draw comfort from this beautiful spot, and I hope you find my letters as comforting as I find yours. I will heed your sage advice and seek the strengths of the man who annoys me. If I don't find any, I'm willing to make the trade. You name the time and place.

The hardware store in Hope Springs carries a good selection of fishing tackle. You can find several kinds of jig-n-pigs there.

May God bless you and keep you.

The Happy Angler

Reading one of the Happy Angler's letters always made him feel better. He didn't have to struggle with his doubts and problems alone. This letter made him almost certain that the Happy Angler was an Amish woman from his community.

She was someone who was familiar with the recent crime spree. She was also someone who advocated forgiveness even as she acknowledged how difficult that could be. Roman's curiosity continued to grow about the identity of his friend. Who could she be? He thought of some of the kindhearted single women in his church district. There was Sally Yoder, Grace Beachy and a whole slew of girls his brother's age. Then there was Lea Belier, the teacher. She would have free time to fish now that school was out for the summer, but who would annoy her at her job? Was she working somewhere else over the summer?

If he started asking his mother questions about the local single maids, she would start harping about grandchildren again. He would simply have to wonder and hope his unknown friend would one day reveal her identity.

Of course, it could be Joann Yoder.

That thought made him flinch. He couldn't see her starting up a correspondence with a stranger. Sure, Leonard was sometimes difficult to work with, but Joann had taken another job. Nothing in this letter indicated the author planned to change where she worked.

He mulled over the advice he'd been given. His friend was a very wise person, indeed. Roman spent the next hour fishing without much success. He caught only three small fish and tossed them all back. As the sun began to set, he wrote:

Dear Happy Angler,

You are so right. We do not travel through this world alone. You are proof of that. Yes, I was talking about the Amish schoolhouse fire and the brick-throwing incident. What will it take to restore peace in our community?

As for forgiveness, I'm working on that. You write with great conviction about the grace forgiveness brings us. I think you are right.

God bless you and keep writing. I do find comfort in your words.

Your Friendly Fisherman

He tucked the brief letter in their makeshift mailbox. He was starting to care a great deal about the woman who wrote such comforting words. Someday, he would tell her in person about the peace her words brought him.

That evening after supper, he waited for a chance to speak to his father alone. His father was a wise man. If anyone could help him with his dilemma, he could.

He followed his dad into the living room. "*Daed,* can I ask you a question?"

His father settled himself in his favorite chair. "Of course."

"I think I know who is behind the attack on Otis and the fire at the school."

"Who?"

"It's a member of Brendan Smith's family. I don't know what to do with the information."

Menlo stroked his beard. "You are considering giving it to the police?"

"*Ja.* I fear others may be attacked."

"I understand your fears. We must trust that God will keep us from harm."

"I know, but is that enough?"

Menlo was silent for long time. Roman waited for his answer. Finally, Menlo spoke. "If I see a house on fire, I will pray for everyone's safety, but I will sound the alarm and try to save what I can, be it my neighbor or his goods, and I will work to keep the fire from spreading. *Gott* put me where I could see the flames and help. You must pray for guidance and ask yourself if *Gott* has put you where you can see the flames."

"*Danki,* Papa. I will do that."

The following morning when Roman arrived at the office, he learned Otis wouldn't be in. Leonard was waiting for him with a note from his aunt. As he read it, Gerald came in.

"What's up?" Gerald looked from Leonard to Roman.

"Otis's headache has gotten worse. My aunt is taking him back to the hospital at the urging of Dr. Zook. She says that Otis wants me to take charge of the business until he returns."

Roman rubbed the back of his neck. The job was beyond him. Without Otis here, he really needed someone who knew what they were doing. Leonard and Otis were both waiting for him to say something. "How are we coming on the schoolbooks?"

"I printed twenty copies of all the first-grade books yesterday," Leonard said.

"I will get the covers on and get them bound today," Gerald said, then looked as if he wanted to say something else.

"What?" Roman asked.

Gerald and Leonard shared a speaking glance. "Otis

wanted all the books done by this weekend," Gerald said. "I don't think we can do it. Not in addition to getting the paper out and finishing all the other orders we have."

"What do you suggest?" Roman wasn't above asking for help.

"Get Joann in here," Leonard stated. "She knows what needs to get done and how to do it."

Roman nodded. "Okay, I will ask her to help us."

"You will?" Gerald asked in surprise. "I didn't think the two of you got along."

Roman scowled at him. "I won't let my uncle's business suffer because of my personal feelings for the woman. Leonard, get started on the second-grade books today. Are there any that we don't have plates for?"

Leonard shook his head. "We have plates for everything that Leah has been using. It's a good thing too, otherwise it would cost more and take more time to set all that type."

"Guess we should get busy," Gerald said. "I sure hope Joann agrees to help."

As the men went to work, Roman sat down at his desk and noticed a note with his name on it. He unfolded the wrinkled paper and saw it was his first attempt at writing his article on law and order. There was a note in the margin. "This one is the best. Use it."

There was no signature, but he knew the note had come from Joann. She must have come in to straighten up after he left and found his discarded attempts to write his article, then salvaged one.

He read through the rough draft again. She was right. This version said what he wanted to say without sounding judgmental and without preaching. He put a new piece of paper in his typewriter and finished the article. When he was done, he felt a keen sense of accomplishment that he'd rarely known.

He opened his desk drawer and pulled out the license plate number that Joann had written down. Had God put him and Joann here so that they might see the flames of this evil and sound the alarm?

Roman prayed he was doing the right thing. He stapled the license number inside a copy of the *Family Hour* magazine and addressed it to Sheriff Bradley, then put it in the mailbox.

He drew a deep breath. Now, he needed to convince Joann to come back to work for him. He wasn't at all certain that she would.

Chapter 12

She was late.

Joann stabled her pony without giving him his hay or grain. He whinnied in protest as she closed the stall door. "I'll be back later to feed you. I promise."

It was only the second day of her part-time job and she was thirty minutes late. Otis would not be happy with her.

She should have waited to go to the lake until after work, but she had been eager to check for another letter and to her delight, there had been one waiting for her. She had lost track of time while writing an answer and now she was late. The letter was tucked in her pocket and the words came back to her now.

Dear Happy Angler,
You are so right. We do not travel through this world alone. You are proof of that.

Her words brought him comfort. She smiled at the thought as she rushed in through the back door of the bookstore and jerked open the supply room door. She grabbed her cleaning supplies and a broom from the corner, spun around and ran into Roman. The handle of her broom smacked the side of his head. She stood speechless with surprise and remorse.

He rubbed his temple. "Come into my uncle's office. I need to talk to you."

That didn't sound good. "I really am sorry. It was an accident."

"I'm just glad it wasn't a brick."

"Let me put this stuff back and I'll be right there." At least he hadn't asked why she was late.

She replaced her cleaning supplies and followed him to the office next door. Otis wasn't in. Roman sat behind his uncle's desk. His grave expression set off alarm bells in her head. "Where is your uncle?"

"He is back in the hospital. Apparently, there was some slow bleeding in his brain. My aunt called the bookstore and told Mabel they are taking him into surgery."

"Oh, no!" Joann sank onto a nearby chair. "What can I do to help?"

"I was hoping you would ask that. Can you come back to work in your old position? I don't know what your pay was, but I will match it."

"Of course. Just tell me what you need me to do."

"My uncle has left me in charge, but I am woefully unprepared to run this business."

He wasn't just being modest, he was worried. She could see it in his eyes. "I will do whatever I can to help. What projects are being run this week, and where do they stand?"

"All the schoolbooks are being reprinted," Roman began. "Otis wanted all of them done by Saturday. We have the first-grade books printed. Gerald is running them through the binder now. Leonard has started on the second-grade books. Fortunately, we have plates for all of them through the eighth grade. If worse comes to worst, we can delay delivery for a few weeks since the children aren't in school. Besides the newspaper, we have two hundred and fifty wedding invitations that need to be done by tomorrow, fifty new menus for the Shoofly Pie Café that were promised for Thursday and a half dozen miscellaneous business announcements."

"In other words, a lot."

A smile tugged at the corner of his mouth. "*Ja,* teacher, we have a lot to do."

She didn't mind her nickname this time. He wasn't being sarcastic. This Roman Weaver, a man determined to do the best for someone else, was a man she could like.

She rose to her feet. "I'll start setting the type for the wedding invitations. We can use the proof press to run them since there aren't very many. If you start on the layout for the newspaper, we should be able to get it out on time."

"*Danki,* Joann. For agreeing to help, and for commenting on my magazine article. I couldn't see the forest for the trees when I wrote it."

She felt herself blushing. She wasn't used to him being nice. "That is often the case with writers. That's why it's helpful to have someone read your stuff."

"I'll remember that."

"Once Otis gets back, I'm sure he'll proofread your work."

Roman's eyes darkened with worry. "I wish we could hear how he is doing."

She longed to ease his burdens. "We can manage without you for a few hours if you want go to the hospital."

He gave her a halfhearted smile. "I'm sure you could manage without me for a lot longer than a few hours, but I feel I have to stay here. This business is important to my uncle. Mabel will let us know something as soon as she hears."

Joann studied him in a new light. Her Friendly Fisherman had suggested that she look for Roman's strengths. She had found them in his writing and even more so in his love for his uncle. She looked forward to telling her friend how well his suggestion had worked.

They received good news about Otis an hour later. His surgery had gone well. He was in intensive care, but he was expected to make a full recovery. The tension in the office lightened perceptibly after that.

When they closed up for the evening, they had made significant inroads into their workload. Leonard was ready to start printing the seventh-grade books, and Joann had finished the wedding announcements. They walked together out the back door to where the horses were stabled. Joann had managed to get away long enough to feed her pony. He seemed eager to be on his way home. She was surprised to realize she wasn't eager to leave. She was enjoying Roman's company.

"Since you're working with us again, why don't I pick you up tomorrow?" Roman said as he headed for his horse's stall.

She frowned as she considered how she could make time to get to the lake now. She couldn't. Her letters would have to wait until things settled back to normal.

Roman led his mare out of the stall. "If you don't want to, that's fine."

"No, I want to, I mean, that's fine and it's nice of you to offer."

"But what?"

She smiled to reassure him. "Never mind. It's something I had planned to do in the mornings since I wasn't working, but it can wait. The usual time?"

He nodded. "*Ja*, the usual time."

She looked forward to spending time in his company more than she cared to admit.

The various jobs at the office kept them busy for the rest of the week, but it gave them something to talk about on their way to and from work. Roman remained approachable and interested in what she had to say. At least it seemed that way.

On Friday, Joann found him in Otis's office, seated behind his uncle's desk. He didn't look comfortable there. She couldn't blame him. His uncle's illness had forced him into a position he wasn't ready for.

He looked up. "Did you need something?"

"Do you have a minute to talk about the schoolbooks we're reprinting?"

He frowned at the paper he held. "Do we really need sixteen reams of copy paper this month?"

"That sounds about right."

"Okay." He jotted a note and closed the order book. "What was it you wanted to discuss?"

She took a step inside the office. "There are some

changes that need to be made in the booklet on learning to drive a horse and buggy safely."

"I read through the book. I didn't see anything that needed changing. Besides, we have the plates for that one. It will cost more if we make changes and we've already agreed on a price with Eli Imhoff for the project."

"I wish you would read through it again."

"I don't have time," he said with exasperation.

"You, of all people, know how important it is to share the road properly."

He scowled at her. "I *was* sharing the road properly until Brendan Smith decided to knock the open door off my buggy with his truck. Either he didn't know or he didn't care that I was standing on the other side of that door."

"There's no denying you suffered a bad experience."

"Thank you, but that doesn't help me move my fingers."

"All I'm asking is for you to take a look at the booklet again, with your own experience in mind, and see if you don't think we can make it better."

"You will nag me until you get your way, won't you?"

She pressed her lips into a tight line. "I would hardly call it nagging."

"Is there anything else?"

"That's all I wanted."

"Fine. Now, I've got work to do."

"And I'll be out here taking a nap," she muttered as she turned away. How could he charm her one day and irritate her so much the next?

Roman heard Joann's remark, but he didn't respond to it. He had far too much on his mind. His uncle's health wasn't improving as rapidly as his doctor had hoped. Roman didn't have time to reread each school-book and make sure they were accurate. They had been good enough in the past. They would be good enough now.

Only, Joann had planted the seed of doubt in his mind. He couldn't dismiss it. He opened a copy of *Learning to Drive a Horse and Buggy* and started reading. Bishop Zook's words came back to him. Driving on well-maintained roads was a privilege, it wasn't a right. The Amish had to share the responsibility for the roadway upkeep and safety, too. Nothing in the text-book addressed this fundamental piece of information.

He, like many Amish, was guilty of being proud that he shunned cars and drove a buggy. Didn't he expect cars to travel at his pace and pass him safely no matter how long he slowed their progress?

The *Englisch* did not intend to slow down to the Amish pace of life. The Amish had to take as much, or even more, responsibility for safety on the roads. It annoyed him that Joann was the one to point it out.

His conscience pricked him as an overlooked truth wormed its way into his thoughts. It wasn't so much that she was annoying. What he found annoying was that she was so often right.

Later that afternoon, he stopped beside her desk. "Rewrite the section that you think needs to be changed, and I'll look it over."

Her eyes grew round. "Really? We're going to change it?"

"You were right, it needs to be updated."

"Oh, that was hard for you to say, wasn't it?"

He struggled to hide a smile. "You have no idea."

"I'm glad you took this job. It suits you."

"Are you going to the school benefit on Saturday?" he asked.

"*Ja,* I planned on it."

"Do you want to help me take the books out there?"

She hesitated, then nodded. "Sure. Shall I meet you here?"

"I'll pick you up at the usual time."

"Can we make it an hour later?" she asked hopefully. "I have something I'd like to do first."

"I don't see why not."

"Great." She smiled brightly and his mood lightened.

He found he was reluctant to walk away. "My mother wants to come with me. *Daed* and Andrew will be along later with the lumber that's needed."

"That will be fine."

He still didn't move.

She raised one eyebrow. "Is there something else?"

He cleared his throat. "*Nee,* I'll let you get back to your nap."

"*Danki.*" She swooped the paperwork on her desk into one large pile and laid her head on it.

He chuckled as he went back to his uncle's office. He had no idea she had such a cute sense of humor. There was more to her than he once suspected.

In spite of the heavy workload, they were able to get everything finished on time.

Roman's good mood lasted until Saturday morning. His mother was bustling around getting food, plates and glasses ready to help feed the people who would be working at the school that day.

She handed him a picnic basket to put in his buggy

and said, "Esta Barkman asked if she could ride along with us. I told her we'd pick her up. I hope that's okay."

Esta and Joann in the same buggy. That should make for an interesting ride to the school. His mother was humming as she worked. That wasn't like her.

He suddenly had a bad feeling about the day.

Joann hurried toward the lake early on Saturday morning. She hadn't had a chance to check for a new letter since she had resumed her old job. It had only been a few days, but it seemed much too long.

When she reached the log, she was disappointed when she saw her letter was still in the same place. The Friendly Fisherman hadn't returned. She sat down and added a short note to the end of her first letter. Content that her friend would know how she had taken his message to heart, she replaced the jar and hurried home.

An hour later, she waited at the end of the lane as Roman pulled up beside her. His mother sat beside him. "*Guder mariye,* Joann," she called out.

"Good morning, Marie Rose. Have you news of your brother?" Joann climbed into the buggy with them.

"He's doing well and has been moved out of intensive care."

"That is wonderful news."

"Roman tells me you are helping at the printing office again until Otis returns."

She had her old job back, but this wasn't how she wanted it. "Roman has things well in hand. I'm just doing what I can to help."

"We have one more stop to make," Roman said. He seemed out of sorts this morning.

His mother said brightly, "We are picking up Esta

Barkman. She wanted to go with me to the hospital after we finish at the school. She's such a thoughtful young woman, and such a good cook, too." She smiled at her son.

Joann wanted to slink away and hide. She hadn't exchanged a single word with Esta since that day in the barn.

Roman turned into the Barkman lane. Esta was waiting on the porch swing. She looked lovely in a crisp new dress of pale lavender. Joann had chosen one of her work dresses to wear. The plain gray fabric and black apron looked shabby next to Esta's cool color.

Esta came down the walk with a wicker basket over her arm. "Hello, everyone. Joann, I'm surprised to see you."

"Roman and I are taking the new books out to the school."

"How kind of you. Very wise to wear your old dress for such work. Isn't she practical, Roman?" She stood beside the buggy looking up at them.

Joann realized they couldn't all sit up front. She got down and climbed in back expecting Esta to sit in back with her.

"*Danki,* Joann." Esta smiled brightly at her and took her place beside Roman's mother up front.

When Roman set the horse in motion, Esta and his mother were engaged in conversation, Joann folded her arms across her chest and stuck her tongue out at Esta's back.

At the publishing office, Joann and Roman loaded the boxes of books while his mother and Esta continued their chat. They were getting ready to leave when Mabel came out with another box of books. "These are some I wanted to donate to the school. They're mostly storybooks and a few songbooks, things I know the kids will enjoy."

Joann put them beside her on the seat. "*Danki,* Mabel. I know Leah will be most grateful."

When they arrived at the school, the work was well under way. A scaffold had been built across the burned opening at the side of the building. Men in straw hats, white shirts and dark pants with suspenders swarmed around the building like ants. Eli Imhoff and Bishop Zook supervised the work and made sure that everyone knew their job.

The sounds of hammers and saws filled the air along with the chatter and laughter of the children who were playing on the school-ground equipment. Long tables had been set up beneath the shade of a nearby tree and women in dark dresses and white *kapps* laid out the food, and made sure everyone had plenty of lemonade or coffee.

Roman's mother and Esta carried their baskets of food toward the tables. Leah came out of the school with Sarah and Sally at her side. "Oh good, you have the books. Bring them inside."

Joann carried the boxes while Roman went to join the men. She and the other women were soon busy shelving books and sorting through the donations that continued to come in.

Later, when they went out to get refreshments, she saw Roman had been put in charge of painting the building. He had seven young boys of various ages wielding paintbrushes beside him. As Joann watched, Esta approached him with a glass of lemonade and a sly smile.

"I can't believe she has set her sights on him again," Sally said as she folded her arms and shook her head.

Joann tried to pretend she didn't care. "His mother likes her. I think she feels it would be a good match."

Sarah stood beside them nibbling on an oatmeal raisin cookie. "I had hoped that you two might hit it off, Joann."

Joann sighed. Sarah always had matchmaking on her mind. "Roman is not my type. He's not sensitive. He doesn't appreciate my quirky sense of humor." She closed her mouth. She had almost revealed her secret.

Sally turned to stare at Joann. "Is there someone who does appreciate your quirky sense of humor?"

Joann couldn't help the blush that heated her cheeks. Sally and Sarah exchanged excited glances and leaned close to Joann. Sarah said, "Out with it. Who is he? Where did you meet him?"

Now she was in a pickle. They both knew something was up. She was going to have to tell the truth, or some version of the truth.

"I haven't actually met him, but I know a lot about him."

"What does that mean?" Sally asked.

"We've been exchanging letters."

Sarah clapped her hands together. "A pen pal courtship, how wonderful. Who is he? Where does he live?"

Joann shook her head. "I'd rather not say."

Sally's eyes narrowed. "Why not? What is this paragon's name?"

"I'd rather not say," Joann answered in a weak voice.

Sarah nodded. "We won't tease you anymore."

Sally fisted her hands on her hips. "You're making it up."

Joann's chin came up. "I am not."

"Well, there is something fishy about this. How come we haven't heard about him before?"

Joann made sure that no one else was close enough to overhear. "We've been leaving letters for each other in a hollow tree at the lake."

Sarah put her arm around Joann's shoulder. "How romantic."

Sally shook her head. "I'm not buying it."

"It's true," Joann insisted. "I lost my new fishing rod in the lake. I was heartbroken. He went fishing and recovered it. Instead of keeping it, he left it with a note beside it. When I went back to the lake, I found my rod and his note. I wrote him a thank-you letter in the same place. It sort of took off from there."

Sarah's gaze grew troubled. "But you know who he is, right?"

"Not exactly." Joann had never considered how lame it would sound when she tried to explain.

Sally scowled at her. "Are you telling us that you're exchanging letters with a complete stranger who happens to fish at the same lake that you do?"

"That about sums it up. I think I'll have another cookie." She started for the table.

Sally grabbed her arm. "Are you crazy? He could be some kind of nut."

Joann didn't want to hear it. "He's not a nut. He's sensitive and troubled and he shares what he's going through with me. What is so wrong with that?"

Sarah clapped a hand over her mouth. "Oh my goodness. He's *Englisch*."

Joann stared at the ground. "I don't think so. His letters sound… Amish."

"Old Amish? Young Amish? Single Amish? Married Amish? Ex-Amish?" Sally waited for an answer. Joann didn't have one.

"I don't know."

Sarah and Sally each grabbed Joann's arm and pulled her to a more secluded spot. Sarah said, "You don't know his name, but he knows yours. Right?"

"I sign my letters the Happy Angler. He signed his letters the Friendly Fisherman."

"Are you telling us he doesn't even know he's writing to a woman?" Sarah's mouth dropped open.

Joann closed her eyes. "I told him I was an Amish woman. It's only letters. I was afraid he would stop writing if he knew. It started out innocent enough. Why are you making it sound so sordid?"

Sally shook her head. "You have to stop. He could be anybody."

Joann walked a few steps away from them. "You don't understand. We have a connection. I don't want to stop writing him."

"Then you have find out who he is."

"I'm not doing anything wrong. I'm exchanging letters with someone who likes to fish as much as I do. We share a joke, talk about our problems, offer suggestions and support. There is nothing wrong with what I'm doing."

Sarah and Sally exchanged pitying glances. Before they could say anything else, Leah joined them. "It's almost done. You can't even tell where the fire was. I'm so thankful for all the people who have come out today. Come, Bishop Zook is going to offer a blessing."

Sarah and Sally followed her, but Joann stayed where she was. In her heart, she knew they were right. She had to end the secrecy. If their friendship was a good thing, it would bear up in the light of day.

If it didn't, she didn't know what she would do.

Chapter 13

Roman managed to stay busy and out of Esta's reach for most of the day. He was thankful when she and his mother left to visit Otis in the hospital with some of his English friends. Before she got in the car, his mother gave his arm a squeeze. With a happy smile, she said, "It's wonderful to see you and Esta together again."

"We're not together."

His mother leaned closer. "She told me that things have been rough between the two of you, but she's willing to work it out."

Esta was already in the backseat of the car. She had the grace to blush. She scooted over to make room for his mother when she got in. He closed the car door and watched as they drove away. It didn't matter if she charmed his mother or not. He didn't see a future with her.

On the ride home, he glanced frequently at Joann. She seemed deep in thought. A small frown put a crease between her eyebrows. He wanted to smooth it away. "Is something troubling?" he asked.

She glanced at him and shook her head. "I have a hard decision to make and I'm not sure what to do."

"That sounds serious. Is there anything I can do to help?"

"I appreciate the offer, but this is something I have to work out for myself."

"If this is about your job, you can stay on until Otis comes back."

"I will be happy to help out again if you get in a bind, but there isn't enough work to keep all of us busy now that the schoolbooks have been finished. On Monday I'll be at the bookstore again."

"You don't mind?"

She sighed. "I believe everything happens for a reason."

"If only we could see what that reason was." He pulled Meg to a stop at the end of Hebron's lane.

"Then we wouldn't need faith, would we?" she asked gently.

"I reckon not. You don't need to come in Monday unless you really want to. I gave Leonard and Gerald the day off. They've both put in a lot of long hours, and so have you."

She nodded and got down. She paused and turned to face him. "I'm glad that Esta has come to her senses. You two make a nice couple."

"You and my mother," he said in disgust. "I'd like to choose my own wife, if you don't mind."

"I know it isn't any of my business, but I hope you

don't hold the things I said in anger against Esta. I was wrong to repeat gossip. I would hate to think that I ruined something between you."

"You didn't ruin anything. You just have a way of making me look at things differently. Good night."

"Good night."

He turned the horse around and drove toward home. As he drew even with the road that led to the lake, he stopped and turned in. He wanted to see if he had a letter. More than that, he wanted to tell his friend about the decisions he'd made.

It took him a while to find the right place. He was used to coming down from the north end of the lake. Once he spotted the faint path leading around the east shore, he left his buggy and walked through the trees.

Roman hoped he might run into his friend on a Saturday evening, but the small glade was empty. There was a note in the jar.

Dear Friendly Fisherman,
I hope your coworker is becoming less of a headache. I think I may have misjudged mine. We are finding our way with each other. I couldn't have done it without you. My mother always used to say a friend is like a rainbow, always there for you after a storm. Thanks, my friend.
A Happy Angler
P.S. I followed your sound advice and searched for my coworker's strengths. I'm happy to say I have discovered that there is much more to him than I first thought. He is committed to taking care of his family, he has a wonderful sense of humor and he is a fine worker. Thank you. With-

out your wise words, I might have continued to overlook his good qualities and focused only on his failings. I find that I like him a lot.

Roman sat back with a smile. He took out his notebook and pen and wrote.

My Friend,
We really do have a lot in common. How wise God was to put us in touch with each other. I don't see my coworker as a headache anymore. In fact, I'm finding I like her a lot, too. Much more than I ever thought I would.

He tapped his lips with the tip of his pen as he decided what else to say.

"I've decided to meet my pen pal."
Joann could barely believe she'd spoken aloud. She glanced at her cousin Sally to gauge her reaction. Sally and her family had come for a visit. It was the off Sunday, the one without a church service, and families frequently traveled to visit each other on that day. The women were gathering morel mushrooms in the woods beyond the house. Sally's little sister and Joann's nieces were playing tag up ahead of them.

"Are you sure you want to do that? What if he is *Englisch?*" Sally's tone was grave.

Joann walked along with her eyes scanning the ground. "If he is *Englisch,* well, I can have an *Englisch* friend."

"Just stop writing him." Sally bent to pick two morels from the base of a tree.

"You haven't read his letters. We share so many of the same doubts and hopes. It has nothing to do with being Amish or being *Englisch*. We're two people trying to find a way to accept God's plan for us."

"I know you feel a connection to this person, but he may not feel the same connection to you."

"I don't believe that." Joann spotted a small cluster of mushrooms and moved toward them.

Sally followed her. "Has your pen pal ever suggested that you meet?"

Joann had trouble meeting Sally's eyes. "No."

Sally stopped and took Joann's hands between her own. "I am the last person who should be giving anyone advice on matters of the heart, but I'm afraid only heartache will come from this meeting."

"I'm not some giddy teenager. This isn't a matter of the heart."

"Isn't it? Aren't you secretly hoping that your pen pal is a handsome, single man?"

Joann pulled away from Sally. "What if I am?"

"Oh, Joann." Sally shook her head sadly. "He's far more likely to be old, fat, bald and married with a half dozen children or just as many grandchildren."

Tears blurred Joann's vision. "Don't you see? I have to find out. I know that I'm not pretty. I know that I'm not likely to marry. This person respects what I think and how I feel. If it's an Amish grandfather who loves fishing as much as I do, that will be wonderful. We'll be friends and go fishing together as often as possible and I won't feel so lonely."

"And if he should be a handsome, unmarried *Englischer*?"

Joann didn't answer. Both she and Sally knew such

a relationship would be forbidden. The only way she could sustain such a relationship would be to leave their Amish community.

Joann turned away from Sally. "I have to know."

She had pined for Levi, but Sarah was the wife God chose for him. Now, she was growing fond of Roman and it seemed that Esta was the one for him.

Joann picked another mushroom and dropped it in her basket. Who was the man for her? "Tomorrow, I'll leave him a note asking to meet."

"If he refuses?"

"I'll stop writing him."

If he agreed to meet, what would happen after that?

Roman didn't have to go in to work early on Monday, so he made his way to the lake. The Happy Angler frequented their spot in the mornings. He had hopes of running into her today. He wanted to meet his friend in person.

He reached the grove of trees and followed the path toward their fishing hole. He rounded the last bend in the path and stopped in his tracks. A woman was sitting on the fallen log. She had her back to him, but she was dressed plain in a gray dress with a white kapp covering her hair.

He took a step off the path into the cover of the woods. His unknown friend was here? It didn't seem possible.

He checked the area for signs of other people. He didn't see anyone else.

The woman turned around with a jar in her hand. It wasn't a stranger. It was Joann, and she held his letter.

Joann Yoder was the Happy Angler? He couldn't believe it.

She tucked the jar in the hollow of the log and picked up a fishing pole, the very pole he had pulled from the lake a few weeks ago. He was too stunned to move.

He tried to think of everything he had written. Written about her! Not much of it had been flattering. He couldn't quite wrap his mind around the fact that she was the one reading his musings. She really would dunk him in the lake if she found out.

Did she know he was the one reading her letters?

No, he didn't think so. He hadn't said anything specific about himself. He took a step back. He had to think this over. He'd become increasingly fond of Happy Angler. How could she be Joann? He tried to reconcile the two in his mind. He had learned to respect Joann. She had a sharp mind and a fine measure of humor. He'd even started to care about her as a woman, but he wasn't sure she returned such feelings. She practically had him married to Esta, but something in the way she looked at him the other evening gave him hope. He'd seen longing in her eyes, but was it a longing for him?

What would she think when she discovered she had been writing to him all this time?

Would she be pleased or mortified? The last thing he wanted was to cause a new break between them. This was going to take some careful thinking. He needed to be certain how she felt about him before he let on that he was the Friendly Fisherman.

He needed to be certain she *was* the Happy Angler. Maybe she'd simply stumbled on this location and accidentally found the letter jar.

He dropped to a crouch and waited for her to leave.

She fished for a while, but didn't catch anything. Soon, she put her rod and tackle box inside the large end of the log and stuffed some grass into the opening.

She hadn't stumbled on this place by accident. He crouched lower as she walked by. When he was certain she had gone, he went to the log and pulled out the jar. His note was gone and there was a brief one in its place.

> Dear Friend,
> As much as I have enjoyed our correspondences,
> I feel it's time we met in person. I have so much
> I want to say to you.
> Sincerely,
> The Happy Angler

The handwriting was the same. Without a doubt, Joann was the one. Someday, he hoped they would look back on these days and laugh about their secret correspondence, but he wasn't laughing yet. He was in trouble.

He pondered how he could make this could come out right as he walked home. The longer he thought about it, the more panicked he became. His brother was crossing the yard. He stopped. "I thought you had gone to work?"

Roman pulled off his hat and raked his fingers through his hair "Not yet. It's her. I couldn't believe my eyes."

"What are you talking about?" His brother looked at him as if he'd gone crazy. Maybe he had.

Roman began pacing. "Joann Yoder."

"I still have no idea what you are talking about."

Roman spun to face him. "I went to the lake today, and she was there. I can't believe this."

"I'm still not following you. Why should you care if Joann Yoder was fishing at the Lake?"

"She wasn't fishing. She was writing a letter."

"I wrote one last month. It's not that amazing that she knows how to do it."

Roman shook his head. "Remember the letter I left for the person whose rod and reel I pulled out of the lake?"

"Sure. He left you a lure as thanks."

"That wasn't the only letter I wrote. We've been exchanging notes ever since, only I thought I was writing to a woman who liked to fish. I never once thought the letters I received came from Joann Yoder."

"Wait a minute. You've been exchanging love letters with Joann Yoder and you didn't know it? What a hoot!" Andrew started laughing.

"They weren't love letters." He began pacing again.

"It's still funny. You and the old maid leaving notes for each other in a hollow tree. That's priceless. Did she know it was you?"

Andrew's question stopped him. Did she? He found it hard to believe. There hadn't been anything in her demeanor or her notes that suggested she was aware of his identity. "I don't think so."

"I reckon you should tell her the truth. I wouldn't want to be in your shoes when she finds out. She's bound to think it was a prank on your part."

That was exactly what he was afraid of. Roman tried to sort out his feelings. The comforting letters that had sustained him through the past few weeks showed him a completely new side of Joann. He thought he knew her. Now he realized he barely knew her at all. That would have to change, and she would have to get to know him, too.

Andrew chuckled. "I've got to get back to work. Tell me how it turns out. The old maid and you, what a hoot."

After his brother left, Roman went in his house and pulled open the drawer of his desk. He took out the letters Joann had written and began to study them. The sound of a car approaching made him look out the window. The sheriff was getting out of his SUV. Roman went to the door and stepped out on the porch to greet him. "Good day, Nick Bradley. What can we do for you?"

"I stopped by the office. Mable from next door said you had given everyone the day off. I hope everything is okay."

"Everything is fine."

"That's good to hear. I got a copy of your uncle's magazine in the mail this week. It had a license plate number stapled inside. Would you know anything about that?"

"*Ja,* I put it there for you."

"I figured it might be from you. Can you tell me if you know a woman named Jenny Morgan?"

"*Nee.* Who is she? Was she involved in that sad business?"

"I mean to find out if she was involved or not. Thanks for your time, Roman." He touched the brim of his hat, got into his vehicle and drove away.

"What are you reading?"

Joann looked up to find Roman watching her intently. How long had he been standing there?

She was getting ready to start her half day at the

bookstore, but she had come to town early so she could stop at the library first. It was such a beautiful summer day that she had decided to read for a few minutes on the bench outside.

She marked her place in the book with the ribbon and closed it. "How are you?"

"Fine. Is it a good book?"

She slipped it into her bag. "I like it."

"Would I like it?" There was something different about his voice today. It was softer, gentler and yet teasing.

Or maybe she was just imagining things. "I doubt it."

"It must be one of those romance novels."

She raised her chin. "There is nothing wrong with a story about two people falling in love."

"I didn't say there was. I believe in love. Who wrote it? Maybe I've even read it." He reached for her book bag. She grabbed the strap. After a brief tug-of-war, he wrestled it away from her.

She crossed her arms and glared at him. "Has anyone told you that you are a bully?"

"Nope." He opened the bag and pulled out her book. His eyes widened in surprise. "Successful Freshwater Bass Fishing. That has to be the most romantic title I've ever heard. Don't tell me how it ends. I have to read it now."

"Ha! Ha!" She snatched the book away from him. He let her take it.

She stuffed the book back in her bag. "Very funny."

"I try. Seriously, I didn't know you liked fishing."

"Everyone likes fishing."

He sat down beside her. "A lot of people like to go fishing, but not a lot of people like to read about it."

"Well, I like to do both." She rose and started walking.

He stood and followed her. "Where are you going?"

"To work."

"I'll walk with you."

She scowled at him. What was wrong with him today? He wore a goofy grin, but he looked nervous.

He fell into step beside her. "Tell me more about the fishing you do."

"Why?"

"You may find this hard to believe, but I enjoy fishing, too."

"What an amazing coincidence!"

"I'm serious. My grandfather used to take me when I was little. I loved sitting on the riverbank beside him and listening to his stories. I didn't even mind if we didn't catch anything."

"Really?" She looked at him in surprise.

"Okay, I enjoyed myself a lot more when the fish were biting."

"That wasn't what I meant. I was just surprised because that's how I learned to love fishing. My grandfather took me with him. He was very old then, and he walked with a cane, but he could look at a stretch of water and tell you right where the fish were. He had a gift. I was named after his wife. I think that's why he liked being with me. Those were the very best days." Joann blinked away the tears in her eyes and hoped Roman hadn't noticed.

He said, "I'm sure he liked being with you because you were a charming child."

She cocked her head to the side. "Now I know you're making fun of me."

"How can you say that?"

"I wasn't a charming child. I was plain." And all but invisible to the people she wanted most to be loved by. Her mother had been sick throughout Joann's childhood. Her father spent all his time caring for her and ignoring his lonely daughter.

"If your grandfather inspired your passion for fishing, who inspired your passion for books?"

"I'm not sure. As soon as I learned to read it was like the entire world opened up and invited me in. I could read about places that are far away, have adventures along with the people in the stories. I was hooked."

"I didn't discover books until I started working for Otis. He opened my eyes to what books can do for people."

"That's what I loved about working for him. How is he?"

"Doing well. He should be out of the hospital by the end of the week."

"That's great."

By this time they had reached the printing office. Roman held the door open for her. She said, "I'm working at the bookstore today."

"Oh, right. Say, my brother and I sometimes go fishing. Maybe you can join us one of these days."

"Sure." She smiled and turned away. He was just being polite. She knew the trip would never materialize.

"Great. I'll see you tomorrow." He went into the office and closed the door.

A second later, the door popped open again. He leaned out and said, "I mean it, teacher. We'll go fishing soon."

She giggled and nodded. "Okay, soon."

She spent the rest of the day smiling as she worked. Her heart was warmed by his thoughtfulness.

Chapter 14

On Saturday afternoon, Joann was on her hands and knees sweeping paper shreds from beneath the largest press when she heard her name called in a secretive whisper. She looked behind her to see Sally peeking under the press.

"How did it go? Your meeting with your pen pal. How did it go? Is he fat and bald?"

Joann crawled out and stood up. "I have no idea. He hasn't been back or at least he hasn't left another letter. Why are you whispering?"

Sally looked around then took a step closer. "Believe me, Joann, exchanging secret letters with a total stranger is not the kind of thing you want getting out. Do you think he's avoiding you?"

Joann shrugged. "I have no idea."

"What are you going to do?"

"Finish cleaning this press and then mop the floors."

Sally wrinkled her nose. "Don't be smart. I mean about your mystery guy."

"There isn't much I can do except wait for him to contact me."

"I'm going to go crazy if he doesn't do it soon."

Joann had trekked to the lake and back every morning for the past six days. "How do you think I feel? Maybe he's just busy."

"Maybe his wife found out. Maybe he fell in the lake and drowned. Maybe he read the note and moved to Montana."

Joann rolled her eyes. "Sally, stop it."

Her cousin pointed a finger at her. "This is all your fault."

"Go home. I've got work to do."

"You'll tell me as soon as you hear from him, right?"

"I promise."

Sally tipped her head to one side as she studied Joann. "Is that a new dress? I've never seen you in that color before. It's nice. Mauve suits you."

"Danki." Joann smoothed the front of her matching apron. Sally waved as she headed for the door. Joann waved back. When she was alone, she spun around once to make the skirt flare out. It was a pretty color. She knew it was vain, but she hoped Roman would notice and like it, too.

When Joann finished her work and left the building, she found Roman waiting outside the office in his buggy with Andrew beside him.

Roman jumped down. "Good afternoon. My brother and I are on our way to do some fishing. I thought I'd swing by and see if you wanted to join us."

"Now?"

"*Ja.* We're going to a creek not far from here."

"I know you said you would invite me soon, but I wasn't expecting this soon."

Roman smiled at her. "It was a last-minute decision on my part. I understand if you're busy and don't want to come."

Of course, I want to come. Don't read more into this than it is, Joann. He's asking me to go fishing, like I'm one of the boys. He's not asking me out on a date.

She struggled to hide her excitement. "I'd like to go, but I don't have a pole."

"That's okay. We have an extra rod. Come on, it will be fun."

She looked at his brother. "Andrew, are you sure you don't mind?"

"I'm just along for the ride. This is Roman's idea."

Roman scowled at him. "He doesn't mind a bit."

Andrew shrugged. "Okay, I don't mind."

Roman waited and watched silently as she struggled with her decision. If he pushed any harder, he knew she would refuse. Andrew wasn't helping anything. He'd have a thing or two to say to him when they got home.

Gaining Joann's trust was what Roman was after, but he had to take it one small step at a time.

She nodded and said, "*Ja,* I reckon I could go for a little while."

He could have jumped for joy, but instead he said, "Fine. Hop in."

Andrew drove as they headed east out of town. A half mile later, they pulled off to the side of the road and tethered the horse, then, the three of them left the buggy and walked across the field to a shady spot on the creek.

The bank was grassy, green and inviting beneath a grove of a maple trees. Roman saw the way Joann relaxed once she had a pole in her hand. He was happy to sit on the bank and watch her while pretending to keep an eye on his cork. Andrew moved farther downstream to try his luck there and to give them some privacy.

Roman said, "There's nothing better than a day spent fishing, if you ask me."

She was studying the rod holder strapped to his leg. "Do you mind if I ask what that is for?"

"Not at all. This is Andrew's invention. It holds my rod so I can crank with one hand."

"How interesting. I'd like to see it in action."

"You will if the fish cooperate."

Joann's cork went under. He sat up. "You've got one."

She jumped to her feet and set the hook. The tip of her rod bent nearly double. Her reel screeched as the fish took more line and ran with it.

Roman was on his feet beside her. "Andrew, bring the net!"

Joann laughed aloud. She hadn't had so much fun in ages. "He's a big one. I don't think I can hold him."

"Yes, you can. Don't let the line go slack. He'll snap it if you do. Work him toward the bank." Roman coached her along.

She managed to crank in a small amount of line. "I'm trying."

Andrew arrived with a dip net. "Wow, you've hooked a monster."

Roman took the net from him and moved to the edge of the bank. "Bring him a little closer."

Joann pulled with all her might, backing up to bring the fish within his reach. He leaned out over the water. She said, "Roman, be careful. You'll fall in."

"Don't worry about me. Land your fish."

She fought on with both men shouting encouragement. Each time she got the fish close to the bank, it darted out again into deeper water.

By this time, Andrew was behind Roman holding on to the waistband of his pants to keep his brother from tumbling headlong into the stream. The fish finally surfaced. Andrew shouted, "It's a carp."

"And a mighty big one," Roman added.

Joann's arms were getting tired. "I could've told you that. Get him in the net or he's going to get away."

The fish was running out of steam. She pulled him closer. Roman leaned out as far as he could. Suddenly, the lip of the bank gave way. Roman fell and pulled Andrew in with him.

Joann shrieked. Roman came up with a net in his hand and the fish safely in the net. His straw hat went floating downstream. Joann sat in the grass and laughed until tears ran down her face. Andrew waded after Roman's hat and pulled it out of the water. He was grinning from ear to ear.

As the two men struggled out of the creek, she pressed a hand to her mouth. "All that for a poor old carp that isn't good to eat anyway."

The men didn't seem to care. They were admiring the size of their prize. Andrew said, "I reckon he's twenty-five pounds."

"At least," Roman agreed. He smiled brightly at her.

Joann's heart took a funny leap. No one had ever smiled at her that way. She couldn't help herself. She had to glance behind her to see if he was looking at someone else. No one was there. She turned back to him. He wasn't looking through her. He was looking right at her with those shining blue eyes that put the sky to shame.

In that instant, she realized she was falling hard for Roman and she had no idea what to do about it.

She gloried in the feeling for a heartbeat and then reality reared its ugly head. She was doomed to love in vain. Someone like Roman would never fall for someone like her.

Joann's practical side quickly asserted itself. "We need to get you guys home and out of those wet things."

"Reckon you're right." Roman seemed reluctant to call a halt to the day.

"Put my poor fish back in the creek. He's gasping already."

Roman carried the carp to the water's edge. Andrew said, "I kinda hate to put him back after all the trouble we went to catch him."

She had to agree, but she would be forever grateful to the silver beauty for showing her how wonderful love could feel, if only for a little while.

When they arrived back at Hebron's farm an hour later, Roman got out and walked with her to the door.

She said, "Thanks for taking me fishing. I had a great time."

"So did I. Are you doing anything tomorrow evening?"

She gave him a puzzled look. "Nothing special, why?"

"I thought you might enjoy going on a picnic after church services. The weather is supposed to be nice."

Was he serious? "A picnic? With you?"

"Ja."

"And who else?" She could understand the invitation if it was to a party.

"No one. Just you and I."

She didn't dare hope that he returned her affections. What was he up to? "Why?"

"Joann, I enjoy your company when we aren't trading insults. What do you say?"

Was he making fun of her? He looked perfectly serious, worried even, as if he were afraid she would say no. "Did Sarah put you up to this?"

He shook his head. "No one put me up to it. If you don't want to go, just say so. I will be disappointed, but I'll live."

"You really want to take me on a picnic?" Joy began to spread through her body.

"I do."

A giddy sensation she hadn't felt since she was a teenager made her smile. "I reckon a picnic sounds like fun."

He smiled brightly. "Great. I'll pick you up at noon, if that's okay with you?"

"Noon will be fine. What shall I bring?"

"Just yourself." He stood there smiling at her, looking so handsome it made her heart ache.

She said, "You should get home. Andrew looks miserable."

"You're right. See you tomorrow." He tipped his hat, climbed into his buggy and drove away.

Joann wasn't sure if she actually touched the floor

when she went inside her brother's home. Roman Weaver had asked her to go out with him. Just him. No one else. She had a date.

She felt like singing, like spinning in circles until she fell to the floor, too dizzy to move. She was going on a picnic with Roman.

She ate her supper without tasting a thing. That night, she lay in bed unable to sleep as anticipation chased sleep away. It was a long time before she finally closed her eyes and slept.

She was awake before dawn brightened the sky. Her giddiness had vanished in the night. What was she thinking? Why had she agreed to go? She was barreling toward heartache. He couldn't possibly care for someone like her.

He must have been joking. He wouldn't come at noon. He wouldn't show up at all. She'd made a terrible mistake by agreeing to go. Right now, he and his brother were sitting somewhere laughing at her gullibility.

When twelve o'clock finally arrived, Hebron came in from finishing his chores. Joann helped her sister-in-law prepare lunch. She was setting the table when Salome burst in. "Aunt Joann, there's someone here to see you."

Joann stopped breathing. "Who is it?"

"It's Roman Weaver." Salome's eyes danced with excitement. "He's driving a courting buggy."

Hebron scowled at Joann. "Why has he come to see you?"

She smoothed the front of her apron to hide her trembling hands. "He's taking me on a picnic."

"Is he really?" Salome demanded.

"*Ja,* he really is." She looked at her sister-in-law. "I

don't expect to be back until late, so don't wait supper on me."

Everyone was staring at her with their mouths open. Joann pulled her book bag off the hook by the door and rushed outside before her courage failed.

Roman slipped a finger under the collar of his shirt to loosen it. He hadn't been this nervous since…ever. It occurred to him that he was rushing things, but he didn't want to keep the truth from Joann a moment longer. He had come to care deeply for her. He wanted their relationship to be based on trust and understanding. He wanted to be more than her friend. Much more.

As she came out the door, she gave him a beautiful smile. His heart flipped over in his chest and started beating like mad. She took his breath away.

She slid in beside him in the buggy. "What a glorious day."

"It sure is." It wasn't the weather that filled him with happiness. It was having her beside him.

"Any ill effects?" Her voice sounded breathy and nervous. Her cheeks were pink and her eyes sparkled. He sure hoped he was the reason.

"From what?"

She giggled. "Your swim with the fishes."

"*Nee,* I'm fine and so is Andrew. We'll have to do that again."

She looked down at her hands. "I'd like that. Where are we going?"

"I thought we might go out to the lake."

Her head snapped up. She stared at him with wide eyes. "The lake?"

Suddenly, it didn't seem like such a great plan. "If that's okay with you?"

"It's okay. *Ja,* it's fine. I like going to the lake."

"So do I. It's peaceful there."

She fell silent, and he drove the rest of the way with growing misgivings.

When they reached the south shore, he parked in the shade of an oak tree. She said, "This is a good spot. Shall I put the blanket out here?"

"No, it's prettier on the east side of the lake. Let's take our stuff over there."

Some of the joy left her eyes. "Okay."

He hated that he was tricking her, but he had arranged for the Friendly Fisherman to introduce himself. It had seemed so clever when he thought of it. He prayed he was doing the right thing. He took the picnic basket from the back of the buggy and started following the path around the lake. When they reached the clearing with the fallen tree, he looked down at her. "I like this spot, don't you?"

She relaxed a little. "It's fine."

He said, "You put out our things. I left the lemonade in the buggy. I'll be right back."

Joann couldn't believe Roman had brought her to the same spot where she exchanged letters with her secret friend. Once he was out of sight, she laid open the blanket and went to the log. Reaching into the knothole, she brought out her mail jar. There was a new note inside. She opened the lid and took it out.

My dear friend,
I would be delighted to meet you face to face. We
do have a lot to talk about. So turn around.
F.F.

Turn around. Her heart skipped a beat and stumbled
onward. Slowly, she looked up. Roman was standing
at the edge of the trees. He lifted his hand in a brief
wave. "Hi."

A terrible buzzing filled her ears. This couldn't be
happening. He hadn't brought her here for a picnic.
He'd brought her here to humiliate her. She should have
known better. What a fool she was.

She pressed a hand to her forehead. "It was you! All
this time I thought I was reading heartfelt letters from
some stranger. Only I wasn't. I was the victim of your
sick joke."

He took a step toward her. "No, Joann, it wasn't
like that."

She was so embarrassed she thought she might die
from shame. When she thought of the things she had
confided to him it made her ill. "Did you know it was
me all along?"

"Of course not."

"You knew before today, didn't you?"

"I couldn't tell you. I wasn't sure you even liked me."

He knew and he'd said nothing. How humiliating. "I
have a newsflash for you, Roman Weaver. I still don't
like you. You are mean and underhanded and dishon-
est. I can't believe I ever thought I did like you. Never
speak to me again."

Joann dashed past him and began running through
the trees. She heard him calling, but she didn't slow

down. She ran past his buggy and across the pasture until she was so out of breath that she had to stop and lean against the gate.

What an idiot she was. He must be laughing his head off. Tears blinded her. She wiped them away. "I don't cry. I never cry."

Only today, she did.

Roman couldn't believe how things had gone from so good to so bad in a heartbeat. He gathered up the remains of their picnic and followed Joann. She had to listen to him. He had to make her understand that he had been afraid of losing her friendship. Only now, it seemed that he'd lost so much more.

She wasn't waiting at the buggy. He repeatedly called her name, but she didn't answer

So much for his bright idea. He left the lake and drove to her brother's house. She wasn't there. She hadn't come back and they didn't know where she might be.

Defeated, Roman went home. Perhaps if he gave her enough time, she would cool off and be able to see that he did care for her.

The next day, he waited impatiently for her to come to work. She didn't show up. He started to worry. He left work early and went back to her brother's house only to be told she still hadn't come home. No one in the family had seen her.

Where could she be? Who would she seek out? Sally perhaps?

He set his tired horse in motion once more and drove out to Sally's home.

Sally was hanging clothes on the line when he drove

in the yard. He left the buggy and crossed the lawn with long strides. "Is she here?"

Sally looked at him as if he were crazy. "Is who here?"

"I don't want to play games. Is Joann here?

"She is not. What's going on?"

"I need to speak to her. I need to make her understand that I care about her. I hurt her without meaning to."

"How?"

Roman hesitated but finally explained what had been going on. Sally was every bit as upset as Joann had been. "You weasel. First, you take her job, she loses the home she's always wanted and then you toy with her affections. I wouldn't want to see you again either."

"Wait a minute. What do you mean I took her job?"

"Her job at the newspaper. She was fired so you could have it. Did you really think she only wanted to clean up after you?"

"I thought it was odd, but she said it was what she wanted."

"No, the job you could care less about is the job she wanted. The job she needed."

"So she could buy a house of her own," he said softly, remembering her letter.

Sally's attitude softened. "You really didn't know?"

"That my uncle put her on the cleaning staff so that I could have her job? No. It never crossed my mind."

"Not only did you get her job, she had to teach you how do it. It wasn't fair of Otis Miller to do that."

"No wonder she seemed to resent me. How can I make this right? I do care about her. You must believe me."

"To start with, you're gonna have to eat a lot of crow."

"I can't tell her how sorry I am if I can't find her. Do you know where she is?"

"Maybe I do, and maybe I don't. If you are sincere about patching things up with her, I'll see what I can do to help."

The truth dawned on him in a blinding flash. "Sally, not only am I sincere about patching things up with her, I want her to be my wife. And I don't care who knows it."

"Well, that puts a slightly different slant on things. Okay, I'll help, but you have to go home now."

"Go home? I can't. Not until I've talked to her."

"Men are so clueless sometimes. You have to give her a little cooling-off time. Joann is a smart woman, but she doesn't have a lot of confidence. She's felt unwanted most of her life. Thinking that someone loves her for herself is not something that she's used to doing. Give her some time to let the idea sink in. If she still isn't willing to talk to you in a few days' time, then drastic measures will be needed."

He didn't like the sound of that. "What kind of drastic measures?"

"Nothing for you to worry about. Go home and wait until I contact you. Trust me."

He didn't want to go home. He wanted to find Joann and make her understand how much he loved her, but it didn't look like that would happen tonight. It was with a heavy heart that he left and drove away.

When he arrived at the sawmill, he saw the sheriff talking to his father. Andrew came and took the horse from Roman. "The sheriff wants to talk to you."

"All right."

Roman walked toward the sheriff and his father. "How can I help you, Nick Bradley?"

"I came to let you know we arrested someone for the arson at the school and for the vandalism at your uncle's business."

"Who?"

"Robert Smith, Brendan's younger brother. The woman who came by the printing office after the attack is his girlfriend. The farmer out on Bent Tree Road was able to give me a description of the car they saw speeding away. When I ran the license plate number I received in the mail, her name came up. Her car matched the description of the one at the haystack fire. When I confronted her, she told me everything."

Roman shoved his hands in his pockets. "Did she say why?"

"She thought they were having some harmless fun. They were getting their kicks out of torching a few haystacks. It wasn't until Robert wanted to burn down the school that she started getting worried. She was the one who called in the tip to us that day. After Otis was hurt, she got scared and broke it off with Robert."

"Why does he hate us so?" Menlo asked.

"She said he hates the Amish because they won't fight for their country. He tried to join the Army, but he was rejected. He thinks the Amish are a bunch of hypocrites."

Shame filled Roman. "If I had asked for leniency for his brother, maybe none of this would've happened."

"In my book, Brendan got what he deserved. He didn't know and he didn't care that you were standing at the side of the road when he sideswiped you. He thought it would be funny to knock the door off your buggy because the Amish don't report crimes to the law. Usually. This time you stopped a crime, Roman. According to Jenny, Robert was planning to torch this place next."

Menlo laid a hand on Roman's shoulder. "God was merciful to us."

The sheriff nodded. "I just wanted you to know that the people around here are safer thanks to you."

As Sheriff Bradley walked away, Roman called after him, "Sheriff, will you do me a favor?"

"If I can. What is it?"

"Will you tell the attorney for Brendan and his brother that I will be pleased to come speak on their behalves? Forgiveness is about more than words. It has taken me a while to understand that."

The sheriff nodded and smiled. "I'll be happy to pass on the message."

Chapter 15

Joann sat on the window seat of Sarah's old house and watched the activity on the street below. She was grateful that Sarah and Levi had allowed her to stay in the empty house. Levi had brought over a cot for her to sleep on. It was all she needed at the moment. A place to hide until her heartache healed.

A buggy pulled up in front of Levi's shop and her cousin Sally stepped out. Tears pricked Joann's eyes. She didn't want to see anybody. She hoped that Sarah wouldn't reveal where she was.

Her hope was in vain. Only a few minutes after entering Levi's shop, Sally emerged with Sarah and they both crossed the street toward her.

She heard the front door open downstairs. Sally's voice called out, "Joann, are you here?"

Maybe if she stayed silent, they would go away. She

should've known better. Sally came tromping up the stairs. "I know you're up here, Joann. Answer me."

"Joann doesn't live here anymore. She ran away and joined the circus."

The bedroom door flew open and Sally breezed in. "I've often thought that being an Amish circus performer would be a truly difficult way to live. But if that's what you want, I'll support you."

Joann sighed. "Go away, Sally. I don't want to talk to anyone."

Sally sat beside her on the window bench. "So don't talk, just listen."

Sarah came into the bedroom and stood with her arms folded. "Don't bully her, Sally."

Sally sat back. "You're right. I am trying to bully her into believing that she is a terrific person and that any man would be blessed to have her be part of his life. Even Roman Weaver."

Joann said, "I appreciate the sentiment, but that is hardly the case. I'm a sad, pathetic excuse of a woman who fell in love with an idea, not with a real man."

Sally said, "I have to admit that he's not much of a catch. Who would want a man who can't hold you in his arms?"

Joann glared at Sally. "He only needs one good arm to put around me. If he lost both arms he would still be smarter and more determined than any man I know."

Sally smiled. "That's a pretty strong defense of someone you don't see as a real man."

"You know what I mean."

Sarah came and sat down on the other side of Joann. "I only have one question for you. Do you love him?"

"How can I love someone who lies to me, who tricks me into thinking that he is something he's not?"

Sarah took Joann's hands in her own. "That wasn't exactly a no."

"Okay, I love him, but that doesn't change anything."

"She's right," Sally said. "We just have to figure out what to do now."

Joann stood and crossed the room before turning to face them. "I've come to a decision."

"Not the circus," Sally said dryly.

"No, not the circus. I have an aunt who lives near Bird-in-Hand, Pennsylvania. She left the Amish years ago. My brothers have forbidden anyone to speak about her, but I believe she'll take me in. I'm family, after all."

Sally slapped her hands on her knees. "Wonderful. Now that that's taken care of, all you have to do is write her and wait for an answer."

Joann frowned at her. "Are you that eager to be rid of me?"

"Of course not," Sarah said. "We just want what is best for you."

Sally stood. "In the meantime, we need to get you a pair of new dresses. You can't go to her looking like a pauper. I'll bring some material over tomorrow and we can get you ready to start a new and different life. Wow, I envy you that."

Sally's eyes grew sad. Before Joann could ask her what was wrong, she perked up and said, "I'll be back first thing tomorrow morning."

She charged out of the room, but Sarah remained. "Joann, you are welcome to stay with Levi and me for as long as you like. I hope you know that."

"I appreciate that, Sarah, but I need to move on with my life. There isn't anything for me here."

"I think you're wrong about that, but I'll accept whatever decision you make."

Sarah left and Joann was alone again.

Roman was almost out of patience.

Sally had told him to have faith and wait until she contacted him, but it had been a week and there was still no sign of Joann. Each day he grew more afraid that he had lost her forever. He was proofreading an article for the magazine when the front door of the shop opened. He looked up hoping it was Joann, but it was finally Sally.

"It's about time. Where is she?" he demanded.

Sally gave him a look of disgust. "I have no idea what she sees in you."

"I'm sorry. Hello, Sally, how may I help you?" He forced a smile to his stiff lips.

"You need to go fishing right now."

"Is this some kind of joke, because if it is…" His voice trailed off. He was in no position to issue an ultimatum and she knew it.

"Joann is packed and ready to go to her aunt's home in Pennsylvania. Her aunt's letter arrived today. She wants to leave on this evening's bus. All that she's lacking is her fishing pole. She went to collect."

"To her brother, Hebron's place?"

Sally shook her head. "He's the one who threw it in the lake. Long story. She said she kept it in a hollow log at the lake. Since that was where you exchanged letters, I assume you know where she is going."

He got up from his desk and grabbed his hat. "I could kiss you, Sally."

"Yuck. Not interested. You should hurry. She left Sarah's home thirty minutes ago."

When Roman reached the lake he prayed he wasn't too late. He rounded the last bend in the path and held his breath.

She was sitting on the fallen log by the edge of the water. For a moment, he was too scared to speak. What if he couldn't make her understand? What if he had to spend the rest of his life without her?

Unless he could convince her of his love, that was exactly what would happen.

He prayed for the strength and wisdom to say what she needed to hear. Suddenly, a deep calm came over him. He knew in his heart that she was the woman God had chosen for him. He took a deep breath and walked into the clearing. "Are they biting today?"

She tensed but didn't look at him. "I don't know."

At least she wasn't running away. He took a seat a few feet away from her on a log.

"What do you want, Roman?" There was so much pain in her voice that he wanted to wrap his arm around her and hold her close, but he knew that would be a mistake.

"I want you to be happy, Joann. I know you don't believe that, but it's the truth."

"You hurt me." Her voice quivered.

"I know, and I am so sorry."

She crossed her arms and raised her chin. "If you have come seeking my forgiveness, I give it freely."

He chose his words carefully. "I didn't come seeking forgiveness."

For the first time she looked at him. "Then why are you here?"

"Because you are here. No matter where I go, I'm lonely if I'm not with you."

She bowed her head. Her voice was barely more than a whisper. "Stop pretending. I'm not the kind of woman a man like you falls for."

How could he make her understand? He moved to stand in front of her and then dropped to his knees. "Oh, sweet Joann, you are exactly the kind of woman I have fallen for. I need you."

"Don't," she whispered, turning her face away.

"I have to say this and you have to hear it. I need someone smart and steadfast who will overlook my mistakes. I need someone kind and patient, someone who can teach me to be a better man. I need you, my darling teacher."

She looked down at her clenched hands. "You could have your pick of the pretty girls for miles around. You don't have to settle for someone like me."

"Why would I want a pretty girl when I have a beautiful woman right in front of me?"

"I may be a lot of things, but I'm not beautiful."

"I know you don't think you are, but my eyes see the face of an angel when I look at you. If you would but smile at me, my heart would be made whole again."

"I don't believe you." She started to rise, but he grabbed her hand.

"What can I say that will make you believe me?"

"Nothing."

He let go and sank back on his heels. "Is it because I'm crippled?"

"Don't be ridiculous, Roman."

"How is it ridiculous to lay open my heart and then have you trod on it?"

He rose to his feet and walked to the edge of the water. With his head bowed, he said, "If my disability repels you, I can accept that."

He felt the touch of her hand on his back. He turned to face her.

Joann had never been more confused and more frightened in her life. Here was everything she wanted and everything she knew she could never have. "I don't find you repulsive. No woman could."

"Then why won't you marry me?"

She bit her lip and looked down. "I'm not the marrying kind. I was born to be an old maid."

He put his finger under her chin and forced her to look at him. "For such an intelligent woman, that is the stupidest thing I've ever heard you say."

There were tears in his eyes. It broke her heart to see him in pain. "It's true."

"No, the truth is that I love you and you love me. You're just afraid to say it."

He was right. She was terrified. What if he changed his mind? What if he realized what a poor bargain she really was? How could she face loving him and losing him?

He kissed her cheek. "Be brave, my darling, Joann. You were chosen by God to be my mate. Have faith in God's mercy. Believe that I love you, that I vow before God to love, honor, and cherish you my entire life. Please, I beg you, say that you love me, too."

How could she refuse him anything? She searched her soul and found the faith and courage she needed.

She closed her eyes and took a plunge into the unknown. "All right. I love you, Roman Weaver."

He cupped her cheek with his hand and kissed her gently. He drew back and gazed into her eyes. "You have made me the happiest man in the world."

She smiled as he pulled her close and wrapped his arm around her. Her arms moved up to circle his neck. It felt so right and so wonderful to hold him. It was like a marvelous dream and she was very much afraid she would wake up to find it wasn't true.

"Tell me the truth, Joann. Does it bother you that I only have one arm to hold you with?"

She pulled back a little so that she could see his face. "*Nee,* it does not bother me. What bothers me is that someday you may not wish to hold me."

"That day will never come."

"How can you be so sure?"

"How can you be sure the sun will rise tomorrow?"

"I guess I can't be. I just have faith that it will."

"Then I ask that you have faith in me, too, for I will love you until the day I die."

"Oh, Roman, what have I done to deserve such joy?"

"I don't know, but I am ever thankful that God has smiled upon us."

She looked out over the waters of the lake. "I'm going to miss coming here to read your letters."

"I don't see why we have to stop writing each other. Our wedding won't be until late November."

"Our wedding. That has a wonderful sound to it."

"It does, doesn't it? Mrs. Roman Weaver. I like the sound of that, too."

She laid her head against his chest. "Mrs. Roman Weaver. I *love* the sound that. You know what's funny?"

"What?"

"Sarah told me that we would be a good match." She looked up at him and smiled.

He kissed the tip of her nose. "Remind me to thank her."

"What is your favorite kind of pie?"

"I like them all, but I guess I would have to say my favorite is pumpkin."

"Pumpkin. I like pumpkin pie. That will be easy enough."

"Do I want to know why you're asking that question?"

"Levi said the way to a man's heart is through his stomach. That looks fade but good cooking never does."

"Obviously, he doesn't know what he's talking about. I've never tasted your cooking. You found the way to my heart with pen and ink and a fishing rod."

She chuckled. "I thought the Friendly Fisherman was an ancient Amish grandfather who shared his wisdom with me. What did you think the Happy Angler was like?"

Suddenly she stepped away from him and fisted her hand on her hips. "You said I was someone who would benefit from a dunking in the lake. That I was stubborn, willful, hard to please, and quick to call attention to your failings."

He reached out and pulled her back against him. "And what part of that isn't true? Be honest, soon-to-be Mrs. Roman Weaver."

"I'm not stubborn."

"Yes, you are, and I love that about you."

"I'm not hard to please."

"Have you ever considered marrying anyone else in Hope Springs?"

"No."

"There are a lot of nice fellows hereabouts. Do you agree?"

She nodded. "There are some nice boys around here."

"And yet you have only agreed to marry me. Therefore, you are hard to please, but you knew that and waiting for the right man to come along was worth the wait."

"You have yet to prove that you are worth the wait."

He cupped the back of her head and leaned down until his forehead rested against hers. "Then I had best get started, hadn't I?"

"*Ja,* you should," she answered and gladly raised her face for his kiss.

A long time later, Roman pulled his horse to a stop in front of Sarah and Levi's home. Joanne hated to see the day end, but she knew it had to.

"I'm glad I had the chance to live in Sarah's house before it was sold."

Roman studied her for a moment. "Is this the house you wanted to buy?"

"This is the one." She smiled at him. "But I will enjoy living anywhere you are."

"I've been thinking about that. My arm may not ever be better than it is now. My younger brother can handle the sawmill with my dad. Otis would like me to take over his business when the time comes."

"You do a wonderful job there."

He leaned close and kissed her nose. "I had a good teacher."

She blushed and laid her head on his shoulder. "There

are many things that we will learn together. How to raise children, how to bring them up to value our way of life, how to grow old together."

"As long as I learn those lessons with you by my side, I will be a content man. Will you work with me at the printing office until our children arrive?"

"Gladly." Her heart turned over with happiness at his request. What could be better than working at his side?

"*Goot,* for I need my teacher and my friend beside me."

"I will always be there for you, my love."

"If I'm going to be working in town for the rest of my life, I'm thinking I may need to buy a house that's closer to where I work. Any suggestions?"

Joann wrapped her arms around his and squeezed. "I know the perfect house, and it's for sale."

"Only God is perfect, my love."

She looked up into the eyes of the most wonderful man she would ever meet. The man God had chosen for her. "It may not be perfect, but with you there, the fence painted white, pansies along the walk, our children playing there and a birdhouse in the corner of the yard, it will be very, very close."

* * * * *

SECOND CHANCE PROPOSAL

Anna Schmidt

To all who have believed in the power of love.

Show me thy ways, O Lord; teach me thy paths.
—*Psalms* 25:4

Chapter 1

Lydia Goodloe. Was he seeing things?
Sweet Liddy.

John Amman closed his eyes, which were crusty with lack of sleep and the dust of days he'd spent making his way west across Florida from one coast to the other. Surely this was nothing more than a mirage born of exhaustion and the need for a solid meal.

But no, there could be no doubt. There she was walking across a fallow field from her father's house to the school. He watched as she entered the school and then a minute later came outside again. She pulled her shawl tighter around her shoulders and began stacking firewood in her arms. They might be in Florida, but it was

January and an unseasonably cold one at that. John pulled up the collar of his canvas jacket to block the wind that swept across the open fields.

Lydia went back inside the school and shut the door, and after a few minutes John saw a stream of smoke rising from the chimney. He closed his eyes, savoring the memory of that warm classroom anchored by a pot-bellied stove in one corner and the teacher's desk in the other. He tried to picture Lydia at that desk, but he could only see her as the girl he'd known—the laughing child with the curly dark hair that flew out behind her as she gathered the skirt of her dark cotton dress and raced with him along the path. The teenager—a quiet beauty, the luxurious hair tamed into braided submission under her bonnet and the black prayer covering girls her age wore after joining the church, as he and Liddy had done when they were both sixteen.

He started running across the field, his heart pounding in anticipation of the reunion with this woman he had loved his whole life. This woman he had come back to find after eight long years—to ask why she had not answered his letters, why she had not believed him when he told her that it had all been for her. He had risked everything even to the point of becoming an outcast from their Amish community and indeed his own family so they could have the life they had planned.

But abruptly he stopped. What was he thinking? That he would go to her and she would explain everything and they would be happy again? How could he face her after all this time and admit that he'd failed? Even if she did open her heart to him, what did he have left to offer her? No job. No money. The disdain of his own family…of the entire community unless he agreed to publicly admit his wrongdoing and seek their forgiveness.

He crouched down—half from the need to catch his breath and half because the wind was so sharp. The door to the school opened again and, this time when she emerged, Liddy was not wearing her bonnet. She hurried back to the woodpile and took two more logs—one in each hand. But it was not the logs that John noticed. It was what she was wearing on her head in place of the bonnet.

When she had entered the school that first time, her head and much of her face had been covered by the familiar black bonnet that Amish girls and women wore when outside. John had assumed that beneath that bonnet she still wore the black prayer *kapp* of a single woman. But the *kapp* he saw now was not black but white—the mark of a married woman, someone else's wife. The loose ties whipped playfully around her cheeks as she gathered a second load of wood.

His heart sank.

"Fool," he muttered. "Did you really think you would come back here after all this time and find her waiting?"

His stomach growled as he caught the scent of bacon frying, and he glanced toward the house where his family had once lived. After he'd left—and been placed under the *bann* for doing so—his mother had gotten word to him when the farm was sold. She'd written that she and his father and the rest of his siblings were moving back to Pennsylvania. After that he had not heard from his family again, and now someone else owned the small produce farm that would have been his.

John scuffed at the sand with the toe of his work boot—the sole was worn through and the inside was lined with old newspaper. He hefted the satchel that held what remained of his worldly goods to one shoulder and pulled his faded red cap low over his eyes. He no longer dressed "plain" as he had when he and Lydia had been sweethearts. He doubted that she would even recognize him were he to approach her. He had changed that much, at least outwardly. His gaze swept over the rest of the small town past the hardware store, the livery turned machine shop, Yoder's Dry Goods Emporium, the bakery Liddy's family had owned and back to the schoolhouse and that thin trail of smoke that curled across the cloudless sky.

Home.

"Not anymore," John whispered as he turned his back on the town for the second time. There was nothing for him here. He'd been following yet another foolish dream in coming back. Behind him he heard the shouts and laughter of the arriving schoolchildren across the frost-covered field. Then he hitched his satchel over his shoulder and headed east, the way he'd come.

Lydia had a warm fire burning by the time she heard the children gathering in the yard. They were playing tag or hide-and-seek and squealing with delight as someone made it to home base without being caught. She flipped down the seats of the desks and stood for a moment as she did every morning, asking God's guidance for the day. Then she pulled hard on the bell cord, taking pleasure in the familiar sound in the cold air calling the children inside.

As the children scurried into the school, pausing only to hang their coats and hats or bonnets on the pegs, Lydia turned to close the door. Then she saw a

man walking across an abandoned produce field that
marked the border between the town and the outlying
farms. He was wearing a light canvas jacket and a red
cap. Her heart went out to him when she realized that
he was not dressed warmly enough for the weather. No
doubt he was another of those men who wandered into
town now and again in search of work or a handout.

She continued to watch the man as the last of her
students—a large lumbering boy who would gladly be
anywhere but inside this classroom—passed by her.
There was something about the way the stranger in the
field moved that was unlike the movements of other vagrants she had observed. Most of those men appeared
worn down by their troubles and the harsh realities of
their circumstances. This man walked with purpose
and a rhythm that fairly shouted defiance and determination. Something about his posture stirred a memory
that she could not quite grasp.

"Teacher?"

Lydia looked up to find her half sister's daughter,
Bettina, standing at the lectern ready to lead the devotions with which they began every day. Bettina had
passed the age when most girls attended school, but she
loved being there so much that Lydia had persuaded
Pleasant and her husband, Jeremiah, to allow the girl
to continue helping her.

She nodded and Bettina opened the Bible, carefully
laying aside the purple satin ribbon that had served as
a bookmark for as long as Lydia could recall, even back
to the days when she and Greta had been students at
the school. The days when they had each taken a turn
reading the morning devotions. She permitted herself
a small smile as she recalled how the girls had eagerly

awaited their turn at reading, but not the boys. And especially not John Amman.

John.

Her eyes, which were normally lowered in reverence for the reading, flew open and focused on the closed door at the back of the room. Something about the man she had seen walking across the fields reminded her of John. The broad shoulders unbowed against the wind. The long, determined stride. Suddenly her heart was racing and she felt quite light-headed, to the point that she pressed herself firmly into the safety of the straight-backed chair.

Was it possible that, after all this time, he had come home? But why now? And why had there been no word from him—to anyone—in all this time? Not a single word.

She closed her eyes as a wave of grief and disappointment swept through her. Even after eight long years the sting of John's leaving was as painful as it had ever been. Bettina continued to read the morning's Scripture. The lesson for the day was the story of the prodigal son and the irony of that reading combined with her memories of John Amman made Lydia wince.

John had walked a good six or seven miles away from Celery Fields before he once again changed his mind. How could Lydia have married another man? But then, how could she not when he had given up writing after a year passed with not one of his letters answered? Still, he had to know who that man was. He had to at least be sure that she had married someone worthy of her.

And if she hadn't? What if he learned that she was

miserable? Exactly what did he think he could do about that?

John might have lost most of his worldly goods, but the one thing he had not lost was his faith in God. And he had no doubt that God was guiding his steps as he made his way back the way he'd come. There was some plan at work here, a plan that was driving him home to Celery Fields. Home to Liddy. He just had to figure out what it was. He closed his eyes and prayed for guidance. When he opened them he saw Lydia and her students come out into the schoolyard, where they formed a circle and played a round of dodgeball. John smiled. Lydia had always been very good at the game, but he had been better.

It occurred to him that the best way to learn what he needed to know was to go directly to her. Oh, not to her house. He did not want to embarrass or confront either her or her husband. No, he would bide his time and choose the right moment, the perfect place. And after so many years of silence from her he would finally have some answers.

The unusually cold weather continued as Tuesday dawned with a cutting wind from the north and a slanting rain that came very close to being sleet. An umbrella was useless in such a wind so Lydia covered her bonnet and face with her shawl as she picked her way across the rutted path that ran from her house to the schoolhouse. She would need to get the fire going quickly, for the weather was too foul for the children to gather in the schoolyard waiting for the bell to ring.

Then as she neared the school, she caught a whiff of smoke and lifted the edge of her shawl so she could see more clearly. Rising from the chimney was a trail of gray smoke. Lydia smiled as she hurried to the school. Her brother-in-law Luke must have started the fire for her. He was a kind man, the perfect match for Greta, her lively and sometimes capricious younger sister.

"Luke?" she called as she entered the school and the door banged shut behind her. She hung her shawl and bonnet on the first of a double row of wooden pegs by the door. "I came early to light the fire, but I see that you…" She froze as she realized that the man kneeling by the door of the woodstove was not her brother-in-law.

She recognized the red cap and light canvas jacket of the man she'd seen crossing the field a day earlier and felt a twinge of alarm. He must have stayed the night in the school. Homes and other buildings in Celery Fields were rarely locked unless they were businesses with wares that had proved worth stealing. Slowly the man turned and pinned her with his gaze as he removed his cap and stood up. He had several days' growth of a beard and his hair curled over his ears. But only one man she'd ever met had those deep-set green eyes.

"Hello, Liddy."

She gasped. "You," she whispered, suddenly unable to find her full voice and at the same time realizing that she should not be speaking to him at all.

John Amman was under the *bann* and as such was to be shunned by all members of the church.

"It's been a long time," he added, his voice hoarse and raspy, and he took a step toward her.

Flustered by the sheer presence of him—taller and broader than she remembered and, in spite of the weariness that lined his face, far more handsome—Lydia resorted to her habit of placing distance between herself and something she could not yet understand. She walked straight past him to the board and began writing the day's assignments on it, her back to him.

"Aren't you going to say anything, Liddy?"

Her fingers tightened on the chalk, snapping it in two. A thousand questions raced through her mind.

Where have you been?

Why didn't you write?

What are you doing here, now?

Do you have a wife? Children?

Are you here to stay?

Do you know that your family moved back north?

What happened to all your plans?

When's the last time you had a decent meal?

And on and on.

She finished writing on the board, laid the chalk precisely in the tray and dusted her hands off by rubbing them together. She kept her back to him, felt the tenseness in her shoulders and listened for his step, praying that he would give up and leave.

But she knew better. John Amman had always been determined to get what he wanted once he set his mind to something. Slowly she turned around. He had not moved from his place next to the stove.

"You're the teacher now," he said with a gesture toward the room filled with desks and the other trappings of the school they had both once attended. "Liddy?" He took another step toward her but stopped when she moved away from him.

"You look terrible," she replied in the voice she used to reprimand a truant student, then she clamped her lips shut. To her surprise he laughed, and the sound of it was a song she had heard again and again over the years whenever she lay awake remembering John Amman.

"I guess I do at that," he said, looking down at his patched and ill-fitted clothing as he ran a hand over his unshaved face.

She placed books on desks, her back to him.

"Are you not glad to see me?"

The question infuriated her because the answer that sprang instantly from deep within her was, *Yes. Oh, yes. How I have worried about you, thought of you, longed to know if you were well. And, most of all, wondered if you ever thought of me.*

"I am pleased to see that you are alive," she replied, unable to prevent the words or stem the tide of years of bitterness in her voice. "As I would be to see any prodigal return," she added, raising her eyes defiantly to his. "And now please go. The children will be here any minute and I…"

"…don't wish to have to explain about me?" He stepped closer and fingered the loose tie of her prayer covering. "When did you marry, Liddy?"

She jerked the tie free and at the same time heard the school door open and shut. She turned to find Bettina standing uncertainly inside the doorway.

"Teacher?"

"Guten morgen," John said, crossing the room to where Bettina waited. "I am John Amman. I expect you know my uncle and aunt, the Hadwells?"

Bettina nodded and looked at Lydia. Lydia considered the best way to get John out of the classroom without raising further questions.

"I am Teacher's niece, Bettina."

"You are Pleasant's daughter?"

Lydia saw Bettina take in John's rumpled clothing, his mud-caked shoes. Her niece was a bright girl, and Lydia knew she was trying to decide if this man was who he said he was or another tramp passing through, trying anything he thought might work to get a hand-out or a meal. Her eyes darted from Lydia to John and back again as she nodded politely. But at the same time she edged closer to the bell rope, ready to pull it if she deemed them to be in any danger.

"John Amman was kind enough to light the fire, Bettina. Now he will be on his way." Lydia was satisfied that in directing her comment to the girl she had not further violated her responsibility to shun him. She moved to the door and opened it, waiting for John to leave.

He paused for just an instant as he passed her, his incredible eyes, the green of a lush tropical jungle, locking on hers.

"You may as well know this now, Lydia Goodloe. I've come home to stay."

As Lydia closed the door firmly behind him she noticed that her hand was shaking and her heart was racing and all of a sudden the room seemed far too warm.

John had not meant to say anything about his plans. He didn't know what his future might hold. There were too many unknowns. How would his aunt and uncle, the only family left here, respond to his return? The night before he'd watched them close up shop and head home together and been glad to know they were still there. But could he seek and be granted their forgiveness? Could he find work and a place to live? And most of all, what kind of fool deliberately tormented himself by living in the same small town where the love of his life had settled into a marriage of her own? Still, as he walked the rest of the way into town, oblivious to the rain and wind, he knew that he had spoken the truth. He had come back to stay, for in reality he had nowhere else to go.

When he entered the hardware store it was as if he had stepped back in time. The same bell jangled over the door as he closed it. Instantly he was certain that he could easily fill any order a customer might have because everything was in the same place it had always been. Including his aunt.

He smiled as he watched Gertrude Hadwell chew the stub of the pencil she used to figure the month's finances. She was behind the counter, the ledger open before her, her elbows resting on either side of it as she hummed softly and entered figures into the narrow columns. She looked as if she hadn't aged a day, adding to his sense that nothing had changed.

"Be right there," she called without glancing up. "Roger Hadwell," she shouted, turning her face toward the back of the store as she closed the ledger and walked toward the storeroom. "Customer."

John understood that she was not being rude. His aunt had always felt that their mostly male customers would far rather deal with her husband than with a woman. He removed his hat and smoothed his wet hair as he moved down the narrow aisle past the barrels of screws and nails until he reached the counter.

"*Guten morgen, Tante* Gert," he said softly, not wanting to startle her more than necessary.

She whipped around to face him and immediately her eyes filled with tears. "Johnny," she whispered. Then she hurried around the counter until they were face-to-face and she grabbed his shoulders, squeezing them hard. "Johnny," she repeated.

Behind her John saw his uncle come from the store-room wiping his hands on a rag as he looked up to welcome his customer. He hesitated when he saw his wife touching a strange man, then rushed forward. "See here, young man," he began, and then his eyes widened. "Gertrude, no," he said firmly, and turned her away from John. "Go in back until he leaves."

John's knees went weak with the realization that his uncle was shunning him. If that were true of these two people whom he had felt closest to all his life then he knew everyone in town would follow their lead. Well, what had he expected? That the entire town would set aside centuries of tradition for him? He sent up a silent prayer begging forgiveness for his prideful ways.

His aunt hesitated, gazing at him as her husband folded his arms across his broad chest and waited for her to follow his instructions.

"Go, Gert," Roger repeated.

"I will not," she replied. "This man needs our help and I would help him the same as we would any stranger." She brushed by her husband and pulled out a chair. "Come sit by the fire. Why, you're soaked." She pulled a horse blanket from a shelf and handed it to him.

Behind her his uncle took one last look at his wife and then left the room.

"It's good to see you, Gert," John said as he savored her motherly nurturing.

"Where have you been?" she fumed, then quickly added, "No, I do not wish to know the details of your foolishness. It is enough that God has brought you back to us in one piece." She studied him critically. "You're too thin, John Amman. When did you last have a decent meal?"

John shrugged as she tucked the blanket around his shoulders then handed him a bakery box that had been sitting on the counter. It was filled with large glazed doughnuts. He bit into one and licked his lips. "I see Pleasant Obermeier still makes the best doughnut anywhere," he said as he devoured the rest of the pastry and licked the sticky sugar coating from his fingers.

"She's Pleasant Troyer now," his aunt informed him as she busied herself setting a teakettle on the wood-burning stove. "Obermeier died a few years back and shortly after that Bishop Troyer's nephew, Jeremiah, came to town. He opened up that ice-cream shop next to the bakery and it wasn't long before Pleasant and him married and adopted all four of Obermeier's children. Now they have a couple of their own."

"But she still has the bakery?"

"She does. After her *dat* died she managed on her own for a while and then once she married Jeremiah…"

Pleasant was not the Goodloe sister John wanted to know about, but he thought it best to hide his curiosity about Lydia until he knew just how much things had changed in Celery Fields. "They live up there in the old Obermeier house at the end of Main Street then?"

Gert perched on the edge of a chair across from him to watch him eat. "No, Jeremiah bought a small farm just outside of town for them. Greta Goodloe married the blacksmith a year after Pleasant married. It was her husband, Luke Starns, who bought the Obermeier place." She poured him a mug of strong black tea. "Drink this. You're shivering."

"And Liddy?" he asked as the hot liquid warmed his insides.

"Still teaching," Gert replied. "Pleasant's oldest girl, Bettina, helps her out, not that there's any need. So few children these days. Lots of folks have moved away and until Greta's brood and a few other little ones reach school age, well, it's getting harder to justify keeping that schoolhouse open."

"She ever marry?" John mumbled around a mouth filled with a second doughnut. He kept his head lowered and steeled himself to hear the name of some former friend, some boy he'd grown up with who had known very well that Liddy Goodloe was taken.

"Liddy?" Gert said, as if the name was unfamiliar. "No. She lives up the lane there in her father's house all alone now that Greta's married. I doubt she has any plans in that direction."

John thought he must be hallucinating. Had he imagined the white prayer covering? No. He'd touched one of the ties and Liddy had pulled it away from him. That had happened. Of course, he could hardly ask his aunt about that unless he was ready to admit he'd already seen Liddy and spoken with her.

"You'll need to see Bishop Troyer and the sooner the better," Gert instructed. "We have services this coming Sunday so there's time enough to have everything in place so that you can make your apology and seek forgiveness and get the *bann* lifted. Then you'll be needing a job and a place to stay." Gert ticked each item off on her fingers as if she were filling a customer's order. "And some decent clothes."

She reached for her shawl and bonnet. "I'm going across to Yoder's to get a few things and when I come back we'll get you settled in." She headed for the rear of the store. "Roger Hadwell, go fetch Bishop Troyer," she instructed. "And then go see if Luke Starns is willing to let John stay in his old rooms above the livery until he gets back on his feet."

John watched as Roger came to the front of the store and retrieved a black rain slicker and his hat from a peg behind the counter. Without so much as a glance at John his uncle left by the front door.

By suppertime John had a place to stay as well as two sets of new clothes. He'd shaved and washed and enjoyed his first solid meal in days, wolfing down three bowls of the beef stew his aunt kept simmering in the back room of the hardware store along with half a loaf of Pleasant's crusty wheat bread. In exchange for being able to live above the blacksmith's shop, Roger had agreed that John would take charge of the stables behind the shop and care for any animals housed there overnight. All of this had been arranged between his uncle and the blacksmith. Roger had yet to utter a single word to John.

But his aunt seemed to have made her choice. It appeared that having him home was worth breaking the traditions of shunning.

"Like old times," she said as she and Roger closed the shop. She turned to John and added, "I left you some of that stew for your supper and there's coffee and enough bread for breakfast tomorrow." She cupped his cheek gently. "You look exhausted, John. Get some rest."

Not wanting to contribute to her disobedience of the shunning, John nodded. It was just as well. He probably could not have gotten his thanks out around the lump of relief and gratitude that clogged his throat. The idea of spending the night sleeping under one of his aunt's handmade quilts seemed unbelievable after all the nights he'd had to find shelter wherever he could.

"Come along, Gert," Roger instructed, refusing to make eye contact with John.

"Oh, stop your fussing," Gert chastised as they walked down the street. "By morning everybody is going to know the prodigal has returned and on Sunday he can put things to right once and for all."

The prodigal. That's what Lydia had called him.

Chapter 2

The day had been unsettling to say the least. After her encounter with John, Lydia had barely been able to concentrate on the lessons she tried to teach the children. After they had eaten their lunches she surrendered to her complete inability to concentrate and let Bettina teach the little ones. In the meantime she gave the older students assignments they could do on their own. Then she sat at her desk studying her Bible in hopes that God would send her answers to the questions that crowded her mind.

At the end of the day she hurried home, thankful that the rain had let up and that John Amman had not waited for her outside as she had feared he might. Perhaps he had come to his senses and walked back the way he came. He clearly thought she was married and, given the shunning, surely no one in town would have told him the real story. She could only pray that this was the case. It was unimaginable to even consider living in the same town with John after all this time, after everything that had happened between them.

"Impossible," she muttered as she climbed the porch steps to her house. She was eager to have a quiet supper and settle in for the evening to correct work she had collected from the students. That would surely calm her nerves. She would retire early and pray that John Amman would not haunt her dreams.

But as she reached for the doorknob, the door swung open and there stood her sister Greta, her baby daughter riding her hip while her two boisterous sons—only a year apart—raced from the kitchen to greet Lydia. "Tante Liddy," they squealed in unison as they threw themselves against her.

She set the large basket that she used to carry books and papers to and from school on the table inside the front hallway and bent to give the boys a hug. "This is a surprise," she said, glancing up at Greta.

"I have news," Greta said in a conspiratorial whisper. "Boys, go finish your milk," she instructed as she led the way into the front room. "You should sit," she instructed as she shifted the baby in her arms.

This could be anything, Lydia warned herself. Greta was given to melodrama, and even the simplest news could seem monumental to her. Lydia sat in her rocking chair and reached for her niece. Greta handed her the child, clearly relieved to sit down herself. She was nearly eight months along in her latest pregnancy, and she sank heavily into the nearest chair.

"John Amman has returned," Greta announced. "Gert Hadwell told Hilda Yoder that he just walked into the hardware store this morning as if he'd last been there yesterday." She waited, her eyebrows raised expectantly. "Well?"

Lydia would not sugarcoat the facts, especially with Greta.

"I know. He was at the school when I arrived this morning. He had started the stove to warm the building."

"Well, what happened? What did you say? What did *he* say? Where's he been all this time and why didn't he ever write to you and why come back now? Is he staying?" All of the questions Lydia had refused to voice came tumbling from her sister's lips. Greta covered her mouth with her fist. "But, of course, you couldn't say anything. He's still under the *bann*."

"Of course. How could I have any information about whether or not he plans to stay?" *But he had said as much as he walked away from the school.*

"Oh, he's staying. He's taken the rooms above Luke's shop. Gert sent Roger to arrange everything with Luke earlier today."

So close? The distance between Lydia's house and Luke's building was less than fifty yards. "Well, there's your answer," Lydia murmured, and wondered at the way her heart lurched at the news that he had found a place to live already. That they were to be neighbors.

"If you ask me, there's more to this than it seems," Greta pressed.

"What do you mean?"

"What if he's come back for *you?*"

Lydia stood and bounced the child as she walked to the window that looked directly down to where the blacksmith shop sat and where even now John might be standing at the kitchen window of the upstairs apartment looking at her house, watching for any sign of her. "Don't be silly," she said briskly. "It's been years. If John has come back to Celery Fields, it's because he needs a place to work and live."

"Then why not go north to his family's farm?"

Because he was never a farmer.

With a sigh she turned to face her sister. "You'll have to ask him that question, Greta."

"Well, I just might," Greta replied. "Of course, I'll wait until he's seen the bishop and makes his plea for forgiveness on Sunday. But if he has any idea that he can just come back here after all this time, after no word to you for years, and…"

"Let the past go, Greta," Lydia warned. "Be happy for the Hadwells. I'm sure Gertrude is beside herself with joy. John was always her favorite nephew."

"I am happy for them," Greta said petulantly. "It's just that…" She frowned.

"It was kind of Luke to offer him the apartment," Lydia said, hoping the shift in the conversation would take Greta's mind off worrying about her.

Her sister sighed. "We took most of the furnishings out of there when we moved to the house, so he's going to need some things if he intends to stay. Luke also says we should invite him to supper on Sunday evening. I don't know what that man is thinking sometimes."

"Luke doesn't know John from the past," Lydia reminded her. "And do I need to remind you that Luke himself was under a similar *bann* when he moved here from Canada?"

Greta blushed. "I guess you've got a point. Luke's more understanding of this whole matter."

"And a kind man always doing what he can for others," Lydia reminded her sister.

"Hmm. Still, Sunday is Samuel's birthday," Greta said with a nod toward the kitchen, where the boys could be heard whispering and giggling. Suddenly her eyes widened. "Even if John comes you'll still be there, won't you? Samuel would be so disappointed if…"

"Of course I'm coming," Lydia assured her.

"I mean I could just tell Luke not to…"

"Greta, if John Amman has indeed come home to stay then we will need to adjust to that—all of us."

"If you're sure…"

"I'm sure. Now shouldn't you be getting home? Luke will be wanting his supper."

Greta smiled as she heaved herself out of the chair and waited a minute to catch her breath. Then she took her daughter from Lydia, called for the boys and herded them onto the porch. "I left you something for your supper," she said as she and the children headed back toward town.

Greta had been the homemaker for Lydia and their father from the time she'd been old enough to reach the stove and counters in the kitchen. Even with her own house and brood to care for she still felt the need to make sure that Lydia was eating.

"I do know how to cook," Lydia reminded her.

"Not well," Greta shot back, and both sisters laughed.

Lydia stood on the porch watching Greta waddle down the path toward her own house at the end of town. As she turned to go back inside, a movement on the landing above the livery caught her eye.

John Amman was standing in the open doorway of the apartment Greta's husband had once occupied. He was watching her and, as Lydia stared back, he raised his hand, palm out flat in the signal they had shared as teenagers.

He remembered.

By week's end everyone in Celery Fields and the surrounding area made up of small produce farms owned by Amish families knew the story of John Amman. And as far as Lydia could see, John did not need a forgiving father on the scene to kill the fatted calf in celebration of his return. He had his aunt. Gertrude Hadwell took John in as if he were her beloved son.

Only a day after his return he was working in the hardware store as if he'd never left. Oh, to be sure, at Roger Hadwell's insistence, John's chores were confined to the loading area in back. That way no customers would be placed in the awkward position of having to openly shun him. But Gert made it clear that by Monday he would take his place behind the counter.

In the meantime his aunt had organized a frolic, the name given to occasions when Amish women gathered for some large work project such as cleaning someone's home or completing a quilt top. To Lydia it seemed exactly the right word for such events. No matter how difficult the work, the women always enjoyed themselves—sharing news and rumors and laughter. This time, the cause for gathering on Saturday morning was to properly clean and furnish the rooms above the livery for John. Of course, everyone in town knew how Gert Hadwell had grieved the fact that she had never had children of her own. It was understandable that people would put their happiness for her above their concern about John's past. Besides, John would not be on-site for the cleaning.

So on Saturday morning Liddy sat on a stool in the barn behind her house squeezing warm milk from the cow as she tried to decide her next course of action. Much as she dreaded it, Lydia could hardly refuse to join the other women. If she failed to attend the frolic the day's chatter would no doubt focus on her at some point. She could not bear the thought of the others gossiping and recalling how she and John had once been sweethearts. The newcomers would have to be filled in on the romance that had ended when John left town. Lydia had no doubt that she would be forced to endure curious glances and abject pity when she attended services on Sunday.

No, better to do whatever seemed prudent to get through the first rush of excitement over John's homecoming. Not much happened in Celery Fields and John's return was, indeed, cause for excitement. It had certainly taken everyone's mind off her own stunning break from tradition a few weeks earlier, when Lydia had decided to forego the black prayer *kapp* of a single woman and the habit of sitting on one of the two front benches with her nieces and the other unmarried girls. Rather, she had taken a seat in the rear of the section reserved for the married women and widows. To punctuate her action she had replaced the black *kapp* that she had worn since joining the church with one of white.

As she had hoped, during the service the other women had not wanted to create a stir and so had simply focused their attention on the words of the hymn and sermon. One or two had gently nudged those girls in the first two rows, who had turned to stare. Of course, once the service ended and the women gathered in the kitchen to prepare the after-services meal, there had been whispers and knowing nods until Lydia had realized she would have to say something.

"It seems plain that there is little likelihood that I shall ever marry," she announced, drawing the immediate and rapt attention of the others. "As I grow older—having nearly reached my thirtieth year now—and having served the community and the congregation for several years since my baptism, is it too much to ask that I be allowed to sit with the women of my age?"

She had taken her time then meeting the eyes of each woman in turn. Some had looked away. Others had registered sympathy, even pity, for her plight. Hilda Yoder, wife of the owner of the dry-goods store, had chewed her lower lip for what seemed an eternity and then given Lydia's decision her blessing.

"Makes perfect sense," she said with the crisp efficiency with which she pronounced most of her edicts. "Now, shall we attend to the business at hand and get this food set out?"

And that had been the end of any public discussion on the matter. So at least John's return had taken people's attention away from that. Of course, if she didn't go to the frolic…

Lydia would go to the frolic—and to supper at Greta's after services on Sunday. By that time John would have contritely sought the forgiveness of the congregation and been officially welcomed home. If she could just get through the next few days, surely by the end of the coming week everything and everyone would settle back into the normal routine of life in Celery

Fields. Oh, no doubt, she and John would cross paths in town or at some gathering, but in time…

"Hello, Liddy."

Lydia had been so lost in thought that she'd been unaware of anyone coming into the barn—much less John Amman. He was dressed "plain" in clothes that were obviously new and store-bought. The pants were half an inch too short and the shirt stretched a little too tightly over his shoulders. He was clean shaven and his face was shaded by the stiff wide brim of his straw hat. His blond hair had been recently washed and trimmed in the style of other Amish men, although it was more wavy and unruly than most.

She turned her attention to the cow, determined not to allow John or any thought of him to further disrupt her plans for the day.

"Why do you wear the prayer covering of a married woman, Liddy?" He leaned against the door frame, one ankle crossed over the other. "My aunt tells me you have never married—and in her view you have little thought of ever doing so."

Lydia bit her lip to keep from speaking. He was to be shunned at least until the congregation could hear from the bishop and take a vote to reinstate him. She squeezed the last of the milk from the cow's udder and stood up.

John reached for the bucket of warm milk and his boldness unnerved her. Someone could be watching— people were always passing by on their way to and from town and it was Saturday, the busiest day for such traffic. If she were seen standing right next to John Amman tongues would surely wag, no matter whether she shunned him or not.

She wrestled the bucket from him and quickened her pace as she headed out into the sunlight. Surely, he would not follow her where everyone could see him.

But he did. He had not changed at all. John Amman had always been one for testing boundaries. "We will talk about this, Liddy," he said. "I think I deserve an explanation."

She almost broke her silence at that. *He* deserved an explanation? This man who had promised to write, had promised to come back to her? This man from whom she had heard nothing for eight long years? This man whose memory had so dogged her through the years that he had made it impossible for her even to consider accepting the attention of any other man in his stead?

She kept her eyes on the sandy lane before her and concentrated on covering the ground between the barn and the house as quickly as possible without spilling the milk. But the path was narrow and he was walking far too closely. Their arms were in real danger of brushing if she wasn't careful. She had to do something before they came into Hilda Yoder's view. Surely at this hour the wife of the dry-goods store owner would be at her usual post by the shop window watching the goings-on in town.

John said nothing more as he continued to keep pace with her. In truth he seemed to be unaware of the awkward situation. Not knowing what else to do, she broke into a run, not caring whether the milk sloshed over the sides of her pail. To her relief he made no attempt to follow her. He just stood where she'd left him on the path watching her go. "See you tomorrow at services, then," he called after her. "And after I've been forgiven and reinstated you'll be free to speak with me. I expect to have your explanation, Liddy."

Her explanation? She ran up the steps to her back door and hurried inside.

Safe in her kitchen with the door tightly closed, she scanned the lane that led to town and the parts of Celery Fields' main street that she could see from her window. She cringed at the idea that anyone might have heard him call out to her. Her breathing was coming in gasps as if she'd run a good distance instead of a mere few feet, and she found it necessary to sit down for a moment.

It was not exertion that caused her breath to suddenly be in short supply. It was John—being close to him like that, remembering all the times they had walked together, and facing the reality that he was back in Celery Fields and gave every appearance of intending to stay.

She moaned as she buried her face in her hands.

After a moment she sat up straight and forced her breathing to calm. She would do what she always did when faced with a challenge. She would set boundaries for herself, and for John Amman, as well. They were no longer children. He would simply have to accept that she had certain duties as a member of the community—duties that did not include answering to him.

With her confidence restored, she stood, smoothed the skirt of her dress and put the milk in a glass pitcher before storing it in the icebox. Then she took a deep breath as if preparing to dive into the sea and set forth once again, this time to do her part to clean and refurbish the place next door where John Amman had taken up residence as her neighbor.

* * *

John knew he should not have called out after Lydia ran from him. Even as a girl she had hated anything that drew attention to her. For that matter the entire encounter could have caused her grave discomfort if anyone had seen or heard. "Not exactly the best way to worm your way back into her good graces," he muttered as he headed for the hardware store.

On the other hand, why should he be the one trying to win her favor? Wasn't she the one who had said she would wait and then shunned him as had everyone else? He'd written to assure her that he had every intention of returning once he'd made enough money to set up a business of his own. She had always understood his aversion to farming. She had even been the one to encourage him to start some sort of shop and they would live above it and she would help out on Saturdays and after school. But when he'd explained to her that it would take money to start a business and his father would never accept the idea that John would not one day take over the family farm, she'd insisted that God would provide.

He knew what she meant. In her mind if owning his own business were God's plan for his life then the opportunity would simply present itself. "You just have to be patient—and vigilant for God's signs," she had instructed.

But patience had never been one of John's attributes. When he reached the age of eighteen with no sign from God, he decided to seek out other possibilities. After all, hadn't Bishop Troyer taught them that God helps those who help themselves?

"And where did that get you?" he grumbled as he put

on the denim apron his aunt had left for him and began sweeping the loading dock behind the hardware store. He brushed the accumulated debris into a dustpan and dumped it in the bin next to the loading dock. Then he set the broom and dustpan inside the door and rubbed his hands together as he moved to a place where he could better listen in on his uncle and Luke Starns as they sat outside Luke's shop. With no one allowed to converse with him, this was his only recourse for gathering information.

"Warmer today," Roger said. "After the last spell of frosty mornings I thought we might be in for a stretch of cold weather."

"Good for the crops that it's passed," replied the blacksmith, who was sipping a cup of coffee. He was a quiet man, as John had observed earlier that morning when the blacksmith handed Gertrude a box of kitchen items that Greta had gathered from her own supply to place in the rooms above his business. The idea of this silent giant of a man married to the vibrant and petite Greta made John smile.

A few minutes passed while the men discussed weather and crops and business. Then Bishop Troyer crossed the street from the dry-goods store and joined them.

"Bishop Troyer," Roger said as he stood and offered the head of their congregation his chair. "Did you speak yet with John Amman?"

"*Yah.* We have spoken already twice. I am convinced that he has learned the error of his ways and come home to make amends," the bishop replied. "Everything seems to be in order for tomorrow's service."

"Then I can have him working the counter come

Monday." This was not a question but something John realized his uncle had been dreading.

"Should bring you a bunch of business," Luke said with a chuckle. "Folks will want to get a look at him after all this time. They'll be curious about where he's been and all."

"They can look all they want at services. On Monday I need him to be working, although I'm not sure how we're going to have enough business to support the three of us."

"I seem to recall that this entire matter had its beginning in John wanting to start a business of his own," Bishop Troyer said.

Roger let out a mirthless laugh. "With what? He has nothing. Gert had to buy him the clothes he's wearing now and he owes a debt of gratitude to Luke here that he has a place to stay."

"Still, he must have a skill if the plan was to open his own shop."

"He's a tolerable woodworker," Roger allowed. "Clocks and furniture mostly. He built that cabinet where Gert keeps her quilting fabrics. And the clock we have in the store—that's his work."

John saw the bishop exchange a look with Luke. "I reckon Josef Bontrager took up that business in John's absence," Luke observed.

Roger stared out at the street. "You've got a point there. Not much call for handmade furniture these days."

Was it John's imagination or had his uncle raised his voice as if to make sure John heard this last bit of information? It hardly mattered. He was in no position to take up his trade. Over the past several months he had sold off his tools one by one or bartered them for a meal or a night's lodging.

"Well, until something comes along he's got work with you. The Lord has surely blessed him in having you and Gertrude still here," the bishop said.

"Speaking of work I'd best get back to it," Luke said as he drained the last of his coffee.

As the bishop took his leave and Roger walked slowly back to the hardware store, John stepped from the shadows of the storeroom into the sunlight that bathed the loading dock. There was work to be done—a pile of newly delivered lumber that his uncle had instructed him to sort and stack by size and type in the pole shed outside the store. But when he stepped into the yard he heard feminine laughter coming from the rooms above the livery.

He took a moment to enjoy the sight of the women moving in and out of the apartment, up and down the outside stairs carrying various items they seemed to think he might need. Then Lydia came out onto the tiny landing at the top of the stairs to shake out a rag rug.

She was laughing at something one of the other women had said, her head thrown back the way he remembered from when they'd been teenagers. And in that laughter he heard more clearly than any words could have expressed exactly why he had decided to return to Celery Fields. He had come back to find answers to the questions that had plagued him. He had come back to the only place where he knew there was a path to forgiveness and from there a safe haven to rest in while he found his way. He had come back because even eight long years had not erased the memory of this girl turned woman whose laughter had always had the power to stir his heart.

Chapter 3

When Lydia glanced up and saw John watching her from the loading dock, the laughter she'd been sharing with the other women died on her lips. How could she possibly have gotten so caught up in the pleasure of the work and companionship with the others that she had been able to forget that he was back in her life, whether she wanted it or not? That the place the women were scouring and setting to order was where John would live—was already living? How had she forgotten who would be eating off those mismatched dishes that she had washed and dried and stacked so precisely on the open shelf above the stove?

She had helped scrub the walls and floors and even made up the narrow bed that occupied one corner while engaged in the normal chatter. At events like this, women enjoyed catching up on news from families that had moved back north when the hard times hit, or the decision of the newest member of their cleaning party and her husband to move to Florida and start fresh after a tornado had destroyed the family's farm in Iowa. And so the morning had passed without a single thought about John Amman. His presence in town was far too recent and their encounters had been rare enough that it was easy to lose herself in the work and the conversation. It was truly amazing how easily she had been able to simply dismiss the man from her mind.

But now seeing him standing in the back doorway of the hardware store, filling the space with his tall, lanky frame, she could not seem to stop the images of him living in that small apartment from coming. He would rinse the dishes she had washed for him at the sink as he looked out the small square window with its view of her house. He would hang his clothes on the pegs that she had wiped free of dust above the bed. He would sleep in that bed under a quilt that Greta had brought to add an extra layer to the one already there. It was a quilt that Lydia and Greta's grandmother had made. A quilt that had once covered the bed Lydia and Greta shared when they were children.

She felt the heat rise to her cheeks as these images assailed her and John stepped closer to the edge of the dock, his bold gaze fixed directly on her. The other women went about their work, glancing shyly in his direction as their laughter and discussion dissolved into expectant silence. Lydia stood frozen on the steps, her fingers gripping the small rag rug until her knuckles went white. She felt as if her cheeks must be glowing like two polished red apples.

Greta stepped onto the porch landing next to her. "He's watching you," she whispered.

Hilda Yoder cleared her throat. "We have more work to do," she instructed with a glance at John and then a lift of her eyebrows to Lydia. "Greta, take this mop bucket and get us some clean rinse water."

"I'll do it," Lydia said firmly. Greta had no business hauling buckets of water up and down that steep staircase.

"I hardly think that…" Hilda began but then pressed her lips into a thin line and said no more.

Lydia handed the rag rug to Greta and took the bucket. She descended the stairs without looking at John, but she knew he was following her every move. Dumping the soapy water, she set the bucket aside and prepared to prime the pump until the faucet spit out fresh water. Above her she knew Hilda Yoder was watching with disapproval. She saw John leap down from the loading dock and walk slowly toward her. She could not help feeling a little like the sandpiper she'd once seen caught in a fisherman's abandoned net at the beach.

She reached for the pump handle but John was there first, his fingers closing around the handle and brushing hers. "Let me," he said softly. Lydia snatched her hand away as if she'd gotten too close to a hot stove. Then, not knowing what else she might do, she looked away while he primed the pump until the faucet squirted clear water into the pail.

Without a word he carried the full, heavy pail up the steps and set it on the landing careful to keep his eyes lowered so as not to give offense to any of the women Hilda had herded quickly inside. His delivery complete, he hurried back down the steps, past Lydia, who had waited in the yard, and back to the loading dock where he turned his back to them and began sorting through a lumber pile of mixed-size pieces.

"That man has been too much out in the world," Hilda Yoder huffed as Lydia mounted the steps and all the women went back to their work.

"It may take him some time to settle back into the old ways," Pleasant said with a glance at Gert, who was clearly embarrassed by her nephew's action. "After all, he has been eight years in their world. Still, the important thing is that he has seen the error of his youthful decision and come home to us."

There was a general murmur of agreement among the women. But Lydia had her doubts that John would ever truly return to their ways. The only reason he'd come back now was because he'd clearly had nowhere else to turn. In Celery Fields he could be assured of forgiveness and the care of the community. From what she knew of outsiders, they were not quite so generous to those who were down on their luck. No, she knew John Amman perhaps better than any of them or, at least, she had once a long time ago. It simply was not possible for a man to change so completely, was it? To have finally learned his lesson and abandoned the wanderlust of his youth? To be satisfied at last with the quiet, simple life of his Amish roots?

"Hilda, you don't think there's any possibility for someone to vote against him tomorrow, do you?" Greta asked, her eyes wide with worry.

"John Amman has sought his forgiveness from Bishop Troyer," Pleasant reminded Greta. "We will wait to hear his recommendation tomorrow."

"Nevertheless, the congregation has to be unified in its acceptance," Hilda reminded them. Lydia saw Gert Hadwell press her fist to her mouth. She hoped, for Gert's sake, that Hilda had not got it into her head to vote against John. Not that she would put it past the older woman. Hilda saw herself as carrying the standard for what was right in their small community. In many ways her opinion carried almost as much weight as the bishop's.

But to Lydia's relief Hilda positioned herself next to Gert in a gesture that could only be read as one of support as she glanced around the room. "I think we have done as best we can here."

Gert smoothed the quilt on the bed and nodded. "It does look nice," she said with a smile. "Perhaps," she added wistfully, "with such nice quarters John will find his peace here."

"Well, I'll say one thing," Pleasant announced. "It smells a good deal better than it did when we came in."

All the women laughed as they gathered their supplies and trooped down the outside steps to the yard below.

All except Lydia.

She lingered to wipe the oilcloth that covered the small wooden table and glance around the room one last time. She told herself she was only making sure they had left none of their cleaning supplies behind. But she knew better.

In spite of the aroma of the strong lye soap they'd used, offset by the sweetness of the furniture wax, John's essence filled the space. And as she closed the door behind her she recalled the scent of John—the sheer warmth of his nearness when he'd bent to take the bucket from her. A memory stirred, of him standing so close to her one time when they had gone to the beach together. That day he had smelled of the sun and the sea. And that was the day they had shared their first kiss. They had been fourteen years old.

A lifetime ago, she thought, shaking off the memory as she followed the others down the steps and into the lane where they said their goodbyes. Greta glanced back at her. "Coming to the house, sister?" she called.

"I'm a little tired," Lydia replied. "You go on." She was aware that John had paused in the sorting of the wood the minute she spoke. He did not turn around, but everything about his posture told her he was listening.

Greta hesitated then nodded. "All right. See you tomorrow then."

Ah, yes, tomorrow. First, the services where John will no doubt be fully embraced back into the community. After all, forgiveness is the very foundation of our Amish faith. And later Samuel's birthday party, Lydia thought. And John would be there for all of it. She drew in a deep breath and forced a smile. It had already been a long and difficult day but the events scheduled for *Sunndaag* promised to test her even further. "*Yah,* tomorrow," she replied.

On Sunday morning John was awake well before dawn. He lay on the narrow bed beneath two faded hand-stitched quilts and thought about the bed he'd slept in as a boy in a room shared by his three brothers. Where were they now? Married with families of their own? And his sisters? He tried to imagine them all grown-up.

And his parents. *Dat. Maemm.* Did they think of him? Speak of him?

He rolled onto his side and watched the rays of sun creep through the window that looked out onto Lydia's property, and his thoughts turned to the day before him. He was confident that the congregation would vote to accept the bishop's recommendation of forgiveness. But what about Lydia?

So far she had given not the slightest sign that once the *bann* was lifted she would be willing to resume the friendship they'd once shared. If he was going to live here they would be neighbors at the very least. And, given the way the community's population had shrunk over the years, they could hardly avoid spending time in each other's company from time to time. There would be gatherings where they would both be present, like the birthday party for Greta and Luke's oldest child. Maybe once the *bann* was lifted Lydia Goodloe would meet his eyes instead of averting her gaze. Or would she? He was certain that part of the way she'd been acting had to do with her thinking she would never see him again. And now that he was here she had no idea what to do.

Well, by this time tomorrow—in fact by later this very evening, when they all gathered at Luke and Greta's for supper, he would have made clear that she could no longer use the excuse of his shunning for refusing to talk to him. The congregation would vote to accept Bishop Troyer's recommendation for forgiveness and full reinstatement, for that was the way of his people. They would vote in his favor for his aunt's sake even if they still had doubts about him. He had missed the traditions of his faith; never in all the years he was gone had he once been tempted to follow the faith of outsiders. Without question there were any number of good and pious people out there, but their ways were far too complicated for John to fully grasp. He liked the simple ways of his own people.

He had made a mistake in not coming home after he'd saved up the money that he needed. Instead, he'd allowed his business partner and friend to invest for him. He'd had no idea what a stock market was, but he had trusted his partner and been drawn in by pure greed at the prospect of doubling his savings in a short time with no work at all. Now he realized that he should have known better. The day he'd turned that money over to his friend was the day he'd realized that he had lost his way—his purpose in leaving Celery Fields in the first place.

But now he was back. He had returned for many reasons—to reconnect with his faith and his community was certainly something that had driven him as he made his way west across the state. He had missed his family, although with them moved north again there was little he could do about that for now. But he had also missed his neighbors and friends. And as hurt and upset as he had been with Liddy, he could not get her out of his mind. Every day as he made his way back to Celery Fields he had thought about her. Through pouring rain and cold, blustery nights when he had to sleep outside, he warmed himself by remembering the times they had spent together, the dreams they had shared, the plans they had made.

Now that he was back he was more confused than ever by her behavior toward him. There was the business of the white prayer *kapp* for one thing, and then she had barely said ten words to him. Of course, that could be explained by his being under the *bann,* but still as a girl Liddy had had little use for such rules if they got in the way of what she thought made more sense.

John kicked the covers off and sat up on the side of the bed. Liddy had always been stubborn. She had her opinion on almost any subject and not much tolerance for those who did not see things as she did. The two of them had always been alike in that way and it had caused them no end of arguments when their individual views on a subject differed. But seeing her these past few days since his return—being able to observe her for the most part without actually being able to talk to her—John's impression was that she had changed. She was more like her half sister, Pleasant, than she'd been as a girl. Then she had been as light-hearted as her younger sister, Greta. But from what he'd observed she had developed the pursed lips and tense posture of their former teacher—a woman Liddy had declared she would never ever want to emulate. But then there had been moments—like when he pumped the water for her—when she had glanced at him and he'd seen the girl he'd fallen in love with, the girl for whom he'd risked everything.

Well, that girl-turned-woman had some explaining to do. And once he'd gotten through the service and then the supper at Luke and Greta's, he fully intended to find out why Lydia Goodloe had never acknowledged his attempts to write to her.

John stood and surrendered to the wide smile that stretched across his face. He raked his fingers through his thick hair and it flopped back over his ears, reminding him that he was once again Amish. In a matter of less than a week he had cast aside the trappings of the outside world and now presented himself as every other man in Celery Fields did. He knew one thing for certain: Liddy Goodloe had always been one who wanted to know exactly what to expect at all times. She liked being in charge. That was one of the things that made her a good teacher. Well, just maybe it was time the teacher became the student. And if anyone could teach her the lessons of surviving and even thriving on the unpredictability of life, it was John Amman.

He dressed and then prepared a hearty breakfast of eggs, fried potatoes and thick slices of Pleasant's rye bread slathered with butter and jam. He set his plate of food on the table and bowed his head, thanking God for leading him back to this place and these people.

Anxious now for the day to begin, for this life he'd come back to retrieve to begin, John gobbled down his breakfast. He set the dishes in water to soak and was out the door and on his way to meet Bishop Troyer and the second preacher before the sun was fully above the horizon.

Usually Luke, Greta and the children called for Lydia early on Sunday morning. Services were held every other week in one of the homes that made up the community. On this day the service would take place in the Yoder house behind the dry-goods store in town and, as was her habit whenever the venue was so close, Lydia planned to walk. There was one problem, though.

To walk from her place to the Yoder house she would have to pass by Luke's shop—and the residence of John Amman. Her plan was to delay leaving her house until she had seen him go. That way there would be no possibility of running into him. And so, dressed for over an hour already, the morning chores done, her breakfast eaten and her dishes washed, dried and back on the shelf, she waited. And waited.

The clock chimed eight and still there had been no sign of life in the rooms above the livery. She would be late. Greta would be worried, perhaps send Luke to fetch her. Everyone would be talking about her, about whether or not she had decided against coming because of John, about...

"Oh, just go," she ordered herself.

She tied the ribbons of her black bonnet and wrapped her shawl around her shoulders. The morning air was still chilly although a soft westerly wind held the promise that by the time services ended she would have no need of the shawl's extra warmth. She picked up the basket holding the jars of pickled beets and peaches that would be her contribution to the community meal that always followed the three-hour service. Then she stood at the door and closed her eyes, praying for God's strength to get her through this day.

By the time she reached the Yoder house her sister had indeed worked herself into a state. "I thought perhaps you weren't coming," she whispered as she relieved Lydia of her basket and handed it to one of the Yoder daughters. "I know how difficult this—"

"I am here," Lydia interrupted as she saw that most of the congregation had already taken their places in the rows of black wooden benches that traveled from house to house depending on where services were scheduled. "We should sit."

Pleasant slid closer to the women next to her, making room for Lydia and Greta. She gave Lydia a sympathetic look, as did two other women who turned to look at her. *Oh, will this ever end?* Lydia thought even as she manufactured a reassuring smile of greeting for each of the women.

She and Greta had barely taken their places when the first hymn began. Lydia felt the comfort of verses that had been passed down from generation to generation for centuries as she chanted the words in unison with her neighbors. There was something so powerful in the sound of many voices chorusing the same words without benefit of a pipe organ or other musical support. By the time the hymn ended twenty minutes later Lydia felt fully prepared to face whatever the day might bring.

Of course, it helped that John was nowhere in sight. No doubt, he was sequestered in one of the bedrooms where the elders and bishop had met with him before the service. Either that or he had lost his nerve and run away again in the dark of night.

That thought gave Lydia a start. What if he had done exactly that? She struggled to focus her attention on the message as Levi Harnischer, the deacon of their congregation, preached. But as he rambled from one Biblical story to another she found her thoughts, as well as her gaze, wandering.

More than once she glanced toward the hallway that she knew led to the bedrooms. Was he there waiting to be called before the congregation to make his plea for forgiveness and reinstatement once the regular service ended?

Greta nudged her as the second hymn began and gave her a strange look. *Are you all right?* she mouthed.

Lydia frowned and nodded but Greta continued to stare at her.

"You are quite pale, Liddy," she whispered.

"I am fine," Lydia assured her, forcing a gentle tone through gritted teeth.

Bishop Troyer's sermon followed the singing, and there could be no doubt of his message. He quoted the story of the prodigal son and then focused much of his attention on the young people seated in the front two rows of benches on either side of a center aisle. For over an hour he spoke of lambs wandering away from the flock, tempted by the promise of greener pastures. He spoke of the dangers that awaited such runaways and the importance of returning to the stability of the fold.

All around her Lydia saw her neighbors sitting up very straight as they listened with rapt attention to the bishop's words. They knew what was coming. At the meeting following the service they expected John would enter the room and face them. Did not one of them entertain the notion that he might once again have lost his nerve and run away?

The final hymn began and as each verse was sung Lydia felt her heart beat faster. She focused her gaze on Gertrude Hadwell, who clearly could barely contain her joy at having John back in her life. If he left again, Gert would be devastated.

Please let him be here, Lydia prayed silently even as she understood that life would be far easier for her if John had surrendered yet again to the temptations of the adventures he'd found in the outside world.

John followed the sounds and silences of the service from his position in one of the small bedrooms near the two large front rooms of the Yoder home. The hymns, chanted slowly in unison verse by verse, had a beauty all their own. It was so different from the music he'd heard on the rare occasions when he'd attended an *Englisch* service. In the outside world hymns were always accompanied by some musical instrument—most often a pipe organ that huffed and thudded as the organist pushed or pulled the stops and pressed down on the row of pedals beneath her feet.

He had missed the quiet rhythm of hymns from the *Ausband*—hymns passed down through the generations, hymns that could run on for dozens of verses, hymns he had memorized as a boy. He heard the drone of the preacher's voice as the first of the two sermons was delivered. Since the door to the bedroom was closed, he did not hear the actual words until he was called to seek his forgiveness.

He folded his hands and leaned his elbows on his knees. He ought to be praying for God's guidance. He ought to be using this time to figure out how he was going to state his case without sounding either arrogant or insincere. He ought to be trying to understand exactly what he hoped to achieve by coming back here—what his life was going to look like after today. He ought to be doing all of that but, instead, his mind was filled with thoughts of Liddy.

She would be there sitting with the other women and girls, all of them dressed in the solid dark-colored dresses and aprons topped by the starched prayer *kapps* of their faith. They would wear their hair the same, as well, for in the Amish world sameness was a sign of commitment to the community at large; individuality in dress or style was seen as rebellious. Male and female would sit shoulder to shoulder on their respective sides of the room, their eyes either on the minister or lowered in prayer. None of them would be distinguishable from their neighbor. For that was their way. The community was everything and the individual was nothing.

That was, of course, why he had to apologize and seek forgiveness. He had put his personal dreams and plans above what was considered in the best interest of the community. In the outside world such actions would be considered laudable. He would be praised for his ambition and determination to make something of himself. But not in Celery Fields or any other Amish community.

And not in the eyes of Liddy Goodloe.

He knew why the rest of the community had failed to understand his purpose in leaving eight years earlier, but he had thought that Liddy of all people knew why he'd done the only thing he'd felt he could do if the two of them were to have a future. She had counseled patience then but how long was he expected to wait? And she, too, had wanted to marry and start their life together. He was certain of that—or at least he had been.

He stood and paced the confines of the room, the leather soles of his new work boots meeting the polished planks of the wooden floor with a distinct click like the ticking of a clock. He straightened his suspenders and tucked his shirt more firmly into the waistband of his wool trousers. He heard more singing and then the hum of Bishop Troyer's deep voice as the elderly man delivered the second and final sermon for the day.

Soon the deacon would come for him.

Soon he would face them.

Soon one way or another it would be decided.

And if someone voted against him? What then?

He would have little choice but to leave Celery Fields for good. Mentally he considered each of his neighbors and friends, picturing them waiting to seal his fate. By this time tomorrow he would either be settled back into the fold of the community or once again miles away from everything he had once cherished.

The final hymn began. John stood next to the closed door listening for the deacon's footsteps. He closed his eyes and prayed for God to show him the way. Liddy would say that if it was God's will he would be forgiven and just like that, in the eyes of the community, the last eight years would be gone. People would greet him as if he had been in town the whole time. Liddy would no longer look at him with the eyes of a cornered animal…or would she?

Chapter 4

The vote was unanimous in John's favor.

The *bann* had been lifted and in the yard, where the members of the congregation had gathered to share the light fare of the after-services meal, the atmosphere was that of a celebration. As Lydia brought out platters of food the women had prepared in Greta's kitchen she saw John surrounded by a circle of men, his full-throated laughter at something one of the men had just said filling the air around her. It was as if the past eight years had never happened. She froze suddenly, her eyes riveted on John, her ears attuned to his voice, so familiar, so dear.

"Oh, it is so good to have this matter decided!" Greta exclaimed as she came alongside Lydia and followed her gaze to where John was standing. "Now things can return to normal around here." She wiped away beads of sweat from her forehead with the back of one hand. "Is it me or is it unusually hot today?"

"It's you and that extra weight you're carrying," Pleasant replied as she nodded toward the protrusion of Greta's pregnancy and relieved Lydia of the platter she'd nearly forgotten she was holding. "Liddy, find your sister a place in the shade before she passes out."

"Please do not make a fuss," Greta protested, but Lydia saw the way her younger sister pressed one hand against her side and the grimace that followed.

"Come and sit, anyway," Lydia instructed. "You still have Samuel's birthday supper to manage. It will do you good to rest some." She saw Luke glance up and excuse himself from the group of men, then move quickly to his wife's side.

"Are you all right?"

"I am fine," Greta assured him.

"I'll get you some water," Luke said, but before he could do so John was there with a glass filled with cold lemonade.

"I seem to remember you liked your lemonade extra tart, Greta." He grinned at her and Greta giggled as she accepted the glass.

"It is so good to have you back, John," she said. "Everyone is truly pleased."

Lydia did not miss the way her sister cut her eyes in her direction as she said this.

"It is certain that we have been losing more people than we have gained here in Celery Fields," Pleasant added. "What are your plans, John Amman?"

Lydia hid her smile at her half sister's well-known habit of speaking her thoughts bluntly, not taking time to temper them with discretion.

John chuckled. "Ah, Pleasant, I've missed your forthright way of coming to the heart of any matter."

"That does not answer my question."

"For now I will work at the hardware store with my uncle. In time…"

Lydia almost gasped when she glanced at John as he paused. In his eyes she saw the faraway look she remembered so well from their youth, as if he were already miles away from this place and time.

He had not changed at all, she thought. He was still the dreamer.

"In time?" Pleasant prompted.

John shrugged. "Only God can say." He focused his gaze on Lydia.

"I forgot the bread," she murmured, and hurried back inside the house. From the kitchen she watched out the window. She saw Gert tug on John's arm and lead him across the yard to be introduced to people who had moved to Celery Fields since his departure.

She saw him smile as he spoke to those families that had moved to Celery Fields since he'd been gone. She saw him nod sympathetically as Gert introduced him to a young couple who had lost everything in a recent fire. She watched as he admired children and bent to their height to speak with them, charming them with some chatter that made their eyes go wide or their faces break out in smiles.

Oh, how she had loved him once long ago. Loved him for all of these things. But he had left her, and seeing the way he had looked away when Pleasant questioned him, Lydia had no doubt that in time he would leave again.

* * *

By the time he walked back to his rooms following the services, John had heard the story of how Lydia had one Sunday simply decided that she would no longer sit with the unmarried girls. He chuckled as he imagined her walking into the service, looking neither left nor right as she took her place in the back row with the married and widowed women. And no one protested.

Of course, that was Liddy. She might not be as free-spirited as he had often been but even as a girl she had demonstrated a streak of independence that had worried her father and older half sister. It had been that very inclination toward questioning things that had attracted John to her. From the first day he'd worked up the nerve to walk home from school with her he had felt she was someone who could perhaps understand his own restless spirit. And as they had spent more and more time together, his certainty had grown that they were meant to be together—destined to share a life filled with happiness beyond anything they could imagine. While at home he had to face his father's constant disapproval, when he was with Liddy none of that mattered. *She* listened. *She* encouraged him to pursue his love of carpentry. *She* believed in him. *She* loved him—or so he had thought.

But in the end she had chosen the community over him, as any good Amish girl would have. She had conducted herself as any Amish girl would when dealing with someone under the *bann*. She had let his letters go unanswered, shunning him as tradition required. That single action had told him more forcefully than any words she might have written that, in her eyes, he had chosen the wrong path and she could not—would not—stand by him.

He stared down at the house he'd visited so often as a boy. He, Liddy and Greta had played tag or hide-and-seek, and he had helped Liddy get through her chores so the two of them could go to the beach. He had sat with Liddy on the porch after a Sunday-evening hymn singing and a ride to her house in the brand-new courting buggy every Amish boy received when joining the congregation. And although no one had spoken openly about it, the expectation had been that he and Liddy would soon marry and start a family of their own.

As he stood at the window lost in memories of the past they had shared—a time when everything had seemed possible—John couldn't help but wonder if the old wooden swing on the porch of Liddy's house still squeaked. He smiled as he recalled a day when he had offered to oil the connection between the hook and the chain that held the swing in place. Liddy's father had thanked him for the offer but said with a wink, "Now, if I let you fix that squeak, how will I know what you and that daughter of mine are up to?"

How Liddy had laughed when he told her that. "We'll just have to find a quieter place, then," she'd said with a twinkle that matched her father's.

And they had. At every opportunity he would meet her at the bay that separated the town of Sarasota from the barrier islands standing between the community and the Gulf of Mexico. At the bay they would walk out on the mudflats where Liddy would collect shells while he fished. In the late afternoon they would walk their bikes along the unpaved roads that led east to Celery Fields. Sometimes they walked the entire distance across the causeway from downtown Sarasota to the islands beyond and the wide sandy beaches of the Gulf of Mexico. They walked instead of riding in his buggy or taking their bicycles because it gave them more time. More time to plan their future together.

"So much for that," John muttered as he plucked his hat from the peg near the door and headed for Greta's house. He was not sure why he had agreed to attend the supper and birthday celebration, but a promise was a promise. At least Greta's boys had been excited to know he would be there.

"He'll be here," Greta murmured as she worked next to Lydia, peeling vegetables for the stew she was making for their supper.

It did no good for Lydia to pretend she didn't care but she tried, anyway. "It hardly matters to me, after all. He's your guest," she said, licking her thumb after she nicked it with the paring knife.

"You're nervous," Greta said with a sharp nod. "It's to be expected. After all, if the congregation had rejected him he would probably be long gone by now. I mean, what would he have left to stay around for? But they didn't reject him and now you have to decide what to do."

"About what?"

"About the fact that you are still in love with him. And about the fact that he has come back here for one reason—you."

Sometimes Greta's certainty could be so annoying. To disguise her irritation, Lydia laughed. "Greta, John Amman and I have not seen each other in years. He was not much more than a boy when he left here and I was…"

"You were both of age to be married," Greta reminded her. "You had both been baptized into the faith and you were on your way to starting a life together." She placed her hand on Lydia's. "What happened? You never talked about it to me or anyone else."

Greta had still been a child oblivious to the heartaches of courtship when John boarded the train that took him away from Celery Fields to a job in St. Augustine on the east coast of Florida—a job he'd only read about in the Sarasota newspaper. A job he did not yet have but one he was certain was the key to their future that did not rely on his becoming a farmer.

"He left." Lydia pulled away from her sister's touch and scooped the chopped vegetables into the boiling water.

"And now he has returned," Greta continued. She sat down in one of the wooden kitchen chairs and pulled a bowl of frosting toward her. "He certainly did not come back to work in the hardware store," she commented as she swirled the creamy confection onto each layer of her son's birthday cake.

"He had nowhere else to go." Lydia clamped her lips together. Why was she even attempting to reason with her romantic sister?

Greta gave a hoot of a laugh. "Admit it, Liddy. He came back because of you. So what are you going to do about it?"

"Nothing," Lydia replied as she picked up a stack of plates and utensils and went to set the long table in the front room. From the yard she could hear the children's laughter as they played and, after a moment, through the open window that overlooked the porch, she heard male voices drifting into where she worked. Her heart skipped a beat as she realized that one of those voices belonged to John. He was talking to her brother-in-law Luke. *This is how it might have been every Sunday evening,* she thought as she centered each plate precisely in front of each chair. *This is the life John and I might have shared if he had not left.*

She felt the sting of tears even as she felt the sting of the memory that not once had he written or tried to contact her after that day. Everyone knew that John Amman was the only boy she'd ever come close to marrying. Almost from that first day when John had caught up to her on her way home from school they had been inseparable. Once they reached their teens their families, as well as the rest of the town, simply assumed that they would wed. But late one night John had left Celery Fields to seek his fortune in the outside world. She fought unsuccessfully against the memory of that night when her entire life had changed forever. It had been raining. She had followed him to the train station hoping to talk sense into him. He had listened impatiently and then he had begged Lydia to come with him, painting her a picture of the adventures they would share, the money he would make, the material things he would buy for her.

"I don't want such a life," she had argued. "I just want you."

"Then promise me you will wait," he'd pleaded. She had known in that instant that nothing she could say would change his mind.

"I will wait for you to come to your senses, John

Amman," she had told him, tears streaming down her cheeks.

But he never had. No one had seen or heard from him—certainly not Lydia. His family had worn their shame like a hair shirt until the day they sold their farm and moved back to Pennsylvania. Lydia's father had forbidden any mention of John in his presence. Her mother was dead. Greta was too young to understand what had happened, and Pleasant—in those days—had not been someone that either Greta or Lydia could go to for solace.

So Lydia had turned all of her attention to her teaching, pouring herself into the lives of her students and their families and quickly establishing her place in the community. Through the years there had been hints that this man or that was interested in her and would be a good provider. But when it had come to even considering a match with any other man, Lydia had refused. She had loved only one man in her life and she would not settle for less—even if that man surely had to be the most obstinate and opinionated man that God had ever set His hand to creating.

She set the rest of the plates around the table and then surrounded them with flatware and glasses, ignoring the low murmur of John's voice and his occasional laughter as he visited with Luke. As she set the last glass in place, the crunch of bicycle tires and buggy wheels on crushed shells told her that other guests were arriving. She gave one final glance at the table to assure herself that nothing was missing and then called out to her sister, "Greta, company." She smoothed her apron and went to greet Pleasant and her family, Levi and Hannah and their children, the bishop and his wife and John's aunt and uncle.

In the clamor surrounding the arrival of the other guests Lydia was certain she would be able to avoid John's presence. Once they sat down for supper she had already planned to let him find a place first and then to take a chair as far from him as possible. The very fact that she was making such elaborate plans told her that John Amman was too much on her mind.

He is here, in Celery Fields and at this party, as he will no doubt be often where you are, she scolded herself silently. *Best get used to it.*

And having made up her mind to face whatever she must to get through the evening Lydia squared her shoulders and went out onto the porch. She greeted the women and invited them to carry their contributions into the kitchen. Then she turned to the men. "Supper is almost ready," she said, and forced herself to meet John's gaze before looking at the gathering of men as a group. "We can sit down as soon as the children have washed their hands."

Clapping her hands, she stepped off the porch and into the yard and called for the children to stop their games. When they immediately abandoned the tree swing and seesaw that Luke had built and came running, she heard Roger Hadwell chuckle.

"The children mind their teacher better than they do their parents," he said. But then Lydia noticed a clouded expression pass over his features. "Just wish there were more of the little ones around," he added softly as he made his way past her and into the house.

"What did he mean by that?" John asked. He and Lydia were the only adults left on the porch.

"Enrollment is down at the school and it may have to be closed," Lydia explained. She was so relieved that his first attempt at conversing with her had nothing to do with their personal history that she was able to speak easily. She saw John's eyes widen in surprise and concern.

"But that's your...that's the way you..."

"Times are hard, John. You know that perhaps better than anyone in Celery Fields. If the school building and land can be put to better purpose for the good of the community then that's the way of it." She herded the children into a single line and pointed to a basin and towel set up on the porch. "Wash your hands," she instructed.

"But what about you—what's best for you?" John persisted. He reached around her to hold open the door so the children could file into the house.

She looked at him for a long moment. "You are still too much with the outside world, John," she said. "You have forgotten the lesson of joy."

"Joy?"

"Jesus first, you last and others in between." She actually ticked off each item on her fingers the same way she might if teaching one of her students the lesson. Embarrassed by her primness, she followed the last child into the house, leaving John standing on the porch.

She had not intended to engage in any true exchange of conversation with him, anything that might let him know more of her life after all this time. Her plan had been to remain polite but distant. Still, the realization that he had forgotten the old ways—the idea that community came first—was just one more bit of evidence that John Amman would struggle against the bonds that the people of Celery Fields lived by.

Why should she concern herself with his happiness? He had left her before and he would leave her again.

After Lydia moved the children into the house, John stayed on the porch staring out over the single street that ran from Luke and Greta's house to the far end of town where the bakery and ice-cream shop sat. He found it hard to absorb how much the community had changed in eight years and yet so much was familiar and comforting about being back here. In the distance he heard a train whistle and he remembered how as a boy he had dreamed about where that train might one day take him, the adventures he might have. The adventures he and Liddy might have together. But the destinations of that train held no attraction for him now. He knew all too well what was out there.

"John?"

Greta stood on the other side of the screen door watching him with an uncertain smile. She was so very different from Lydia in both physical appearance and demeanor. Greta's smile came readily while Lydia's had to be coaxed. Greta's vivacious personality drew people to her while Lydia's reserve kept them at arm's length.

"We are ready for supper," Greta said.

John pulled open the screen door. *"Gut,"* he said with a grin intended to erase the lines of concern from Greta's forehead. "It's been three hours since I last ate."

Greta glanced back at him and then she giggled. "Ah, John Amman, it is good to have you back. We have missed you."

They were still talking and laughing when they entered the large front room where a table stretched into the hallway to accommodate all the adults and children. John paused for a moment to enjoy the scene. This was one of the things he had missed most about the life he'd left behind—this gathering of friends and family on any excuse to share in food and conversation and the special occasions of life. He recalled one time when he had attended a Thanksgiving dinner at the home of his business partner in the outside world. There the adults had sat at a dining-room table set with such obviously expensive crystal and china that John had spent the entire meal worrying that he might break something. The children had been shooed away to the kitchen and a separate table set for them with the more practical everyday crockery.

He liked the Amish way of having all generations in one room much better, he decided as he pulled out a vacant chair. He glanced around until he located Lydia taking a seat on the same side of the table but with the safety of his aunt and three small children separating them. Luke took his place at the head of the table and all conversation stopped as every head bowed in silent prayer.

John thanked God for the food and for the willingness of the townspeople to forgive him and take him back into the fold of the community—and for second chances. After a long moment he heard Luke clear his throat, signaling that the meal could begin. Instantly the room came alive with the clink of dishes being passed. Conversation buzzed as the adults talked crops and weather while the children whispered excitedly. No doubt they were all anticipating a piece of Samuel's birthday cake—a treat Greta told them would not be forthcoming until every child had devoured all of his or her peas.

From farther down the table he picked out the low murmur of Lydia's voice and found himself leaning forward, straining to catch whatever she was saying to Pleasant's husband, Jeremiah. She was smiling as she cut small slices of the sausage and then placed the meat on Samuel's plate.

It struck John that she performed this task so naturally that she might have been the boy's mother. And for the rest of the meal, while he fielded the questions of those around him about his plans for the future, John found his thoughts going back to a time when he had first thought what a good mother Liddy would be. The time when he had imagined her as the mother of the children they would have together. And he could not help but wonder if she regretted never marrying.

She glanced up then, her gaze meeting his and she did not look away as she continued to speak to young Samuel, reassuring the boy that she had seen his birthday cake and it was his favorite—banana with chocolate frosting. John wondered if she was remembering that this was his favorite, as well. He wondered if she was remembering a day when the two of them had shared a single piece of cake, their fingers sticky with the frosting as they fed each other bites while sitting in the loft of her father's barn.

How they had laughed together that day, and on so many other days. But now her expression was as serious as it had been each time he had seen her since his return. In her eyes he saw questions and could not help but wonder if her questions were the same as his.

Chapter 5

Lydia had managed to convince herself that once she settled into the daily routine of morning and evening chores separated by her duties as teacher, John Amman would be less of a problem for her. Surely, once everyone in Celery Fields returned to the regular business of living and working, John would cease to be the topic of discussion and speculation. He would be busy with his work at the hardware store all day every day except Sundays. The chores he had taken on for Luke in exchange for living above the livery would occupy him in the early mornings and after the store had closed for the day.

But when she returned home on Monday she found a basket filled with oranges next to her door. There were orange trees in Greta's yard and her first thought was that the gift had come from her sister. But she and

Greta had sat on the back porch after they'd finished cleaning up after the party on Sunday and Lydia had noticed that the fruit on her sister's tree was not quite ripe enough to pick yet.

"The tree outside Luke's shop is loaded with fruit," Greta had said. "Every day he brings me a basket filled with the largest, sweetest oranges I've ever tasted."

Lydia hesitated before reaching for the basket. She glanced down toward the livery where she could see the tree, its orange bounty reflected in the bright sunlight of late afternoon. The tree stood just outside the stables at the back of Luke's shop and she was well aware it was a tree that John passed every time he descended or climbed the stairs to his living quarters.

A square of white paper tucked in with the fruit caught her eye.

"Remember the day we picked oranges?"

She folded the paper slowly as the memory he'd awakened overcame her. They could not have been much more than ten or eleven. It had been Christmastime and the children and their teacher had planned a special program to celebrate the season. Their teacher had sent the older children—Lydia and John among them—to pick oranges from a grove of trees at the Harnischer farm to be handed out as a treat at the end of the evening.

"We will need a gross at least," their teacher had instructed. "How many is that, John Amman?"

"One hundred and forty-four," he'd replied without hesitation. Even then John was good with numbers.

"And there are how many dozen?"

"Twelve."

Their teacher had smiled and then counted the older

children. "There are six of you so how many must each of you bring back?"

"Two dozen," the students had chorused.

"Two dozen of the most perfect specimens you can gather," their teacher had added. "Now off you go."

The other children had finished the task within half an hour of arriving at the orange grove. And so had John. But Lydia had lingered over every orange until he'd lost patience. This one was not as large as that one was. Another had a slight blemish. And wasn't it more desirable to have the fruit's stem and perhaps a leaf or two still showing? But the leaves would dry and wither and that was no good.

"We're going back!" he had shouted.

"I'll be right there," she had replied as she made her way deeper into the grove, oblivious to the waning daylight. The Harnischers had gone away for the holidays to visit relatives and as the shadows lengthened Lydia had been unaware that all the other students, including John, had returned to the school. By the time she realized she was alone and she had wandered to the farthest end of the large grove of trees, it was dark.

She shuddered as she recalled how terrified she'd been as she fumbled blindly along the rows of trees trying to find her way back to the farmhouse and the road so she could return to town. Every night sound that she thought of as almost a lullaby when she lay safe in her bed seemed ominous in the dark. Fallen fruit made the way more challenging as she tripped over the oranges on the ground. By the time she reached the Harnischers' house she was choking back tears.

She knew it was not that late, but in the country the darkness was like a blanket thrown over any possibility of light. There was no moon that night. She knew that her family thought she was at the school rehearsing the pageant with the other children. No one would come looking for her for hours. She had sat on the steps of the porch, her arms wrapped around herself as she cried and tried to think what to do.

Then she had heard a sound, faint and in the distance—someone was calling her name.

"Here!" she had shouted, running toward the sound. "I am here."

She had slipped on the root of a banyan tree and gone sprawling onto her stomach, the breath knocked out of her as she tried without success to call again.

"Liddy Goodloe!"

It was the voice of John Amman. Although the two of them had had their differences over the years, she had never been so happy to hear him calling out to her.

"Here," she managed, and only minutes later he was there beside her, placing a kerosene lantern carefully on the ground as he bent to help her.

"What hurts?" he asked.

"I scraped my palms when I fell," she admitted, holding her hands out to him, "but really, I am all right." She started to stand up but he blocked her way.

"Stay still," he ordered, and he removed his wide-brimmed hat, as if it might block the light while he examined her palms.

"Really, I am…"

He let out a heavy sigh. "Why do you always have to be so stubborn, Liddy Goodloe?"

"I am certainly not as stubborn as you are, John Amman. Now, please move so I can stand up. It's a long way back to town and Dat will be worried."

But instead of doing what she asked, he continued holding her hands as he ran his thumbs lightly over her palms. "You frightened me, Liddy," he said softly. "You said you would be along shortly so I went back with the others. But when it got dark and you still had not come…"

Liddy pulled her fingers free and, with one hand, brushed back his flaxen hair from his forehead. "I did not mean to frighten you, John," she said. She thought she might faint from the rush of pure joy she felt at the realization that he cared, truly cared for her the way she did for him. "We should go back," she said softly.

Without a word John replaced his hat and retrieved the lantern and her basket of oranges. He handed her the lantern, and as they walked back toward town she slipped her hand in his and did not let go.

Remember the day we picked oranges?

"I remember," she whispered as she carried the basket of fruit inside and set it on the table. Then she went to place John's note in the box where she had kept all of her special treasures when she and John were courting.

By the end of his second week in Celery Fields John had settled back into life in the town as if the years he'd spent in the *Englischer* world had been no more than a bad dream. He took up his duties in his uncle's hardware store with a familiarity born of the years he had worked there as a teenager. He waited on customers, filled and delivered orders, and even managed the store on his own one day when his uncle took ill and Gert stayed home to care for him.

He was aware that gossip around town had it that he would one day take over the business permanently, but the Hadwells were still in their prime and it would be years before anything like that might happen. In the meantime, stretching the income of the business to cover the needs of three adults took some doing. To make matters easier on his aunt and uncle, John continued the arrangement of bartering his services at the stables with Luke so that he had no rent to pay and his uncle could keep his wages low. He had revived his habit of going to the bay after finishing work. Twice already he'd brought back buckets of clams and a string of fresh-caught fish that his aunt prepared for the noon meal the three of them always shared at the store. He also planted a kitchen garden behind the store so he could tend it when business was slow, which was often. He planned to give the harvest to his aunt in return for the steady supply of covered dishes she kept bringing him for his supper.

The main problem John faced was trying to decide whether he and Liddy might have a future, after all. She did not appear to be trying to avoid him. They were both so busy with their work that most days he barely caught a glimpse of her and, when he did, she was usually surrounded by others—her sister, her students or some of the women in town. On the one hand he was glad he had some time to consider his options. If he and Liddy were to find their way back to each other he wanted to make sure that this time he would be fully ready for them to start the life they had postponed for all these years.

The one thing his father had taught him was the responsibility of a man to provide properly for his wife and children. Of course, his father had insisted that farming was the only way to do that. In his eyes—

weather notwithstanding—the land was God's gift and the only living a man needed to secure a future for his family. He had never understood John's attraction to building things and found his curiosity about how some machine or tool worked as bordering on dangerous.

"Never mind how it works," he would grumble. "Just thank the Lord that it does."

In spite of his father's disapproval, John had continued to focus his interest on ways he might make a living other than by farming. And Liddy had encouraged that. How many hours had they spent thinking about all the ways he might put his talent for carpentry to use to establish a business once they were married?

They had finally settled on the idea of John setting himself up as a clockmaker and furniture builder. Liddy had assured him that in time his father would come around, even when his father accused him of willfully disobeying his elders and from that day refused to speak further of John's future. Instead, he focused all of his attention and praise on John's younger brothers—boys as dedicated to farming as their father was.

"We'll be fine," Liddy had said repeatedly. But he could not help but recall how her small hands had tightened into fists as if she alone would make sure that everything turned out for the best.

But providing for the family was a man's job and he had been determined to prove himself—to his father and to Liddy. He'd been so sure that she would understand why it was so important for him to succeed.

"But you haven't succeeded, have you?" he muttered to himself as he loaded lumber for a neighbor's new barn onto his uncle's delivery wagon. "It's going to take years before you have enough to support a family—even if Liddy were willing…even if you and she…"

They were both almost thirty years old. Not that age mattered, but if they wanted children…and they did…. Or at least they had once upon a time. Surely she still did want children of her own. In their courting days they had talked often of the offspring they would have, how things would be different for them, how John would encourage them to find the talents God had given them and build a future with those. They had so often talked about how their children would be native Floridians, not transplants like their parents and grandparents. They would have different opportunities.

But what if Lydia had changed her mind? What if having spent years teaching other people's children she had decided that was enough? Night after night John had fought his inclination to go to Liddy's house and ask her point-blank what she was thinking, feeling. And as he considered how he'd failed to achieve anything he began to understand why Lydia might have decided to make a clean break of it with him by refusing to answer his letters. He had asked for and received the forgiveness of his friends and neighbors, but he wondered if God had truly forgiven him for his foolish and prideful ways. What if never having enough to support Liddy and make a home with her was to be God's punishment?

"You're getting ahead of yourself," he muttered as he scooped up the last of the powdered cleaning compound that his uncle used to sweep out the store at the end of every day. "What makes you think she's even interested in a future?"

The bell above the front door jangled. "Be right there," John called, chastising himself for forgetting the turn the latch on the door. On the other hand a customer was a customer. He wiped his hands on a clean rag as he walked to the front of the store.

Of all the people he imagined might be standing just inside the door, her hand still on the doorknob as if she might change her mind and leave, the last person he would have guessed was Liddy Goodloe.

"Oh," she said when she saw him coming toward her, "I thought… I had wanted to… Is Gertrude not here?"

John slowed his step, keeping some distance between them as he might have were he approaching a skittish mare. "Just me, I'm afraid," he replied with a smile. "Can I help?" She was clutching a basket.

"I brought her…these are scraps she needs for… We're making a quilt for Greta's baby," she finally managed. She fumbled with the doorknob. "I'll just…."

John stepped forward and relieved her of the basket. "My aunt will be back tomorrow. I can give these to her then if you like."

"She wanted to work on the quilt this evening. I got delayed at the school and…"

"It's not that far. Why don't I walk them over to Gert's house?"

"I can manage," she replied, seeming to conquer her obvious bout of nerves. She held out her hand for the basket. "Thank you for offering." Her tone again was prim and proper.

"Liddy, don't be stubborn. It's nearly dark and you know there have been some incidents in the town—vagrants wandering through and such."

"The last incident like that was months ago, before…" She pressed her hand to her lips as if to stem the tide of her words.

"Before I wandered into town?" He handed her the basket. "Humor me, Liddy. Let me walk with you to my uncle's house. If you like I'll wait in the shadows. They won't even know I'm there."

"Gert will want me to come inside."

He bit back a smile, knowing she was wavering. "I can wait," he said softly. *For as long as it takes to win you back.*

She chewed her bottom lip as she looked around the store, dimly lit now as the shadows of evening gathered. "All right," she agreed, and then her eyes pinned him with their glitter of determination. "But you will stay back and no one is to know…"

"I'll just put these away," John said, picking up the push broom and bucket of cleaning compound. "Won't be a minute," he added, backing away and afraid that the minute she saw her opportunity she would change her mind and leave.

In the back room he took a minute to remove his hat and smooth his hair, then brush sawdust off his trousers. At the same time he sent up a silent prayer of thanks that God had provided this unexpected opportunity for him to walk with Liddy. It would bring back all the wonderful memories of the times they had kept company together, the times they had laughed together. The times they had stopped under the shadow of a live oak tree and shared a kiss.

"Are you coming or not?" Liddy demanded using her teacher's voice.

"Yah. Ich bin…" He gave his trousers one more swipe with his palms and headed for the front of the store.

Once they were outside he noticed that Liddy kept

glancing around as if she feared being spotted by one of their neighbors. At the end of the street kerosene lanterns lighted her sister's house, but otherwise the thoroughfare was dark. All of the shops were closed for the night, their owners at home finishing their suppers, readying their children for bed or reading their evening Scripture.

"Do you think it might be too late?" Liddy wondered aloud.

"I don't think so. Gert was late leaving the shop this evening and Roger was out making a delivery. I expect they might just be sitting down to their meal."

Lydia stopped walking and seemed about to turn away from the lane leading to the Hadwell house. "I wouldn't want to interrupt their supper," she said.

"But if my aunt needs the scraps for the quilt..." he reminded her. To his relief this seemed to give her the impetus she needed to press on. "When is the baby coming?" he asked, and immediately realized that such a statement could be taken as the invasion of a private family matter among the Amish. "Sorry," he muttered.

"You are going to have to watch your ways, John, if you truly wish to make your place in this community," Liddy admonished him, and the fact that she was frowning in disapproval was evident in her tone.

"Perhaps, but when we were younger Greta was like a sister to me." He chuckled at the memory. "A pesky little sister but nevertheless..."

To his surprise and delight, Liddy laughed. "You came up with so many schemes for escaping her notice," she said.

"And not one of them worked. I doubt those children of hers can get away with much," he added.

Liddy sighed. "It is hard to believe that she's a mother herself, almost four times over now."

"She is certainly providing future students for you to teach," he said. When Liddy grew quiet as they walked away from town and down the lane that led to his uncle's house he knew that once again he had said the wrong thing. Still, having broached the subject, he decided to persevere. "Tell me more about this business of shutting down the school."

"I told you, John. The elders are thinking that for the time being the building and land might be put to better use. They will do what is best."

"But if a community is to thrive, surely it needs to have a school," he argued.

"Whatever the children need to learn can be taught at home," she replied, but her voice sounded as if she were simply repeating some argument given for closing the school. "And these hard times are bound to pass. Once more people come here to live, we can start another school."

"And what about—"

"Ah, here we are," she interrupted as they approached the gate that led to the small cottage his uncle and aunt occupied. "Wait here. I won't be long."

He crouched down in the gathering darkness, resting his elbows on his knees while she walked up the path and knocked on the front door. Her voice and his aunt's were muffled, but the tone of their words told him that Gert had invited her inside and she had refused. He heard her laugh as she retreated down the porch steps and called out her good-night. How he had missed the lilt of that laughter!

He was about to rise to meet her when he heard her

hiss, "Stay down." Then she turned back toward the house and waved. *"Guten nacht,"* she called out.

John watched as Liddy continued on her way back toward town. If his aunt were watching she would see only Liddy walking with her usual determined stride.

"Well, come along," she said in a normal tone when she'd already gotten several yards past him.

He caught up to her and she started to walk faster. He kept pace and even moved a little ahead of her as he turned to face her. She giggled as she raced past him. Then they both started to run as they had when they were children and had just gotten away with avoiding Greta or John's stern father and were running off to the shore to wade in the shallow water and collect shells. And it was the most natural thing in the world for John to grasp her hand in his as they ran back toward town.

Lydia was not only giggling like one of her students, she was also gasping for breath by the time she and John reached her front porch. It felt like old times—the two of them out together on some adventure, the wind in their faces and hair, her one hand clutching his while the other held fast to her bonnet. Their fingers were so entwined that it was as if he never intended to let go and Lydia found that she liked that feeling—she liked it very much.

Too much, she thought as caution and common sense overcame her giddiness. She slid her hand from his and pressed it to her chest as she forced her breathing to slow. "Thank you for going with me, John. You were right—I would have been nervous in the dark alone," she admitted. "And I did not thank you for the oranges you left for me. They were very…sweet."

It was the wrong word but the only one that came to mind. She found that she could not look at him, and yet even if she closed her eyes she could see him clearly: the wide smile that lit his entire face as if his features had been bathed in sunlight; the eyes that twinkled and teased and dared her to take the kinds of risks that he had more often than she cared to recall talked her into taking as teenagers; the mouth that so often had kissed hers in those long ago years.

A moment before she had been babbling like a brook, the words tumbling out almost faster than she could think them. But with the sudden image of his lips meeting hers she felt as if she had been struck dumb.

"Guten nacht, John," she whispered as she prepared to flee such thoughts of him in favor of the secure isolation of her house. But he caught hold of her hand before she could move more than a step away from him.

And then he waited. John had never been more eloquent than when he said nothing. Everything he might have said was contained in the compelling silence that was heavy with expectation and unasked questions.

"John," she whispered, and her voice was a plea that she could not have defined. Was she asking him to stop or to come closer? Did she want him to leave or to stay? She had no idea what her feelings were. "You confuse me," she added petulantly.

He chuckled and stroked her cheek with the tips of his fingers. She closed her eyes, savoring that touch.

"Gut," he replied as he kissed her lightly on her forehead.

And then he was gone.

* * *

Slow and steady, John reminded himself as he walked from Lydia's house to his rooms above the stables. And although he had to fight against the urge to look back at her, he kept walking, knowing she was still standing where he'd left her. He could not keep the smile off his face. He had his answer. Whatever she had felt about his leaving all those years earlier he was sure now she was glad he was back. A man could build something on that.

Later, as he lay in bed waiting for sleep to come, he thought about the many good days he'd had since returning to Celery Fields. That first day when he'd gone to the school and Lydia had walked into the schoolroom. Later, when he'd surprised his aunt. The meeting with Bishop Troyer when he'd known by the man's kindness and complete absence of censure that he would be forgiven. Then, that Sunday when he had stood before the congregation—some faces familiar while others were new to him—and without question they had welcomed him back into the fold of their community.

All except Lydia.

She had maintained her caution and reserve, while remaining polite.

Until tonight.

He folded his hands behind his head and gazed out the small window at a strip of clouds sailing across the moon. The way things were going he had every reason to hope that he might win her back. They might have a real future just like the one they had planned years earlier.

Slowly John's smile and the high spirits behind it dissolved into the worried frown that had been his con-

stant companion when he and Lydia had first talked of
marriage. Nothing had changed. Or maybe now things
were worse than they'd been when he left. He still had
no means to start a business of his own—he was a carpenter with no tools. And he could hardly expect to earn
enough from clerking at the hardware store to make the
kind of life he wanted for Liddy.

He sat up, his bare feet resting on the polished floor,
his fingers buried in his hair as he realized that unlike
before when he'd so foolishly left, these days he lit-
erally had nothing to offer Liddy. Everything he had
earned in the world was gone, taken by creditors along
with the business he'd built with George Stevens, the
son of a wealthy *Englischer* family. The Stevenses had
absorbed their son's part of the losses. They had even
offered John some money "to tide him over" but he
had refused.

"You'll do all right," his partner had assured him.
"You've got a gift for building things, fine things that
one day people will be wanting again," he added.
"These hard times won't last forever, John, and one
day…"

John couldn't afford to dwell on *one day*. He needed
to find work he could do today and tomorrow and next
year. He thought about some of the furniture pieces he
had designed and built—pieces that were then mass
produced in their factory and sold to stores all up and
down the East Coast. Tables and chests and bureaus
and desks. And the clocks. How he had loved figuring
out the intricate workings of fine clocks—each cog and
wheel and wire set just so.

But those days are gone, as are my tools, he reminded himself as he flopped back on the bed and

stared at the ceiling. He had a trade, a skill with which he might make a decent living, but without the tools or the money it would take to purchase lumber and the other materials he would need, how was he going to build a business? And without a way of earning a living, there could be no future for him with Liddy.

He closed his eyes against the sting of tears. What a mess he'd made of everything. He and Liddy were no longer teenagers flush with the certainty of youth that all things were possible. "Oh, Liddy, what are we going to do?"

He got up and paced the confines of the tiny apartment, finally coming to rest at the kitchen window that looked down on Liddy's house, which was dark now. She would be sleeping. But then he saw a light in the window of an upstairs room and the silhouette of Liddy herself seated in a chair, her head bent as if in prayer. And even though he had no idea whether she was also struggling with thoughts of the evening they had shared—of his touch, his light kiss on her forehead—he needed to believe that such a thing was likely. Because believing that she held him in her thoughts and prayers, he would find a way.

God would show him a way.

Chapter 6

Lydia saw John only from a distance over the next several days. Sometimes when she was on her way to school she would see him grooming one of the horses from Luke's livery. He would pause for a moment in his work and lift his hand, palm out, to her. At first she simply nodded in his direction and kept walking. But after a week of such silent greetings she found herself responding in kind. She took some pleasure in the blossoming of his smile when he saw her return the special signal they had devised in their youth.

Each of them worked long hours and they both had chores. Ever since the evening that John had walked with her to the Hadwells' and then seen her home again, Lydia had begun staying after school to tutor a child, correct the children's work or prepare the lessons for the following day. After a few days she realized that she was unconsciously timing her departure from the school for when John might be finishing his work at the hardware store. Such schoolgirl foolishness was more Greta's way than Lydia's and yet she simply could not seem to help herself. John Amman was constantly in her thoughts.

Not that her careful timing did any good. Even if she stayed at school until nearly suppertime, John was always still at the hardware store. She knew Roger and Gert closed at five, as did every other merchant in Celery Fields. But many an evening John stayed there until well after dark. What could he be doing?

Unable to suppress her curiosity, she left school one day at her regular time, went home and spent some time squeezing lemons from Greta's garden to make lemonade. She told herself that her purpose was to use the lemons before they spoiled, and then she ended up with far more of the product than she could hope to use herself. It was only prudent that she share.

Through her open kitchen window she heard the rhythmic sound of a handsaw passing back and forth across a piece of lumber. The sound was faint but definitely coming from the rear of the hardware. It was well past five. The sun was low on the horizon, but the heat and humidity that earlier had led Lydia to release the children to sit under the shade of a banyan tree to work on their lessons had not abated.

Before she could change her mind or overanalyze her motives, Lydia filled a crockery pitcher with the fresh lemonade, chipped in some ice from the block that Jeremiah had delivered to her earlier that week and carried the pitcher and two glasses outside to the porch. Her plan was to sit on the swing and wait until she saw

John walking from the store to the steps leading up to his rooms. She would offer him the lemonade, as she would to any neighbor she saw coming home from a long, hot working day, she told herself firmly.

With her plan decided she took her place on the swing. From this vantage point she had a clear view of the stables with the stairway that led up to John's rooms as well as the hardware store. She poured half a glass of lemonade for herself. Then she realized that it would be odd for her to simply be sitting idly sipping lemonade at this time of day. She should be doing something—reading or needlework.

She went back inside and retrieved her sewing basket. Taking her place again on the porch swing, she pulled out the pieces for a nine-patch quilt square and began stitching them together. Yes, this was better. She could keep an eye on things and yet not appear to be laying in wait.

But as the shadows lengthened and it became harder to see the small pieces of the patchwork, much less measure her stitches properly, Lydia grew restless. The sounds of the wind rustling the large palm fronds, dry from the days without rain, were usually a comfort to her after a long day at school. Tonight the sound grated on her nerves. Through the open window she could hear the clock in the front room clicking off the seconds as the brass hands made their way toward six-thirty. The chatter of the birds as they settled into the shrubs surrounding her house for the night seemed louder than usual. A horse in the stables whinnied. The ice in the pitcher settled into melting.

And still John stayed at the hardware. She saw the unmistakable glow of a lantern spilling its light onto the loading dock through the open back door of the shop. The sawing had been replaced by hammering, a light tapping that matched the restless rhythm of her foot.

"This is ridiculous," Lydia muttered as she put aside her sewing and stood. Without bothering to retrieve her bonnet, she picked up the extra glass and the pitcher of watery lemonade and struck out across the yard toward the rear of the hardware store. With each step she told herself that she simply needed to satisfy her curiosity about what John was doing at the shop so late. It was nothing more than that. She would take him the cool beverage on the pretense of having noticed that he was still working. She would see whatever he was doing and, satisfied at last, she would walk home and get some rest.

But when she reached the hardware's loading dock, she stopped short, her mouth open in surprise and admiration. Inside John had set his hammer aside and was sanding the arms of the most beautiful rocking chair Lydia had ever seen. It was small and slender and the lines were as graceful as the woman who would surely sit there cradling her child.

"Is that for Greta?" she asked as she climbed the three steps to the loading dock.

John glanced up and grinned. "Shh," he whispered, putting his finger to his lips. "Luke wants it to be a surprise." He stood and set the sanding block on a stool near the chair. "Is that for me?" he asked, nodding toward the pitcher and glass she held as he wiped his forehead with the back of his arm.

He was so incredibly handsome, his features lit by the soft glow of the lantern. Lydia felt her heart race, and her hand shook a little as she filled a glass and handed it to him. "It's watery," she said.

He drank it down without pausing for breath and held the glass out for her to refill. "It's perfect," he replied.

He was not wearing his hat. His hair was damp with sweat and clung to the edges of his face. He had rolled back his sleeves, exposing tanned and muscular forearms, and he was covered in a fine coat of sawdust.

"This is very kind of you, making a chair for Greta," she began, needing to say something to break the silence that surrounded them, a silence filled with unspoken possibilities.

"Not kind at all. Luke hired me to do it. Seems he preferred not to do business with Josef Bontrager even though from what I've been told Josef has the furniture-making trade pretty well sewn up in these parts."

"Greta will be very surprised. She already has a rocking chair, the one our mother used when we were born."

John frowned. "Do you think she won't want to replace that one? Luke tells me that after three children already, the chair is in need of some repair. Maybe he should have…"

Instinctively she placed her hand on his arm. "She will be very, very pleased," she assured him.

John drank the second glass of lemonade more slowly than the first. "Come to think of it, I seem to recall that Greta and Josef Bontrager were pretty close. What happened?"

"They were just children in those days. Greta and Luke are a good match and Josef seems to have made an equally good match with the Yoders' eldest daughter, Esther. It has all turned out well, as God intended," Lydia assured him.

John grinned. "It certainly has for me. Luke is paying

me a nice sum to make this chair for Greta, and if others see the work, perhaps they will…" He stopped abruptly.

She hated the shadow of defeat that passed over his features. He set down the empty glass and took up his sanding block again.

"It's just something I was able to do for Luke," he told her. "Roger said I could use the space here and his tools in the evenings to work on it. With the money Luke is paying me I can start replacing some of the tools that I used to have."

Lydia waited for him to say more but he just worked the sanding block across the curve of the rockers.

"Will you tell me what happened, John?" Lydia set the pitcher next to his glass and folded her arms in her apron as she leaned against the doorjamb. She knew that she should simply let the past go, but she had so many questions.

He shrugged and kept on working, not looking at her. "Surely you know the story. It's the same for everyone out there. Things were going well—and then they weren't."

"You made a good living then?"

"For a while. Most of the time."

She could see that the memory caused him pain so she stopped asking about it. Instead, she watched him work. "Have you eaten?" she asked after several minutes.

"Yah." He did not look at her and she wondered if he was still lost in the thoughts of happier times, before he'd been forced to come back to Celery Fields. And from there logic took her to the more obvious point.

He had come home to Celery Fields. That did not mean he had come back because of her. John had a ready smile and friendly wave for everyone he saw. Why was she imagining that she was special to him? Or was it John's true motive to win her back because out in the world he had fallen so far that he had decided she represented a safe haven? He had come back to his past and she was nothing more to him than a part of that past. She was making a fool of herself for all the town to see.

Without a word she collected the pitcher and glass and walked back out to the loading dock.

"Wait," he called.

"It's late," she replied, and kept walking.

John caught up to her before she cleared the last step of the loading dock. He closed his fingers around her upper arms and turned her so that she was facing him. "It's hard, Liddy," he said. "Going back over those times—the fool I made of myself, the losses I suffered."

"But you are back now and safe again."

"And you think that's what I want? When did I want what was safe, Liddy? When did *you* want that?"

Finally she looked up at him and in the light spilling out from the shop he saw that she studied him not with the longing and love he'd hoped for, but with pity. He released her arm and stepped back.

"We were so young then, John." He hated the way her lips pursed in the disapproving manner of their former teacher.

"You were not a child that Sunday when you decided to take your place with the married women at services," he reminded her. "That was an act of defiance by the girl I once knew, the girl I…"

Her expression softened as she pressed her fingers

over his lips. "Do not say things you will regret," she whispered. "Please. You are too soon trying to set things the way you remember them, the way you want them to be. But you are not the boy who left here, John. And I am not that girl. We cannot go back in this world— only forward."

She pulled away from him and continued walking back to her house—*her* house, *her* school, *her* life.

"We could be if you're willing to work things out with me," he said, and was gratified to see her step falter. "We could find a way to…"

She turned around but her features remained in shadow. "I am glad that you've come home, John. Is that not enough for now?"

"It's a beginning," he admitted. "But…"

"And that's the point, John Amman. We are beginning again and you must allow time for things to develop according to God's will." She took half a step toward him and stopped. "You must think of me as someone you are just getting to know, John."

"Is that how you see me? As some stranger?"

"Not a stranger exactly. Just not…" Her voice trailed off.

"Just not the same person you once loved?"

For a long moment she said nothing. Then very softly she said, "There are glimpses of him, John Amman. That I will grant you, but it has been eight years and whether you are willing to admit it or not, each of us has changed—grown, hopefully—taught and shaped by the lives we have lived while apart."

He knew she was right but he didn't want her to be. "So what are we, Liddy?" He knew he sounded annoyed.

"We have made a good start as neighbors."

He snorted. "Neighbors? I barely see you these days."

"Friends, then—friends who have not seen each other for many years and are looking forward to getting reacquainted."

He could see that it was the best answer he was likely to get on this occasion. "Truly? You're looking forward to getting to know me again?"

She laughed and the lightness of it floated on the air between them. "I am, John Amman. I seem to remember that you were always a most interesting man. Now, *guten nacht.*"

He let her go, watching until she let herself into the dark house, waiting for the light in the window of the front room that never came.

Lydia was actually shaking as she stepped inside the dark house and closed the door behind her with a soft click. It wasn't a chill or fear that overcame her. It was her understanding that after all these years—after assuring herself that she had made a life for herself—she still had deep feelings for John. But surely such feelings were born of reflection on things past. John's very presence in Celery Fields was bound to stir up scenes they had shared when they were younger. His laughter would naturally bring back those times when they had laughed together. His touch would evoke the sensation of times in the past when he had held her hand, stroked her cheek, kissed her.

She closed her eyes against the flood of sensations that swept through her as she leaned against the closed door. Having John Amman back in town was going to be much harder than she could have imagined.

"Well, there's nothing for it but to take things one day at a time," she admonished herself. She pushed away from the door and in the dark went through the familiar regimen of preparing for the next day's teaching and for bed. But, after assembling the items she would need for the following school day, she bypassed the rocking chair in the front room where she was accustomed to ending her day by reading passages from her Bible and silently praying for her students, her family and her neighbors.

Her chair, the one her father had sat in when he was alive, was nothing at all like the chair that John had been making for Greta. But it was enough that it was a rocking chair and that alone brought to mind the image of the beautifully shaped wood, the smooth gracefulness of the back and arms, the sheer simple beauty of John's handiwork. From there it took little to make the leap to recalling her fingers touching his lips. She found herself standing next to her father's rocking chair, her fingers moving slowly over her own lips.

"You are being ridiculous, Lydia Goodloe," she said as if she were lecturing one of her students. "Go to bed."

She followed her own advice but sleep did not come. Instead, she lay awake next to the open window. Every night sound seemed exaggerated and she kept thinking she was hearing the swoosh of a handsaw slicing into wood or the light tapping of a hammer. Surely John was not still at work on the chair. Like her he had to work long hours the following day, and yet she recalled that even as a boy he had been single-minded when it came to completing an important project. And John would see the perfection of that chair as vital to his goal of impressing Luke and anyone else who might see his handiwork.

Lydia frowned. He was clearly aware that Josef Bontrager had been the carpenter that the people of Celery Fields had turned to for years. John must understand that loyalty, if nothing else, would keep them from abandoning Josef in favor of buying from him. And, besides, there were two other issues that made questionable his chances of succeeding in establishing himself as a furniture maker. For one thing, the families still living in Celery Fields had been there for years and their homes were already furnished. And second, even if someone did need to replace a cabinet or chair, most likely the purchase would be postponed until the economy was stable again.

She should warn him of the folly of his plan.

Why me? Surely his uncle…

But I know him so well.

She sat up and pulled the heavy braid of her hair over one shoulder, fingering the ends that curled round her forefinger as she tried to calm herself. Again she thought John Amman was too much on her mind. From the moment she'd seen him kneeling next to the stove at the schoolhouse he had been a constant presence, and she was only fooling herself if she believed that living practically next door to the man was going to be easy.

Didn't she have troubles enough of her own to worry about? If the school closed and she had no income she would have to consider selling this house, and then what? Move in with Greta? Pleasant? She shuddered at the image of the rest of her life spent as the spinster aunt whose only purpose in life was to make herself useful so as not to be a burden to her sisters and their husbands. Yes, she had more than enough to worry about without adding John Amman to the list. Neighbors? Fine. Friends? Of course. But anything more? Far too risky.

After Liddy left, John returned to the shop and continued working on the chair. Only now, as he sanded and stained the smooth wood, he imagined he was making a chair for Liddy. He imagined them married and her rocking their child and singing softly to the baby. As he recalled she had a lovely voice, as sweet and clear as the air on a spring morning. He pictured the way she would look up at him from under her long lashes, her eyes brimming with love for him and their baby.

Liddy would be a wonderful mother.

But what kind of a father would he be? How would his natural inclination toward restlessness and adventure affect their children?

He paused in his work and closed his eyes.

How long would it be before he could no longer stand the sameness of the life he'd come home to in Celery Fields? At least when he was building something, he had the freedom of his creative imagination. There were always problems to be solved so that the piece turned out different.

He set down his paintbrush and wiped his hands on a rag. That was the crux of it. John had always been different, had always needed to stray from the path set for him first by his parents and then by his community. But, while he readily admitted that he had rebelled against those norms, he had never in all of his life felt that he was straying from the way God was leading him. Even when he left Celery Fields, he had felt he was doing what God intended him to do.

At first, he reminded himself sternly. For he had left with the best of intentions to go out and earn the money he would need to return, establish a business and marry Liddy. But when she had not replied to his letters—when there had been no word at all—he had turned his mind to the ways of the outsiders. Making his fortune became the one driving force that got him up every morning, and in time it had replaced everything else—his family, his religion…even Liddy.

Liddy. Liddy. Liddy.

She was everything he wanted in this life and yet he had nothing to offer her.

Chapter 7

After that night, Lydia managed to keep her distance from John until the community gathered once again for their biweekly worship. But avoiding him at Sunday services and especially at the social gathering afterward proved more difficult. As she carried food out to the gathering in Josef Bontrager's large yard, John never seemed to be more than a few feet away from her. And even though he was engaged in conversation with the other men, his soft voice settled around her like blossoms from an orange tree blown free by a tropical breeze. When she sought refuge inside the large farmhouse, assuring Josef's wife, Esther, that she simply needed a break from the heat, she certainly did not expect to wander into the front room and find John there.

He was running the flat of his palm over the closed cover of Josef's tilt-top desk. The piece dominated one corner of the otherwise mostly barren front room. The expression on John's face was hard to read, but Lydia decided that it showed something between admiration and disappointment. Either way, she felt that it would not do for her to interrupt his reverie or for others to see them alone together. She turned to go.

"Josef Bontrager is a fine carpenter," John said without turning.

"Yah." She was rooted to the spot, one foot half-turned to leave.

"I can see why he's earned the loyalty of his customers," he continued, moving on to the fireplace, studying the way Josef had so expertly matched the wood grain of each side piece and crossbeam the way a woman might precisely match the square of a quilt to form a border between the rows.

As the sun streamed in through the open windows, Lydia was glad for the breeze that filled the room with the fragrance of the bougainvillea blossoms matting the trellis outside the open window. She stepped into the room, the leather heels of her shoes echoing on the bare wooden floor that an hour earlier had been filled with the benches used for worship, benches now moved outside.

John turned to her with a wry smile. "My uncle has repeatedly reminded me that there is not much call for handmade furniture these days—hard times."

The words held an aura of bitterness and regret that seemed to cover him like a cloak. Lydia instinctively stepped closer as she searched for any gesture that might offer some comfort. "The chair you are making for Greta is fine," she said.

He smiled. "Are you complimenting me twice in one week, Lydia Goodloe?"

"I am simply stating a truth," she replied, hating the edge of contention that colored her words. Why did she always have to sound so prudish when she spoke with him?

"I could make you a chair—or a desk or anything you might like," he said, moving away from the fireplace and closer to her.

"My father furnished our home when he was alive. Besides, I have no money for such…" He kept coming until he was standing so near that if she moved an inch his breath would surely fan her suddenly hot cheeks.

"It would be a gift," he said, his eyes roaming over her features, her hair and finally settling on her eyes. "I have missed seeing you these last days, Liddy."

As have I missed you. "I was at the school and the evenings I spent with Greta helping her with the little ones. She has not been feeling well." *That's right. Stay with mundane, impersonal topics. Neighborly, friendly topics.*

John frowned. "The baby?"

It was not appropriate that she should discuss such matters with him—no woman would. But she was worried and, because she had promised Greta that she would say nothing to anyone lest talk get back to Luke, she had kept her concerns to herself. But this was John and she had always been able to confide in him.

"I'm worried," she admitted.

He lifted his hand as if to touch her then lowered it back to his side. "Can I help?"

She realized that he already was. The relief that flooded her with the ability to finally say aloud the thoughts she had carried with her for days now was like a great weight had been taken from her.

"You know Greta," she said, the words flowing like a rushing stream now. "She is determined to put on a brave face, but when it is just the two of us I see that she is so very uncomfortable. With the first three babies she had no problems at all, but this time is different."

"I can see now that Luke is also concerned. He's been quieter than usual these last days. I thought perhaps his distraction was due to the fact that business is slow, as it is for everyone. I expect he understands more than Greta realizes."

"Yes, they are so loving and caring with each other. Luke wants her to agree to see one of his customers, an *Englischer* doctor from Sarasota, but she refuses. She insists that she will be fine with the catcher."

John smiled. "I haven't heard that term for a very long time, Liddy."

"Do they not have catchers in the outside?"

His smile broadened. "Only in the game of baseball," he said with a chuckle. "Never applied to the woman who attends the mother in a birthing."

"Greta will be in good hands."

"Hilda Yoder is still the catcher for Celery Fields?" Lydia nodded.

"She has certainly been present for the delivery of her share of the children of Celery Fields," John said. "And if Greta trusts her…"

"Oh, she does. Everyone does. It's just that…" Unexpectedly her eyes filled with tears. "Oh, John if I were to lose Greta…"

He caught the single escaping tear with his thumb. "She's not going to die," he said softly.

"You can't know that," she argued, but she did not pull away from his touch.

"No," he said softly. "Just like you can't be sure that she might, so why worry about something we cannot control?"

He had a point. Lydia gave him a tentative smile. "You were always one to find the brighter side of the matter," she said.

He chuckled, his thumb still lightly touching her cheek. "And you were always the worrier."

Behind them a woman cleared her throat and they turned to find Hilda Yoder frowning at them. "Here you are, Lydia," she said, as if making a pronouncement for all those in the yard to hear. "I thought you must have already gone back to town to see how Greta is doing. I cannot recall a time when she and Luke missed services. We are all quite worried."

Lydia put several steps between herself and John by heading for the door where Hilda stood waiting. "There's no need for concern, Hilda. Greta is just a bit under the weather."

"Still, it would ease all our minds to know that you were with her—at this time," she added with a look that conveyed her reluctance to mention Greta's pregnancy.

"Yes, you are right. I was just about to…"

"Let me drive you there," John said.

"I really do not think that you and Lydia should be seen…" Hilda began.

But John gave her the smile that Lydia remembered charming every female in Celery Fields, regardless of her age, from the time John was a young boy. "Ah, now Hilda Yoder, let me do my part in setting your mind at rest. As it happens my uncle and aunt and I were late coming this morning so there was no time to stable their horse. Why spend time hitching up Liddy's buggy when God has already seen to our having one ready to go?"

Lydia saw what he was doing. By turning things around so that he seemed to be trying to put Hilda at ease he would no doubt win her approval.

"Well, I suppose…perhaps I should ride along, then."

"That might be all right," John said hesitantly as he frowned and scratched his clean-shaven chin.

"But?" Hilda asked impatiently.

"Well, that might give folks the wrong idea about Liddy here. With you appearing to be acting as chaperone, it might look like we had taken up courting again and, well, it's just that…"

Lydia thought her cheeks must be ready to burst into actual flames. "Really, John, I can—"

"No, John is absolutely right," Hilda interrupted. "The two of you go along, and should there be speculation I'll be here to assure everyone that it is exactly what it appears to be—John giving you a ride so you can get to Greta's as quickly as possible. You should take along some of the food we haven't yet put out," she added, leading the way to the kitchen, where she loaded a basket with partially filled containers of their meal. She handed the basket to Lydia. "For Luke and the children, even if Greta doesn't feel like eating."

"Greta will appreciate your thoughtfulness," Lydia said.

"Well, go on," Hilda instructed. "I'll tell Roger and Gert that they need to drive your buggy back to town, Lydia." She shooed the two of them out the back door in the direction of the barn, where a row of identical black buggies sat lined up at precise angles to one another.

John helped Lydia onto the seat and then waved to Hilda as he climbed up and took the reins. "That was close," he murmured with a grin.

Lydia could not help herself. She burst into laughter and nearly choked trying to cover her mirth as he guided the buggy past the house and out to the road with Hilda Yoder still watching them from the back porch. The tears that spilled down her cheeks were of pure joy, and she could not remember a time when she had felt so lighthearted.

Then she saw John give her a sideways glance, his own face wreathed in a smile, his eyes twinkling with mischief, and she remembered that there had been times—many of them—when she had felt this way. Back when she and John had been courting, there had been so many times like this.

"I see Hilda Yoder hasn't changed much," John said as he let the reins go slack, knowing the horse would find the way back to town without his help. "When we were children she was always kind of the town overseer, and that seems to still be her role."

"She means well."

He glanced at Lydia, aware that in the close confines of the buggy their shoulders would touch whenever the vehicle swayed. He sent up a silent prayer of thanks for rutted roads.

"I expect there is someone like Hilda in most small communities," Liddy added, "someone who takes it upon herself to make sure things run smoothly—or at least the way she believes is right and proper."

"You've got a point. My partner's mother was that woman when…"

He stopped talking. Rarely, since he'd returned to Celery Fields, had he allowed himself to speak of those years he'd spent living in the outside world. He knew that his neighbors did not wish to hear about such things—certainly Liddy would not want to know the details of his life then. Even if she had raised the question herself that night when he was working on Greta's chair.

They rode in silence for several minutes, the mood now stifled by his slip of the tongue.

"What was it like?" Liddy murmured so softly that at first he wasn't certain she had really spoken. "Out there, what was it like, John?"

He took a moment to consider his answer. How much should he say? How much did she really want to know?

"Did you like that life?" Liddy asked before he could find words to answer her initial question.

"It was…it was so very different from life here," he began, glad that the horse seemed content to plod slowly along, giving them more time. "At first it was all so strange. Their ways are not our ways. It took time for me to find my place."

"And did you find your place in their world?" There was no accusation or judgment in her words, just curiosity.

"Once I met George Stevens, things got easier." He smiled at the memory of that first meeting with the man who would become his friend and business partner. "I had taken a job with his father's company. The building industry was booming and new orders were coming every day. One day George's father brought George to me and told me that my job was to take him in hand, teach him how to do the work I was doing."

"And you became friends?"

John chuckled. "Not at first. George certainly wasn't used to working with his hands. I think he began to hate me a little in those early days, but I knew that his father was preparing him to take over the business and he believed that to be successful you had to know everything about it."

"So you became a teacher."

"I suppose you could say that. In time, as we worked, we started to talk. He'd had a harder life than I first thought. His father was a true taskmaster, and especially with George. Then his father was in an accident and suddenly George was in charge." He shook his head. "It's still hard for me to understand, but the very next day he called me to his father's office—his office then—and promoted me to foreman for the entire company. A year later, after his father died, he made me a partner in the business."

"But surely as a partner you would need money to invest…"

"I had built up quite a savings by then," he said, and swallowed the words that would have reminded her that his whole purpose in going away had been to make the money necessary to return and start his own business and marry her. "George could never understand what he called my 'living on the cheap.'" He smiled. "He spent money almost before he had it in hand. Anyway, he offered me stock in the company at a price that would take all my savings—two years' worth—but would make me a major shareholder."

"And you gave him your money?"

Now he heard the faintest hint of disapproval creep into her voice. He tightened his grip on the reins. *"Yah,"* he said, and snapped the reins to urge the horse into a faster pace.

"So what happened?"

John's lips thinned into a hard line as he recalled those difficult times. "The stock market crashed and it seemed like overnight everything just changed. People had no money for clocks or furniture—or to pay for furniture that they had already ordered. The company was heavily invested in bad stocks and had to close up shop."

"And the money you had invested?"

"Gone. Everything was gone—my savings, my job, my ability to find work…" *You and the life we had planned together.*

"But surely your friend was in the same position and the two of you…"

"First of all, he'd lost his business and a lot of money in the bargain, but he still had his family and the means to make it through. Times would be hard, but he assured me that the day would come when things would be better again and then the two of us would start fresh."

"So he was able to help see you through these—"

"That is not their way, Liddy. He offered me a loan, but how was I ever going to repay him?"

"What did you do?"

This was the part of his story that John was most reluctant to talk about. He shut his eyes against the images of begging for handouts and working in the citrus groves picking fruit for hours and hours in exchange for a place to sleep and a hot meal. "I came back here," he said after a moment. *I came home to you.*

In silence they approached the cluster of shops and homes that made up the center of Celery Fields. Just before John turned the buggy onto the street that led to

Greta and Luke's house, Liddy reached over and covered his hand with hers.

"You made the right decision," she said, and her hand remained on his, her warmth seeping into his fingers and spreading up his arm to settle in his chest as he pulled the buggy to a stop.

Lydia was glad for the wide brim of her bonnet that hid her face from John. His story of the years he had spent away from her had not only touched her, it had infuriated her. So much time wasted and lost when they might have shared those years. And what of this so-called friend and business partner? Did he not care that while he apparently remained in his home with his family, John was left to make do as best he could? What kind of people were these *Englischers?* By the time she stepped down from the buggy she was fuming about how the people who had called themselves John's friends had abandoned him. So lost in her own thoughts was she that she marched straight up to the front door and entered her sister's house without knocking.

"Tante Lydia!" Samuel shouted as he came racing toward her from the back of the house.

Almost immediately Luke stepped into the hallway, shushing the boy as he tried to balance the two younger children, one in each arm. Lydia immediately reached to relieve him of one of the children, but he shook his head. "I've got them. Could you go and see about Greta?" His eyes shifted toward the stairs and Lydia saw that he looked more haggard and worried than usual. "She's been ill all through the afternoon."

Lydia turned to mount the stairs and saw John waiting uncertainly in the doorway, the basket of food in his hand. "We brought this for you and the children, Luke. Perhaps John could help feed the children while you make Greta some tea?"

To her relief John did not shy away from the duty she had assigned him. Instead, he looped the handle of the basket over one arm and scooped Samuel into the other. "I'm starving," he announced. "How about you?"

"Me, too," Samuel agreed, and the other two children echoed his words.

As he passed the stairway on his way to follow Luke to the kitchen, John glanced up at her. In his eyes she saw his concern for her and for Greta and also his assurance that he had things in hand with Luke and the children. She could focus on her sister.

Lydia removed her bonnet on her way up the stairs, and when she reached the landing she followed the sound of low moaning to the large bedroom at the end of the hall. As soon as she saw her sister, she dropped her bonnet onto a dresser and ran to the bedside where Greta was thrashing about. Her eyes were closed, her lips were parched and her forehead gleamed with perspiration.

Lydia soaked a cloth in a nearby basin of tepid water and wiped her sister's face, smoothing back the strands of golden hair that clung to Greta's cheeks. "Shh," she crooned. "I'm here now."

Greta's eyes flew open and she tried to sit up. "Services are over? What time is it? Luke and the children haven't eaten and…"

Gently Lydia pushed her back onto the pillows. "They are eating now. I brought a basket of food from services and John is downstairs helping Luke with the children."

"John? Here? With you?" She managed a smile. "Progress at last," she murmured as she relaxed against the pillows and closed her eyes. After several more minutes of restlessness, her breathing settled into the steady rhythm of sleep.

Lydia studied her sister's wan face. After a moment she rested her hand on the mound of Greta's stomach and then instantly removed it when she felt the movement of the child inside. What would it feel like to carry a living being? What would a child of hers look like were she to ever know the joy of motherhood?

John, she thought as she imagined a towheaded boy running from the house where she lived down to the hardware where John worked. *His child—and mine.*

She heard steps in the hallway and got up expecting to see Luke bringing the tea. "She's resting," she said softly at the same moment that John entered the room carrying a tray with a teapot and two cups. "You shouldn't be here," she said, but at the same time she felt such gladness that he was.

"Luke has his hands full downstairs. I'll just set this here and go." He kept his eyes averted from the bed and Greta's sleeping form. "Is she…?"

"Resting a little easier," Lydia assured him. She did not look at him as she relieved him of the tray and set it on the top of a bureau next to the door. "When she wakes, I'll try to get her to sip a little tea."

"You should have a cup, as well," John said, and she could feel him watching her.

"I'll be fine. Thank you for…everything," she said, and knew that it came out as if she were dismissing him even as everything inside her cried out for him to stay.

"I'll go, then." He turned back toward the stairs and she followed him. "You'll be all right?"

"It is Greta we must pray for," she reminded him.

"I know, but she has a whole town looking out for her. Who do you have, Liddy? Who takes care of you?"

There was a time when I hoped you and I would take care of each other, she thought as she met his intense stare that demanded an answer. "I am fine," she said instead.

She walked with him to the top of the stairs. From below, Lydia heard the laughter of the children. Behind her she heard Greta begin to moan again. "I have to go to her," she said, but it came out a whisper as if she weren't yet ready to let John go.

"I know," he answered as he took hold of her hand and brought her fingertips to his lips. "Drink the tea," he added. He kissed her fingers then walked slowly back down the stairs and out the front door.

Could they find their way back to each other? Was it possible to re-create the past—the time when they had been everything the other needed or wanted?

"Liddy," Greta moaned.

"Coming," she replied.

Chapter 8

John knew that he could not work on Sunday without enduring the disapproval of Hilda Yoder, not to mention his uncle. Sundays were reserved for the activities of faith and family. Even though the Amish met only every other week for formal services, the alternate Sundays were given to more leisure activities. On Sunday evenings the single young people in the community would gather for a hymn singing and, more important, a rare opportunity to explore the possibility of a courtship that could eventually lead to marriage. In their youth he and Liddy had attended such gatherings and afterward he had driven her home in his courting buggy as the two of them talked of the day when they would marry and start a home of their own.

Many times they had sat long into the night on the front porch of her father's house planning their future, oblivious to hours passing or the oppressive summer heat, the mosquitoes and pesky gnats known as no-see-ums that were native to Florida. On Sundays when there were no services they often went to the beach. John would borrow a small rowboat and row them along the shore, weaving close to the tangled roots of the mangrove trees that formed a barrier between the water and land. Liddy would bring a picnic lunch and they would spend the whole day together.

Having been assured that there was no more he could do for Luke and the children, John drove his uncle's buggy to the Hadwell house on the edge of town and arrived just as Gert and Roger did with Liddy's buggy.

"Is everything all right, John?" Gert asked.

"Liddy's with her. Luke thinks it might be something she caught from one of the children—a stomach bug." He unhitched and stabled their horse, then returned to climb onto the seat of Liddy's buggy. "I'll take care of this for her," he said.

"You'll come back?" Gert called from her position at the back door of their small cottage.

The idea of sitting for an entire evening with his aunt and uncle in the small, dark house while Gert read Scripture and Roger dozed was not at all appealing. "I thought I might keep Luke company—maybe carve the children a soap animal to keep them quiet while Greta rests."

"Tell Luke I'll bring them some supper," Gert said.

By the time John had unhitched and stabled Liddy's horse and walked back down the street toward Luke and Greta's he saw another buggy parked outside the house. Luke was sitting on the porch with one child while the other two played in the yard. Sitting across from him was Jeremiah Troyer, Liddy's half brother-in-law and Bishop Troyer's great-nephew.

Jeremiah's story was not all that different from John's. He'd left home, settled in a new community, started one business—the ice-cream shop—and eventually bought another—the ice-packing company.

Not so different in some ways. Worlds of difference in others, John thought as he walked down the street. For one thing, Jeremiah Troyer had had the good sense to seek out a new Amish community instead of trying to make his way in the *Englischer* world. For another, by the time he was ready to court Pleasant, he was making a good living and had a secure future to offer her.

And what do you have to offer Liddy? The question was never far from his thoughts.

He should stay away from her. But he willingly admitted that the reason he was heading back to Luke's house had little to do with wanting to help out. It was because Liddy was there and he was drawn like a moth to a lantern to wherever she might be.

"John Amman!" Samuel shouted when he saw John approaching. John smiled as he recalled how George's son had once called him by his given name and been reprimanded by George's wife. "This is *Mr. Amman,* young man," she had instructed. But in the Amish world such titles were never used, although often a person would be called by his or her full name.

"Did you forget something?" Samuel asked, his eyes wide with curiosity as he walked alongside John up the steps of the porch.

"In a way I did," he said as he nodded to Luke and Jeremiah and took a seat on the top porch step. He pulled out his pocketknife and the bar of soap he'd picked up after stabling Liddy's horse. "Do you like horses, Samuel Starns?" he asked as he started to carve the soap made pliable by the warmth of the day.

"Yah."

Samuel's younger brother scrambled down from his father's lap and took his position beside her brother. "I do, too," he announced.

"Das ist gut," John replied as he concentrated on shaping the rectangular bar into the form of a pony. "Ask your *dat* if he might have an extra bar of soap around and we'll make a team of horses."

Behind him Luke chuckled as the boy, Eli, looked imploringly at him. "In the house," he said. "By the kitchen sink."

Eli was gone and back in an instant, presenting the partially used bar of lye soap to John as if it were a bar of gold. "Ah, looks like these ponies will be a matched set," John said, showing him that the two bars were identical in color.

Eli giggled. "They'll be *bruders* like me and Samuel." Then he frowned as he glanced back to where his little sister was crawling around the porch. "My *maet* is getting a brother or sister for Sarah there," he whispered. "We're not supposed to talk about it. It's a surprise."

John nodded. "I won't tell anyone," he whispered, and Eli giggled again.

He finished Samuel's horse and turned his attention to carving one for Eli. "Greta feeling any better?" he asked as the two children sat apart, admiring Samuel's soap horse and plotting out the game they would play as soon as John finished the second one.

"Lydia and Pleasant are with her. Pleasant said they

were able to get her to take a little of the clear broth that she brought." Luke sounded tired and more than a little worried. "She's never had trouble before," he added, and his voice trailed off as if he hadn't meant to say this part aloud.

Jeremiah cleared his throat. "John, Luke tells me that you're making a rocking chair for him to give Greta. That's your trade, then? Making furniture?"

Normally John was reluctant to discuss his work, always aware that the discussion might eventually stray to those years he'd spent in the outside world. But he understood what Jeremiah was doing. He wanted to turn Luke's attention away from his sick wife. "It is a gift that God has given me," he replied.

"I'm in need of some extra tables for the ice-cream shop," Jeremiah continued. "If you have the time you could stop by the shop tomorrow and see if that might be something that would interest you."

Ever since John had lost everything he'd ever acquired, he had been especially sensitive to strangers who might think they were doing him a favor by offering some charity. He glanced up at Jeremiah, trying to gauge the man's purpose.

"I have a bid from Josef Bontrager for the work," Jeremiah continued. "Seems high."

"Josef has not known much competition in this," Luke said, and John realized that Luke was encouraging him to agree to at least consider the project.

"Tomorrow, then," John said as he blew the last shavings off the second horse and handed it to Eli. The youngster squealed with delight and ran off with his brother to play under the shade of the live oak tree that dominated the front yard.

John leaned back against the column that supported the porch roof. He could hear the women moving around upstairs and speaking softly to each other, their voices drifting out through the open windows.

"Have the elders come to a decision about the school?" Jeremiah asked Luke.

John's ears perked up.

"It's still under discussion."

"But Liddy…" John blurted. The other two men exchanged a look. "Teaching is her whole life," he added.

"She'll still be able to teach—privately in her home," Luke said.

"But in Celery Fields not many have money for private lessons. How will she make her way?"

"The final decision is not yet made," Jeremiah assured him. "Perhaps there will be a way that the elders have not yet seen. God will show us in time the decision we must make for the good of the community."

And Liddy?

Lydia was sure that she must be imagining things. She thought she heard John's voice rising up to the open windows from the porch. He sounded upset. She edged closer to the window and listened.

She sighed. They were talking about closing the school. It was a topic that was often discussed when men gathered these days. Waiting for the decision to be finalized had been a little like waiting for the next nibble on her line in the days when she and her father used to go fishing in the bay. But she had no doubt that the school would close. She was a practical woman with simple needs. She had put aside a portion of her stipend from the past year in preparation for the time after the school closed. And she had other skills. If all else failed she could clean houses for families in Sarasota, although she did not like the idea of working for outsiders. She took comfort in knowing that whatever happened with the school, this was Celery Fields. Her family and friends would make sure she had everything she needed.

What truly bothered her about John's comment was the focus on her and not what was best for the community. Perhaps his coming back here had been a mistake. Still, she had begun to allow herself to hope that in time...

"Liddy?"

Pleasant was studying her curiously and Lydia realized that a question had been posed to her, one she had not heard. "Sorry," she said, moving away from the window.

"I was just saying that the worst seems to have passed. Greta's fever is down and she's likely to sleep through the night now. Jeremiah and I need to get back for the milking and other chores. But I can send Bettina to take charge of the little ones and stay the night so Luke can get some sleep. What do you think?"

"It is a good plan, Pleasant. I'll stay until Bettina gets here. I can fix supper for Luke and the children."

"And eat something yourself?"

Lydia smiled sheepishly. It was well-known that she often got so caught up in her teaching or her chores at home or some other project that she forgot all about meals. "I will eat."

"Bettina will bring back one of the peach pies I made for services today. No one touched it," Pleasant grumbled. As the town's bakery owner she was frequently irritated when others did not line up to devour her wares, especially when they were freely offered as they were at any community gathering.

"Your peach pie is my favorite—you know that," Lydia replied, and was relieved to see her half sister smile.

From outside they heard a buggy approach and then stop outside the gate. Pleasant glanced out the window. "It's Roger and Gert Hadwell," she announced. "From the looks of it they've brought enough supper for half the town."

"I'll go help them bring things to the kitchen," Lydia said, glad of the excuse to go downstairs and see for herself that John was there, that he had returned. *Because of me?* Her heart beat a little faster as she digested that thought. But then she forced her steps to a slower pace as she descended the stairs. Sitting with Greta while she slept, Liddy had allowed herself to get lost in the memories of the Sunday afternoons she had shared with John when they were younger. She had gotten so caught up in those pleasant daydreams that she'd actually begun to convince herself that maybe they might find their way back to what they once felt for each other.

But she had seen that faraway look cross John's handsome features more often than it should if indeed he had come back to stay. He might be deceiving himself but she knew him too well. His determination to make a success of himself was the one thing that had not changed. And she could think of nothing that she might do to persuade him that such things did not matter to her and *should* not matter to him.

You are a foolish woman, Lydia Goodloe.

The chorus of voices from the gathering on the porch

brought Lydia back to the present. She smoothed her apron over her dress, tucked a wisp of her hair back under her prayer covering and then went to open the screen door for Gert.

"Let me take that for you," she said as she relieved John's aunt of a heavy basket and led the way to the kitchen. "You'll stay for supper?"

"That's the plan," Roger Hadwell said with a chuckle as he set down a second basket filled to the brim. "I don't think my wife left us a single thing to eat at home."

"Oh, stop that," Gert said, but she was smiling.

It had been a day for Lydia to be surrounded with couples whose marriages were strong and even inspiring. Watching Luke worry and fuss over Greta, then seeing how Jeremiah took his lead from Pleasant and got Luke and the children settled on the porch so that she and Pleasant could minister to Greta, had made Lydia more aware than usual of the beauty of a shared life. Now the Hadwells were taking over Greta's kitchen, their gentle teasing and laughter a testimony to the comfort and security they had found in each other's company.

There was a time when she and John had thought to have a marriage like any one of these. There was a time when they had assumed that they would grow old together. But at this moment she had to face reality. And the reality was that she was a single woman and would likely always be so.

She turned to get a platter from Greta's cabinet and found John watching her. Surely in time she would not feel her heart lurch with unexpected joy every time their eyes met. Surely in time they would be able to settle into the kind of easy friendship she shared with her brothers-in-law. She stood on tiptoe to reach the platter from the top shelf.

"I can get it," John said as he stood behind her and easily retrieved the platter. He stepped back so that she could turn and take it from him. "What else?" he asked.

"Nothing," she said, her voice barely audible. "It's fine. I'm…."

"You men go back outside while Liddy and I take care of things here," Gert instructed, shooing the men from the kitchen. "We'll never get this meal on the table with you in the way," she added as she swatted at Roger's hand when he tried to take a slice of the cheese she'd just unwrapped.

In the commotion that followed, John leaned in closer. "May I come by tonight?"

Lydia's nod of agreement was automatic. She should have refused. She should have used the excuse that Greta might need her. But Greta would be fine under Bettina's care. He was asking to see her in a way that could hold only one meaning.

John Amman is asking to court me again.

The shy smile that thought carried to her lips froze when he added, "We need to talk about this business with the school."

"That will be decided by others," she replied curtly, and walked back to the kitchen.

While the others ate supper together in Greta's large kitchen, Lydia insisted on sitting with Greta.

"She's sleeping," Gert said. "And you have to eat something. You came directly from services and Pleasant told me that you haven't eaten a thing since I arrived."

"I'll take a tray up with some broth for Greta and

something for myself, as well. I don't want to leave her alone until we're certain her fever has run its course."

Gert wasn't one to give up easily, but she agreed to Lydia's terms on the promise that she would let the older woman prepare the tray of food and send it up with Bettina as soon as the girl arrived.

Over Gert's shoulder Lydia saw John watching her from his position on the front porch. He was scowling at her. John had never been pleased when she dared to dispute something he had said. But the closing of the school was not for him to decide, or her, either. The elders would do what was best for all, and John's need to discuss the matter only served as more evidence that he might have moved back to Celery Fields but he had not entirely left the ways of the outside world behind.

John left as soon as supper was over. He accepted Luke's heartfelt thanks for his part in bringing Lydia to care for Greta and encouraged him to follow up on giving Jeremiah a bid for the tables he needed for the ice-cream shop. His aunt tried hard to get him to stay for a second piece of pie but he declined, having realized that Liddy had no intention of coming downstairs as long as he was still there.

He walked back down the main street, deserted now and nearly dark with shadows. The woman was as stubborn as ever. Did she not understand that what he wanted to do was help her devise some alternate plan that she could bring to the elders to perhaps keep the school open and her job secure?

She hadn't even given him the opportunity to discuss the possibilities, rejecting any such conversation out of hand from sheer obstinacy. It was becoming an old story with them, this refusal to even consider his ideas for making things better. It was as if, having not trusted him when he left to make enough money to get his business going, she had decided never to trust his thinking again.

He frowned. What kind of a marriage could they build on that? He would agree that his leaving Celery Fields had not turned out at all the way he'd intended. In fact, he had made matters far worse. If he had stayed and worked for his uncle through the good years they might be married by now with a house filled with children of their own. On the other hand he had stayed away far longer than he had intended mostly because she had rejected him. He had written her time and again, trying with each letter to make her understand his intention to return as soon as he had earned his financial stake. But her refusal to even acknowledge his letters had been his answer.

So why are you here? Why do you care so much whether she maintains her job or not? Why should it matter to you when it doesn't seem to matter to her?

Because, having failed her once, he was intent on making certain that she was happy and content in her life, even if he were not to be a part of it beyond living in the same community. If John was sure of anything it was that Liddy loved teaching and that taking that away from her would be devastating, whether she wanted to admit it or not. And whether she wanted his help or not he was determined to find some way that the school could hold on for at least a couple of years. By that time Luke and Greta's children would be ready to attend, as would other youngsters from the outlying farms that he had seen at Sunday services.

Instead of going directly to his rooms above the stables he walked over to the schoolhouse and stood outside the closed double doors considering the possibilities. The building was in good shape—no peeling paint, no loose shingles on the steep-pitched roof. The windows were not cracked or broken and the yard surrounding it was well tended and neat. It was close enough to the businesses in town that John could understand why the elders might be thinking it would bring in some much-needed income if turned into a shop of some sort.

He stepped onto the well-worn footpath that connected the school to Liddy's house. No doubt she had walked this path thousands of times over the years. In those first days after he'd left, he imagined her walking slowly from her father's house to the school, her head bent low, her heart missing him as he had missed her. But then as the weeks and months and years passed, being Liddy, she would have raised her eyes from the ground to the school itself and walked with new purpose. She would have set her mind on becoming the very best teacher she possibly could.

And these days? He thought about the woman he'd watched making her daily trips to and from the school and realized that there had been little difference in her posture or stride even as she must have already been facing the likelihood that this would be her last year of teaching. She would simply accept that whatever happened was God's will and that there would be some new purpose for her life.

So why bother trying to change things?

Because I love her—always have and always will.

"Whether she wants me to or not," he muttered aloud

as he crossed the yard. He stomped his way up the outside stairs and into the rooms that Liddy and the other women had made into a home for him. But the home he truly wanted was the house across the way, shared with Liddy and their children. In spite of everything that had happened, he still wanted to marry her. Nothing about that had changed. All he had to do was persuade her that being with him was surely God's will.

Chapter 9

If the week in late January that John returned to Celery Fields had been unseasonably cold, six weeks later saw the humidity and unsettled skies of storms that usually did not arrive until the hurricane season began in early summer. There was no need for a fire at the school on these days. Instead, Lydia made sure the windows were open to allow whatever breeze there might be to flow freely through the single room.

As Greta's time to deliver grew nearer, Lydia spent most of her days either at school or caring for Luke, Greta and their children. To Greta's dismay Hilda Yoder—in her role as the town's midwife—had injured her back in a fall and was laid up in bed on doctor's orders until it had a chance to heal. On Hilda's orders Greta was also confined to complete bed rest for the duration of her pregnancy. So Lydia closed up her own house and moved in with her sister and Luke. The irony of her circumstances did not escape her. She believed that God was offering them the opportunity to become accustomed to an arrangement that would almost certainly be their future—the school shut down and Lydia living with Greta and Luke.

It also did not escape her notice that there was a blessing in all of this. By living with Luke and Greta she could avoid seeing John. Her feelings for John were incredibly confusing and rushed at her like a wave on the beach whenever she was in his presence. Her only defense seemed to be avoiding him whenever possible. No longer would he be able to watch from the vantage point of his uncle's hardware or his own living quarters above Luke's business as she came from and went to school or did chores around her house. Luke now handled milking Lydia's cow and gathering the eggs her chickens laid.

She also had not attended any of the community gatherings in town since moving to Greta's, offering the excuse that someone needed to be with her sister at all times. This included missing services for the first time in her life. And although John had stopped by on several occasions, she had always made sure to be sequestered upstairs with Greta, an area of the house off-limits to him.

"Is it your intention to avoid him forever?" Greta asked one afternoon as Lydia sat by her bedside mending some of the children's clothing. Greta had been feeling much better the past few days, enough so that she and Lydia had both urged Luke to go to Sarasota on business for the day. He was not expected back until late that evening. Pleasant had insisted on taking the children and Lydia had turned her duties at school over to Bettina in order to stay with Greta.

"I am not avoiding anyone."

Greta snorted and shifted her large bulk so that she lay on her side. "Yes, you are. What I want to know is why? In the weeks that have passed since his return has John Amman not proven his sincerity in wanting to be part of the community again? When will you let go of the past, Liddy?"

Lydia put down her sewing as she faced her sister with a sigh. She knew Greta would not give up on this conversation so they might as well have it. "I am not clinging to the past, Greta," she explained patiently. "John Amman left Celery Fields—and me—eight years ago. We are both very different people now. Why, it is almost as if he is a stranger to me, he's so unlike the boy he was."

"The boy you loved, have always loved, will always love," Greta insisted. "And he seems quite the same to me." Her eyes went all dreamy, the way they sometimes did when she thought or spoke of her husband. "That smile of his has not changed one bit and, if anything, age has made him more handsome. And the way he looks at you."

Outside the open window, thunder roiled in the distance like a giant's unsettled stomach. They would have the welcome relief of rain before the day was out. Lydia could smell it in the heavy air that hung over the room. It reminded her of the day that John had left. It had rained then, a harsh, cold, pelting rain that had slapped at her face as she watched him go. She pressed back a wisp of her hair that had clung to her cheek as she took up her sewing again. "That boy is no more," she reminded her sister.

"No he is now a man, a very eligible man. You'd best wake up, sister, before some other single woman sets her eye on him."

Lydia felt the color rise to her cheeks. John was indeed handsome, in the way that drew attention especially from women, despite the Amish leaning toward sameness. He stood out. He was taller and broader than many of the men in Celery Fields. "And that is exactly the point. Since he is so fine looking, why would he be interested in a spinster like me?" She felt she was making an excellent argument.

"Because he does not see the years, Liddy. He sees you. Everyone can see it except you. I don't understand why you think you must ignore the reality before you." She twisted around to reach for the cardboard fan they sometimes used during summer services and let out a cry of distress.

Lydia kicked over her sewing basket as she stood up. "What is it?" she asked as she eased Greta back onto the pillows. She noticed that her sister was biting hard on her lower lip to keep further cries at bay. "Where does it hurt, Greta?"

"Everywhere," Greta managed through gritted teeth.

"I'll go make you some peppermint tea. That always eases the cramping."

Greta nodded as she closed her eyes against the pain.

Downstairs, Lydia hurried to prepare the tea. From the day she had moved into the house, she had made sure a kettle was always filled and kept simmering on the wood stove in the kitchen. And as Greta's time grew closer she had made other preparations, as well—a stack of clean rags placed on the bureau in the bedroom, along with newspaper and two pads they would use to line the bed during the delivery. Greta had finally finished stitching the dark blue gown and blankets that she had made to wrap the newborn in after the delivery.

They had planned that when the time came, Luke would go fetch Hilda, who would attend Greta through the delivery with Lydia's help. Luke would be there, too, while the children would go to stay with Pleasant again. Everything was prepared. And Greta had been through the entire process three times already. There was no need to worry, Lydia assured herself as she prepared the tea and carried a steaming mug back up the stairs as large drops of rain splattered against the windows. Except, if the baby came today, Luke was not there and Hilda was still confined to bed.

By the time Lydia reached the room Greta was collapsed against the pile of pillows, her eyes closed, her breathing coming in shallow gasps. Rain was dripping onto the wood-planked floor through the open window. Lydia set the mug of tea on the bedside table and closed the window then sat on the side of the bed.

"Greta? I have some tea," she said softly.

Greta's eyes fluttered opened. "Did you send for Hilda?"

"Hilda cannot come, remember? She took a fall and injured her back."

Greta closed her eyes again and nodded as a single tear leaked down her cheek. "Something is not right, Liddy," she said, and her voice shook with fear. "This isn't like any of the others. I know that something is terribly wrong."

"Lie still," Lydia instructed as Greta began to writhe

in pain. "I'm going for help." She set the tea aside and ran back down the stairs and out onto the porch. The sky was pitch-black and the rain now fell in sheets that made seeing more than a couple of feet impossible.

Normally someone was always out on the street in Celery Fields at this time of day, but with the storm everyone had sought shelter. She needed to send someone to fetch the *Englisch* doctor that the citizens of Celery Fields hesitated to call except in emergencies. Well, this was definitely an emergency, and the only telephone in town was the one at Hadwell's Hardware.

From upstairs she heard Greta cry out and she did not wait another second before dashing into the street and running as fast as she could to the hardware. She was soaked through by the time she pushed open the door and clutched at a counter displaying a variety of pocketknives to catch her breath.

"It's Greta," she gasped when Gert glanced up and then hurried forward. "I think the baby is coming but there is a problem—a serious problem. I think we should call for the doctor."

Gert ran to the wall phone and lifted the receiver. She yelled into the phone. "Hello! Hello?" Her shouts into the phone brought John and Roger from the storeroom.

"It's dead," Gert announced. "The wires must be down with this wind."

"What's going on?" Roger demanded.

Once again Lydia explained the urgency to reach the doctor, and all the while her mind raced with thoughts of what she would do if they couldn't get him there in time. "I need to get back. Greta is alone and..."

"I'll go for the doctor," Roger said, grabbing his rain slicker. "John, you go with Lydia."

"Shouldn't I…" Gert began but she was already shaking like a leaf, her nerves evident to all.

"Someone has to manage the store," Roger reminded her gently. And although Lydia knew the store could simply be closed for the time being, she also understood that Roger was protecting Gert. Gertrude Hadwell tended toward hysteria when faced with any crisis.

"John?" Roger nodded toward Lydia.

John took down a second black rain slicker and held it over his head and shoulders indicating that Lydia should join him under the shelter of the coat. "Let's go," he ordered as he held out one arm, ready to envelope her against him under the coat.

"I…"

"For once in your life stop worrying about what is proper, Liddy. Greta needs you."

Her sister's name galvanized Lydia into action. She huddled close to John as he opened the shop's door, and together they headed out into the storm. All around them thunder rumbled and lightning cracked the blackness of the sky in jagged flashes. John held her close, half carrying her forward as they ran back to the house.

The front door stood open. As they stepped into the front hallway and John dropped the coat and shut the door against the noise of the storm, Lydia realized that the house had an eerie, empty sound. She glanced up the stairway, her ears peeled for any cry from Greta.

Nothing.

"Oh, please, do not let her have…" Lydia did not finish her prayer as she raced up the stairs with John right behind her.

When they reached the bedroom, Greta was on her hands and knees in the middle of the bed. Because her face was buried in a pillow they could barely hear her moans. The linens on the bed were soaked through with perspiration as well as what Lydia realized was the rush of water that was a preamble to the baby's coming.

"There's water simmering on the stove. Fill this basin," she instructed John, thrusting a washbasin at him as she rushed to her sister's side. "Greta, we're right here."

"Luke?"

"Not yet. Remember, he had to go out on a job and there's a storm? I'm sure he'll be back as soon as he can." As she talked, she took a clean rag from the stack by the bed and wiped Greta's forehead.

"The mattress," Greta said. "It's ruined."

"It's wet," Lydia corrected, "and it will dry."

To her surprise Greta managed a laugh. "Oh, Liddy, there is ever so much more than water coming," she said. "Get the newspapers and pads."

Relieved to have her sister take charge Lydia did as she was told, managing to spread the pad, layers of papers and another pad while she helped Greta balance back and forth on her hands and knees. "Do you want to lie down?"

"No. This is better," Greta said, and then gasped as another contraction took hold.

What was taking John so long?

As if in answer, she heard footsteps on the stairs and he came to the door with the basin of steaming water. "There wasn't enough in the kettle," he said, and Lydia remembered that she had taken water for the peppermint tea earlier.

"I refilled the kettle." He sounded as nervous as she felt.

She took the water from him. "How long before Roger comes with the doctor?" she whispered.

John glanced at the window where the wind was so strong that palm fronds lashed at the sides of the house like fingers scratching on a chalkboard. The sky was so dark that it seemed more like midnight than midafternoon. He shook his head. "Just tell me what to do, Liddy, and we'll get through this together."

I don't know what to do, she wanted to tell him, but behind her Greta let out a half moan and half cry and rolled onto her side. "Just stay close in case I need you, and watch for the doctor," she said as she returned to Greta's bedside. "Right here, Greta," she chanted as she dipped a rag in the water and pressed it to her sister's swollen belly as she had seen Hilda do when delivering Greta's other children. "Just tell me what to do," she whispered, and was not at all sure if she was directing this plea to Greta or to God.

"That's good," Greta managed as the contraction passed and she shifted into a half sitting position. "The heat helps." She sounded almost normal, but her face was flushed a blotched red and her breathing sounded as if she had run a great distance. "Better," she added, and found the strength to smile at Lydia and clutch her hand.

Within seconds she was squeezing Lydia's fingers as her face contorted into a grimace. "Coming," she managed to gasp as she pushed herself higher onto the pillows.

Lydia had never found the term "catcher" more accurate than she did as she watched the head of the baby appear. Surrounded by the sounds of the storm, Greta's labored breathing and John pacing back and forth just outside the bedroom door, she instinctively cradled the emerging head of the child in one hand as she gently guided this wonder into the world. She looked up once to find Greta grimacing through the strain of one final push and suddenly the rest of the baby landed in Lydia's hands.

She was shaking and laughing at the same time and there were tears of pure joy rolling down her cheeks. "It's a girl, Greta. A beautiful daughter," she said. She turned the child, still connected to her mother by the umbilical cord, so Greta could see her. But then her heart raced with panic as she realized the baby was making no sound and was not breathing.

"You need to give her a slap," Greta instructed, her voice faint.

Lydia was horrified at the very idea of striking such a precious being.

"Get her breathing," Greta urged, half leaning forward as if to do it herself.

Lydia patted the baby girl sharply on her tiny back still slick with the afterbirth. After what seemed like an eternity the baby gasped and then let out a wail. Lydia smiled and turned to her sister. "She's lovely, Greta."

Greta smiled as she cradled her newborn. "Another girl," she whispered.

Lydia laughed. "*Yah*. You have a pair of boys and now a pair of girls."

She felt more confident now that the baby was out and breathing. The rest would not be that different from the time she had helped her father deliver a calf. There would be the afterbirth that Luke would take and bury in the field behind the house. Once she had cut the cord, she would take the baby away to wash her and coat her in baby oil before dressing her in the gown that Greta had prepared and wrapping her in the blankets.

"John!" she shouted, and heard him come running. When he got to the door his eyes were wide with fear. "Is it…?" But as soon as he saw the baby, he started to smile. "You did it," he said, softly edging into the room and peering over Lydia, who stood between him and Greta as she tried to protect her sister's modesty.

"I was only the catcher," she said, handing him the basin that now held the afterbirth. "Take this downstairs so Luke can bury it when he gets home. Then I need you to bring me fresh water and warm these blankets on the stove—try not to let them catch fire. Oh, and Greta will need a cup of that mint tea."

She shooed him from the room as he struggled to balance the basin and the blankets she had draped over his arm. Just then a crack of thunder shook the house and was followed immediately by a flash of lightning that seemed to arc right through the window in Greta's bedroom. Lydia turned back to her sister and newest niece and cried out in panic as she saw Greta's eyes roll back and a gush of bright red blood soak the padding.

John was halfway down the stairs when he heard Liddy's shriek of sheer terror. Carefully he set down the basin on a step and, still clutching the blankets, he raced back up the stairs. When he entered the room, Lydia thrust the tiny slippery, squirming bundle into his hands and then turned back to her sister, grabbing rags from a pile on the bedside and placing them between Greta's legs.

"The doctor has to come now, John. I don't know what to do." He realized that she was crying and shaking and he wanted to pull her into his arms and reassure her. But he was holding the baby and he could see the blood that soaked through the rags even as Liddy added more. Spying the cradle in the corner of the room, John laid the baby girl down and covered her as best he could with the blankets still clutched in his arms.

"I'm going for help," he said.

"Don't leave me," Lydia begged.

It was exactly what she had said to him that day eight years earlier when he had boarded the train. She had been sobbing then and she was sobbing now. Then he had left, certain that he knew best. Now he hesitated, knowing that what they needed was for him to find help and yet feeling reluctant to leave her alone.

He crossed the small room and placed his hands on her shoulders. "I'm going for help, Liddy. I'll be back."

She caught her breath and nodded. Then she looked up at him, her eyes pleading with him to make this all right. "Yes, go," she whispered as she cupped his cheek with one bloodstained hand. "Go now."

He kissed her forehead damp with perspiration. "I won't be long," he promised. On his way out the front door, John grabbed the still-wet rain slicker and covered his head as he dashed into the street and barely missed being run over by a motorcar coming toward the house. The car squealed to a stop and a gray-haired man carrying a doctor's bag got out. "Is this the house? Starns?" he shouted above the driving wind and rain.

"Yah. Kommen Sie," John urged, reverting to the German his grandparents and parents had spoken. He led the way back inside the house and up the stairs. "This way."

"You're the father?"

"A friend," he replied as he stood aside for the doctor to enter Greta and Luke's room.

"Mrs. Starns," the doctor said in a loud, firm voice. "I'm Dr. Benson."

John heard Greta give a low moan of acknowledgment and then he heard Lydia answer the questions the doctor asked as he opened his bag and began examining Greta. Not knowing what else to do, John took the bowl with the afterbirth down to the kitchen and left it so Luke could bury it. He returned and waited outside the door as the sounds coming from the bedroom took on a rhythm of their own. Liddy's voice, calm now, then the doctor's. Occasionally, the gurgle or cry of the baby.

The clock in the front room chimed five o'clock. Outside, the wind had calmed and the rain let up. His uncle had brought Pleasant, who immediately joined the doctor and her half sisters in the bedroom. "Bettina is staying with the other children," Roger explained. "I thought it best. Is Luke back?"

"Not yet," John said. He glanced toward the closed bedroom door. "What if…"

His uncle clasped his shoulder. "God will show us the way, John. Come downstairs."

John followed his uncle down to the kitchen and accepted the cup of tea Pleasant handed him. The house seemed suddenly filled with people and he could not help but wonder where they had all come from and why they hadn't arrived sooner. He could not shake off the feeling that only the intervention of God's own hand had made everything turn out right for Greta and Luke and their new baby. He understood just how close this young family had come to the day ending in tragedy. And he could not help but put himself in Luke's place—

Luke who knew nothing as he drove his wagon back from Sarasota where he had gone on business that day. What if Luke had come home to find that Greta had died in childbirth?

He wandered out to the back porch, sipping his tea as he stared at the fields that lay beyond the town. Fields he and his father had once plowed and planted together. Fields he had abandoned in his zeal to do things his way. The time he had squandered on his foolish pride were years he and Liddy might have shared the joys of marriage and started a family of their own. What did it matter if he farmed or ran a business like his uncle did? What mattered was Liddy.

He glanced up at the sky, beginning to clear now that the storm had passed. A double rainbow arched its way across the horizon, enveloping the house and town in prisms of color. John felt his chest tighten with tears of gratitude, for surely this was a sign that he'd been given a second chance. And this time he was determined to get things right.

When Luke arrived and heard the news, he raced up the stairs and into the bedroom without even bothering to shed his rain slicker. Greta was sitting up holding their daughter, an exhausted smile on her lips. Lydia made the excuse of showing the doctor out and closed the door behind her with a soft click before leading the way back downstairs.

"Thank you for coming," she said.

"You did everything right for your sister," he told her. "These things happen. I'm just glad I was able to help. Tell your sister and her husband that they have a fine, healthy baby girl there and, given the demanding nature of her cries, I expect they will have their hands full raising her." He chuckled as he stepped off the porch and climbed into his car.

Lydia wrapped her arms in her apron and hugged herself as she closed her eyes and thanked God for the way this day had turned out. She was bone weary and there was still a great deal to be done, but she felt happy.

"Liddy?" John stepped out onto the porch and stood next to her. "We need to talk," he said, and she saw that the deep lines of a frown creased his brow.

"Oh, John, not right now. Can you not be happy for my sister and Luke, for the blessing of this new life?"

"It is because of their joy that we need to talk," he persisted. "What happened today and the way things might have gone had God not blessed them with your quick thinking has brought me to my senses. I have wasted so much time, Liddy, so many years I might have shared with you and the children we might have had."

Lydia felt her cheeks go pink as she glanced toward the open front door, hoping no one was close enough to overhear this very personal conversation. "John Amman, this is neither the time nor—"

"This is exactly the time, Liddy," he argued as he stepped closer, his fists clenched at his sides as he stared down at her. "This is past the time."

"You are speaking in riddles, John Amman, and I am very tired and have no patience for—"

"Will you marry me or not, Lydia Goodloe?"

Her first instinct was to laugh. Surely he was making a joke, a cruel one at that. But she did not laugh. Instead, she met his gaze. "I answered this question once before—eight years ago," she reminded him. "It was you who…"

"You said yes then. Are you saying the same now?"

Without warning, the years fell away and the man she was looking up at was the man she had loved then. The man against whom all others had been measured and come up short. "I…" She swallowed hard and shook her head to clear it. Had there ever been a stranger day than this one had turned out to be?

She closed her eyes and thought of the hours just past, the baby she had lovingly washed and wiped with baby oil while the doctor worked with Greta to stop the bleeding. She thought about the cotton birthing gown and the soft blankets she had wrapped the baby in before presenting Greta with her new daughter. It had been like handing her sister a very precious gift. And yes, she thought of the envy she had felt that this gift was not hers, might never be hers.

But perhaps God was giving her another chance, giving John and her another chance to make a fresh start and have the life together they had planned.

"Liddy?" His voice was husky with pleading. "Open your eyes. I am right here. Can we not begin again?"

Oh, how she wanted to say yes to his plea. How she wanted to set aside the doubts that had hardened inside her in the years he had been gone and sent no word. But if he left again surely her heart would be shattered forever. Caution had become her proverb and she would not abandon it now. "I will stay here for the next month caring for Greta and her family," she said slowly. "I cannot stop you should you decide to call on Luke and Greta in the evenings after your work is finished." She watched as a grin twitched at the corners of his mouth and knew that he understood she was giving him permission to court her.

"And you will sit with me sometimes on those evenings, Liddy?"

His smile was contagious, and to hide the joy she felt building inside her she ducked her head. "It would be rude not to," she admitted.

"And at the end of that month, will I have my answer?"

It was a reasonable request especially given their ages. And she did love him, had always loved only him. But would a month be long enough for her to find trust again? "You will have your answer," she said softly.

Chapter 10

On more than one occasion John had heard his partner, George, use the expression "walking on air" to describe his feelings whenever he had a business success. Finally John thought he understood what George had meant. On his way home from Luke's house, with Liddy's promise echoing in his mind, he did feel a certain bounce in his step. Oh, she had doubts and they would not be easily put to rest, but he had a month to prove to her that he was home to stay and intent on making a life with her.

He stopped by the hardware store to check on the rocking chair he had finished only the evening before. Luke had asked him to deliver it as soon as possible but, with so many people crowded into the house to meet the newest member of the Starns family, John thought it best to hold the delivery until the following day.

"On the other hand," he muttered to himself as he ran a soft cloth over the finish to remove any remaining sawdust, "no time like the present." He grinned as he realized delivering the chair later that very evening would be the perfect opportunity to spend a little time alone with Liddy. Luke would be with Greta and the baby, the other children would surely be in bed and all the rest of the company would have returned to their homes. It would just be Liddy and him—alone.

He looked down at the sawdust that had formed a fine covering down the front of his trousers. He should go to his rooms and make himself more presentable. Before his partner had married, George would take his lady a gift like flowers or candy. But the Amish did not believe in such things, and what could John possibly bring Liddy, anyway?

Your heart.

And suddenly he fully grasped the mistake he had made in leaving. Liddy had tried repeatedly to tell him that material goods did not matter to her. She had always believed and assured him that all they needed was each other and God would take care of the rest. Now he understood she'd been saying that the only thing that mattered to her was that he loved her.

But John knew that love could not last on an empty stomach. He had seen families fall apart—good, solid families where there had once been bonds of love that had seemed unbreakable. When hard times came even those bonds weakened and unraveled. And his bonds to Liddy had come unraveled, as well. Hard times had had little to do with it. It had been her stubborn refusal to trust in him that had been their undoing.

Okay, that wasn't exactly true. But maybe now that

her livelihood was in jeopardy, she would come to some understanding of why he had gone away. Maybe now he could convince her that work—money—was important. Of course, there was always work to be had. He had heard her tell Greta that she could no doubt find a position cleaning houses in Sarasota, an idea that caused him to cringe. The very idea of his Liddy on her hands and knees scrubbing floors for some wealthy family in Sarasota was unimaginable. He had to come up with some viable way to show her he could earn a living that would be enough for both of them to live on.

"First things first," he said as he reached for the brush his aunt kept on the tool rack and whisked the dust from his trousers. "First step is to ease her fears about whether or not you've changed. Once you've earned her trust, then you can worry about how you're going to earn a living."

He placed the brush back on its hook, then wrapped the rocking chair in an old clean blanket. His purpose was not only to protect the finish from any lingering raindrops but also to hide it from Greta should she look out the window of the upstairs bedroom and see him coming up the street.

Not likely, he thought as he recalled the cries of the newborn filling the house. Liddy—his Liddy—had delivered that baby girl all by herself. He grinned as he remembered the way her eyes had glittered with pure triumph as she held that baby. He could only imagine how beautiful she would be holding their child.

Lydia had finally gotten the other children settled for the night and all of the friends and neighbors had left. The house was quiet as she sat by her sister's bedside. Luke had gone to see Dr. Benson to his car. The doctor had stopped by unexpectedly "just to be sure everything is all right."

Dr. Benson had assured her, "I'm just here for the extra innings," using a baseball phrase that Luke had had to explain to her. "Mother and daughter are doing just fine, thanks to you, young lady."

Lydia had blushed at that. No one had called her either young or a lady in a very long time. It was the kind of meaningless flattery outsiders doled out on a regular basis. Lydia had bowed her head to acknowledge the compliment but said nothing. Still, she found that she liked the gray-haired doctor. He reminded her of her father, and his willingness to come whenever someone in Celery Fields called had endeared him to the entire community.

"Get some rest," he had advised. "All of you. That daughter of yours strikes me as one determined to have her way." He actually winked at Greta. "Seems to me she might be a lot like her mother."

Greta smiled, her features revealing nothing of the trauma she had been through earlier that day. Years earlier Dr. Benson had been called for the delivery of both Greta and Lydia and in that moment he reminded Lydia even more of their beloved father. How she missed him. She couldn't help wondering what he would say about John's return.

Her father had always been wary of John. "That boy has his head in the clouds," he would tell her. "Be careful, Liddy, that he doesn't lead you astray." It had been the only topic of contention between them. After John left, Lydia had consoled herself in the stronger bond she and her father developed as he turned his attention toward worrying about Greta and her capricious nature.

Greta was sleeping by the time Lydia heard Luke close the front door and climb the stairs. But she realized he was not alone and, when she turned toward the door, she saw John entering the room carrying a large blanket-wrapped object. She could just see the graceful curve of the rocker peeking out from beneath the covering. Luke grinned and signaled for her to remain quiet while he silently directed the placement of the chair next to the crib. He moved their mother's rocking chair into the hall.

John removed the blanket and then adjusted the position of the chair. He touched his handiwork with such reverence that Lydia believed he was reluctant to part with it. Then he stood for a long moment looking down at the sleeping newborn in the crib. She saw him swipe the back of one hand across his cheek before he turned around, grinned at Luke and tiptoed out of the room.

"I'll just see him out," Lydia whispered, but Luke had already taken her place next to Greta's bedside. He was holding his wife's hand as he watched her sleep.

John was downstairs and reaching for the doorknob. "The chair will serve them well," she said softly. It was as close as people of their faith ever came to handing out a compliment.

"Maybe one day," he said as he watched her descend the stairs, "I can make such a chair for you—for us and our child."

"Perhaps," she whispered as she reached the foot of the stairs and walked without hesitation into his embrace. She could not have said whether it was the emotional drama of the day or simply that the dark silent house made her bold. What she did know without a single doubt was that with John's arms embracing her and his strong heartbeat thudding in her ear, which was pressed to his chest, she was home.

After a moment John took her hand and led her out to the porch where he sat down in the swing with her curled against his side. She was asleep in less than a minute as he kept a steady pace rocking the swing like a cradle.

The mist of the humid dawn curled around them as the reality that Lydia had spent the entire night sleeping next to John roused her. She leaped up from the swing, her hands flying to her prayer covering to check that it was still there. "John, wake up," she whispered, glancing around to see if any of the neighbors were out and about yet. "You have to go."

He blinked and then grinned as he stretched out his arms and legs and yawned loudly.

"Shh," she hissed. "You'll wake the entire town."

"I doubt that," he said in his normal voice. "My guess is that most people in town are already awake and going about their morning chores." He grinned up at her and showed no sign at all of leaving as he stretched his long arms along the back of the swing and set it in motion. "How did you sleep?"

She ignored the question as she retrieved the hat that had fallen off sometime during the night and handed it to him. "Go," she ordered. "Now."

"Going," he said as he stood up and accepted the hat. And then his expression sobered as he cupped her cheek with the palm of one hand. "But I'll be back this evening and the one after that and the one after that until the month you need has come and gone, Liddy."

The man was impossible.

Impossibly handsome.

Impossibly stubborn.

Impossibly charming.

Long after he had gone Lydia stood on the porch, her hand on her cheek holding on to the warmth of his hand caressing her. As she heard the sounds of Greta's family stirring and headed inside to start breakfast, she realized that she was smiling.

Her high spirits stayed with her throughout the day as she went about the business of caring for Greta, the baby and the other children. She prepared meals and carried a tray up to Greta, who was dressed and sat rocking her newborn. She washed and hung out the sheets and other linens used in the birthing all the while keeping an eye on the children playing in the yard. Pleasant brought sweets and three pies from the bakery and told Lydia that Jeremiah was churning up a fresh batch of strawberry ice cream as a special treat for Greta. She also reported that she had stopped by the school and she assured Lydia that Bettina had everything under control.

Later that evening, after they had finished supper and Luke had taken the children upstairs to sit with their mother and new sister before going to bed, Hilda Yoder's youngest daughter stopped by with a basket of food and detailed instructions for Lydia to follow in caring for Greta and the baby. Hilda did not approve of calling for help from outsiders and her daughter made it clear that Hilda was adamant that there should be no need for Dr. Benson or his noisy vehicle to disturb them further. Her aversion to relying on outsiders for anything was the sole reason that the town's only telephone was located at the hardware when it more logically should have been at the dry-goods store that already housed the post office. And yet it had not escaped anyone's notice that when tourists vacationing in Sarasota found their way to Celery Fields it was Hilda who welcomed them into her shop.

"That's just good business," she had protested when Pleasant commented on the double standard one day after watching Hilda fuss over a trio of *Englisch* women who had made multiple purchases. Hilda had glanced at Lydia then and added, "Perhaps if enough tourists visit and buy from us we can afford to keep the school going."

Now as she completed her final chore for the day, scrubbing the kitchen floor, this particular train of thought was not helping to sustain Lydia's good mood. She paused in her scrubbing and considered whether or not she might truly make a home and future with John, one that would give her the same sense of purpose and security she had always felt in teaching. *God's will be done,* she reminded herself sternly. And she attacked the floor more vigorously with the brush and soapy water.

"You'll rub that wood to splinters if you keep scrubbing so hard," John said with a hint of laughter.

She had not heard him enter the kitchen. She resisted the urge to drop everything and walk into the welcome haven of his embrace. Instead, she exchanged the scrub brush for a rag soaked in clear water and wiped up the soapy residue from the floor. "You are late, John Amman," she said.

"Ah, you missed me. This is progress and we're only

on the second day of our month of decision." He was grinning as he relieved her of the rag, dropped it into the bucket and then offered her his hand to help her to her feet. "Haven't you done enough for one day, Liddy?" he asked as he studied her features.

"Work does not wait for sleep," she said, quoting one of Pleasant's maxims as she picked up the pail of soapy water and headed outside to dump it. The pure joy she felt at being in his presence was overwhelming. She needed to take this more slowly. He had left her once, after all, and she could not convince herself that he would not be struck by wanderlust yet again.

"Dr. Benson is on his way over," John said as he leaned against the door frame and watched her wash out the soapy bucket and set it in its place. "I saw him when I was in Sarasota making a delivery for my uncle."

Lydia shot him a look. "Is he worried that Greta might...will there be problems?"

"He didn't say, but he also did not seem particularly worried. I think he just likes seeing the babies he helps bring into this world."

Just then they both heard the rumble of a motorcar coming closer.

"I should put the kettle on," Lydia murmured as she stepped past John and started preparing a tea tray.

"I'll get the door," John offered as he headed down the hall as if they were a married couple preparing to welcome a guest to their home. It was a feeling that Lydia felt was surely not proper, but it was also one that brought the smile back to her face. She barely noticed she was humming as she sliced the loaf of banana bread that Gert had sent earlier with John.

After the doctor had checked on Greta and the baby,

he joined Luke, John and Lydia at the kitchen table. "Right as rain they are," he assured Luke, then turned his attention to John. "I was admiring that rocking chair, young man. Greta tells me you made it."

"Yah."

"It's a fine piece of carpentry. My wife has been after me to buy her a cabinet for displaying her china and knickknacks. Do you do that sort of thing?"

"I have work at the hardware and Jeremiah Troyer has asked me to build some tables for his ice-cream shop."

"No hurry. Her birthday's in summer. I just thought I could surprise her." Dr. Benson glanced at Luke and grinned. "Women do like surprises, right, Luke?" He finished the last of his tea and stood up. "Think about it, John. You have a gift and I know a number of people in my community who would pay top dollar for that rocking chair. If the rest of your work is that fine, you'd have more orders than you could fill in no time once word got around."

Lydia could practically see the wheels turning in John's mind. This was the opportunity he'd been hoping for and, while she did not especially like the idea of John doing his business primarily with outsiders, the other side of that coin was that if he had enough work here he would not be tempted to go elsewhere.

"You could perhaps draw up a sketch for Dr. Benson to consider," she said quietly.

"Good idea," the doctor boomed as he donned his fedora and picked up his medical bag. "I'll get you some measurements. My wife has already picked out the exact place in our dining room where she wants the cabinet to sit." He chuckled. "Come to think of it, the only surprise in all of this would be if I didn't do something about getting that cabinet for her—and that wouldn't be good." Luke walked him down the hall to the front door while Lydia cleared the dishes.

"It could be our future, Liddy," John said quietly as he remained at the kitchen table and picked at the crumbs of the banana bread.

"You've always wanted a business of your own," she replied.

"Uncle Roger would be relieved if I could start making my own way without having to rely on him."

"A few tables for Jeremiah and a cabinet for the doctor are not a business, John," she warned, worried suddenly that he was setting himself up for disappointment. "Perhaps your uncle would keep you on—just until…"

"I know this will take time." He stood up and carried the plate to her for washing. He leaned in close to her ear and whispered, "But I've got almost a whole month before you say you'll marry me—plenty of time to get this business going." He kissed her on the cheek. "You will say yes," he added.

As Luke walked back into the kitchen and cleared his throat, Lydia realized that this had not been a question. "You are sometimes too sure of yourself, John Amman," she said as she brushed past him to wipe the table.

"Ah, Liddy, have a little faith."

If Lydia had thought a month was ample time to decide her future, she had not counted on the way the days—and especially the evenings she sat with John on Greta's front porch—seemed to race by. They laughed a lot together, recalling the adventures they had shared as teenagers.

"Remember that time we went to the beach?" he asked one evening, chuckling and shaking his head.

And although there had been many trips to the beach to wade in the Gulf of Mexico and look for her favorite olive and moon shells, Lydia knew exactly which time he was recalling. "I had never seen you so nervous before."

"Well, I had never before borrowed a boat without actual permission although I did know the fisherman who owned it. Remember on our way over we saw the police patrolling the waters?"

Lydia giggled. "I thought you were going to faint when they came so close to us. And then they just waved and went on about their business."

"And then it was your turn to be nervous when the waves they left in their wake rocked that little rowboat to the point of practically tipping it over." He put his arm around her shoulder. "You clung to the sides so fiercely that your knuckles turned as white as the clouds above us."

"And you rowed all the faster. By the time we reached the islands you were breathing as if you had just run a footrace and, oh, the blisters you had." She ran her thumb over his callused palm then rested her head against his shoulder as they let the motion of the swing and the whispers of the night breeze in the palm trees lull them into silence.

"Let's go to the beach, Liddy," he said.

"Now?"

"Tomorrow. It's Saturday and we can ride our bicycles over the causeway and take a picnic. It will be like before."

Oh, how she wanted to believe that such a thing could be true, but the truth was that in all the years that had passed they had both changed—the world had changed. "I don't know, John. Isn't it dangerous trying to relive old memories?"

"Maybe. On the other hand, I thought we had decided to spend this month trying to build some new memories."

"I do love the beach," she admitted. "But you have to work and…"

"We'll go after the hardware closes for the day. We can watch the sunset together."

"It sounds nice," she admitted. "You wouldn't say anything to Gert, would you? I mean everyone knows about your visits in the evenings, but riding off together on our bikes in broad daylight…"

John sighed. "You leave whenever you think best and I'll meet you at the start of the causeway. No one need know, not that it matters to me one way or another."

"But it should matter, John Amman. Of course, others know, or at least have their suspicions, but they also respect that our seeing each other is meant to be a private matter and…"

"Then how come I feel like shouting it out to every person passing by?" He took her hands. "I promised to do things your way, Liddy, and if that means going separately to the beach, that is the way of it. Just promise me that we will come back together."

"Well, of course," she said primly, and then she smiled mischievously. "By then it will be dark."

* * *

The following afternoon Lydia had only been at the foot of the causeway for ten minutes before she saw John pedaling toward her. The sight of him took her breath away. His broad shoulders hunched over the handlebars of the black bicycle, his long legs pumping furiously as if to cover the distance separating them as quickly as possible. And the smile that said, more than any words, how seeing her made him as happy as it did her.

"Ready?" he asked as he slowed his bike and balanced it with one foot on the ground while she mounted hers.

"Ready," she agreed happily. "I'll race you to the circle!" she shouted as she took off.

"Not fair!" John called back. "You have a head start."

She laughed and pedaled all the harder, determined to outdistance him. She thought she was well ahead of him, but when she reached the circle of shops and restaurants that stood at the entrance to Lido Key and the road that led north to Longboat Key, she saw that he had deliberately lingered just behind her until they reached the circle. Once there he grinned and shot past her then eased his speed down to coasting, waiting for her to catch up.

"Beat you," he teased as, side by side, they dodged traffic on the circle until they came to the road that turned off and led to the beach on Lido Key.

"Maybe I let you win," she challenged.

He laughed at that. "Not likely." They both knew that as a girl Lydia had been very competitive and she usually won once she set her mind to something. They rode along the path that followed the beach until they reached an area shaded by a small cluster of cypress trees. "Looks like a good place for a picnic."

She leaned her bike against a tree and removed the sheet she had packed for them to sit on. While John spread it on the ground, anchoring the edges with stones, she unpacked the sandwiches, oranges, cookies and thermos of tea that she had brought for their supper. John had devoured two whole ham sandwiches before she had finished a half. She found herself thinking about what it would be like to prepare food for him every day. What would he want for breakfast? Would they, like most families in Celery Fields, take their main meal at midday, or had he come to prefer the ways of the *Englisch,* having his main meal in the evening?

As he ate he stared out toward the Gulf, his eyes watching the waves rush at the beach, break and retreat. She tried to imagine what he was thinking and took his silence and his attention to a distant horizon as evidence that he still longed for unexplored shores.

She was surprised when he said, "You know, ever since I got back to Celery Fields I have felt such a sense of homecoming. I don't think I was ever in my life so reluctant to leave a place—to leave friends and family. To leave you especially."

Then why did you? She wanted so badly to ask. But she would not risk spoiling the moment. "It is your home, John. It has been since the day your family first moved here when you were, what? Eight?"

"Nine." He chuckled. "It seemed to me like we must be moving to the ends of the earth. The trip was long and then when we got here everything seemed very different from what we had known in Pennsylvania."

He cut his eyes her way and then immediately back to the water. "Then I met you and I was glad we came."

She felt heat rise to her cheeks. "You exaggerate. As I recall, you were not at all sure about me in those early days. Especially not when I bested you at dodgeball in the schoolyard."

He shrugged. "I let you win then." He stuffed the last of the cookies into his mouth. "Made up for it today, though," he teased. He stood, brushed the crumbs from his shirt and trousers and held out his hand to her. "Walk with me, Liddy. The sun will set soon."

They gathered the wax paper wrappings of their picnic and John carried them to a trash barrel while Lydia folded the sheet and replaced it and the thermos in the basket of her bicycle. Then she fell into step with him as they walked hand in hand across the wide expanse of the beach, nearly deserted now as the last of the tourists packed up their belongings and headed away.

Close to the edge of the water they removed their shoes and set them well away from the rising tide, marking the spot they would return to once their walk was done. They stepped into the clear water that had gone calm now, the waves barely breaking over their bare feet, then headed north to where they knew the beach would curve and bend. There they stood on a point looking across a pass that separated Lido Key from Longboat.

Occasionally Lydia would stop and retrieve a shell, show it to John and then return it to the water.

"Keep one to remember," he said after she had repeated this process half-a-dozen times.

"You find one for me to keep."

Chapter 11

The shadows lengthened as the sun turned to a fiery orange low on the horizon. As they walked along, they were both focused on the water.

"Let's stop here and watch the last of it," John said, and gently turned her attention to the sun half-gone already. He stood behind her and wrapped his arms around her as they watched in silence. "Here," he said, handing her a perfect but tiny Florida conch shell that was the exact color that the sun had been. "To remember."

She turned to face him and cradled his cheek with her hand. She removed his hat and ran her fingers through his thick hair.

"Next week it will be a month, Liddy." His voice was raspy with emotion.

"I know." And although she knew he wanted his

answer, she also knew that she could trust him not to press her.

She could trust him.

Not only had John shown no recent signs of wanderlust, he seemed perfectly satisfied to give her the time she might need. He was content. He worked every day at the hardware store and in the evenings and on Saturdays he worked at establishing his carpentry business. He had even gone so far as to make needed repairs and renovations for members of the congregation at no charge. He had especially endeared himself to those women in Celery Fields who were widowed and perhaps reluctant to become too dependent on their neighbors, although that was the Amish way of things. John had a way of just showing up as if he had simply been passing by and noticed a loose hurricane shutter or a wall with some rotted boards. He would assure the women that they were the ones helping him to make amends for his past.

Everyone in town knew that he was courting Lydia, but it was not their habit to speak of such matters. Courtship was private and that was a good thing as far as Lydia was concerned. For if things did not work out for them she could be sure that others would not speak of it—at least openly.

But things were working out. These days she could hardly get through an hour without some thought of John that brought a smile to her lips. He was wonderful with Luke and Greta's children, and sometimes he even came by the school during classes on some pretext or another. Her students looked forward to these impromptu visits. Even Pleasant seemed to be working hard to accept the idea that John was back to stay and that he intended to marry Lydia if she would have him.

If she would have him.

It was up to her. In so many ways it had always been up to her. "John," she said now as she wrapped her arms around him and rested her cheek against his chest. "Is there a reason that we need to wait out the entire month?"

She actually felt his heart beat a little faster. "I cannot think of one."

"Neither can I," she whispered, and stood on tiptoe to kiss his cheek.

He placed his finger under her chin, holding her up-lifted face to the minuscule amount of dusky light left, trying to see her face. "Do not tease me, Liddy."

"Do you still wish to marry me?"

"You know that it is all I have ever—"

She pressed her fingers to his lips to silence him. She would not allow him to lie. There had been all those years when he was away and thought only of his life in that world beyond Celery Fields, a life that had not included her. "Then you should see the deacon so he can meet with my family, and the bishop can make the announcement at services week after next."

"You are certain?"

"I am," she assured him, and she brushed his hair back from his forehead. "We have wasted far too many years, John Amman. I will not waste another day."

He pulled her tight against him, his lips brushing her ear. "I love you, Liddy. I have always loved you. We are going to have a good life together. I promise you that."

"As God wills it," she added, with a silent prayer of thanksgiving that God had brought John home to her.

* * *

John hardly slept that night so anxious was he to call on Levi Harnischer, the deacon of their congregation, after services the following day. His uncle was not especially pleased that he wanted to take an hour off first thing on a day when he had orders to fill and customers to serve, but his aunt intervened.

"Really, Roger Hadwell, the boy has been working tirelessly for weeks now. Would you deny him one hour?" Gert demanded.

"An hour—no more," Roger instructed, wagging his finger at John.

And so the planning for his wedding with Liddy was set in motion. Once he had met with Levi, he knew that later that evening Levi would go to Luke and Greta's house to meet with Liddy and her family, making sure marriage was what Liddy wanted and her family approved. Levi would then go to Bishop Troyer's house to let him know that the planned nuptials should be made public.

After returning from Levi's and making sure he went straight to work unloading supplies and restocking shelves, John glanced at the calendar that his aunt kept hanging behind the counter. It was the fifteenth of March. Ten days hence the community would gather for the biweekly service, after which Bishop Troyer would make the announcement. By the middle of April he and Liddy would be married.

But as he stacked lumber in the shed behind the store, he overheard his uncle talking with Jeremiah Troyer.

"…no choice," Roger said. "I mean if it has to be, perhaps now is the best time. We're coming to the end of the term and, with Lydia and John planning their wedding, maybe this is God's will."

John tightened his grip on a board and felt a splinter prick his palm. He bristled at the idea that it might be God's will to take away the one thing that Lydia loved almost as much as he believed she loved him. What about the fact that God had blessed Liddy with a gift for teaching? What about the remaining children of school age who would not have the privilege of learning from her? What about...

"Perhaps Lydia could offer private lessons in her home for the time being," Jeremiah suggested. "After all, these hard times will not last indefinitely. In time the community will start to grow again and we can re-open the school."

John felt a whisper of hope. With their wedding only weeks away, the one thing John wanted more than anything was to assure Liddy's happiness. She would be saddened by the closing of the school, but Jeremiah had offered a possible solution at least for the short term. Private lessons. In spite of his earlier reservations, it was an idea worth considering. There was certainly plenty of room to set up the front room of Liddy's house—soon to be their home—for such lessons. And Liddy was such a practical woman. He had no doubt that she, like Roger and Jeremiah, would take the closing of the schoolhouse where she had spent so many years simply as God's will.

In the meantime he felt a real urgency to work doubly hard on building his business. For without Liddy's stipend as the community's teacher they would struggle to make ends meet on the small wages his uncle could afford. And if they should be blessed with children the financial burden would grow.

With all of these responsibilities dogging him through the rest of the day John could hardly wait to finish his work. He would not be expected to call on Liddy that evening, because Levi would go to Luke's house after dark to maintain the privacy of the matter. So, as soon as possible after bidding his aunt and uncle a good evening, John took a large piece of the wrapping paper his aunt used for purchases and rolled it up. Then he spent the rest of the evening making signs to post in Sarasota advertising his furniture-making business. And before dawn he rode into town and put up signs on every public bulletin board that he could find and still make it back to Celery Fields before the hardware store opened for the day.

To his delight and surprise he didn't have to wait long for his first order. That very afternoon Dr. Benson walked into the store and asked to speak with him. John knew the unusual request aroused Gert's curiosity, but to her credit she called him and then left him alone with the doctor to talk business.

"I'd like to order that cabinet we spoke about for my wife," Dr. Benson said. "I showed her the sketch you made and she said it was exactly the thing. Name your price."

John's heart was beating so hard he thought surely the doctor must hear it. He knew it was important to give a price that would cover materials and still leave a decent profit. Yet, it was also important that he not price his skill so high it would discourage other orders.

When he hesitated, Dr. Benson named a figure that

was higher than John had been considering. "If you think that's fair," John managed.

The doctor laughed. "If you knew what they're charging for these things in the stores you'd know it's a bargain." He stuck out his hand. "Do we have a deal, then?"

John shook Dr. Benson's hand and grinned. "We do."

"Remember now. I need the thing finished and delivered on her birthday—June the first." He tipped his hat to Gert, who had lingered in the back of the store and left.

"You are doing business with the *Englisch* now?" she asked.

"I need to earn a living."

"You have a job here." She tapped her pencil on the counter. "Your uncle will not—"

"This is work that I do after hours."

"Using your uncle's tools," she reminded him.

"And how am I ever to have the money I need to buy tools of my own, Tante Gert? How am I to build a secure future and start a family?"

Her scowl softened. "Oh, Johnny, is it never enough for you?" He understood that her use of his childhood name was deliberate. She intended to remind him of mistakes brought on by his decision to go out into the world to seek a future instead of building one with his own kind in Celery Fields.

"It's not the same," he said, and was surprised to see tears well in his aunt's eyes.

"I hope not, Johnny. We would hate to lose you twice."

The bell above the door jangled and she hastily wiped her eyes on the hem of her apron before calling out, "Be right with you." She turned then and walked to the back of the store, leaving John to serve the customer.

That evening Lydia waited eagerly for Levi's visit. At supper she had told Luke and Greta that she would be moving back to her house at the end of the week. Greta and the baby were thriving and the other children had settled into the new routine of having a newborn in the house. They no longer needed Lydia to help manage her sister's household.

"I must make plans for the closing of the school," she told them.

"That's not been decided," Greta protested.

"I am speaking of the end of the term, Greta," she corrected. "But the truth of the matter is the elders are leaning toward a permanent closing for the time being, and that will require a great deal of work, as well."

"How can you be so calm about this?" Greta asked her later as the two of them washed the dishes after supper while Luke read the older children a story. "I do not see why the school can't remain open," she fumed. "In time...."

"But until such time, Greta, it is the practical solution."

Still, Lydia was concerned about losing the income that her stipend provided. But surely with John's wages they could make do. After all, they would have a roof over their heads and it was Florida, where the growing season gave ample opportunity for raising a variety of fruits and vegetables in the garden that lay between the house and the livery. Their needs were simple. Of course, if they were blessed with children...

Knowing that Levi would not come until well after

dark, Lydia walked down to her father's house, that she and John would share once they married. She wandered through the rooms, smiling as she mentally arranged the furnishings to suit their new life. This small bedroom had once been a nursery for her and Greta, then it had been Greta's sewing room and most recently the place where Lydia prepared her lessons and graded her students' work. "By this time next year perhaps it will again be a nursery," she said aloud, testing the sound of the words against a vision of the room furnished with a brand-new crib and rocking chair made by John for their baby.

She pressed her palms over her flat stomach and closed her eyes as she considered all the changes that would surely come once she and John were married. "May it be Your will that they are happy changes," she whispered.

"Liddy!"

John's voice echoed through the house, filling Lydia's heart with such joy that she could not help but hurry back down the hall to greet him. "I am here," she called out.

His eyes glittered with excitement and she was sure that he had brought good news, perhaps about the school. Perhaps, it would not have to be closed, after all. Perhaps...

"I have been given a commission," he said. "Dr. Benson has officially ordered a china cabinet for his wife's birthday. And he will pay handsomely for it."

"John, that's wonderful news."

"It's more than wonderful, Liddy. With the money he is paying me we can manage a proper wedding trip, and with his influence there are sure to be more orders. Things are getting better all across the country and people are once again looking for ways to spend their money."

"Englischers," she said. She wanted to share in his excitement, but the idea that he might once again be drawn to building a business based on the patronage of outsiders gave her pause.

"People in Sarasota, yes. It's always been a town that attracted people of wealth. They come down for the weather, to escape the cold, and many of them stay on. Or if they don't they build winter homes here—homes that need furnishing." A little of his initial excitement had faded. "I'm not leaving, if that's got you worried," he added, and this time she heard the hurt in his tone.

She laid her hand on his wrist. "I am sorry, John. It is good news."

"For both of us," he said, his eyes holding hers.

"For both of us," she repeated, because that seemed to be the assurance he needed. But instead of the smile of relief that she had expected, he frowned. "What else?"

"I overheard my uncle talking to Jeremiah Troyer," he said, and he did not have to say the rest aloud.

"It's decided, then," she whispered, and looked down at the floor, suddenly aware that her shoes needed a good polishing.

John pulled her into his arms and rocked with her from side to side. "We will be fine," he said huskily. "I will make things good for us. Don't worry. I will provide for you."

She raised her face to his. "We will do it together, John. With God's help." She saw the slight frown that marred his handsome features. "We have each weathered hard times before, John, and now we will have each other to lean upon when challenges come."

The frown was conquered by his smile. "I love you, Lydia Goodloe."

She rested her cheek against his chest, taking comfort from the hard strength of him. Surely God would not have reunited them if a match between them was not to prosper and thrive. Still, for all her happiness at having John back in her life, she could not quell the dull pain of disappointment that the school would close and her role as teacher was coming to an end.

"Jeremiah suggested to my uncle that perhaps after the school is closed you might offer private lessons here. You could use the front room. The extra money could be a blessing when we have children of our own."

Lydia stepped back from him. "I could never charge our neighbors and friends for lessons. Of course, I will teach any child but I will take no money for doing it."

"Why not? You are offering a service in the same way Luke offers his services to shoe horses or repair machinery. Besides, you are already being paid for that work."

"Luke is in business. What I am paid comes from a general fund for services that benefit the entire community. Yes, everyone contributes to that but no one is asked to pay individually." She saw that her answer did not satisfy him and once again realized that in the world where he had spent much of his adult life the very idea that a person might simply give away something that could bring a fee was not likely. "John, these are the children of our neighbors, my sisters. How can I ask them to pay?"

There was a beat of silence between them and then

John smiled uneasily. "Then we will make do. I will work at the hardware and build furniture and in time…"

She hugged him. "It will all work out, John. I am certain of it." But it was only a half-truth. Liddy wasn't sure at all, mostly because she could see that John was not convinced.

He kissed her forehead and grinned. "Enough talk of finances," he announced. "I believe that we have a wedding in need of planning."

"So we do," she agreed, happy to have the discussion of how they would make their way behind them. "Will you want to live here, John, in my father's house?" She had really never thought they would do otherwise, but their discussion of money had reminded her of the many times her father had expressed objections to her spending time with John.

"It is your house now, Liddy, and if it suits you then it suits me, as well. Or we can start fresh somewhere else."

"I want to be close to Greta," she replied.

"Then this is the place." He gave her a hug and then stepped back. "I have to get to work on that china cabinet," he said. "Will you come to the hardware store after Levi leaves and keep me company?"

"I will," she promised as they walked together through the kitchen to the back door. "I'll bring some of that strudel Greta makes that you like so much. We can have a picnic on the loading dock."

"You aren't worried about someone seeing us?"

"Let them look," she said with a recklessness that was completely out of character for her. She felt giddy with her love for John, and for once in her adult life she was going to permit herself to enjoy that feeling.

After John left, Lydia walked back to her sister's

house at the end of town. In her absence Pleasant and Jeremiah had arrived, bringing Bettina along in case the baby started to fuss while the family met with the deacon. It seemed as good a time as any to prepare Bettina for the news of the school's closing that would soon be spread throughout the community.

"But they can't," Bettina protested. "I had thought that after you and John Amman married…" She blushed scarlet, realizing her mistake in mentioning a courtship and marriage that were not yet properly announced.

"You had thought that one day you might become the teacher." Lydia finished the thought for her. "I would not leave my position, Bettina."

"But if you and John Amman married and had children…"

"We would still need my income and, besides, we have known for some time, Bettina, that the school's future was precarious at best."

"But I had planned… Caleb and I had…" She stopped speaking again, this time shoving her fist against her lips as if to stem any further admissions.

It was well-known that Caleb Harnischer was intent on marrying Bettina one day. In so many ways the young couple reminded Lydia of herself and John when they were that age. So filled with plans for the future they were. And, just as with John and Lydia, it did not occur to this young couple that God might have other plans for their lives. She could only hope that neither of them would make a decision as John had that would separate them for eight long years.

"It will all work out," she promised Bettina. "You must simply trust that God will send you in the right direction even as he is guiding the elders regarding the school. Besides, it is not forever. In time the population will grow again and there will be children in need of schooling and the school will be reopened."

"But I have heard that they plan to tear it down and use the land for other purposes," Bettina protested,

Lydia had heard the same thing. "Then when the time comes the elders will build another school."

Bettina made a face. "But by then…"

"Shh. God will show us the way. We may not always see His path clearly, but in the end…"

Bettina's face brightened. "Just like He did for you and John Amman, you mean."

"That's right. Just like that."

But as she watched Bettina climb the stairs to care for the crying baby, she could not help worrying about Caleb and her niece. They might face a great deal of heartache before they found their way together, if that was God's intent for them at all.

Outside she heard the crunch of buggy wheels on crushed shell and the muffled snort of a horse. Levi had come at last. It was time to put aside any worries she had about the school and give all of her attention to the happy task of planning her wedding.

Chapter 12

As the days passed leading up to Sunday services and the bishop's announcement of their wedding, nothing could dampen Lydia's good mood. Not the closing of the school—the news public now. Not even her previous concerns about John taking orders from outsiders. For if Lydia had suffered doubts about John attracting *Englisch* customers, such doubts were soon put to rest as word spread of his gift for making fine furniture. Besides, as Greta repeatedly reminded her, Luke served many in the Sarasota community with no ill effects. Thanks to Luke, John now had half-a-dozen small orders in addition to the china cabinet for the doctor's wife.

Even his uncle, as well as Hilda Yoder, came around to seeing the benefit of John's growing business. Hardly a customer who came to place an order with John left town without purchasing something from the hardware store or crossing the street to browse the wares of the dry-goods store. And if Lydia had worried that Josef Bontrager might not like the fact that John was in competition with him, she needn't have. One Sunday after services, as they all enjoyed the communal meal, Josef had approached John.

"I saw the cabinet you are building for Dr. Benson's wife," he said. "It reminded me that I have a supply of wood in my barn that I have no use for. I need the room that it's taking up, so if it is something you could use…"

John was on his feet immediately. "I'll stop by and have a look at it, but I would pay you…"

Josef held up his hands. "You would be doing me a favor, John Amman. Managing my land holdings and farm takes all my time these days. I am out of practice with crafting furniture and it would be good to see the wood put to some use."

"I'll come tomorrow evening if that suits," John said.

"That'll do nicely," Josef replied, and walked back to the table where his wife and her parents sat.

"So looks like you're to be the resident woodworker," Luke said after Josef left.

John grinned. "Life is *sehr gut*," he said. "I'll have to think about a place to store the lumber, though."

"You can use the stables for now," Luke offered. "Not that much call for livery services these days. There's plenty of room."

Lydia didn't know when she had felt so certain that God's plan was playing out exactly as He had intended. How could she ever have doubted it? It was true that most of the orders were for small things—caning a chair seat, building a small side table or a simple bookcase.

But over time John's business would grow. Times were clearly getting better. They might struggle in the beginning, especially after the school closed, but for the first time since John's return she realized that she was clear of any doubt that he might leave again. He had found his place in Celery Fields.

With the joy of a future she had only dared dream of in her heart, she scrubbed the iron skillet. Just after breakfast John had gone to make a delivery with Roger and after that he would go to Sarasota to call on a prospective customer. Lydia intended to finish scouring the skillet before settling in to prepare the lessons she would teach the following day. A knock at the front door interrupted her work.

"Coming," she called out as she set the pan aside. Using her apron, she wiped her hands, reddened now by the hot water, and made her way down the hall. She could not imagine who of her neighbors might be calling at this time of day. Besides, anyone she knew would surely have come to the kitchen door.

A stranger waited patiently on her front porch, *Englisch* by his dress. He was a short, stocky man who looked, given his tan linen suit and soft straw hat, as if he had done well in the world. He carried a walking stick and was looking around when Lydia reached the door. "May I help you?"

His smile showed brilliantly white teeth set off by the ruddy color of his skin. This was a man who had spent a good deal of time in the sun but not necessarily doing hard work. She could not help but notice that his hands, folded on top of the walking stick, featured clean fingernails polished to a high sheen. Behind him she saw a motorcar parked in front of the house and a uniformed driver waiting next to it.

"Good day, ma'am," he said, removing his hat in the gesture of respect for women common to outsiders. "I wonder if you might help me. My name is George Stevens and I am looking for an old friend of mine—John Amman?"

Lydia felt a wave of panic sweep through her. George Stevens had been John's business partner and whenever John spoke of the man it was always with admiration, even a certain nostalgia. *Not now,* Lydia silently prayed. *Not when he's finally come back to me.*

"I apologize for disturbing you at home," George Stevens hastened to add. "We—my driver and I—tried several of the businesses, but they all seemed to have closed for the day. A boy sent me to the apartment above the livery, but also said if I didn't find him there I should try coming here."

"John Amman is not here." Lydia forced out the words.

The stranger frowned as he glanced back toward the town and the setting sun. "I was certain that he told me…this is the town of Celery Fields, is it not?"

She should not be explaining anything to this man— she should not even be speaking with him. She was relieved to see Luke coming up the path. "May I help you?" he asked politely as he positioned himself between the stranger and the still-closed screen door.

George Stevens repeated his question. But it was clear that he was less sure of himself when facing Luke. It was as if he realized for the first time that he had left his world behind and was now standing in the midst of theirs. "I… John Amman and I were friends and busi-

ness partners at one time. Unfortunately, the economy
ended the business, but we parted as good friends and
I had hoped…" The man was babbling to fill up the silence that Luke and Lydia greeted him with. It was an
Englisch habit that Lydia had always found especially
annoying.

"John Amman will be in town tomorrow—at the
hardware store," Luke said. "We will let him know that
you were here. *Guten abend.*" And with that he stepped
inside the house and closed the inner door. He handed
Lydia a basket. "Greta said you needed these things for
the wedding supper."

"*Yah.* It could have waited until tomorrow, but I'm
glad you came."

"Would you like me to stay until we're sure he's
gone?"

Outside, the motor of the car rumbled to life. "I think
it is all fine now," Lydia replied.

"*Gut.* Then I will go." He opened the door and
stepped onto the porch, looking down the street to
where the car was making a turn that would take George
Stevens away from Celery Fields.

"But, Luke, what if…" Lydia's hands started to shake
and she felt the sting of tears filling her eyes.

Luke grasped her concern at once. "He's not going
to leave you a second time, Liddy," Luke said softly.
"No man could be so dumb."

"But…"

"Do you not trust him, Liddy?"

And there was the crux of it. She was certain of her
love for John and of his for her. But John had once been
drawn to that other world. Look where he was at this
very moment, sitting with some *Englischer* hoping to

get an order for a clock or piece of his furniture. Oh, why could he not be satisfied to wait for orders from his friends and neighbors in Celery Fields?

"It's not the same as before, Liddy," Luke said as if reading her thoughts. "All of us trade from time to time with them. I could not have made it these last two years without their business. But my place is here with my own people, and so is John's."

She took some comfort from Luke's words. "You do know that were you ever to decide otherwise Greta would come after you," she said, and smiled up at him.

He grinned. "*Yah.* She keeps me in line, your sister." Then his expression sobered. "You will tell John that his friend stopped by."

Lydia bristled. "Of course. I would not keep it from him."

"Then you will have your answer," Luke said softly as he turned and headed for home.

John was just leaving his meeting with two men preparing to open a new restaurant on Main Street in downtown Sarasota. In his hand he held the order for the tables where patrons would be served. He had turned down their request for him to also build a bar. John was certain Lydia would draw the line at him making anything remotely associated with the sale of spirits. He already was concerned that she would object to his accepting the order to build the tables.

The men had acquired the chairs they wanted and it was from the simple design of those chairs that they wanted John to design the two dozen tables. He could not wait to tell Liddy. With an order of this size he could afford to cut back his hours at the hardware store, giving him more time to work on his carpentry orders. His uncle would no doubt grumble something about him being unappreciative. But that would pass the moment John reminded him that fewer hours also meant less wages.

He was crossing the main street, bustling even at this hour with traffic and people, when he had to jump out of the way of a long sleek Packard automobile coming toward him. The car braked and stopped just as John made it safely to the other side of the street. From the corner of his eye he saw a man get out.

"John Amman? Is that you?"

John turned and broke into a grin as he saw his friend and former business partner coming toward him. A wave of nostalgia for all the times, good and bad, that he had shared with his friend swept through John and propelled him forward. He walked straight into George's bear hug.

"Look at you," George said as he held John at arm's length and took in the straw hat, shirt with no buttons, collar or cuffs, and homespun trousers held up by black suspenders. "I hardly recognized you."

"What are you doing here?" John asked, suddenly a little self-conscious to be standing in the middle of a busy sidewalk talking to someone who was not Amish.

"I came to find you," George replied. "Come have something to eat with me at the hotel. I'm staying there and word has it that they serve a fine shrimp dinner. It'll be like old times."

Only it wouldn't—couldn't. John was not the man he had been when he and George had worked together. "I can't," he said. "It is not our way."

George blinked and studied him as if trying to decide whether or not John was teasing him. Back east they had often played practical jokes on each other. "I want to talk to you, John. There's a new business opportunity that's come my way."

John indicated a park bench in front of a business that had closed for the night. "We can sit here and talk," he said.

George motioned to his driver to leave without him and sat down next to John. He glanced up and down the street. "Things seem to be prospering here," he said.

"Times are better," John agreed. "How are Bonnie and the children?"

"They are fine." A moment of awkward silence passed. "I met your Lydia," George said.

"How? Where?"

"I went to Celery Fields and asked for you and eventually ended up at the house behind the livery. She's lovely, John."

"We're to be married in two weeks."

"Congratulations! That's wonderful news."

The sun had set and before long it would be dark. The streets that had been so busy just minutes earlier were more deserted now. He should be getting back to Celery Fields, back to Liddy, but he was curious. George had come west to see him. "What is this business opportunity you have?"

"How much do you folks keep up with world news, John?"

You folks? There had been a time when George would not have thought to make such a distinction. "We hear some things," John hedged. Once he had been very aware of all that was happening in the outside world. George had talked of nothing else.

"There's every possibility that war is coming to Europe," George continued. "Several of the countries that allied themselves with the wrong side in the Great War now seem to think they got the short end of the stick in the peace. There's a lot of unrest and political upheaval, especially in Germany."

"I do not understand what this has to do with your business opportunity."

"It has everything to do with it. The American government mostly wants to stay out of things, but on the other hand, they are concerned about our allies— England, France..."

John did not understand where this was heading, but he could see that George was very excited. "Go on," he encouraged, hoping that his friend would soon come to the point.

"I—*we* if you want in—have been offered a government contract to build parts for submarines. They want us to reopen the factory and retool it for the work. The government will pay for everything—refurbishing the factory, raw materials, everything. In less than a month you'd recoup the losses you took when the market crashed, John."

"This is a good opportunity for you," John said.

"For us," George corrected. "The government won't just hand over the money. They're going to need proof that we can do this. Without you to design the parts, there's no chance of getting the contract. I can't do it without you, John."

"I know nothing of submarines."

"You are a design wizard," George said. "We have to figure out how to make the parts so that they can be mass-produced. That's where you come in."

"I am to be married," John reminded him.

"Bring her east."

John fought a smile. It was all so easy for George. It had been that way when they worked together. For him obstacles simply did not exist, or if they did they were merely challenges to be overcome. "Our home is here with our own people," he reminded his friend.

George frowned. "Did I mention what the government is offering to pay us, John?" He named a figure that was more money than John had ever dreamed of earning. "With that kind of money you could work with me for a couple of years and then retire for good."

With that kind of money I could assure the future for Liddy and our children. For Gert and Roger Hadwell.

"Talk to your Liddy about this, John. She seems to me to be a levelheaded young woman, one who would see the advantages for both of you." George stood up and extended his hand to John.

John also stood and accepted his friend's handshake. "I will discuss it," he promised.

"I need your answer by tomorrow, John. The government doesn't wait."

John nodded.

"We'd have to get started right away."

"Before the wedding?"

George chuckled. "Not that soon. Get yourself hitched, my friend. But I'll need you out east by the end of the month at the latest."

All the way back to Celery Fields, John thought about the offer George had made him. It was true that in their business before, John's role had been one of figuring things out—how best to design a piece of furniture so that it not only served its purpose but also looked good alone and with the other furnishings in the room.

But this was different. This was designing parts, like for a clock. Like for a missile or bomb. The thought gave him pause. No one in Celery Fields would approve of him building anything connected with war. The Amish were a peace-loving people. They did not take part in war or anything to do with it. He snapped the reins, urging the team of horses into a trot. He needed to talk to Liddy. She would know what to do.

"You cannot seriously be considering this," Liddy said after he explained everything to her. Her voice came out in little gasps as she struggled to catch her breath and force out the words. Her head was pounding and her heart was racing as she fought to suppress the image of her world falling apart yet again.

"It is not for the war, Liddy. George says that the Americans are trying to maintain the peace. All they want to do is protect the shoreline and the best way to do that apparently is with submarines."

"Those ships are instruments of war, John." Surely, it was the excitement of seeing his friend after all these months. Surely, it was the fact that it was now nearly eleven o'clock and he was exhausted after his long day. He was not thinking clearly.

"They are also instruments for keeping the peace. Why can't you understand that I would do this for us, for our future? It would not be forever, Liddy. I am not leaving you. George says—"

"I do not care what George says," she said through gritted teeth. "This man is not of our faith, and he knows nothing of our ways."

"He has been a good friend to me."

"And for that I am grateful, but John, can you not see that I am afraid?"

"And can you not see that all I want is to make sure you never have anything to fear ever again?"

"You cannot control what happens to us, John. If it be God's will that—"

"Why then might you not consider that *this* is God's will, that the sudden appearance of my former business partner is part of God's plan for us?"

"Or perhaps George Stevens with his fancy motor-car and his driver and his expensive clothes is nothing more than temptation, John Amman, a test to see if you have conquered your wanderlust once and for all and will never again be tempted by the outside world."

The light of excitement that had lit his eyes—indeed, his entire face—from the moment he'd come to tell her the news dimmed. "Will you never have trust in me, Liddy?"

"Oh, John, I love you so very much and…"

"But you do not trust me, Liddy."

"I…" She struggled to find the words. "You can understand that I have doubts. You were away for eight years, John, and while it's true that you have returned to us—to me—you cannot deny the pull of that outside world still works within you."

"They are not our enemy, Liddy."

"I know, but they are also not of our ways."

"And in our ways, is it not the duty of the man to provide for his wife and children? To make sure they have shelter and food and the children have a future?"

"This is true, but…"

"This is all I am trying to do, Liddy. We are getting

a later start on our life together than most. We do not have the years younger couples have to build a business and a future. Our need is now."

"We have shelter and food enough. You have work and in time…"

He stood up and started to pace. He turned once as if to say something more and then paced again. Lydia sat in her chair, hands folded in her lap, and waited.

"There is another side to this, Liddy. George Stevens is my friend. He has told me that if I turn this down he will not be awarded the contract. The government wants to begin at once."

"There must be others who can do what he wishes you to do in this project."

"No doubt. But finding that man would take time that George doesn't have. He has also suffered great financial losses these last years and…"

Lydia could not suppress a laugh. "Yet he arrived here in a shiny motorcar with a driver," she reminded him.

John shrugged. "That's George. He has a habit of spending before he earns. He thinks it is important to make the good impression. I expect he is deeply in debt for his trouble."

"Then all the more reason not to become involved in his plan," Lydia argued. "He is not to be trusted."

"His father hired me when no one else would. George made me an equal partner in that business. He is my friend."

Would it truly come to this? That she would have to demand that he choose her or his friend? "I am so very tired, John, and not thinking clearly. Can we not discuss this tomorrow?"

"George needs my answer tomorrow," he replied as he stood at the window staring into the darkness.

Lydia let out a sigh of resignation. "Then do what you must," she said quietly, all the while silently praying that he would choose her this time.

Instead, he picked up his hat and walked to the door. "I would like your blessing, Liddy, and your trust that I am doing this for us as much as for George."

So he was going away again. "I cannot…" she began, and her voice broke as the sobs she'd been holding back spilled out. "Please just go," she managed when he started to cross the room to her. She looked up at him. "Go," she whispered.

His lips hardened into a thin line and he turned away and stalked to the door. "I'm going, then, and this time I won't bother to write, Liddy," he said as he left.

When Lydia woke the following morning after most of the night spent pacing the floor, fighting the desire to run across the yard that separated them and up to John's apartment, Greta was in the kitchen frying bacon.

"What are you doing here?" Lydia croaked, her throat raw from crying most of the night.

"I came to find out what is going on. I mean it is perfectly understandable that as you and John approach your wedding day one or both of you will get a case of nerves but this business is ridiculous. Luke says that John has packed up and left with that man. How could you let this happen yet again, Liddy?" She scooped up two strips of the bacon and plopped them onto a plate that she set in front of Lydia. "Eat," she commanded as she pulled out a chair opposite Lydia and sat down.

"I did not let this happen this time nor the time before," Lydia protested. "John is a grown man and…"

"A man who loves you," Greta reminded her.

"Then why did he leave?" Lydia said quietly as the tears once again leaked down her cheeks.

Greta grasped her sister's hand and squeezed it. "Oh, Liddy, he wants to make a good life for you. The wages Roger Hadwell pays him wouldn't be enough to support John alone if Luke hadn't bartered the living space for John maintaining the stables."

"He has orders for his furniture."

"And in time there will be more orders, enough to build a proper business, but that will all take time, Liddy, and Luke says that with the school closing and the loss of your stipend…"

"I can get other work," Lydia protested.

"Doing what? There are no jobs in Celery Fields. Are you truly going to go out into the Sarasota community and clean houses?"

"It's honorable work."

"It is, but I seem to recall that you were the one who was concerned about John taking orders for his furniture business from outsiders. How could you work for them?"

Greta's occasional burst of logic could be maddening. She had a point, of course. "Still…" Lydia began searching for some counterargument. "The point is that John keeps returning to their world and I am afraid…"

"Ah, finally we get to the root of it. You are afraid of losing him. Well, look around, Liddy. He's already gone. Now, the question is what will you do about it?"

"He has made his choice."

"And who placed him in the position of having to

choose?" Greta rolled her eyes. "The way he explained the whole thing to Luke when he came by late last night, his friend needs his help. Would you have him ignore that?"

"No, but..."

Greta continued as if Liddy had not spoken. "What would Luke have done when his business burned to the ground if friends and neighbors from both Celery Fields and Sarasota had not stepped up to help him rebuild? It's what we do, Liddy, and if you needed some reassurance that John has indeed returned to his roots, this should surely be it."

"Now you are truly making no sense," Lydia fumed as she picked at a strip of bacon. "John has chosen, all right. He has chosen the outside world."

"No. He has chosen to help his friend. He will come back once that is done just like Luke's customers from Sarasota went back to their lives after helping him after the fire."

This time I will not write.

John's parting words rang in her ears. He hadn't written last time, either, so why say such a thing? "It's over," she said wearily as she carried her dishes to the sink. She stood there for a long moment and looked across the yard to John's rooms. There was no difference that she could see, but in her heart she felt his absence as surely as if there had been some physical sign that he had left. "Where are the children?" she asked.

"Bettina is watching them." Greta got up and began wiping the kitchen table and clearing away the skillet she'd used for the bacon. "Pleasant will need to be told," she said.

"I expect that Gertrude Hadwell has already let her

know, along with Hilda Yoder and others." It would be some time before the gossips in the community stopped talking about this. "I am sorry for Gert," she added wistfully. "She has gotten so used to having John back again."

"I am not worried about Gertrude Hadwell, Liddy. I am worried about you—to have your heart broken once is bad enough, but to repeat that experience?" She actually shuddered. "I can't begin to imagine what…"

"I will be fine, Greta."

But would she? She had lost her livelihood, work she truly loved and now John had left her for a second time. Would she ever be fine again?

Chapter 13

It had been a long time since John had ridden in a motorcar, especially one as fine as George Stevens's Packard. His Amish faith allowed him to ride in such a vehicle when necessary as long as he neither operated nor owned the car. He had to wonder if the elders would consider this trip "necessary." He ran his palm over the soft cloth seat, marveling at the space available for a third person to sit comfortably between George and him.

George had dozed off almost as soon as his driver had pulled away from the Sarasota hotel. He had asked no questions when John had showed up at his suite and said that he was ready to accept his former partner's offer. John suspected that George was just relieved to hear his decision and didn't want to risk jinxing it by asking too many questions. All through breakfast

George had talked about his wife, Bonnie. But not once had he asked about Lydia.

John studied the folders of papers George had handed him at breakfast. His education had stopped after eight years, as did formal learning for all Amish boys, but in the years he'd spent working with George and other *Englischers* his reading and understanding of the written word had increased significantly. Still, the government contract and the specifications for submarine parts that George expected him to design made little sense to him. Not for the first time he wished Liddy were riding in the car with him.

He laid the papers on the seat next to George and pinched the bridge of his nose as he squinted his eyes closed and then opened them again to stare out the open window. Florida was flatland dotted with orchards of citrus trees, fields planted with vegetables, swamps, horse farms and small towns. The recent drought had turned the landscape a greenish-brown and the fronds of the tall, slender coconut palms drooped toward the ground as if willing the water to rise up and satisfy their thirst. He watched an egret fly next to the car, keeping pace with it for a bit before veering off to land in a ditch. He saw a flock of roseate spoonbills fly across the sky in the distance, their pink bodies reminding him of the sunset that he had watched with Liddy at the bay.

Liddy. Beautiful. Stubborn. Impossible.

Why couldn't he make her understand that everything he did, every decision he made, was for one purpose only? Her happiness was everything to him. After returning to Celery Fields and learning that he still had a chance to make things right with her, to win her heart this time forever, how many nights had he paced the small confines of his rooms above the stables thinking of how best to build a life with her?

He frowned.

And why did he need to prove himself to her over and over again? After all, she had been the one to put community ahead of their happiness. And he had come to accept that decision, so why was it so difficult for her to accept that he was doing this partly because George needed his help? She had refused even to consider the possibility that George Stevens might have been sent to them, a blessing in disguise. She was always talking about how God would provide. Well, to John's way of thinking, a person had to be open to such messages and opportunities. Annoyed by thoughts of Liddy's obstinacy, he set his lips in a tight, hard line, folded his arms across his chest and closed his eyes.

But sleep did not come. Instead, his mind reeled with memories of Liddy's laughter, her smile, her touch, her kiss. Not even George's snoring or the thud of the car's tires on the uneven road could block out the sweetness of those times that he and Liddy had shared recently. He felt his features relax into a smile as he recalled her story of Greta's plans for their wedding.

"You would think she was planning her own nuptials," Liddy had said with a shake of her head after describing the menu for the wedding supper that Greta had suggested. "I keep trying to tell her that we need everything plain, the way it should be, but she seems determined to find a way to turn the entire event into some kind of community celebration."

"Well, isn't it?" he asked, suddenly unsure whether or not Liddy truly loved him or simply saw this as her last chance to marry.

"Oh, John, of course it is. But we have waited for so long and all that truly matters is that we will finally be together. A wedding is an event, a celebration. But it is the marriage that I am looking forward to—the years we are going to share together with God's blessing."

And after that he'd entertained no more doubts.

Until now.

"Are you hungry, John?"

John opened his eyes and found George watching him, a puzzled expression on his face.

"Do you want to stop?" he replied, not wanting to be any trouble.

George chuckled. "You haven't changed a bit, my friend. Still answering a question with another question." He leaned forward. "Henry, next diner you see let's pull in."

Over lunch George explained the project in a way that set John on the path to understanding the task before them. He realized that the work was exactly as George had described it, like building the workings of a clock. As they ate John made some detailed sketches on a napkin and showed them to George.

His partner grinned. "That's the ticket," he said. "I see what you've done. Just in changing the angle of that piece, it will eliminate the necessity of this connector and…" He released a low, satisfied whistle. "If we get this order done early, there's every possibility that the government will give us another project and then another and before you know it, my friend, we will be right back where we were before."

John forced a smile. *"Yah."*

But the truth was that he didn't wanted to be back

where he was with George and their business. What he really wanted was to be back with Liddy.

After John left, Lydia found that she could not stand being in the house alone. Over the weeks that had passed since she had accepted John's proposal she had spent most of her time imagining them living there together. She had even started to make small changes in preparation for John moving in after the wedding. The chair she knew he favored had replaced the one her father had used in the front room. She had taken down the hat her father used to wear from the peg by the back door where it had hung since his death a few years earlier. Now the peg was empty. The house seemed to be waiting for John's arrival.

"An arrival that will never happen," she muttered as she shook out the small rag rug she had placed on the floor by the bed they would have shared.

"You are talking to yourself, Lydia." Her half sister, Pleasant, frowned with concern as she crossed the yard.

Lydia gave Pleasant a weak smile. "So I am. Come in. I just squeezed some fresh juice from the oranges you brought me yesterday."

Pleasant sat at the table in the chair that Lydia had imagined John using for their shared meals. Lydia could feel Pleasant watching her closely. "You look tired," she said when Lydia set two glasses of juice and a plate of ginger cookies on the table.

Lydia shrugged. "There's a lot to be done to finish the school year and then prepare the building to be permanently closed."

They sipped their juice in silence. "You haven't heard from John?"

He'd been gone for ten days. "I don't expect I will. After all his parting words were that this time he would not write." She gave a bitter bark of a laugh. "As if somehow this time were any different than…"

To her shock she began to cry and because this was Pleasant, ever practical and stoic, rather than the more excitable Greta, Lydia gave in to the tears she had held inside for days now.

Pleasant waited for the storm of tears to pass, acknowledging the outburst only by passing Lydia a napkin to use for wiping her eyes and blowing her nose. It was their way to not make a fuss. The two of them had always enjoyed this special bond.

"In time I suppose…" Lydia began but did not finish the thought as she took a sip of her juice.

Pleasant tapped her fingers nervously on the tabletop. "I have something I must tell you, Liddy," she said softly. "Jeremiah says that I should have told you long ago, but that is the way he is."

"Has something happened with one of the children?" Lydia felt ashamed that she had been so focused on her own misery that she might have overlooked something that would be a concern for Pleasant.

"This has nothing to do with my family, Lydia," Pleasant replied brusquely. "We are speaking of you— and John."

With a weary sigh, Lydia started to rise from her chair to refill their glasses. "It is over, Pleasant. I would expect Greta would continue to live in blind hope, but surely not you, as well."

"Sit down, Liddy." She waited until Lydia was facing her across the table. "When John went away before— all those years ago—he did write to you."

"He didn't, Pleasant. Are you trying to say that I have forgotten?"

"I am saying that you never knew. Our *dat* asked Hilda Yoder to make sure anything that looked as if it might have come from John be first given to him. There were letters, Lydia, several of them."

"But why…?"

"He did not wish to see you hurt and he was afraid."

"Of what? John is…"

"He was not afraid of John. He was afraid of losing you. He was afraid that you would follow John and be lost to us forever."

"But I wrote John, as well, and…"

"Those letters were never sent."

Lydia felt a tightening of her chest that she recognized as fury at Hilda Yoder for her part in this. But when she lifted her gaze to meet her half sister's eyes, that fury was directed at Pleasant. "You knew and said nothing?"

"I am not pleased with my actions, Lydia. It was a time in my life when I suffered from the sin of envy. You and Greta held such a special place in our father's heart. You represented your mother to him and he had loved her so very much and grieved for her untimely death. Perhaps if I had known Jeremiah then, I might have—"

"What happened to the letters?" Lydia felt a twinge of hope that perhaps somehow they had been saved.

"He burned them, both yours and John's."

"And John never knew? Would not Gertrude have known or John's mother?"

"No one knew but Hilda, *Dat* and me."

"I thought that he had abandoned me—all those years, Pleasant…lost."

This time when the tears began Pleasant did not sit by and wait. She knelt next to Lydia and wrapped her arms around her. "I know. I am truly sorry for my part in all of this, Liddy. I wish I could make amends. Jeremiah said that I could by telling you the truth, but now I see I have only upset you further."

"He thinks I don't care, Pleasant. For eight long years he thought I had turned from him, and still he came back."

"He loves you in spite of the fact that he believes you turned away from him. He has always loved you, Lydia, as you have always loved him—as you love him now. There may yet be time to salvage this. Write to him at once. I will post the letter myself and this time there will be no question that it is sent."

"It's been almost two weeks since he left," Lydia moaned. "What if…"

"You will have no answers if you do not try, Liddy." Pleasant led Lydia to the front room and the small desk in the corner. "Write to him. I will clean up in the kitchen."

"But what can I say that will change anything?"

Pleasant cupped Lydia's cheek. "Tell him what I told you. Tell him you love him. Ask him to come home to you."

Lydia sat at the desk for nearly half an hour, the words pouring onto the page before her. Finally she could write no more. She folded the thin pages and placed them in an envelope and sealed it. "We have no address," she said, carrying the letter to the kitchen, where Pleasant sat waiting patiently at the table.

Pleasant smiled. "That man, George Stevens, stayed at the hotel in Sarasota. Jeremiah was able to get his address. We will send the letter in his care and it is sure to reach John."

Lydia watched Pleasant head back to town, to the ice-cream shop her husband owned, and a few minutes later she saw Pleasant and Jeremiah in their buggy headed for Sarasota. She closed her eyes and sent up a silent prayer that the words she had written would bring John back to her.

A week passed with no word. And then half of another week.

Finally, one evening after he returned from Sarasota and the ice-packing business he ran there, Jeremiah walked slowly up to her house and handed her an envelope—her envelope, her handwriting. She turned it over in her hands and saw that the seal had not been broken. The letter had been returned to her unread.

She had her answer.

At the biweekly services that Sunday, Lydia once again endured the barely concealed glances of pity and sympathy cast her way. By now everyone had heard the story. John was gone—again. And this time not a single person in the community believed he would come back, not even Lydia. And yet in the still-dark hours before dawn as she had stood looking out toward the windows of the rooms above the stable, she felt something in her heart that she could only describe as hope.

Foolish, foolish woman, she thought as she bowed her head for the first prayer of the morning. She prayed for understanding, for God to reveal His purpose for her life. The school would be closed in another week and John was gone. What was she supposed to do?

She barely heard the first sermon so focused was she on thoughts of John. Was he happy? Was he well? She prayed that both were true. But oh, how she missed him—his smile and his laughter. Missed his hand holding hers, his arm around her as they sat on her porch swing planning their future.

Every day that he'd been gone she told herself that in time the pain would lessen. In time the memories would not sting so much. In time...

But the truth was that her every waking moment was spent thinking about John. If only she had known about the letters her father had intercepted and burned. Those letters were proof that John had kept his promise. Pleasant had told her that they had come for months after he left—one a day at first and then, later, one a week, and finally they had stopped.

And suddenly she knew her purpose. Her eyes flew open as the decision came to her. This time she would be the one to go and find John. And even if there was no chance of rekindling their love a third time at least he would know the truth as she now did. He deserved that. Yes, as soon as school was closed, she would pack up her things and take the train east. She would leave notes of explanation for Greta and Pleasant, but she would not let anyone know of her plan.

And then?

She closed her eyes and clasped her hands together. She was certain that God had brought John back into her life for some purpose. Perhaps that purpose was only to lead both of them to an understanding of the past that had caused each of them pain and kept them from moving forward in their lives. Now she was certain that God was leading her to John to explain what neither of them had known. And would God be gracious and bless them with a reunion that brought John home to Celery Fields, home to her?

One step at a time.

The remainder of the three-hour service went by in a flash, so preoccupied was Lydia with crafting her plan for leaving to find John. She had the address for George Stevens. He had seemed a kind man. She thought that if she went to him first he would help her arrange a meeting with John. Yes, that was the best idea.

She rose with the rest of the congregation for the closing hymn. And by the time she and the other women had gathered in the kitchen to lay out the meal, she felt a new lightness of spirit.

John's first time back inside the large, rambling factory where he and George had built their earlier fortunes brought back a flood of memories, some pleasant and some incredibly painful. There had been the day that the workers they'd hired had completed the first large order of grandfather clocks to be shipped to a chain of department stores in New York. George had declared the day a holiday and given each employee a cash bonus.

Then there had been the day when he and George had called the remaining employees that they had not already had to let go onto the floor of the factory. Behind the dozen or so men the machinery stood silent and unused. Everyone knew what was coming. They were closing the factory for good. It was Christmas Eve and George had bought each of the men the makings for a turkey and ham Christmas dinner to take home to their families. It was the best he could offer and John remembered how, after the last man was gone and the doors of the factory closed behind them for the final time, George had cried like a small boy.

But when John walked into the factory after the drive across the state, he was surprised to see some of their former employees already at work cleaning and oiling machinery and painting walls—walls they were also lining with patriotic posters. They greeted him with smiles that spoke of trust and optimism and John's heart was filled with a determination to make this work, if not for him, then for these men and their families.

Refusing George's offer of a room at his parents' mansion, John chose instead to set up a cot in the factory office, citing the need to be near the work when ideas for design changes came to him in the night. He did not admit even to himself that the nights were when he did most of his work. At least if he could force himself to focus on the designs and patterns for the pieces the factory would produce, he could get through the night without constantly thinking of Liddy.

Or so he thought.

The truth was that thoughts of her haunted him day and night. He tried to remind himself that he had been in this position before, that in time the memories and the pain of them would lessen. In time he would fill his days and nights with work and the joy of seeing the business that he and George had built together thrive once again. But every time he walked out onto the factory floor to try modeling one of the parts they would be producing his thoughts went back to Celery Fields. The stables that Luke had told him he could use for his woodworking. The smell of fresh-cut wood mingling with the smoky fire of Luke's blacksmithing. The rocking chair he had made for Greta and the china cabinet he had built for Dr. Benson's wife.

And there had been the orders from Luke's customers—orders he had stayed up all night before leaving to finish. He thought about the kitchen table and chair set he had started making for Liddy as a wedding gift. Those pieces sat unfinished at the back of Luke's stables. Remembering the smoothness of the tabletop John ran his hand absently over one of the worktables in the factory and was stung by a sliver of metal filing that nicked his palm. They would work in metal now, the machinery having already been retooled. They would not build clocks, cabinets, tables or rocking chairs. The assignment was for small parts that would have to fit perfectly with other parts being made in other factories. Parts for submarines that would silently patrol the waters offshore.

In Liddy's eyes the work he was doing would be used in instruments of war and, as she had reminded him, their faith was rooted in peace and forgiveness. It was hard not to face the fact that war would come, if not to the shores of America then surely to Europe. He could tell himself anything he liked, but he knew in his heart that Liddy was right. And as each day passed he watched his designs and patterns turned into actual parts that the men on the factory floor produced. His certainty that agreeing to George's plan had been a mistake hardened into a lump of solid regret that lodged in the very center of his chest.

There was no doubt that he could make enough money to secure a future for himself. The government contract had provided separate funding for the creation of the designs and patterns that could be easily transferred to other factories making the same parts in other places. After John had been back only two weeks George had presented him with a check. "With the gratitude of the United States government," he had said.

But John had refused to take the money. Liddy was right. Any way he looked at it, the factory was running on what George called "war time" whenever he reminded the employees of the urgency of meeting production numbers on time.

Then one night George came to the factory late. John assumed that he had come to be sure the night shift was running smoothly as he often did when they were approaching a delivery deadline. Only this time George came straight to the office and he was carrying a large new toolbox. The men from the third shift crowded into the doorway behind him. For once the machinery behind them that ran round the clock was silent.

"You won't take the money. I get that—sort of. But without the work you did to make the patterns, John, we would all be unemployed. So, the men and I decided to get you a present to show our appreciation. This has nothing to do with the government, you understand. Just a bunch of once-out-of-work guys wanting to say 'thanks.'"

He placed the toolbox on the desk. When John just stared, he said, "Well, open it." Behind George the men pressed forward, their excitement palpable in the small office.

John unhooked the locks and raised the lid. The box was completely outfitted with a set of woodworking tools—hammers, chisels, handsaws, clamps—everything anyone would need to build furniture by hand.

"One day," George said softly, "you'll go home again to Celery Fields and we want you to have a good start on that shop you're going to open."

"I don't know what to say," John whispered as he lifted a tack hammer from the toolbox to admire it, feel the fit of his fingers around the grip.

One of the men broke the uncomfortable silence that fell over the room by starting up a chorus of "For He's a Jolly Good Fellow" and the others joined in. When the song ended George was grinning broadly as he wrapped his arm around John's shoulders. "We might be a bunch of outsiders, John Amman, but every man here is your friend." Then he turned to those crowded into the office and with a good-natured sternness shooed them all back to work.

After the others had left George closed the office door and sat down at the desk watching John go through the toolbox, admiring each implement.

"Go home, John," George said softly. "Go home to your furniture building and your lady. I don't think you've slept more than two or three hours a night since you got here. It's pretty obvious to me that it hasn't been the work here keeping you up at night. You miss her—you miss the whole place. Go home, my friend."

"What if there's nothing to go back for?"

"You think she won't forgive you? She did once before, didn't she?"

John shrugged. "That was different. We were young and…"

George stood up and put on his fedora as he pulled an envelope from the inside pocket of his suit jacket. "Go home to your people, John. Your work here is done, and once this war comes and goes I'm going to be calling on you for some of those furniture designs we used to make before the bottom dropped out." He placed the envelope on the desk next to the toolbox. "This is a check, John. It's from me not the government. I'm buying you out."

"But…"

"I know what you're going to say but we went into this together, and you may not have invested money, but you deserve something for the designs you developed. I'm buying the rights to those."

John thought about all the times that Liddy had reminded him that God would show him the way. And all of a sudden his path seemed clearer than it had been at any time in his life. He grinned at his friend and extended his hand. "Thank you, George."

"I expect to be invited to the wedding," George said as he left the office and closed the door behind him.

John stood at the desk long after George and the others had left as he once again examined each tool in the box. They were of the finest quality, especially the wood-carving chisels and knives. He could do excellent work with these replicas of the tools he had once bought with the money he and George had made in their first venture. In those days, as apparently he continued to do now, George had spent his money on clothes and dining out at fine restaurants. He had even bought himself a diamond ring for his little finger. But John had had no such wants. For him the luxury of a hand-crafted tool intended for crafting wood into usable objects was enough.

As he replaced each item in its designated space in the large metal box, he realized that what George had given him was far more precious than the simple hand tools. He picked up the envelope, opened it and found inside crisp new bills totaling more cash than he had ever held before and a one-way railway ticket to Sarasota. *Go home,* his friend had advised him.

For perhaps the first time in his life, it was advice that John fully intended to heed.

Lydia was counting down until the last day of school and the next, when she would finish packing up the supplies and books and maps she used for teaching and move them to her house. The morning after that she would board the train for St. Augustine and even if John refused to see her she would tell his friend, George Stevens, the story of the intercepted letters and plead with him to act as an intermediary between John and her.

From the moment she had devised her plan she had thought of little else. Fortunately Greta and Pleasant assumed she was simply mourning John's departure and the loss of her job. The two of them were constant in their suggestions for what she might do now that she would have no responsibilities for teaching the children. Luke had come by one day to invite her to move in with them if she chose. "Or, if you won't accept our help, then Jeremiah and I will provide you with a monthly stipend to replace your lost wages so you can continue living in this house."

She had thanked them and begged for time to attend to her remaining duties before she made any decision about her life going forward. And then she sat up late into the night working out the details of her journey to find John and bring him home. She studied the train schedule, set aside the money she would need for the ticket, packed some spare clothing in the basket she normally used for carrying her books to and from the schoolhouse. That way if anyone saw her, they would not think anything of it.

As anxious as she was to go to John, she had a duty to the community. The school was closing and her students and their families deserved the best she could offer them. But at night she sat at her desk, writing letter after letter trying to find the words that might explain how her late father had duped both of them. She tore up every single letter. From the little she had seen of George Stevens she had no doubt that he would find words far more persuasive than hers could ever be for bringing John home.

But then George Stevens might not agree that Celery Fields was the best place for John. After all, the man had a business venture that was dependent on John's skills as a draftsman and designer. What if he decided to sabotage her efforts to reunite with John? What if he laughed at her?

Lydia gritted her teeth. Well, God would show her the way. She felt more strongly than ever before in her life that God was guiding her steps. Never in her life would she have even considered leaving Celery Fields for so much as a day, much less for the week or more that it might take to find John and persuade him to forgive her. Such reckless actions were more Greta's style. And yet here Lydia sat, night after night, plotting and planning every little detail of her adventure.

It occurred to her that she might be feeling what John had felt when he had left that first time. Like her, he had set a purpose for his journey. Like her, he had been certain of his cause. Like her, he must have had moments when he questioned the wisdom of his actions. And, like her, he had cast all doubts aside and moved forward. She would tell him all of that and more once she found him. She would tell him how she now realized that it had been her own fears that had prevented her from seeing his true purpose.

She shook off all such thoughts. There was only one thing she needed to tell him and make him understand: that she loved him, and if only he would give her one more chance she would show him how happy a life they could build together.

In just two days she would say goodbye to her students for the last time. The day after that she would pack up her supplies and close the school for good. And the day after that?

She would set out in search of the only man she had ever loved.

Chapter 14

George insisted on driving John to the train station and seeing him off. "I have a confession to make," he said as the two of them stood on the platform, the train hissing and belching next to them while men loaded the freight and passenger luggage.

John had noticed how quiet his friend had been on the ride to the station. He had assumed George was struggling with the reality that John was leaving. "Look, George, let's not…"

"There was a letter," George blurted. "From her. From your Lydia."

John thought he must have heard wrong. The noise from the train and shouts between the men loading it had surely distorted George's words.

"It came after you'd been here for a couple of weeks. We were in the midst of everything by then and the pressure to get the designs completed and the patterns developed— Well, I just didn't want you to have any distractions."

"Distractions?" John felt his grip tighten on the toolbox that he fully intended to keep by his side for the entire journey. "Lydia is not a distraction, George. She is…"

George looked away, his cheeks blotched with red. "I know. I'm sorry. I assumed that she would write again and by then…" He turned back to face John. "Besides, when we left Sarasota you were so hurt that I figured you wanted nothing more to do with her. As you told me, it wasn't the first time that she had—"

"The letter," John interrupted. "Give it to me."

"I don't have it."

"You destroyed a letter meant for me?"

"I sent it back unopened."

A dozen scenarios danced through John's brain as he tried to imagine what Liddy must have thought when her letter was returned. In his heart he knew that there was only one true reaction she could have had. She would have thought he had refused her letter and was cutting all ties to her, this time for good.

"I'm so sorry, John. I don't know what I was thinking. I've never met anyone like your Lydia and I thought that in time you would meet someone else. But then as the days passed I realized how miserable you were and I knew I had done the wrong thing. That's why I encouraged you to go home. That's why…"

"But you made sure you had gotten what you needed from me first," John said, fighting to keep his temper in check. He set down the toolbox and fished out the envelope that held the cash and his train ticket. "You would buy my forgiveness, George?"

George pressed the envelope into John's hands. "The money is yours, John. You would not take payment for your designs and patterns and so per your wishes I divided that money among our employees. But this is payment for your part of the factory building and machinery. We owned that together. I am simply buying you out."

"And the tools?"

George looked down at the box between them. "Yes, that part was guilt. I hoped to make it up to you by giving you a stake to start your business. But the men insisted on being part of it when they learned that their bonus money had come from you. They wanted to show their appreciation."

"I did not give the money to be handed it back in another form," John argued as the conductor moved along the platform making his first call for passengers to board the train. "I cannot accept…"

"The men are innocents in this, John. Do not reject their gratitude out of some false sense of pride or hurt."

"All aboard!" the conductor shouted for a second time. All around them people were saying their farewells and heading for the entrances to the passenger cars.

"I am asking you to forgive me," George said. "I do not deserve it and I fully understand that I may well have ruined any chance you might have had to make things right with Lydia. I've never had someone in my life that I cared about so deeply, much less anyone who cared about me beyond what I could buy her. But then I realized that what you had with Lydia was the kind of love we all search for in this life. I just hope I didn't realize that too late."

John stared at his friend, a myriad of emotions throbbing in his veins. He felt anger and pity and regret and, oddly, hope. "Maybe it's not too late," he said as he picked up the tool chest and handed it up to the porter. "Goodbye, George," he called as he stood on the landing between cars and waved to his friend.

"Write to me," George shouted back as he ran alongside the train.

John laughed at the irony of George's words. Letters sent and returned. Letters sent and never answered. As far as John was concerned, letters were a poor way of saying what a man needed to say. This time he intended to talk to Liddy in person. This time there would be no more room for misunderstanding.

And if she rejects you?

"Then God's will be done," he murmured as he found his seat and the porter slid the heavy toolbox onto the floor next to him.

On the last day of classes the children were almost beside themselves with excitement. Lydia knew that for them this was just the same as other years when they would be off school for a few months and then return. Only Bettina and one or two of the good students seemed to realize that the school would be closing for good.

"Do you want me to help you pack up everything tomorrow?" Bettina asked at the end of the day as the children enjoyed the picnic that Lydia and some of the other women had prepared for them.

Lydia smiled and patted the girl's hand. "You are

kind to offer but I would prefer to do it alone. There are many memories here and I need to savor them a bit before I close that door one last time."

"Do you think the elders will truly tear it down and sell the land?"

"That is for them to decide." She saw a tear trickle down Bettina's cheek. "Come now, this is not a day for sadness. Look at the children, how happy they are."

"I had so wanted to teach…"

"And if it be God's will, one day I have no doubt that you will lead a classroom full of children, Bettina. But it won't be in this building. You must accept that."

Bettina nodded and dabbed at her eyes with the hem of her apron. "What will you do now?"

Lydia's heart swelled with the excitement that had lodged there now for days, but she could hardly reveal her plan. "Oh, I will be fine, Bettina. You mustn't concern yourself about me." She stood up and clapped her hands loudly, her signal for the children to make a circle and join hands. "Let us all give thanks," she said once their chatter had settled into a low murmur of whispers and giggles.

And as every head bowed, Lydia silently prayed that she would have the courage to follow through on her plan to travel east and find John. And she dared to add a plea that God would soften John's heart and make him receptive to her gesture of reconciliation.

The following day she arrived at the school early. It was a hot, humid day and her first job was to open all of the windows and block open the double doors hoping to capture as much of a breeze as possible. Next she packed up her books in the cartons that Roger Hadwell had left for her and loaded them onto the cart waiting just outside the door. Luke would come by at the end of the day and move the cart up to her house where Bettina and her sweetheart, Caleb, would help unload it.

At first Lydia had protested the elders' decision that she should take everything that was usable from the building. "You have earned it, Lydia," Jeremiah told her. "By the time we can reopen a school the maps and such will surely be outdated. And, besides, if you plan to offer private lessons you need something with which to teach."

It was simply assumed by most people in town that once she had closed up the school Lydia would set up her house for private lessons, not that anyone in Celery Fields had the money for such a thing. It was further assumed that either she would continue living in her father's house alone or that more likely, in the absence of an income, she would move in with either Greta or Pleasant. The women in town had it all planned out for her and Lydia had been annoyed more than once over the past few weeks at their assumptions.

The truth was that as her plan had developed she had rediscovered the impetuous girl she had once been, the girl John had fallen in love with. More than once she had almost blurted out her intentions during a conversation with Greta. Her sister had developed a habit of looking at her with pity, and it seemed nothing Lydia said or did would convince Greta that she was not yet defeated when it came to John Amman.

She smiled at the thought of him. She did a lot of that these days, imagining his surprise when she simply appeared one day at the factory he owned with George Stevens. She had debated whether or not to write to George and let him know she was coming but, from what John had told her about his friend and business partner, she was not sure the man could be trusted to keep a secret.

No, better to simply go there. The train would arrive midday, so there was plenty of time for her to seek directions and make her way from the railway station to the factory. She refused to even consider the horrid thought that had awakened her one stormy night—the idea that John might have found someone else.

Once the books had been packed and she had loaded the rest of the supplies onto the cart, she began the process of cleaning the single room. How she had loved being here. It had been her refuge in those weeks and months that passed with no word from John after he left that first time. And in the years that followed it had given her a purpose for rising each day. The children needed her.

The shadows lengthened into late afternoon, and she climbed to the top of a ladder so that she could use the broom wrapped with a dust rag to sweep away any cobwebs that might be lingering in the corners. As she stretched to reach the high peak of the beamed ceiling she heard someone enter the foyer where normally the children would leave their coats. "I'll be right there," she called out, assuming it was Luke coming to deliver the loaded cart up to her house.

"I had not thought it would be necessary to do so thorough a cleaning if the school is to be closed." The voice was familiar but not that of her brother-in-law. She grasped the top of the ladder as the broom fell from her hands and clattered onto the floor. Below her, John Amman was walking around the now-barren room, running his hand over the wide sill of a window and then standing before the chalkboard that she had washed earlier. He picked up a piece of chalk from the tray and lightly tossed it in the air, catching it each time as he continued to stare at the board.

"You came back," she said, and realized that her voice was no stronger than a whisper, so unsure was she that weariness had not created a mirage before her.

If this were a vision then it was one she savored. Unlike the time before, when she had discovered him kneeling next to the woodstove feeding kindling into the fire, he was not a bedraggled man. This time he was dressed plain but everything about him was pristine—from his white shirt tucked into black trousers supported by wide suspenders to his black straw wide-brimmed hat resting on top of his golden hair. Only his shoes showed any signs of the dust of travel.

He used the chalk to begin sketching on the board and, as Lydia descended the ladders and moved closer, she saw that he was drawing a floor plan for the building where they stood. "I have just washed that board," she said, reverting to her usual habit of reprimanding him whenever she was unsure of what to say to this man.

He shrugged and kept drawing. "I had thought perhaps to place a counter here with a desk there where we might take orders and manage the accounts. That way when customers first come through the door, they will be welcomed." He sketched in the counter and desk leaving most of the rest of the space open. "We will need to add a door here and a loading dock." He added these two features to the back wall of the plan.

"John, the building is not yours to change," she said softly.

He glanced at her, cocked one eyebrow and gave her half a smile before turning back to his sketch. "I think we'll keep the chalkboard. I like having it available to work out measurements and such."

"John, what…"

"And the building is mine to do with as I please—I just bought it."

"I…you…how…"

The smile tugged at his cheeks, fighting to break free as he continued his study of the sketch. "I paid the money the elders thought was fair and we shook hands and I am now here. Come to think of it, it is good that you have done such a thorough job of cleaning, although why you insisted on doing the job alone is beyond me. Nevertheless, it gives us a clean slate for planning the renovations."

"What renovations? What are you talking about, John Amman?" She placed her hands on her hips as she stepped around him so that she stood between him and the chalkboard.

"This building will house my furniture-building and carpentry business, Liddy. It's near enough to my uncle's hardware and the rest of the businesses in town to draw customers. Tourists, I suspect, will make up the bulk of the business. Those *Englischers* do have an appetite for our simple ways. Not that they would ever change their ways, but they enjoy pretending. We can build a business on that."

"What about the factory and the government contract and George Stevens?"

"George bought me out and that gave me the money to buy this place. It's taken me nearly a decade, Liddy, but it's all I ever wanted. And now…" His voice trailed off as he studied her as if truly seeing her for the first time. "The question is, Liddy, do you want what I want?"

He sounded almost wistful. She would have expected him to be angry or dismissive given the fact that he had returned her letter unopened. "I want you to find peace," she said, uncertain of what he was asking her. "If building furniture for outsiders is the path to that, then I am pleased for you."

He reached around her and replaced the chalk in the tray, then dusted his hands off by rubbing them together. "I did not know about your letter, Liddy," he said quietly. "Surely you know that I would have answered you."

"I knew nothing of the sort." She moved away from him, busying herself by wiping a thin film of dust from the desk she had used all the years of her teaching. "And if you did not know of it, if you did not refuse to accept it, then how do you know of it now?"

He told her about George's admission at the train station. "I don't think I have ever come so close to striking another man as I did when he told me what he had done."

She saw him clench and unclench his fingers.

"I do not think, John, that you and I should trust the habit of communicating by letter," she said softly. "After you left—this time—Pleasant told me some startling news. My father destroyed your letters to me and mine to you. He was afraid that I would follow you, that he would lose me as your family had lost you."

"They did not lose me," John protested. "I always intended to return. But we had no future, Liddy. How was I supposed to provide for you and our children?"

"You had work on your father's farm," she reminded him.

"I was never a farmer, Liddy."

"That was not for you to decide. Only God can guide the path we will take."

"And do you not see God's hand in all of this?" He waved his hand to encompass the bare schoolroom. "Do you know how I have prayed constantly for God to show me His way?"

"As have I," she replied defensively.

"And yet here we stand. Why would God keep finding ways to reunite us if we are not meant to be together?"

"You must not question or test or bend His plan to fit what you want, John."

John removed his hat and set it on the desk, then ran his fingers through his hair, drawing it back from his face—a face she now realized reflected hours without sleep and the weariness of all that they had been through separately and together. "Will you marry me or not, Lydia Goodloe?"

The words that she would have hoped to hear uttered sweetly and softly came out as if he had reached the end of his patience. She bristled at his tone.

"I wouldn't wish to upset your plans," she replied and turned away.

John caught her forearm and held on. "Just yes or no, Liddy."

"How do I know that you won't decide that God has called you into the outside world yet again?"

"Because my purpose in leaving—both then and recently—was the same. To find a way that we might build our future together. I have secured that for us now."

"And what about George Stevens and his plans? How do I know that one fine day he won't show up at our door wanting you to join him in yet another business venture?"

John closed his eyes, his lips working in exasperation. "How many times do I have to explain myself, woman?"

She felt her heart soften at that. After all, because of her father's actions she was every bit as much at fault for the lost years they had endured as he was. "I suppose you will have to start over—go to Levi Harnischer and seek his approval and then call on my sisters and…"

Slowly John opened his eyes and looked at her. Doubt and hope flickered across his handsome features. "Do not tease me, Liddy," he pleaded. "Give me your answer."

She cupped her hand around his cheek. "*Yah,* I will marry you, John Amman."

With a victorious yelp of joy, John picked Lydia up and spun around the room with her. He stopped just as Luke Starns stepped inside the school.

"Here we go again," Luke muttered as he retraced his steps and started pushing the loaded cart up the path to Lydia's house.

Lydia giggled and rested her forehead against John's. He was still holding her so that her feet did not touch the floor. Somehow she doubted that even after years with this incredible man she would ever again feel as if she were standing on firm ground. The feeling gave her such a rush of joy that she threw back her head and laughed.

John grinned up at her. "Why are you laughing?"

"Because I have never been happier."

"Just wait," he said, and sealed the unspoken promise with his kiss.

John certainly understood what Liddy meant when she said she had never been happier. The pure joy that seemed to flow through his body in the place of normal breathing was remarkable. How could he ever have thought that going away and leaving her was the answer? He had been a fool and he saw now that because she never received or even know of his letters, and her own to him had also been destroyed, they had not had a chance to work things out. Oddly he understood her father's actions, his need to protect Liddy from hurt and perhaps harm if she had chosen to follow him into that world of outsiders. If she had been his daughter he knew he would have done the same.

But he had not allowed for such possibilities then. He had, instead, permitted his hurt and disappointment to dictate his actions. Making the money he needed to start a proper business had become less about getting the stake he needed and more about proving to Liddy that he could be a huge success. He had seen the way his partner lived and he had recalled the way that Levi Harnischer had once lived in such luxury when he owned the circus. Once he and Liddy had taken their bikes all the way to the place where Levi's former mansion was set on the shores of Sarasota Bay. The house had been huge and beautiful.

But he recalled now that Liddy's only comment as she stood next to him staring at the house with its stained-glass windows and tower that soared three whole stories into the blue sky was, "It must take days to clean that place properly."

Still, John could not get the image of such wealth out of his mind. He told himself that it wasn't some grand mansion he wanted for Liddy, but he did want what that mansion represented—security and a future. What he had refused to remember was the story well-known in Celery Fields of how truly miserable Levi had been in those days and how deeply happy he was now that he had turned his back on all of that and married Hannah. He had not sold his worldly goods for money. The story was that he had given everything away to his former employees. He had returned to the people of his youth empty-handed, needing nothing more than Hannah's love.

And now that Liddy had agreed to marry him John was determined to follow the example that Levi had set. He would take whatever time necessary to build a business that would support her and the children he hoped they would have. Twice he had left her, with his only thought being gathering enough money to set them up for the future. Twice she had taken him back. He would not risk testing her a third time.

Later that evening, when Levi Harnischer came to call on Lydia and her family—this time at Lydia's house, Pleasant seemed more than a little reluctant to give the proposed union her blessing. "He has left you twice already," she reminded Lydia as the two of them stood in the kitchen preparing glasses of sweet tea while Greta waited in the front room with Levi.

"But now we understand why," Lydia protested. "The letters that our *dat* destroyed without either my knowledge or John's and more recently the letter that George Stevens returned without even so much as showing it to John. You were the one who encouraged me to write to explain everything."

"This is not about letters, Lydia." She held up her hand to stop further protest. "Hear me out, for I have given this a great deal of thought. This is about the fact that John left in the first place. Against everything his family and the elders taught him, against the very foundation of the faith in which we were raised he went out into the world—and stayed there."

"*Yah,* but he had his reasons. He thought that he was doing what God was leading him to do."

Pleasant shook her head. "That might be forgivable for a lad of seventeen, but what I cannot ignore is the fact that John is a grown man now and still he left you again."

"He did not leave *me,*" Lydia argued, although deep inside she could find little fault with Pleasant's reasoning.

"Nor did he stay when you asked him—no, when you *pleaded* with him to do so," Pleasant said softly. She placed her hand on Lydia's and then picked up the tray and carried it into the front room. "My concern is for you. I do not wish to see you hurt."

Lydia stood for a long moment staring out the window. It was a moonless night and she could only just make out the silhouette of the livery and a single lamp set in the upstairs window where she knew John was watching for Levi's buggy to leave their house. After that he would wait until he saw Greta and Pleasant leave, as well, and then he would come to her. He would expect that nothing would have changed, that her sis-

ters would have given their blessing, that Levi would
be on his way to let the bishop know to announce their
planned union the following Sunday at services.

But if Pleasant had doubts…

"Lydia Goodloe, I wonder if I might speak with you
privately." Levi stood at the door of the kitchen. "I have
asked your sisters to wait for us in the front room."

Lydia indicated a kitchen chair for him to sit and
pulled out one for herself. "Pleasant is not…"

Levi held up one hand. "Please hear me out."

Lydia nodded and folded her hands in her lap.

"You know, Lydia, there was a time when I was
also drawn into the outside world, where I remained
for years. I, too, thought that I would find happiness
there. And, like John, I was wrong."

Lydia smiled. The tale of Levi and his wife, Hannah, was well-known in Celery Fields. Levi had run
away from his family as a boy and eventually became
the owner of one of the most successful circus com-
panies in all the land. Years later Caleb, Hannah's son
from her first marriage to Pleasant's brother, had also
run away to join Levi's circus. Hannah had been beside
herself and she, along with Pleasant and Lydia's father,
had boarded the circus train with Levi to go bring the
boy home again. Along the way Levi had fallen in love
with Hannah. More to the point, he had realized that all
the financial success and material wealth he might gain
in that outside world could never satisfy him the way
the plain and simple ways that Hannah brought back
to his life did. Eventually he had renounced his former
lifestyle, sold his company to his business partner and
come to Celery Fields seeking Hannah.

"Your story is different from John's," Lydia reminded

him. "You ran away as a boy. John had already joined the church when he left."

Levi chuckled. "Some would say that I had the longest *Rumspringa* ever."

Lydia could not help but smile. The very idea that a successful businessman could be seen as enjoying the time set aside for Amish teens to test their wings before joining the church and renouncing all things connected with the world of the *Englisch* was ridiculous. "Still, John made his choice."

Levi nodded. "That he did and it seems to me that in both cases his choice was his desire to do what he thought best for you, for the two of you to build a future."

"He tells himself that now, Levi, but the first time he left…"

"He has paid for that, Lydia. He has sought and been granted forgiveness."

"And this time?"

He took a swallow of his orangeade. "Times are changing, Lydia, and if we are to remain strong in our beliefs and practices we must face the fact that we will be tested many times over."

"So, you are agreeing with Pleasant? You believe that this is a test for me?"

"I believe that you must look into your heart and open yourself to God's will. If you truly are convinced that marrying John is the path God wants you to follow then take it. As for Pleasant…" He smiled as he stood up and carried his now-empty glass to the sink. "As I recall she made her own journey, one no easier than the one you face now. It seems to me that it has turned out well. Now come, your sisters are waiting."

Lydia followed Levi back to the front room, dimly lit by the single lamp on the table by the window. Both Greta and Pleasant looked up expectantly.

"Well?" Pleasant asked.

"Here is what I propose," Levi said, taking the chair that Lydia had placed by the window with the idea that in time it would be John's place. "We will spend some time now in silent prayer, each searching our hearts for God's guidance. We will not dwell on what we as individuals might think best but open our hearts to receive His will."

Greta nodded and sat upright with hands folded, prepared to bow her head in prayer.

"And then?" Pleasant pressed.

"Then we will all accept the will of God when Lydia Goodloe gives us her answer as to whether or not she wishes to marry John Amman."

Lydia met Pleasant's gaze and saw her half sister purse her lips as if about to protest. But then she nodded and took her seat.

"Let us pray," Levi said softly, and a silence settled over the room, interrupted only by the steady ticking of the clock on the fireplace mantel.

Chapter 15

John kept a watch for Levi's buggy to leave but the time stretched from minutes to over an hour and he was still there. What could be taking so long? It wasn't as if Pleasant and Greta didn't know what was coming. Was Levi expressing doubts of his own, perhaps making Liddy think twice before agreeing to marry him? Pointing out that she would not wish to do something rash simply to fill the hole left in her life by the closing of the school?

These were all things that John had certainly considered. The idea that Liddy still wanted to marry him after all that he had put her through was sometimes a mystery to him. But in spite of everything she had accepted his proposal—again. Almost from the moment she had learned that he had bought the schoolhouse and its land and planned to open his business there she had enthusiastically joined him in planning the space, in planning the future they would share.

"We could perhaps add a porch to the front of the building," she had suggested. "A place to display your rocking chairs. The tourists will be drawn to those, I'm sure. Perhaps you could even design a smaller version for children."

"I can see that you are going to have me working round the clock," he had teased. Now as he stood on the loading dock of the hardware store after closing up for the day he wondered if perhaps Liddy was having doubts.

He could hardly blame her and yet when, on the night that he'd returned, they had sat on her porch talking until the sun streaked the eastern sky, he had thought she had accepted his reasoning for leaving a second time.

"I cannot deny that everything seems to have worked out," she had told him, and he had ignored the hesitancy in her voice.

But what if she had had second doubts through the day while he had been at work at the hardware store and she had been occupied sorting the materials that she had taken to her house from the school? What if instead of dwelling on the future, she had spent her time reliving the eight long years when she'd had no word from him?

The familiar creak of Liddy's front screen door brought his attention back to the moment. He saw Levi standing on the porch and Liddy was there with him. Their voices were muffled, but he did not need to hear their words to know that something was missing. At a time when their voices should have been filled with the joy of a happy event, there was no lightness in either their tone nor their posture. Liddy stood rigidly on the porch, her arms folded into her apron as she watched Levi walk to his buggy.

"You are certain?" he called before taking up the reins.

"Yah."

Levi drove away and Liddy continued to stand on the porch watching him go. After a moment Greta and Pleasant joined her. The three women talked in low tones and then Pleasant walked away and Greta hurried after her, catching up to her on the path that led into town. Greta seemed to be making some point, her hands fluttering around the way they did when she talked. Pleasant strode along looking neither left nor right and seeming to have nothing to say.

John turned his attention back to the porch and saw that Liddy had gone back inside the house. His heart thudded with apprehension. Something was not right here. Without bothering to take off his work apron, he jumped down from the loading dock. After only a few steps his pace quickened to a run. *Please,* he prayed as he covered the distance between the store and the house. *Not now.*

The front door was closed and the house was dark when he reached it, but he was undeterred. He hammered on the wood with his fist. "Liddy?"

The house was silent.

"I know you're in there," he said more softly, pressing his face close to the door. "Please, Liddy, open the door."

After what seemed like forever he saw the knob turn.

"The door is not locked," she said, her voice heavy

with weariness as she opened the door and then walked away from him toward the kitchen.

He saw that a single lamp burned in the back of the house. Some of the dishes she had used for serving Levi and the others were soaking in the dishpan while the rest had been washed and set to drain on the side counter. He followed her to the kitchen and pulled out a chair at the table while she returned to her chore.

"What happened, Liddy?"

Her shoulders lifted and then collapsed in defeat. "It's Pleasant," she said softly, her hands pausing mid-motion as if she had momentarily forgotten what she was doing. "She has had a change of heart concerning…us."

"I am not marrying Pleasant," John replied. And when Lydia said nothing, he added, "The question is, am I to marry *you?*"

She let the dish slide into the soapy water as she turned to him, her eyes wide with surprise. "Oh, John, yes. We will marry. It's just that I had hoped for ours to be such a happy day."

He went to her and wrapped his arms around her. "And it will be—the happiest of days in our life together so far," he promised. "Pleasant will come around." He did not need to ask what Liddy's half sister's doubts might be. After all, Pleasant had known all along about the destroyed letters and never said a word. "You do not need her permission, Liddy."

"It is not her permission I was seeking. I want her blessing. She is family as much as Greta is, and you and I are not in a position to take such ties lightly, John Amman."

She turned back to her washing up.

John picked up a dish towel and began drying the glasses and plates, setting each carefully on the open shelves that ran along one wall. He rummaged around in his brain for words that might offer comfort but decided against trying to make things better when he might make them worse.

"That was unkind of me," Liddy murmured as she placed the last glass on the counter and then wrung the soapy water from the dishrag before turning to wipe the table. "I am sorry, John."

"Perhaps if I spoke to Pleasant, gave her the chance to state her concerns, maybe I could put her doubts to rest," John said, choosing his words carefully.

Liddy took the towel from him and dried the last of the dishes. "No. Greta has tried that. I have tried that, as has Levi."

"Levi is on our side, then?"

"Oh, John, there are no sides in this. It is not some schoolyard game we are playing. Pleasant is concerned and that concern comes from her love for me. She wants only the best."

"But Levi…"

She told him then about the silent prayer that Levi had counseled and how when it was done Levi had asked each of the three sisters if she approved the union. He had begun with Greta, as the youngest, and her endorsement had been enthusiastic. Then he had asked Lydia.

"I love this man with all my heart," she told him she had said quietly. "I believe God would not have brought him back to Celery Fields not once but twice were it not His divine will that we should spend our lives together from this time forward."

Liddy bowed her head as she recalled the evening's events.

"And Pleasant?" John coaxed.

"She was silent for some time, opening her lips as if about to speak and then closing them again."

"And when she finally did speak?"

A shudder ran through Lydia's shoulders. "She said that she was afraid for me, for us. She said that only time would tell what the future might bring. She spoke of her marriage to Merle Obermeier, how unhappy they had made each other."

"You told me that Pleasant and Merle did not love each other," John reminded her. "That he married her for the sake of his children and she married him because…"

"She thought it would be her only opportunity. Her fear for me is that I am making this decision for that same reason."

"I have no children in need of a mother, Liddy," John said as he took her hands in his. "Not yet, anyway," he added with a hesitant grin.

"Oh, John, we will make a good life, won't we?" she asked, tightening her grip on his fingers. "I mean Pleasant is right that we cannot know what the future may bring, but I so firmly believe that our being together is God's will."

John let his smile broaden into a grin. "And everyone knows, when you have made up your mind as to God's purpose in your life, nothing and no one can change it."

Liddy met his smile with one of her own. "That's almost exactly what Pleasant said. So when Levi asked if she had intentions of disputing the union, she said that she did not. But John, she is wary."

"With good cause given her history—and ours. Time will put her fears to rest, Liddy. You will see. By this time next year she will understand that we have made the right decision."

He saw in her eyes that she wanted to believe him and he prayed that it would not take an entire year for him to prove to Pleasant that everything he had ever done, good decision or bad, had been for one reason: his love for Lydia Goodloe.

Pleasant made no further comment on the proposed marriage, but over the next several days Lydia was well aware that her half sister could not put aside her doubts and concerns. So on Saturday she was thinking of going to the bakery to speak with Pleasant and to try to persuade her to be happy for them. She was pacing the kitchen floor putting together the points she thought most likely to sway Pleasant when she saw Hannah Harnischer coming up the back porch steps.

"Lydia?" she called as she shaded her eyes and peered in through the screened door.

"This is a surprise, Hannah," Lydia said as she welcomed the woman inside. Hannah had been married to Pleasant's brother—Lydia and Greta's half brother—and years after he died she had met and married Levi. The story of their romance had been quite the talk of the town at one time, as no doubt John and Lydia were the objects of much speculation these days. In spite of the fact that she and Hannah were not especially close, Lydia felt a kinship to this woman.

"I have some sweet tea, freshly made," Lydia offered.

"Just a glass of cold water."

Lydia got two glasses from the shelf and pumped

water into the dry sink to fill them while Hannah took a seat at the kitchen table. She accepted the water and nodded toward the door where Lydia's shopping basket sat. "Were you on your way out?"

"I was going to the bakery, but that can wait. I am glad you have come, Hannah."

Hannah's smile was kind but concerned. "Pleasant tells me that she has concerns about your proposed union with John Amman."

Over the years Hannah and Pleasant had become close friends, as were their husbands. The two couples and their children spent lots of time together. Lately Greta and her family often joined that circle of friends and family. They always invited Lydia to partake in the meal or outing they had planned, but she felt like the person she was—the spinster aunt tagging along.

"She has said that she will not protest the union," Lydia said quietly. "Has she changed her mind?"

Hannah set down her glass and held up her hands. "Oh, no, Lydia. She simply wants you to be happy and she knows the future is in God's hands."

"Then why…"

"Why have I come?" Hannah smiled. "I have come because we brides of Celery Fields must stand together. I have come because I think you have doubts of your own, as each of us did in those days before we married. I have come, Lydia, to do whatever I can to assist you in making your wedding a happy time that has been far too long coming in your life."

Lydia's eyes welled with tears and she reached across the table and clasped Hannah's hand. "You are too kind," she whispered.

To her surprise Hannah laughed. "Not at all. Levi

says that I am an incurable romantic who simply cannot stand it if two people I care deeply about are not completely 'over the moon'—that's what he calls it. An expression that lingers from his days as a circus man."

Lydia giggled and felt much of the worry and anxiety she'd carried since meeting with her sisters and Levi melt away. "Oh, Hannah, will it be like this always? This feeling that you could actually fly because your heart is so light and at the same time so full?"

"Heavens no. There will surely be days when you will wonder if you haven't made the biggest mistake of your life," Hannah assured her. "Unfortunately, men do not seem to lose any of their headstrong ways simply because they have married. It will take time and patience, but you have both in abundance so there is no reason to believe that things will not go well for you and John. That's what I told Pleasant."

"And did she believe you?"

This time Hannah's reassuring smile was slower to come. "She'll come around, Lydia." She stood and took her glass to the sink. "Now then, have you made your dress yet?"

"I am not much of a seamstress," Lydia admitted.

"Well, fortunately, Pleasant is. Now let's go shopping for the fabric she'll need and…"

"I cannot ask Pleasant to make a dress for my wedding."

Hannah handed Lydia the bonnet hanging on a peg by the back door. "Of course you can."

They stopped first at the bakery where Bettina was helping out now that the school was closed. "Bettina can manage," Hannah said, overriding Pleasant's protest that she could not be expected to simply close up shop for the day. "And it's not like you to exaggerate. Half an hour for choosing some fabric—no more. Now come along."

Lydia was fascinated to see Pleasant remove her apron and take down her bonnet without further protest. "I suppose you have decided on a color already," she grumbled as the three of them walked to Yoder's Dry Goods.

"I hadn't really given it much thought," Lydia admitted.

"Well, as this is the second time you have decided on marrying John Amman, what color had you planned on wearing before?"

"Blue," Lydia replied with a smile as she remembered how John had once compared the color of her eyes to a summer sky.

"Blue will do," Pleasant declared. "I had feared you might be inclined toward something…less proper."

Hannah smothered a giggle.

"What?" Pleasant snapped as they entered the shop.

"Forgive me, Pleasant, but I was just imagining our Lydia here all dressed in pink or bright purple for the occasion."

Pleasant frowned and then looked away and Lydia feared she was about to lose her temper with the two of them. But then she heard Pleasant's well-known laugh. It was a laugh that bubbled up from somewhere deep inside her on the rare occasions when something struck her as funny. And once it began, Lydia and most everyone else in town knew that it would take time for Pleasant to regain control. There was nothing to do but join in.

So as the three of them approached Hilda Yoder at

the counter they were hard-pressed to get out the words they needed to tell the shopkeeper what they wanted. "Fabric," Pleasant finally managed. "Blue..."

"Or did we decide on the purple?" Hannah whispered mischievously, and the three of them broke into fresh gales of giggles like three schoolgirls out on a lark.

Hilda frowned and took down three bolts of fabric in shades of blue. "This just came in," she said, tapping the thickest of the bolts.

Pleasant pushed it aside in favor of the bolt with the least amount of yardage left. "This one if there is enough," she said, and began unfurling the fabric and measuring the yardage by extending it length by length from her nose to her outstretched fingertips. "That should so it," she announced. "And we will need fabric for a prayer *kapp,* as well."

"I already have..." Lydia began fingering one of the white ties of the covering she wore beneath her bonnet. But under Pleasant's gaze she abandoned any protest. "Yes, a *kapp* and an apron," she added, winning Pleasant's approving glance for the first time in days.

It was tradition that the clothing a woman wore for her wedding was the clothing she would be buried in at the end of her life. It was not different in the sense of being made of special fabric or with lace trim. At her wedding Lydia would look little different from every other woman there. But she would always know that this dress and apron were unique and she would always know that she had chosen the fabric for the outfit in the company of her beloved half sister, a woman who had been more of a mother to her than any other.

Hilda prepared to wrap their selections in brown

paper and tie the package with string. "Is there anything else? Thread? Needles?"

"That will do," Pleasant replied. "I will send Jeremiah in to pay."

"Oh, no," Lydia began, but Pleasant's look told her that this was as close as her half sister was going to come to openly giving her blessing to the marriage. She would buy the material for Lydia's dress as their father would surely have done had he been still living. *"Dienki."*

"I'll come by after I close up for the day to take your measure," Pleasant said, studying Lydia's tall thin frame as if truly seeing her for the first time. "You've lost weight."

It was Hannah who laughed. "Well, I shouldn't wonder. The poor woman has been through a great deal these last several weeks with the closing of the school and…everything else."

Pleasant's eyes softened as she studied Lydia for a long moment. *"Yah,* there has been too much of that. Hannah, why don't you come tonight, as well, and I will ask Greta. We have a wedding to plan and a dress to make." And with that she turned from them and went back to the bakery.

"So we do," Hannah said softly as she squeezed Lydia's hand and winked at her.

On the Monday morning after Bishop Troyer had announced the plan for John and Lydia to marry, John woke well before dawn. Today was the day he would begin renovations on the former schoolhouse. His plan was to spend at least three hours there in the mornings before going to work at the hardware and then return in the evenings to work for several more hours before retiring for the night. If he could keep to this schedule he was fairly certain he would be able to have his business ready to open the day after the wedding, which would take place in just ten days.

He dressed in the predawn darkness, drank a cup of black coffee and packed up some cold biscuits and sausage he'd prepared the night before. The air was already heavy with humidity as he made his way to the schoolhouse. He wondered if he would ever stop thinking of the building as a school. Liddy had suggested that he call his business something like The Old Schoolhouse Clock Shop. It had a nice ring to it and he did plan to make clocks his primary ware in these early days. He was still thinking about the name and envisioning the sign he would eventually mount above the double front doors when he reached the school and found the double doors standing wide-open. He heard the buzz of male voices inside the building.

"Hello?" he called out.

Luke Starns, Jeremiah Troyer and Levi Harnischer all turned to greet him. Then he saw Liddy pouring mugs of coffee and passing one to each man. "You're late, John Amman," she called out in the voice he was sure had struck fear into the hearts of her students.

But then she turned to him and her smile was as radiant as the morning sun just beginning to make its way through the tall thin windows. "Surprise."

"What's all this?" he asked as he moved into the room and took the coffee she handed him.

"This is what neighbors do for neighbors," Luke said. "I know you've spent some time out there in the world, John, but surely you have not forgotten all our ways."

From outside John heard others arriving and soon the building was filled with men talking and drinking their coffee as they studied the chalkboard and John's plans for converting the schoolhouse to his business. "Let's get started," his uncle announced. "If you three men will come with me we can start bringing over the lumber and supplies I've been storing at the hardware."

Roger Hadwell paused next to John. "It's a good plan you have, John. I think we can have you up and in business by the end of the week." John understood that this was his uncle's way of giving his blessing.

As the others went about their assigned tasks, John saw Liddy watching him from across the room. "You knew?" he asked as he moved next to her.

"I suspected," she corrected. "Greta's boys let something slip when I was there the other day." She picked up the tray of used coffee mugs. "I'll just wash these and bring them back with a fresh pot of coffee. Cover those cinnamon rolls that Pleasant sent over so the flies don't get to them," she instructed, nodding toward a tea towel draped over a sawhorse.

"Liddy?"

She turned and smiled and he knew that for the rest of his life he would ask for nothing more than the blessing of awaking every day to this face, these lovely eyes bathing him with their trust and their devotion. "I love you."

Her hands shook slightly, rattling the cups on the tray, but she met his gaze without hesitation. "I know," she assured him. "I think I have always known. That's why I waited."

Epilogue

Five years later...

"Liddy!"

Lydia wiped her hands on a towel and walked out to the back porch. She had noticed early in their marriage that whenever John called out for her to come to him there was an urgency in his voice. Early on she had gone running to him every time, especially after the children started coming. Her heart would pound within her chest as she imagined all sorts of mishaps. Their son, Joshua, perhaps bleeding from some cut. Their daughter, Rose, almost certainly nursing some bruises from a fall. But then she would see them and John would look at her, smiling as he pointed to the blossom of an orchid that he and the children had planted for her in a tree, or at a butterfly that had come to rest on Rose's finger.

Now she rested one hand on the mound of her pregnancy as she shaded her eyes against the bright noonday sun with the other. In the yard outside their barn she saw Joshua sitting astride their horse, his short, chubby legs dangling to either side as his laughter rang out across the yard. John was holding the reins as he led the animal in a large circle.

"My turn," Rose shouted. "My turn now," she demanded sounding very much like her aunt Greta had at that age.

"Be careful," Lydia shouted as she watched John lift Rose onto the huge animal so that she was sitting in front of her brother.

Joshua wrapped his arms around Rose as she shrieked her delight. "Faster, *Daadi*."

Her cries brought John's aunt and uncle out onto the loading dock of the hardware store and Lydia saw Gert press her fist to her mouth in alarm. "John Amman, those children are far too young..." she shouted.

"Never too young, *Tante* Gert," John called back, but Lydia saw him glance her way and knew that if she told him to stop, he would.

"Come wash up," she said instead as she turned to go back inside. But suddenly she was seized by a familiar pain in her back and she reached for the door to steady herself until it passed.

"Liddy!" John's voice seemed to come from far way but this time there could be no doubt of the edge of panic.

Don't leave the children astride that horse, she mentally instructed even as she gritted her teeth and willed the pain to subside. "I'm all right," she managed to call out to him.

"You are not all right," he fumed, reaching her side and leading her to one of the rocking chairs he'd built for them. "I'm going for the doctor."

"You will do no such thing, John Amman. Now, get those children down off that horse and…"

"Luke is tending to them. Said something about taking them for ice cream."

"It's too close to suppertime and…" She looked up at him with surprise as she felt her water break.

Please, no, she prayed. She was not due for weeks.

Dr. Benson had warned them that having another baby would be dangerous. Both Joshua and Rose had been difficult births for Lydia. "You are thirty-five years old, Lydia Amman," Dr. Benson had warned.

"Many women in our community have children late in life," she had replied. "If it be God's will that John and I should be blessed with more…"

Dr. Benson had sighed heavily. "Just take time to heal, all right?"

Lydia had not wanted to explain to him that whether she would have another child or not—and when—was in God's hands. But it did seem as if God had heeded the doctor's warning, because it had been three years before Lydia had become pregnant again. By that time she had almost given up and John had assured her that two healthy children were blessing enough. Still, she had not missed the look of pure joy he had given her when she had announced that he might want to get started on a set of bunk beds for either Joshua or Rose's small bedrooms.

"Of course," she had mused, "if the twins are one of each…"

"Twins?" he had exclaimed hardly able to believe what he was hearing.

"So, Dr. Benson seems to believe."

The one thing that John had insisted on from her first pregnancy was that the doctor should manage everything. "I will not have Hilda Yoder catching our babies," he declared. "Something could go wrong and I will take no chances on your health or the child's."

To Lydia's surprise Hilda had been in complete agreement with John's decree. "Times are changing, Lydia," she had said when Lydia tried to explain John's wishes without hurting the older woman's feelings. "And you are not so young anymore yourself. John is being very wise."

"Maybe you should call Dr. Benson…" Lydia said to John.

He turned back toward the hardware store and shouted, "Call for the doctor, Tante Gert. The twins are coming."

It thrilled Lydia to hear the tone of pure unadulterated joy with which he delivered this news. "Well, you don't have to tell the entire town," she teased, and started to rise from the chair.

"Just sit there," he ordered as he knelt next to her. He dipped the towel she'd wiped her hands with into the bucket of water they kept on the back porch for washing up and wiped her forehead. "Where is that doctor?" he muttered after no more than five minutes had passed.

"He'll be here," Lydia assured him and took hold of his hand, forcing his attention to her face. "John, I know it's before my time, but I am sure that God knows best. Pray with me until the doctor arrives." It warmed her heart knowing how John had settled into the strength of their faith following their marriage. Together they had built a home and were raising a family and they were doing both with the support and bond that they had found together in their congregation and community.

He folded the towel and laid it across her forehead and then took both of her hands in his and bowed his head.

John had prayed often in his life. Early on his prayers had been selfish pleas for something he wanted or felt he needed. In those earlier years when he had left Celery Fields he had prayed for God to make Liddy come to her senses and understand that everything he was doing was for her, for them. But since marrying Liddy his prayers had all focused on the well-being of Liddy and the children.

And he believed with all his heart that God had heard his prayers. Over the past five years his business had blossomed and enough new families had moved to the area that the elders had announced plans to build and open a new school. Bettina would be the teacher, since Liddy's time was taken up with their children and managing their household as well as taking orders and keeping the books for his business. Their son, Joshua, would be in the first class to occupy the new building, one that John had worked side by side with their neighbors to build.

So God had blessed them many times over, so much so that when Liddy warned him that hard times were bound to come again, he had assured her that they could weather any storm as long as they were together. But hard times came in many disguises, he realized as he held on to Liddy's hands. It was too soon for the babies to come and the doctor had warned them both of the danger of another pregnancy at her age.

Please, God, we need her—the children and I. Please let the twins be all right and protect Liddy.

He opened his eyes, first checking on Liddy, who sat with her eyes closed and the sweetest smile on her face. Then he turned his gaze toward the lane that passed their house, willing the sound of the doctor's automobile even as he saw his aunt crossing the space between the hardware store and their house at a run. "He's coming," she called out. "He's on his way."

In the moment John realized that what had seemed like hours had in fact only been a matter of minutes since he'd first seen Liddy grab for the door frame and grimace in pain. "Her water…" he said when Gert stepped onto the porch and knelt beside him.

"It's only a little," Lydia told Gert.

But Gert—having never had children of her own—tended toward hysteria in times like this. "Roger Amman!" she shouted. "Leave the store and come now."

In seconds John saw his uncle running toward the house.

"Let's get her inside out of this hot sun," Gert ordered as she held open the screen door and waited for the two men to help Liddy inside.

"I can walk on my own," Lydia protested.

By the time they reached the bedroom Gert had already prepared the bed for the birthing by lining the mattress with newspapers and padding. "Lay her down here."

"Truly, you are all getting ahead of yourselves," Lydia fumed.

The sound of a car outside had them turning toward the open window. "That'll be the doctor," Roger muttered, and headed back through the house to meet him.

As the doctor came through the front door, Pleasant and Greta came through the back and suddenly the bedroom that John had always thought spacious was so filled with people that he had no choice but to stand in the doorway trying to see his wife.

"Liddy, I'm here," he said, and the others turned to him.

"Come," Pleasant urged, making a place for him as they crowded around the bed. "She needs your strength, John Amman. She needs to know you are here with her."

"I would never leave her," John replied, annoyed at the implication that there was cause for Liddy to doubt his devotion.

Pleasant placed her hand gently on his forearm, forcing him to look at her. She smiled. "I know that, John. There was a time when I doubted that you...." She sniffed loudly and pursed her lips. "I was wrong."

It was as close as Pleasant Troyer would ever come to an outright apology and John understood that. He patted her hand and then turned his attention back to his wife.

"This is ridiculous," she said, ignoring her family and addressing the doctor.

"Tell me about the pain," he said. "When did it begin?"

"Twenty minutes ago and there's been nothing since," she reported. "Now..." She started to raise herself up from the bed, but Dr. Benson gently pushed her back.

"Lie still please. We have work to do here and then you can go do whatever you seem to be in such a worry to take care of."

John was not at all sure that he liked the doctor's brusque tone, but it seemed to work. Liddy fell back onto the pillows and almost immediately she grimaced and half sat up as a fresh pain grabbed her. John glanced at the doctor.

"Now Herr Amman, you know well enough how this goes. She's going to have some pain. You can either hold her hand and offer her comfort or wait out there," he told John as he indicated the hallway outside the bedroom.

"I will not leave her," John said. "Tell me what is needed and let me help."

Dr. Benson glanced at Pleasant, who nodded. "Very well, position yourself behind her there so that she is partially sitting up and leaning against you. If you start to feel queasy you will need to fight against that. The only person whose comfort matters right now is your wife's and once we begin you cannot leave her. Understood?"

"This is not my first time doing this," John grumbled as he positioned himself at the head of the bed and pulled Lydia against him. "I'm not going anywhere," he added in a tone that defied anyone to dispute him. Then he leaned close to Liddy's ear and repeated his promise. "Ever again." He smoothed back her hair after Greta took away her prayer covering and handed him a cloth that she had dipped in cold water. Recalling the births of their two older children, he prepared himself for a long siege of Liddy fighting gripping pain followed by long periods of her collapsed in exhaustion against him. It had taken nearly twelve hours to bring Joshua into this world and seven for Rose.

He tightened his embrace on Lydia as she cried out and the doctor ordered her to push. In what seemed only a matter of a few seconds the doctor handed Pleasant a bundle that John realized was their child.

"A boy," Pleasant told him, her face wreathed in smiles as the doctor cut the cord and she handed the child to Greta for washing.

"And here comes the other one," Dr. Benson announced.

The second child was a girl and once freed of the umbilical cord that had wrapped itself around her neck, she let the world know with her cries that she had fought her way into a world that she clearly intended to take by storm. Once again Pleasant handed the child to Greta and turned back to assist the doctor.

Lydia could not recall a time when she had felt quite so filled with joy—or quite so exhausted. She closed her eyes.

"Liddy," John whispered.

"She'll need her rest," Lydia heard the doctor say as he completed his work.

"I'll be fine," Lydia insisted, forcing her eyes open and holding out her arms to receive her babies.

Dr. Benson handed Pleasant a vial of pills and gave her instructions for administering them. "I'll stop by later tonight," he said.

Lydia barely heard him as she and John cradled the newest members of their family. "They're so very small," John murmured.

"They'll be bigger soon enough," Pleasant advised as she and Greta continued to clear away the refuse from the birthing.

"Do you…did you and Lydia choose names?" Greta asked as she bent down for a closer look at the red-faced infants.

"Noah and Ruth," Lydia and John said in unison, and then they both laughed.

Pleasant laid out a fresh nightgown for Lydia, her take-charge demeanor reminding them all that the world did not stop even for the birthing of twins. "Go get yourself cleaned up and have something to eat, John," she ordered. "Gert has made some supper for you. Greta and I will take care of things here while you and Luke tend to the chores and keep Joshua and Rose occupied."

"You won't leave her," John cautioned.

"Not for an instant," Pleasant promised.

"John Amman, there is work to be done and children to be fed," Lydia instructed. "Now go."

Gently John handed baby Noah to Greta and eased himself from behind Liddy. He walked to the door and then turned around and walked back to her, grinning. "You'd think at a time like this you might be the one to take orders not give them," he teased as he kissed her temple.

Lydia could not seem to open her eyes although she tried to do so. She could hear the low murmur of John's voice from somewhere very close to her and yet he seemed so very far away.

She felt a damp breeze pass over her and realized that somewhere a window was open. She could smell lemons mingling with the telltale scent of baby oil.

The babies!

She was very tired and so much wanted to sink back into the sleep that called to her. But her children needed her—her four precious children. John was hopeless when it came to managing the children. They would be spoiled rotten in no time if he were left to tend to them. Look how he had spoiled Joshua and Rose already. The man could refuse them nothing and those children knew it. She felt a smile play over her parched lips. On the other hand they were good children, caring of each other and their many cousins and friends. So what if John gave in to their pleas for one more story at bedtime or one more slice of cake because they had indeed finished eating all their vegetables?

She forced her eyes open and waited for the hazy image of him to clear. He was sitting in the rocking chair he'd clearly brought inside from the porch. "Well, hello there. It's about time you came back to us. Were you planning to sleep through the first year of our babies' lives?"

"I have always been right here and you know it." She was upset with herself for having left all the work to others. "You are the one who left, not once but twice."

He smiled and sat on the bed next to her. "Are you never going to let that go, Lydia Amman?"

"Probably not," she said as she reached up and

cupped his cheek. "Otherwise, you might just forget how miserable you were without me."

"And were you not just as miserable without me?"

She stroked his face, smoothed back his hair and then placed her fingertips against his lips. "I thought that I might die from that misery," she said.

"Then it is good that God saw fit to lead us back to each other every time," John murmured as he leaned in to kiss her.

"The babies? I mean it was early and…"

"Noah and Ruth are fine, Liddy. Doc Benson was here while you were sleeping and has pronounced them hale and hearty."

"Bring them to me."

"You're sure you don't need more rest?"

"Oh, John, what I need is my family—you and the children."

"All right, but if you tire… I'm going," he promised when she presented him with the expression she had perfected in all her years of teaching to get her students to follow her instructions.

He was gone only a minute and then back, a baby cradled in each powerful arm and their two older children peeking at her shyly from next to him. Behind him Pleasant and Greta peered in, their faces wreathed in smiles.

Before she could say a word, all of them were crowded around the bed. John handed her a bundle. "Your son Noah," he said, even as the bundle still in his arms started to writhe and fuss. "And this," he said, pulling back the covers from the second baby's face, "is your daughter Ruth, and I fear that she is going to be very much like her mother."

"God willing," Lydia murmured as she held out her free arm to receive her daughter. They were perfect, she saw as she examined them. And as Joshua and Rose scrambled onto the bed and took up places on either side of her, Lydia met John's gaze.

He looked a good deal like the man she had found kneeling next to the stove at the schoolhouse that morning. His clothing was just as rumpled and his hair was as tousled as it had been that day. But this time his unkempt appearance was not because he had been away from her for eight long years. It was because he had been—and with God's blessing would be right there at her side—for years to come.

* * * * *

REQUEST YOUR FREE BOOKS!

2 FREE INSPIRATIONAL NOVELS
PLUS 2
FREE
MYSTERY GIFTS

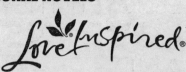

Save $1.00

on the purchase of any
Love Inspired®,
Love Inspired® Suspense or
Love Inspired® Historical book.

Available wherever books are sold, including most bookstores, supermarkets, drugstores and discount stores.

Save $1.00

on the purchase of any Love Inspired®, Love Inspired® Suspense or Love Inspired® Historical book.

Coupon valid until April 30, 2017. Redeemable at participating retail outlets in the U.S. and Canada only. Limit one coupon per customer.

52614590

5 65373 00076 2   (8100)0 12248

Canadian Retailers: Harlequin Enterprises Limited will pay the face value of this coupon plus 10.25¢ if submitted by customer for this product only. Any other use constitutes fraud. Coupon is nonassignable. Void if taxed, prohibited or restricted by law. Consumer must pay any government taxes. Void if copied. Inmar Promotional Services ("IPS") customers submit coupons and proof of sales to Harlequin Enterprises Limited, P.O. Box 3000, Saint John, NB E2L 4L3, Canada. Non-IPS retailer—for reimbursement submit coupons and proof of sales directly to Harlequin Enterprises Limited, Retail Marketing Department, 225 Duncan Mill Rd., Don Mills, ON M3B 3K9, Canada.

U.S. Retailers: Harlequin Enterprises Limited will pay the face value of this coupon plus 8¢ if submitted by customer for this product only. Any other use constitutes fraud. Coupon is nonassignable. Void if taxed, prohibited or restricted by law. Consumer must pay any government taxes. Void if copied. For reimbursement submit coupons and proof of sales directly to Harlequin Enterprises, Ltd 482, NCH Marketing Services, P.O. Box 880001, El Paso, TX 88588-0001, U.S.A. Cash value 1/100 cents.

LIINCICOUP0117

SPECIAL EXCERPT FROM

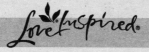

*Discovering he has a two-year-old son is a huge
surprise for veterinarian Wyatt Harrow. But so are his
lingering feelings for the boy's pretty mom…*

*Read on for a sneak preview
of the fifth book in the*
LONE STAR COWBOY LEAGUE: BOYS RANCH
miniseries, *THE DOCTOR'S TEXAS BABY*
by *Deb Kastner*.

Wyatt glanced at Carolina, but she wouldn't meet his
eyes.

Was she feeling guilty over all Matty's firsts that she'd
denied Wyatt? First breath, first word, the first step Matty
took?

He couldn't say he felt sorry for her. She should be
feeling guilty. She'd made the decision to walk away.
She'd created these consequences for herself, and for
Wyatt, and most of all, for Matty.

But today wasn't a day for anger. Today was about
spending time with his son.

"What do you say, little man?" he asked, scooping
Matty into his arms and leading Carolina to his truck.
"Do you want to play ball?"

Not knowing what Matty would like, he'd pretty
much loaded up every kind of sports ball imaginable—a
football, a baseball, a soccer ball and a basketball.

Carolina flashed him half a smile and shrugged
apologetically. "I'm afraid I don't know much about

these games beyond being able to identify which ball goes with which sport."

"That's what Matty's got a dad for."

He didn't really think about what he was saying until the words had already left his lips.

Their gazes met and locked. She was silently challenging him, but he didn't know about what. Still, he kept his gaze firmly on hers. His words might not have been premeditated, but that didn't make them any less true. He was sorry if he'd hurt her feelings, though. He wanted to keep things friendly between them.

"There's plenty of room on the green for three. What do you say? Do you want to play soccer with us?"

Shock registered in her face, but it was no more than what he was feeling. This was all so new. Untested waters.

Somehow, they had to work things out, but kicking a ball around together at the park?

Why, that almost felt as if they were a family.

And although in a sense that was technically true, Wyatt didn't even want to go down that road.

He had every intention of being the best father he could to Matty. And in so doing, he would establish some sort of a working relationship with Carolina, some way they could both be comfortable without it getting awkward. He just couldn't bring himself to think about that right now.

Or maybe he just didn't want to.

Don't miss
THE DOCTOR'S TEXAS BABY
by Deb Kastner, available February 2017
wherever Love Inspired® books and ebooks are sold.

www.LoveInspired.com

LIEXP0117

Forced to marry her father's new employee after being caught overnight in a storm, can Caroline find love with her unlikely husband?

Read on for an excerpt from
WED BY NECESSITY,
the next heartwarming book in the
SMOKY MOUNTAIN MATCHES *series.*

Gatlinburg, Tennessee
July 1887

As a holiday, Independence Day left a lot to be desired. Independence was a dream Caroline Turner wasn't likely to ever attain.

The fireworks' blue-green light flickered over the sea of faces, followed by red, white and gold. She schooled her features and made her way along the edge of the field to where the musicians were playing patriotic tunes.

"Caroline, we're running low on lemonade."

"Then make more," she snapped at eighteen-year-old Wanda Smith.

"We've misplaced the lemon crates."

At the distress in the younger girl's countenance, Caroline relented. "Fine. I'll look for them. You may return to your station."

It took her a quarter of an hour to locate the missing lemons. By then, the last of the fireworks had been shot off and attendees were ready for more food and drink.

The celebration was far from over, yet she wished she could return home to her bedroom and solitude.

A trio of young women approached and engaged her in conversation. As usual, they wanted to know about her outfit, whether she'd had it made by a local seamstress or her mother had had it shipped from New York. Before they'd exhausted their talk of fashion, a stranger inserted himself into their group.

"Excuse me."

Caroline didn't recognize the hulking figure. Well over six feet tall, he was as broad and solid as an oak tree and looked as if he hadn't seen civilization in months. He was dressed in common clothing, and his shirt and pants were clean but wrinkled. Dirt caked the heels of his sturdy brown boots. His thick reddish-brown hair was tied back with a strip of leather. While he appeared to have a strong facial structure, his mustache and beard obscured the lower half of his face. His mouth was wide and generous. Sparkling blue eyes assessed her.

"Would you care to dance?" He spoke in a rolling brogue that identified him as a foreigner.

Don't miss
WED BY NECESSITY by Karen Kirst,
available wherever Love Inspired® Historical books
and ebooks are sold.

www.LoveInspired.com